AMISH
WEDDINGS

Books by Leslie Gould

THE COURTSHIPS OF LANCASTER COUNTY

Courting Cate
Adoring Addie
Minding Molly
Becoming Bea

NEIGHBORS OF LANCASTER COUNTY

Amish Promises
Amish Sweethearts
Amish Weddings

Neighbors of LANCASTER COUNTY
• *BOOK THREE* •

AMISH WEDDINGS

LESLIE GOULD

BETHANYHOUSE
a division of Baker Publishing Group
Minneapolis, Minnesota

Published by Bethany House Publishers
11400 Hampshire Avenue South
Bloomington, Minnesota 55438
www.bethanyhouse.com

Bethany House Publishers is a division of
Baker Publishing Group, Grand Rapids, Michigan

Printed in the United States of America

Library of Congress Cataloging-in-Publication Data
Names: Gould, Leslie, author.
Title: Amish weddings / Leslie Gould.
Description: Minneapolis, Minnesota : Bethany House, a division of Baker
    Publishing Group, [2017] | Series: Neighbors of Lancaster County ; book 3
Identifiers: LCCN 2016034656 | ISBN 9780764230042 (hardcover) | ISBN
    9780764216947 (softcover)
Subjects: LCSH: Amish—Fiction. | Mate selection—Fiction. | Lancaster County
    (Pa.)—Fiction. | GSAFD: Christian fiction. | Love stories.
Classification: LCC PS3607.O89 A86 2017 | DDC 813/.6—dc23
LC record available at https://lccn.loc.gov/2016034656

Scripture quotations are from the King James Version of the Bible or from the Holy
Bible, New International Version®. NIV®. Copyright © 1973, 1978, 1984, 2011 by
Biblica, Inc.™ Used by permission of Zondervan. All rights reserved worldwide. www.
zondervan.com

Cover design by John Hamilton Design

Author represented by MacGregor Literary, Inc.

17   18   19   20   21   22   23   7   6   5   4   3   2   1

1

September 2015

Rose Lehman sat on a bench toward the back of the Bylers' large shed, halfway listening to the sermon as she resigned herself to the upcoming announcement. Just the thought of what was ahead made her grateful, again, that Bishop Gideon Byler and his wife had hosted the day's church service.

It was always an ordeal for the Lehman family to take their turn, with their small barn and house. At the Bylers', the meal could be served in their large airy home that seated the entire congregation. And their shed easily housed the service, with room to spare.

Rose shifted on the bench a little, as her thoughts wandered to Reuben Byler. He didn't live with his *Dat* and stepmom—no, he had his own house next to the lumberyard he managed. True, the house needed some work. New paint, inside and out. And new furniture. But Reuben had the means to provide all of that and more.

And he wanted to marry her. They just needed to set the date.

The minister sat down, interrupting Rose's thoughts, and Bishop Byler stood. The time had come.

"We have a *Hochzeit* to announce," he said.

Rose's youngest sister, Trudy, jabbed an elbow into Rose's side and smiled. *Jah*, today was the day.

The Bishop's voice grew louder. "Zane Beck and Lila Lehman will be married on October seventeenth." The date was only a month away. Rose sighed. For a time, she had been sure she'd marry before her older sister. That wouldn't happen now.

Lila and Zane's upcoming wedding was the reason Bishop Byler and his wife, Monika, had agreed to host the service. The Lehmans were working frantically to get everything ready for the wedding, although Dat wasn't doing as much as Lila wished he would, such as finishing the basement in case of rain. Rose hoped he'd be more cooperative when it was her turn to marry, which she still expected would be soon.

"Join me as we ask for God's blessing on this couple," Bishop Byler said. "And that we'll all do what we can to support them."

Lila sat a few rows ahead with her head bowed. Zane was probably in the back of the men's side, possibly late because he couldn't control his new horse. Watching him drive a buggy was a laugh. He tried so hard to be Amish, really. Yet it was so obvious he was a newcomer.

Rose knew there were some in the district who were suspicious of Zane, saying he'd only joined the church to marry Lila. Rose couldn't quite imagine him living the Plain way for the rest of his life, not after being in the Army for four years. And especially not after he'd owned a big pickup truck. That, in contrast to his horse and buggy, he could handle with ease.

If he left someday, Lila would have to go with him.

As Bishop Byler prayed, Rose snuck a look at Reuben, who sat in the middle on the men's side. With his head bowed, his brown hair fell across his forehead. He was older than she was by eight years, but that didn't seem to bother him. It certainly didn't bother her. No, if anything it made him a better catch.

When she turned sixteen, she'd planned to have a *Rumschpringe* time, as her brothers did. She'd imagined getting to know a new group of *Youngie*, becoming a part of a gang who partied together. She'd planned on such antics, even with Dat watching her like a hawk.

But then Lila broke up with Reuben, and everything changed for Rose. She'd set her sights on Reuben and had never looked back.

She had no desire to run with other Youngie and soon joined the church. She'd worked at becoming less selfish and more aware of the needs of others. Her relationship with her sisters and Dat improved too. Jah, Reuben had been a positive influence on her. She was one hundred percent certain he was the man for her to marry.

The prayer ended, and Trudy grabbed Rose's hand. "Let's go help Monika," she said, dragging Rose to her feet, toward the door, and out into the bright September sunshine. Trudy was blond like Lila, while Rose had dark hair.

Members of the district were already greeting the soon-to-be groom. Rose still couldn't get used to Zane with a blunt haircut and wearing a white shirt and suspenders. On the outside it seemed he'd embraced the Amish lifestyle, and he did have the advantage of being able to understand and speak Pennsylvania Dutch. But only time would tell if he could truly become part of their community.

Lila stepped to Zane's side, and their eyes met as a sweet look passed between them. Rose was happy for her sister—she truly was. She just hoped her wedding didn't interfere too much with Rose's own plans.

Dat stood off in the distance, with a pained expression on

his face and his massive arms crossed over his chest. He'd had his own problems lately, issues that Bishop Byler was trying to deal with. Rose followed to where Dat's eyes were focused.

She wasn't surprised he was watching Beth Yoder, Trudy's teacher. The woman had gray hair and was a little plump, but by the expression on Dat's face you would think she was the most beautiful woman in the world. Unfortunately she had a husband. One who had divorced her years ago, but in the eyes of the church they were still married.

It had bothered Reuben that his father hadn't put an end to the friendship, but Rose believed it was mostly harmless and hated to see it end, because Dat's friendship with Beth had brought a sense of calm to the Lehman household.

That didn't matter though—Dat and Beth's relationship was against the *Ordnung*, the unwritten rules Plain people followed. Someone must have said something to the bishop, because Dat and Beth had started avoiding each other a couple of weeks ago.

"Dat," Rose called out as she passed by.

He blinked, as if confused, and then finally turned toward her.

"Bishop Byler needs help with the benches." The men would carry them into the house.

Dat nodded and started his slow lumber back toward the shed.

Trudy tugged on Rose's hand, and the two continued walking, past the oak tree where Daniel, Lila's twin, stood with his wife, Jenny. She was Monika's youngest daughter, the bishop's stepdaughter, and Reuben's stepsister. Jenny was pregnant and due soon after Lila's wedding, which meant she wouldn't be much help.

As they headed up the back stairs to the kitchen, someone called out Rose's name. She turned. It was Reuben. Rose smiled and waved and then said to Trudy, "Go on ahead. I'll be right there."

She hurried back down the steps and then pointed away from the crowd, toward the garden. On the other side was the *Dawdi Haus* where Zane had lived for the last year. Bishop Byler thought he'd have a better chance of success as an Amish man if he lived on the same property as a Plain couple instead of with his Englisch family.

Reuben met Rose by the pumpkins. He held his black hat in his hands. He didn't have the presence his father did, but he was honest, loyal, and trustworthy. And well established. Rose had decided a couple of years ago that he was the best catch in the county, and no other boy had tempted her to change her mind.

After they greeted each other, Reuben asked, "How long have you known about Lila and Zane's plan?"

"Lila told me last Sunday night, after you dropped me off."

"Oh. I thought she would have given you more notice."

Rose shrugged. "You know Lila. She keeps things to herself."

Reuben nodded. He looked disappointed, just as Rose had been when she found out. He ran his hand through his hair. "Could I give you a ride home this afternoon?"

"I'd like that." Rose wrapped her finger around the tie of her *Kapp*.

He smiled at her, his hazel eyes kind. "*Gut*. I'll see you then." He stepped away, waved, and headed back to the group gathered around Lila and Zane.

Rose stayed by the garden. Reuben greeted Zane first, shaking his hand. Then he said something to Lila, and she smiled. Rose crossed her arms. Her sister and Reuben had courted for years. Everyone in the district had been certain they'd marry, but then Lila broke things off with him.

The gossip in the district was that she'd left him for Zane, and that was how Rose usually remembered it too. But if she was honest, she had to acknowledge that Lila broke things off with Reuben months before she and Zane began courting—though Lila and Zane clearly cared about each other during that time. In fact, there was no doubt they loved each other and had since childhood, but Lila had done her best to ignore her feelings for Zane for years.

"Rose!" She turned toward the porch. Trudy stood with one hand on her hip. "Come on!"

Rose waved at her little sister and then gave Reuben one last glance. He turned toward her and smiled. Her heart fluttered. She wished he'd had his eyes on her all those years, but that couldn't be helped. He was interested in her now—that was all that mattered.

She smiled back at him and then turned quickly. Trudy watched her from the porch, but she was sure that Reuben had his eyes on her too. She was used to that. Men—both Amish and Englisch—often watched her. For many years it had given her the idea that she was special, even though she knew it was a dangerous thought. No one was more special than anyone else. Still, she couldn't help noticing that men thought her special. And knowing that Reuben did too gave her a thrill. Perhaps today would be the day he'd bring up a wedding date.

~~~~~

Beth helped Rose dry the dishes, while Lila washed them and Monika put away the food. The conversation was stilted at first as everyone avoided any mention of Dat, but then Beth asked Lila how the wedding plans were coming along. Before Lila could answer, Monika said that their *Mamm* would be so happy about the upcoming wedding. Everyone paused for a moment.

Rose couldn't remember their Mamm very well, although it seemed she should be able to. Rose had been seven when she died. She did remember the funeral, mostly because Lila wouldn't stop crying. Rose always felt as if their Mamm "belonged" to Lila. Maybe because everyone said Lila looked like their Mamm or because Lila wasn't Dat's biological child and that seemed to make her entirely Mamm's. Not that anyone ever mentioned Lila and Daniel's biological father. No one even acknowledged he existed.

Rose clearly remembered when the Becks moved to Juneberry Lane, however. She'd been fascinated with them. But then Lila ended up being closer to the Becks than Rose, and soon she felt as if they "belonged" to Lila too. It was as if Lila ended up owning everyone.

But Reuben's family would belong to Rose. Bishop Byler and Monika. Reuben's brothers, sister, and stepsisters. It was a big happy family, and Rose knew they were all hoping she and Reuben would marry soon.

Rose wiped her hands on her apron and smiled at Reuben as he carted a table out of the room with Daniel's help. He smiled back, and Zane gave him a playful nudge with his elbow.

As they finished the dishes, Monika offered Lila a gallon jar of bean soup and a plastic container of peanut butter spread to take home. "I know you won't have much time to cook this week, considering you'll need to deliver your wedding invitations."

"*Denki,*" Lila said.

Rose was grateful too. Since their Mamm had died it seemed they were always receiving help from someone—usually Monika or their *Aenti,* Eve, or Zane's mother, Shani, who lived up the lane.

"Ready?" Reuben asked as Rose hung up the dish towel.

"Jah." She dried her hands on her apron and followed him out the door. He already had his horse hitched to his buggy. Some of the young men bought a courting buggy, but Reuben's was a practical family-style design. And his horse was slow.

Behind him, Dat had his buggy ready to go and also Beth's. The sight of the separate buggies stabbed at Rose's heart for just a moment. She was afraid Dat had accidentally fallen in love with Beth, if such a thing were possible. She was sure he hadn't intended to.

Reuben helped her into his buggy and stepped around to his side as Zane zipped by in his buggy, frantically pulling it to a stop. Lila came down the back steps of Monika's house, laughing. Rose admired her sister's courage.

Rose watched the Youngie playing volleyball on the plush lawn of the side yard as she and Reuben passed by. The girls were all barefoot, the ties of their Kappa blowing in the breeze along with the skirts of their dresses. Everyone appeared to be having fun. A year ago, Rose would have been in the middle of the action.

She smiled at Reuben, but he was concentrating on staying on his side of the narrow lane as a car zoomed by on the other.

Rose shaded her eyes from the autumn sun as Reuben turned onto the highway. His horse clip-clopped along at a slow pace. Ahead, in a grove of trees, the first of the fall leaves had started to change color. A herd of cows grazed in an emerald field. Rows and rows of golden cornstalks swayed in the breeze. Surely there was nowhere in the world as beautiful as Lancaster County.

Rose leaned back against the seat, enjoying the lull before the craziness of putting on Lila's wedding overwhelmed them all. The only thing that would make the day better would be if she and Reuben talked about a date for their wedding. True, they couldn't marry as soon as she'd hoped, thanks to Lila. But they only needed to wait a month or two. She scooted closer to Reuben. He smiled but didn't turn toward her. A few times in the last couple of months, she was sure he was going to kiss her—and then he didn't. She was getting tired of waiting.

She cleared her throat and said, "What are you thinking about?"

He smiled again, just a little, and said, "The order I need

to finish up tomorrow. It's for an Englisch man—actually, the county sheriff. He hopes to get a fence and deck done before the weather turns."

"Oh." Rose didn't know much about Reuben's job, even though Dat had worked part time at the lumberyard with him for as long as Rose could remember. Everyone seemed to think Reuben was brilliant with measurements and figuring out designs and such things. He liked math and often spoke about percentages and angles. Rose had liked math in school too, especially fractions and percentages. But she didn't use either in everyday life the way Reuben did, except in cooking.

Today she didn't care much about his work though. She was more interested in what he thought about her. She made her voice as lighthearted as possible. "Are you thinking about anything else?"

He pulled back on the reins as they approached the stop sign.

She put her hand to her chest. "Perhaps about me?"

He glanced at her and chuckled. "I'm always thinking about you, Rose."

Her heart beat faster. She dropped her voice to a whisper. "And about us?"

"Of course," he said.

She leaned closer. "What exactly do you think about?"

"Well, right now I'm thinking about more than just us. Your family has a wedding coming up, and everyone will be busy for the next month. I've been wondering how I can help."

Rose inhaled. It wasn't the answer she'd hoped for.

"Rose," he said. "Our time will come." Now he sounded as if he were teasing.

"Jah, but I thought it would be sooner rather than later. We won't have to wait long, will we?"

"We can talk about it after Lila and Zane are married and settled. Maybe we can set a date in the spring."

She couldn't hide the disappointment in her voice. "That long?"

All along she had worried that perhaps Reuben thought she was too young to marry—maybe he did. Lila had strung him along when she was eighteen, but Rose had done nothing of the kind. "I'm the complete opposite of my sister." Her face grew warm as soon as she spoke, realizing her comment would make little sense to Reuben.

But he chuckled as if he understood. "Jah," he said. "I'm very aware of that. You are opposites. Absolutely."

She took his agreement as a compliment, but his words didn't lessen her disappointment. She'd never been a patient person. A pout started to form on her face. Perhaps she should have taken time for her Rumschpringe after all. She'd been waiting forever for Reuben to set a wedding date.

"I'd hoped we'd marry sooner too." Reuben turned off the highway onto Juneberry Lane. "But it would be a lot for your family to host two weddings close together. This way, we can be supportive of Lila and Zane, and your Dat will have some time to regroup before another big event. Besides, your Dat's under extra stress right now."

Rose bristled. "Did you say something to your Dat about them?"

Reuben shook his head.

"Are you sure? Because they've been avoiding each other. Something's going on."

"A lot of people have noticed the amount of time they've been spending together," Reuben said. "Not just me."

Reuben wouldn't lie to her. Someone else had brought it up with Bishop Byler. As they reached the driveway, Rose focused on the autumn clematis growing along the fence. She wouldn't think about Dat and Beth. No, she'd concentrate on the things she longed for. Marriage. Sharing Reuben's home. A kiss.

She'd shared a couple with boys she'd gone to school with, but they hadn't really counted. A kiss from Reuben would help her accept the delay in their plans. It would give her something to think about during the month of chaos before Lila's wedding.

Reuben parked the buggy by the barn, with the chicken coop blocking sight of the house. Rose turned toward him. He smiled at her, placed his hand on her shoulder, and leaned toward her. It was as if he could read her mind. She lifted her mouth toward his.

A car horn honked and then a horse neighed loudly.

Someone yelled, "Whoa!"

Reuben's horse jerked backward, sending the buggy lurching. Reuben quickly set his brake as the horn blared again.

"Knock that off!" Dat yelled.

Rose's curiosity won, and she jumped down from the buggy, quickly stepping to the other side of the coop where she could see what was going on. Zane handed his reins to Lila, jumped down, and walked back toward a red sports car.

An Englischer climbed out. He wore jeans and a long-sleeved T-shirt, the sleeves tight against his arms.

"Anderson!" Zane called out. "What are you doing?"

"Your parents said you might be down here." The man wore his sandy hair short and his face had a sculpted look. He could have passed for one of those celebrities on the cover of the magazines Rose saw in the stores—and sometimes bought.

"Dude, you really did it, didn't you? You joined the Amish." The man shook his head. "Suspenders, a hat, weird pants. You're the real deal."

"Who's that?" Reuben asked as he stepped to Rose's side.

Rose shrugged. "Maybe one of Zane's Army buddies." His hair looked like an Army cut.

"What's he doing here?"

"I don't know," she answered.

Reuben took a step closer to the action and then asked, over his shoulder, "Do you think he's here for the wedding?"

Rose shook her head. "It's too early. Besides, no one said anything about a friend coming."

Zane put out his hand, and the men shook hands. Then they hugged. "Trevor," Zane said, "it's great to see you."

Lila jumped down from the buggy and grabbed Zane's horse, holding him steady.

An alarming sound—a sob, it seemed—escaped between Zane and the Englisch man. Rose stepped away from Reuben so she could see better. She couldn't imagine Zane was crying. The other man's shoulders shook.

Zane patted his back.

Neither Rose nor Reuben said anything for a long moment, but then Reuben took off his hat, ran his hand through his hair, and said, "I'd better get going."

"Jah," Rose replied, wishing he'd take her with him, but she knew he wouldn't. She'd never been in his house alone with him, and he wouldn't change his thinking on that now.

Rose's hand brushed against Reuben's. For a moment she thought he might grab hers, but he didn't. She wished he'd pull her close and say something like, *We'll pick up where we left off.* But he didn't. He didn't say anything at all. Maybe he was taking her for granted, thinking she should be happy to wait until spring to get married.

She gave him a heartless good-bye and started toward the house.

Zane had taken the reins back and softly spoke to his horse, the Englischer standing beside him, his back to the rest of them. Rose reached her sisters, and they walked toward the house.

"Who is that?" Rose asked as they climbed the back steps.

"Hush," Lila answered.

When they reached the kitchen, Trudy hurried toward the

dining room window, but Lila called her back. "His name is Trevor Anderson," Lila explained. "He served in Afghanistan with Zane. He was the driver of the vehicle . . ." Her voice trailed off. Rose remembered that Zane had been in some sort of big van or something that ran over an explosive. Lila probably didn't want to say any more in front of Trudy. "He's been having some problems," Lila added.

"What kind of problems?" Trudy asked.

"Depression. Maybe PTSD."

"What's that?" Trudy stepped back toward the window.

"Post-traumatic stress disorder. From combat."

"Does Zane have that?"

"I don't think so," Lila answered.

Trudy wrinkled her nose. "How about Simon?"

"Hush," Rose said to her little sister.

"No, it's fine." Lila stepped close and patted Trudy's shoulder. "I don't think Simon has PTSD." He'd been in Afghanistan but was stateside again. He'd seen his girlfriend, Casey—who had served with Zane—but hadn't made his way home yet.

"What's Trevor doing here?" Rose stepped toward the window. Zane now had one arm around the Englisch man. Rose couldn't help but feel sorry for Trevor.

"He wrote Zane a while back and said he wanted to visit." Lila's gaze drifted toward the window. "He didn't say he wanted to visit *now* though. I thought he'd come after the wedding."

2

The next evening a chill filled the air, causing Lila to pull her cloak tighter as she breathed in the acrid smell of the lingering smoke from Dat's leaf pile. The day before, after Trevor drove back to Shani and Joel's house, Zane had asked her to meet him at their old fort tonight, at eight. He said he had a surprise for her. She hurried through the gate and into the field, anticipating what he wanted to show her.

After returning from the Army last year, Zane had immediately taken a construction job, started taking instruction to join the Amish church, and moved into Monika and Gideon's Dawdi Haus. That, along with Lila's job at the Plain Buffet and her chores, didn't give them much time together. After he joined the church last November, and people started to accept that he was sincere, they had more freedom, but for the last three months Zane's spare time had been taken building a little house for them near his parents'. She hoped he planned to show it to her tonight.

She walked along the poplar trees and then stopped at the

bank of the creek, casting her flashlight beam down into the water. The level was low after the hot summer, but still the creek murmured along. Below, their fort stood sturdy after so many years. Above, the trees swayed in the breeze. Lila breathed deeply, relishing the crisp air. She'd spent the afternoon cooped up inside, addressing the wedding invitations she and Zane would deliver over the next week.

There were moments when she had to pinch herself to truly believe that she would marry Zane in a month. There were other moments when she feared something would still go wrong.

Zane was her person, the one she most wanted to be with, to spend her life with. Sometimes she feared she loved him too much, held on to him too tightly. Sometimes she feared God had a lesson for her to learn to trust him more and Zane less, but then she told herself she was simply being superstitious.

A rustling caused her to turn toward the field. Zane called out, "Sorry I'm late!" He held his hand on top of his hat as he ran, and he wore his old down jacket instead of his new black coat. Under his hat, his blond bangs were pushed to the side—a sure sign that he'd been working hard.

Lila nodded toward their fort. "Do you want to talk down there?"

He grinned and grabbed her hand. "No. I have a surprise. Remember?"

She smiled, anticipating that he was ready to show her the house. When he first planned it, he'd asked her opinion about the layout and the details, but then he'd asked her to stay away. She was excited to see what he'd done.

He led her through the field. "Trevor's going to stay with Mom and Dad for a few days, although Mom doesn't seem thrilled to have him around. She says he's too charming." Zane shrugged. "Dad told him to go down to the Center and get some help." Zane's father worked for an organization that assisted veterans. "He says he enjoys construction and his back seems to be doing okay." Lila knew, from what Zane had said a few months ago, that Trevor had a rough time after the accident in Afghanistan. First he was at an Army hospital in Texas. Then he went home to Delaware, to live with his father. Now he'd found his way to Lancaster County.

"Is he going to be okay? He seemed pretty upset yesterday."

"I think so," Zane said. "He's been having problems with his girlfriend—he's been a little vague, mostly saying she nags him all the time. But I wonder if he has a hard time committing. Plus, it sounds as if he had a drinking problem, but he says that's all in the past."

Lila winced. Zane's little brother, Adam, was only ten.

Zane shrugged. "Trevor has promised not to drink—at all—while staying at our house."

"He's only staying for a few days? For sure?"

Zane hesitated a moment. "Well, Dad said he'll look for another place if he decides to stay in Lancaster County longer. Charlie and Eve might take him."

Lila wrinkled her nose. Her aunt and uncle had taken in vets who needed a place to stay in the past, but they'd recently started caring for a foster child.

"We have too much going on right now with the wedding and everything to give him much time." He smiled down at her. "Anyway, let's not think about Trevor right now."

She handed him the flashlight.

Zane took it and pointed it toward the Becks' barn. "Like I said, I have something I want to show you."

"Not your horse again." She couldn't help but laugh.

"Ha ha. I am going to take you up on your offer to work with him."

Lila halfway regretted saying she'd train Billie, but Zane hadn't grown up driving a horse and buggy the way she had.

He wasn't firm enough with the horse, which had turned out to be quite spirited.

"All right," Lila said. "I'll start tomorrow." She'd take him on her regular errands, that sort of thing. "So, if we're not going into the barn, are we . . ." She pointed toward where the little house was.

Zane wrapped his arm around her, shining the light toward the grove of trees. "Jah," he said. "Finally. You don't know how many times I've regretted asking you to stay away." He pulled her close. "Although, I should probably show you tomorrow, in the light."

"No!" Lila laughed at her reaction.

Zane pulled her closer. "I take it you feel strongly about this?"

"Jah," she answered, her heart swelling. They stepped through the opening in the hedge and then around the Becks' old *Hinkle* coop that Zane had repaired. She'd buy chicks once they were married and start a flock. She'd share the eggs with Shani and help with her garden too, although she suspected she'd still tend the garden at her Dat's place as well. Rose had grown up a lot in the last couple of years, but she would still need help managing the house.

When Lila was a girl, she used to dream of marrying Zane and having a home on Juneberry Lane. They'd have chickens and sheep and horses and cows. A big garden. Six *Kinder*. That had been her dream. However, she never believed the dream could come true.

But now it was.

Zane held the flashlight higher, and the beam fell on their house—right in front of them.

It was small, jah, and it would only work for a few years. Once they had more than a couple of babies, they'd need a bigger home. But by then they'd hopefully have enough money saved for a down payment on a property of their own. She hated the thought of leaving Juneberry Lane someday, but it was probably inevitable.

The beam of the flashlight darted from one side of the house to the other.

"Zane, it's beautiful." And it was. The exterior was painted white, like most of the Amish houses in Lancaster County. A wide front porch led to the door. Two gables were pitched above the first-story windows. Zane had built a concrete ramp into the house, instead of a step, to make it easier for his father, who walked with a cane.

"Come inside," Zane said, squeezing her hand and pulling her along. They hurried up the ramp onto the porch and then into the house. Zane turned to a table right inside the front door and quickly turned on a battery-powered lamp. The light filled the small living room. All the walls were wood and stained a rich maple color. Lila knew Zane had gotten all of the building materials from Reuben's lumberyard.

The far wall was lined with bookshelves, an old-fashioned braided rug covered a good portion of the wood floor, and a wood stove sat in the far corner. The room was cozy and warm.

"We'll get a rocking chair for you," Zane said, pointing to the opposite corner. In less than a year, they could be parents, God willing. The thought warmed her soul almost as much as her love for Zane did.

He held the lamp high and turned to the left. "Come see the kitchen."

As she stepped through the doorway, Lila gushed, "Oh, Zane." She'd never seen anything like it. The countertops were made of stone, and the sink, refrigerator, and stove were all stainless steel. "This is too much," she said. "It must have cost a fortune."

He shook his head. "The granite was left over from a project we did at work. And the stove and refrigerator both have dents, but on the sides. No one will ever know."

"How about the cabinets?" They appeared to be high quality.

"I got a deal from a contractor we work with. An Amish man near Paradise."

She opened a cabinet door. It was smooth and easy to maneuver, nothing like the old cupboards back home. She pulled open a drawer—the spoon, fork, and knife dividers were all built in.

"I've never been so spoiled," she said.

Zane put his hands on her shoulders. "I'd do anything for you."

She swallowed hard, unable to speak. She knew he would.

He pointed to a doorway past the refrigerator. "There's a small pantry there."

Lila stepped to the door and opened it as Zane held the lamp up. It was perfect.

"And then there's a little half bath." He opened the next door. "But I haven't done anything with it yet. I'll finish it up last." She knew Zane had included the half bath so his father wouldn't have to go upstairs when he was visiting. The room wasn't any bigger than a closet, but a toilet and sink would fit. Right now it was an empty shell with capped pipes.

"I'll show you the second floor," he said.

The staircase was open with a simple but well-constructed banister, and the little landing at the top had a matching, high railing with slats that were close together. All designed with future children in mind, Lila was sure.

Zane pointed to the door at the far end of the landing. "Here's our room." The door was closed, and Zane stepped forward and opened it wide, holding the lamp high again. The first thing Lila noticed was the window seat.

"Oh, Zane," she said.

He smiled.

"It's lovely." She could imagine someday stealing an hour to read, with children at her side.

There was already a bureau in the room. And a bed with one of the quilts her mother made on top of it. It was the shadow quilt Aenti Eve had given Zane's mom, and then Shani had given it back to Eve. Made from jewel-toned squares and diamonds—sapphire, burgundy, and forest green against a black background—it had always been Lila's favorite. She had intended to use the crazy quilt she'd made, but she was thrilled to have the quilt her Mamm designed. Regardless she said, "Eve shouldn't have given it back."

"Of course she should have." Zane broke out into a smile.

She sat down on the bed, running her hand over the soft fabric and fine stitching. A branch outside the window swayed in the wind. An owl hooted in the woods behind the house. Zane plopped down beside her. He put his arm around her and pulled her close, tucking her head under his chin. He smelled of wood stain and the crisp fall air.

This was their house. Their room. The future she'd longed for since she was eleven had finally arrived. Well, nearly. Another month and it would be here.

She turned her head up to him and their lips met. Waiting for each other hadn't been easy. Passion filled her.

Zane pulled away. "This was a bad idea," he said, struggling to his feet. "I shouldn't have brought you up here, not like this."

Lila exhaled.

"I'm sorry," he said.

"Don't be." She smiled a little and then scooted off the bed.

He headed to the door. "Want to see the *Bobbli*'s room?"

She shook her head. "Not tonight. Let's come back tomorrow afternoon. We can bring your mom with us. . . ."

"I volunteer at the station tomorrow."

"Oh," Lila said. "I thought we'd get started delivering the

invitations." They were on the landing now, walking past the Bobbli's room with its door closed, headed to the stairs.

"We can do that Wednesday." Zane started down the stairs.

"I'll go see Eve tomorrow, then." Lila had the day off from the Plain Buffet, and she'd been meaning to visit her aunt for the last week to see their foster child. Eve was taking a month-long leave of absence from her teaching job. "I'll take Billie," Lila added. The sooner she could get the horse into shape, the better. She knew driving a buggy was one of those things that worried Zane. Most Amish children grew up learning how to handle horses. She certainly had.

Zane reached the front door.

"Wait," Lila said.

He turned toward her.

"Hold me," she said.

He did but not in the same way he had in the bedroom. "One more month," she whispered.

"I need to get you home," he responded, pulling away and turning the doorknob.

⁂

When they arrived at her back steps, Zane quickly told Lila good-bye and then retreated back to the lane. Under the moon-light, she watched until he disappeared into the darkness. They would soon be together, in their little house, in their bed, with their someday Bobbli's room across the landing. One more month was all.

She took the steps slowly, hoping everyone would be asleep. She entered the house quietly, hung up her cape, and tiptoed into the kitchen as the smell of coffee greeted her. Someone must have made a pot after she left. The lamp burned on the table. Dat must have left it on for her, but there was a light coming from the living room too. He wouldn't have left that lamp burning. Perhaps he was getting ready for bed.

She heard a soft murmur. Then another. Dat's voice and someone else's. "How ill is he?" Dat asked.

"Quite. And it seems he has been for some time. He'd need a heart transplant to recover." It was Beth's voice.

Lila strained to listen.

"I can't wish ill on someone else," Dat said. "Not for my own gain."

"No," Beth said. "I pray for his recovery. And yet it doesn't seem likely that—"

"I could talk to Gideon about this," Dat said. "Perhaps he'd understand."

"Wait," Beth said. "Give it a few weeks."

"Gideon didn't say we couldn't ever see each other, just that we shouldn't spend as much time together," Dat said.

"Jah," Beth said. "But he's right. I'm surprised it took so long for people to start to gossip. I shouldn't be here tonight. . . ."

Lila's face grew warm, sure they were talking about Beth's ex-husband. She continued on to the hallway and the bathroom. She knew Dat and Beth cared about each other, but hearing them whispering in the dark made them seem so vulnerable.

She was certain they would marry if Beth's husband died. But would they feel horrible about it, under the circumstances? They might not wish him dead, but they would certainly benefit from his demise. Perhaps Lila would have a stepmother after all, and soon.

She would be out of the house by then and happily married, with a life and home of her own. Rose would soon too. But how wonderful it would be for Trudy to have Beth as her mother.

Lila paused at the bathroom door in the dark hallway, ashamed of herself. She shouldn't be hoping for a future contingent on the death of Beth's ex-husband either. None of them should. It would be best not to think about it until it happened. Hopefully that's what Dat and Beth would do too.

Ten minutes later as she crawled into her bed, Rose whispered from across the room, "How do you like your house?"

"It's wonderful," Lila said.

"Jah," Rose said. "I stopped by late last week. Zane did a good job."

"Why are you still awake?"

Rose turned on a flashlight and held up a book. "I was looking at recipes."

"Share the best ones with me."

"I will." Rose turned off the light. "Did you see Trevor?"

"No," Lila said. "Why do you ask?"

"I just wondered how he was doing. . . . He seemed so lost."

"He'll be all right," Lila said, rolling onto her back. "*Guder Nacht.*"

Within a few minutes Rose's breathing slowed, followed by a little snore. Then she flopped over to her other side, obviously sound asleep. Rose had changed since she started courting Reuben. She'd become less lippy and selfish, and she'd taken on more of the household chores, including the cooking and baking.

There was still a part of Rose that craved attention though. Lila hoped she'd stay focused on Reuben—and not shift her interest to an ex-soldier struggling to cope with day-to-day life.

No, that wouldn't happen. Maybe it would have two years ago, but Rose had truly changed. She wouldn't be distracted by Trevor, no matter how good-looking he was.

⁂

The next afternoon Lila stood in the doorway of the baby's room in Eve and Charlie's house, watching as Eve lifted a little boy with red hair out of the crib. Light from the window bounced off the lemon-colored walls of the room. The curtains were a sheer yellow and the crib a contrasting white. A small chest of drawers and a changing table were pushed against the far wall.

For a moment Lila regretted not peeking into the Bobbli's room in her house. Had Zane painted the walls? Surely he hadn't furnished the room. Just the thought of the little house and the way she felt the night before made her face grow warm.

Eve turned toward her. "Here he is," she cooed. "Just up from his nap."

Lila knew the baby's name was Jackson, and that he was five months old. He looked smaller though. He wrinkled up his face and started to cry.

Eve put him to her shoulder and patted his back. "There, there," she said. She was a natural. Lila couldn't help but remember how well Eve had cared for Trudy when she was a baby—how well she'd cared for all of them.

Eve kept talking as she changed his diaper and then carried him out to the kitchen. As Eve grabbed the bottle that she'd prepared a few minutes before, Lila said, "He's really cute."

Eve nodded in agreement as she positioned the bottle in the baby's mouth. He latched on and relaxed against Eve's arm.

"How long do you think you'll have him?"

"It could be a while. In fact there's the possibility his mother might relinquish him."

"And then what?"

"We'd like to adopt him if no family members come forward to do so."

"Oh," Lila said, thinking that sounded risky.

After the baby drained the bottle and Eve burped him, she asked Lila if she wanted to hold him. "Of course," she said, taking him and then settling down on the sofa. The little one looked up at her and smiled, just a little.

"Oh, look at that." Lila stroked the side of his face, and he smiled again, his blue eyes lighting up. She glanced up at her aunt. "He's so alert." He was small, true, but he seemed healthy.

Eve nodded. "His reflexes are good, and he's on schedule as far as all of his developmental steps. If he falls behind, we'll get the support he'll need."

The women talked more about the baby and then about Charlie. Finally Eve asked about Zane.

"He's volunteering at the station this afternoon and evening," Lila said.

"Oh, great. Charlie didn't mention that."

Zane considered Charlie one of his best friends even though there was a fifteen-year age difference between them. After Zane was discharged from the Army and came home to Lancaster, he began volunteering at the station during the same time he took instruction to join the church.

He now carried a beeper for emergencies, and he'd been known to arrive at the station on a scooter he bought at a yard sale—which he claimed was faster than hitching up his horse to his buggy. Lila teased him that was because he was so slow at hitching a horse. That made him laugh. But she guessed the truth was he was afraid Billie might take off and never get him to the station at all.

Eve asked, "How's the house coming along?"

Lila's face grew warm again at the thought of it. "It's mostly done—Zane did such a good job." She smiled. "Although I'm guessing Charlie helped him."

Eve smiled back. "I think quite a few people helped."

"Like who?" Lila asked. Zane had been secretive, hardly talking with her at all about the project.

"Well, Charlie. And your Dat."

Lila nodded. She'd suspected that.

"And Daniel, and even Reuben."

"Reuben?" Lila wrinkled her nose.

Eve laughed. "Jah, he seems to be over you."

A smile spread across her face. "No doubt. He'll be much happier with Rose."

Jackson blew a bubble and then smiled again.

"What time is it?" Lila asked.

Eve pulled her phone from the pocket of her sweater. "Two forty-five."

"Uh oh, I need to get going." She stood. "Time to pick up Trudy."

"I thought Rose was handling that." Eve stood too and put out her arms for the baby.

"No, she's working as a mother's helper today—she should be home when I get back with Trudy." Her sister had never gotten a steady job like Lila had, but she helped out mothers in the area a couple of times a week at least.

A few minutes later, Lila was sweet-talking Billie and feeding him an apple. Once he'd finished it, she drove the buggy toward the highway. Billie's blinders flapped in the warm breeze, and his stride was steady. He hadn't startled at anything all day. Lila was confident that he would be a good buggy horse, and that even Zane would be able to handle him soon.

She hoped her wedding day would be as bright and warm as the weather had been all week, but there was no way to know. The only thing she could be certain of was that the house would be crowded. Dat had said he'd finish the basement, but he hadn't done a thing, and it would soon be too late.

Her mind went back to Eve as she half listened to the clippity-clop of Billie's hooves on the pavement. Lila hoped, if it was the Lord's will, that Eve and Charlie would be able to adopt the little boy. And hopefully there would be more children in their future too. They'd waited a long time to be parents.

Lila had never wondered whether she'd be able to have children. Most Amish women could, but every once in a while she'd hear of someone who couldn't. No one expected such a thing before they married.

But what if a woman knew before? What if Eve had known, would Charlie still have married her? She imagined so. She thought of how badly Zane wanted to be a father and wondered how he would react.

She glanced in the rearview mirror as a semi approached and pulled the horse as far to the right as she could. A second later the truck blew past her. Billie kept trotting along, seemingly oblivious to the leaves, dirt, and debris swirling around him. A few minutes later she turned off the highway, slowed for the covered bridge, and then bounced over the wooden slats through the dark tunnel, peering through the railings on the side into the creek. She was only a mile from the school.

The buggy bounced back into the sunlight, and the creek turned, bubbling alongside the road now. An Amish farmer cut his hay, probably his last crop of the year. In the next field a group of young men heaped dry hay into a wagon. One of the horses nickered, causing Billie to turn his head some, but he didn't break his stride. Across the road a cow mooed, and a farm dog ran along the fence line, barking at the buggy.

Or maybe at another vehicle. Lila sensed something behind her. She glanced toward her rearview mirror. But before she could register the image, something rammed into the back of the buggy. She flew forward, the reins slipping from her grasp, and hurtled through the windshield. She sailed over the top of Billie as the buggy flew apart behind her. The very last thing she remembered was flying toward the creek.

3

The alarm sounded in the station as Zane and the fire-fighters ate a late lunch, having returned to the station after responding to a car accident on Village Road. Thankfully it had been minor, with only one transfer to the hospital. No one had been badly hurt.

Zane pushed back his chair, rushing with the rest of the firefighters through the kitchen door to the bay, hoping this next event would be minor too. Charlie led the way, listening to his radio as he ran.

"It's a buggy accident," he called out. "An SUV is involved."

Zane cringed. Those were the worst, and he couldn't help but fear it might be someone he knew. The paramedics and firefighters filed out, quickly put on their gear, and headed toward the trucks. Charlie climbed into the driver's seat of the ambulance while Zane climbed into the passenger seat of the fire truck and buckled up as the driver, Bob, started the engine. A moment later they lurched forward and out of the open garage door, swinging left onto the street and then through the outskirts of Strasburg, following the ambulance.

Vehicles pulled to the side of the street as the sirens blared. The ambulance turned onto the highway and then a few minutes later onto a side road and headed toward Juneberry Lane.

Zane breathed in deeply. Just because they were headed that way didn't mean the accident involved anyone in the Lehman family. A few minutes later, the ambulance turned again. Zane exhaled in relief—until he realized they were headed toward Trudy's school. His heart raced faster. The ambulance turned again, but the driver of the fire truck went straight.

"We can't go over the covered bridge," Bob said. "We'll take a detour."

By the time they arrived, the ambulance had stopped not quite fifty feet in front of a black SUV on the shoulder of the road. Bob parked the fire truck behind the SUV. Zane jumped down. A group of both Amish and Englisch were gathered beyond it.

An Englischer stood with his hands on his knees beside the SUV, his head down as if he was sick. He appeared uninjured.

Zane headed toward the crowd, past the SUV, with its dented front bumper, and past the remnants of a buggy and the orange caution sign toward the group, just as a police car pulled up to the scene. Gideon stepped from the crowd toward Zane.

"It's Lila," he said. "She's injured badly."

Zane plunged forward.

"She's unconscious." Gideon grabbed Zane's arm. "You should wait here. She landed in the creek, and the horse fell on top of her."

"No," Zane choked, propelling himself forward, out of Gideon's grasp. She was now on the edge of the road. Beyond her was Billie. Two Amish men worked at freeing him from the torn harness as another tried to hold the horse steady. If Lila wasn't so good with Billie, Zane would fear the horse had spooked and caused the accident, but he doubted that was the case.

Charlie looked up. "She has a pulse," he said.

Zane squatted down beside her on the other side, relieved. She had cuts on her forearms, hands, and face. She was bleeding on her forehead and left cheek, but it seemed her arms took the brunt of the cuts. They were covered in blood, but the cuts seemed superficial. Her dress was soaked with water. He touched her forearm—her skin was cold and clammy. Thank goodness it was September and the creek was low.

Her eyelids fluttered a little as he said, "Baby, it's me. We're going to take care of you."

"Let's get her on the board," Charlie said. "After we get the neck brace on."

She could easily have a spine injury. Definitely internal injuries. And probably broken bones too.

The other paramedic handed Zane the neck brace. He reached around her neck, pulling away the hair that had fallen around her face, and fastened the brace. Her face was nearly as white as her Kapp, which lay on the ground next to her. Zane took a deep breath, trying not to panic.

Charlie knelt beside him, and they carefully rolled Lila onto the board. After they strapped her down, the other paramedic stepped forward and took one side of the board while Charlie took the other. Several men, including Gideon, rushed to help. The police had the road completely closed and one officer was questioning the driver of the SUV. He was around thirty, wore work boots, and kept running his hand through his hair.

Another policeman joined the Amish men attending to the horse.

As they neared the ambulance, Gideon stepped toward the driver of the SUV. Zane guessed the bishop would have some words of comfort for the man.

Zane was thankful for that because if it were up to him to say something, it probably wouldn't be very nice. He heard Gideon call the man "Donald" and then say something Zane couldn't understand. He turned his attention back to Lila. She looked so small on the board. So fragile. Panic welled up inside of him again. *Please, God! Let her be all right.*

Once they slid the board into the back of the ambulance, Charlie climbed in and then said to Zane, "Ride up front."

Bob stepped to Zane's side and said, "Give me your gear. You won't need it at the hospital."

Zane quickly stripped out of his pants and jacket and turned it over, along with his helmet, grateful others were thinking for him.

As Zane hurried to the cab, the Englisch man spoke loudly. "The horse veered to the left and pulled the buggy in front of me." Zane stopped and turned.

"I tried to stop," the man said. "Honestly."

Gideon, still standing beside the man, motioned for Zane to get into the ambulance. "I'll get Trudy home," he called out, "and then talk to Tim. Get going."

Zane seethed as he did. If he'd been driving the buggy, yeah, Billie might have done what the man said. But there was no way it happened that way with Lila. She was a good, cautious driver. And she knew how to control a horse, even Billie.

"Man, I'm sorry," the driver of the ambulance said, flipping on the siren. "I'm really sorry. Do you need to call anyone? Want to borrow my cell?"

Zane nodded, took the phone, and punched in his mom's number. As the ambulance turned around in the road, he could see the school ahead and the students who had gathered in the yard, watching the accident scene. He couldn't make out Trudy—but his heart lurched at what she might have seen.

His mom's voice came on with her usual, "Hello, this is Shani."

"It's Zane," he said. "You need to go get Tim and meet us at the hospital. But wait until Gideon gets Trudy home."

His mom gasped. "What's happened?"

"It's Lila. She's been in an accident." He swallowed hard. "It's bad. She's alive but not conscious. Hurry."

～✦～

As the ambulance pulled up to Lancaster General several doctors and nurses hurried out to meet it. Zane jumped down from the cab and then raced around to the back, explaining what had happened.

They pulled Lila out of the ambulance first, and Charlie followed. "She's been in and out of consciousness," he said. "Lacerations on her arms and face. Probable concussion. Possible internal injuries. Symptoms of a ruptured spleen. Possible broken bones."

Charlie turned toward Zane. "She asked for you."

Relief flooded through Zane, but he couldn't get past the threat of a ruptured spleen. Or what other internal injuries there could be.

"Has the family been notified?" an older nurse asked.

Zane nodded. "I'm her fiancé. Her father should be here soon."

The nurse gave him a sympathetic look. "Did you just happen to get the call?"

Zane nodded again, taking Lila's hand as they made their way through the double doors. She turned her head toward him and opened her eyes. "You're here."

"I am," he said.

"What happened?"

"You were in an accident," Zane said. "You're at the hospital now. The doctors will run some tests and find out what's wrong." He squeezed her hand. "You're going to be all right." She had to be.

As they made their way down the hall, the older nurse said, "Hey, you look familiar. Aren't you Shani's son?"

"Yes," Zane said. His mom had worked at the hospital for over ten years, up in pediatrics, but she knew most everyone.

The nurse glanced back down at Lila and then at Zane again. "I'm sorry," she said.

Zane simply nodded again as the emergency department doc directed the group into a bay. Charlie spoke more with the doctor as the nurses tended to Lila. The doctor began the examination as a nurse hooked Lila up to the blood-pressure cuff. Immediately the machine began to beep. The reading was 80/50.

"Affirmative on the ruptured spleen," the doctor said, his hands on Lila's abdomen. "We need to get her into surgery now."

The nurse grabbed the phone as the doctor began pushing Lila's gurney out of the bay.

Lila reached for Zane. He grabbed her hand and jogged beside the gurney.

"Your spleen ruptured," Zane said. "They need to remove it. That's what's most important now." She could die if they didn't stop the bleeding. They'd figure out the rest later. What other internal damage there might be. How bad her concussion was. If she had any broken bones.

"I'll be here when you get out," he said, letting go of her hand.

Charlie caught up with Zane and said, "I'll stay here with you."

"They need you at the station."

Charlie shook his head. "Someone will cover."

As they sat, Zane covered his face with his hands, thinking about his first day in Lancaster County, back when he was twelve. His father and Simon were both in Lancaster General that night. A workhorse Zane had spooked kicked Simon, and Dad had fallen and reinjured his leg that had been torn up in

Iraq. Zane had seen Lila for the first time through the field gate that day, and he'd been enchanted with her ever since.

Charlie put an arm around Zane's shoulders. The physical comfort helped.

Zane tried to pray a second time, but still couldn't get past *Please, God!* God wanted him to trust, no matter what. All Zane could think of was that Lila had to live. He couldn't lose her now.

He wrestled with himself, going back and forth as far as trusting, until Mom and Tim rushed into the waiting room. Charlie explained the spleen injury.

"It's not uncommon in accidents," Mom said to Tim.

"So she's not in danger, then?"

"We hope not," Charlie said. "But it is very serious. Any internal bleeding is. And she could have more."

Mom's eyes grew even more concerned.

"Jah," Tim said. "I figured with the horse landing on her and all there could be lots of injuries."

No one said anything for a few minutes, but then Zane said, "I forgot to ask Gideon to get the horse home."

Tim nodded. "He told a couple of the other men to deliver him, after he'd calmed down, to our place."

"It didn't look like Billie was badly hurt," Zane said.

"We'll see," Tim answered. "Most horses don't escape injury in such a bad accident. I'll call the vet."

Zane wasn't sure if that meant Tim believed Billie needed to be examined—or put down. And he didn't want to think about it now. "How's Trudy?"

"She seems to be doing all right," Tim said.

Zane didn't trust him to truly notice. He wasn't known for taking his children's feelings into account. Zane glanced at his mom.

"Gideon dropped her off at the house just before I left with Tim," she said. "She stayed with Rose."

"Did she see what was going on from the schoolyard?"

"I don't think so," Mom answered. "But she thought the accident probably involved Lila, because she was so late."

Everyone was silent for a long moment until Charlie said, "We should go to the operating waiting room. The surgery shouldn't take too long."

Nearly two hours later the surgeon appeared—a woman, with her mask in her hand. Zane jumped to his feet and quickly introduced Tim as Lila's father. The doctor shook their hands and then said to Tim, "Your girl is lucky to be alive. The spleen had ruptured, plus she has a bruised liver and bladder. She had quite a bit of internal bleeding."

Zane grabbed the back of a chair for support.

The doctor continued. "I had an orthopedic surgeon check in. Lila also has a crushed pelvis. He's ordered X rays to see exactly where the damage is. And we'll also do a CT scan to make sure we didn't miss anything in the abdominal cavity. Right now she's critical but stable, so that's a relief, but she has a long road of recovery ahead of her."

Tim exhaled as Mom put her arm around him. Then she grabbed Zane's free hand. He held on as tight as he could.

Lila was alive. That was what mattered. His knees grew weak. He'd almost lost her—after all they'd gone through, she'd nearly been killed.

He needed to thank God, but all he could do was fight back his tears.

4

Reuben stood in the doorway of the Lehmans' barn, his eyes adjusting to the dim light. His Dat had called and told him to close down the lumberyard early because Lila had been in an accident, and Reuben needed to help Rose with the milking.

As his eyes adjusted, he could see Rose at the far end of the barn, standing in a stream of light from the open door. Specks of dust floated around her, and she wore a vinyl apron, cinched around her waist, and a kerchief over her hair. "Denki for coming," she said, giving him a wave.

"Jah," he answered. "Have you heard anything more about Lila?"

Rose shook her head. "But it sounds as if it was a bad wreck."

Reuben glanced toward Trudy, who'd stopped shoveling. She'd turned eleven in March and had grown taller in the last year, but she still wore the baggie dresses and long aprons that little girls did. He didn't want to burden her with more fear than she probably already felt by asking Rose for details.

"I'll go get more cows." He grabbed a vinyl apron from a peg by the office door as Rose herded a cow into the first slot and secured the animal's head.

He started for the other end of the barn to herd in the cows that had gathered near the door. Maybe they could tell he was worried or maybe it was his lack of skill with animals, but he had trouble with several of the cows. He didn't particularly like to do the milking, even though he helped the Lehmans in the past, especially when he was courting Lila.

Now here she was, soon to marry someone else in a month, if her injuries weren't too bad. He shivered. He wanted her to be all right. He held no ill feelings toward her.

Rose was a far better match for him.

He gently pushed on a cow's neck, trying to nudge her next to the milking machine. She balked. Tim had such a way with animals that the cows practically waltzed into place for him. It wasn't how they behaved for Reuben.

"You have to be really firm with her," Rose said. "Or she won't cooperate."

Reuben pushed harder. The cow sidestepped toward him. Rose came around from the trough and pushed from the other side. The cow kicked.

"Oh, you . . ." Rose sputtered, shoving harder against the cow.

"Need some help?"

Reuben turned toward the door. The Englisch man from the day before was headed toward them.

"Hi, Trevor," Rose said, speaking in a friendly manner. That was her way.

"Hi." Trevor glanced from Rose to Reuben. "I worked on a dairy back in Delaware. Want some help?"

"Sure!" Rose's face lit up.

Reuben moved away from the cow as Trevor stepped forward.

The man was tall—nearly a head taller than Reuben—and muscular. He wore a long-sleeved T-shirt, but his muscles bulged enough for their outline to be apparent through the fabric. He stepped up to the cow with confidence. He didn't shove her, not exactly. He simply leaned against her and walked forward with confidence. The cow moved with him, stopping when she reached the trough. Trevor quickly secured the cow and then hooked up the machine.

There was no sign of the emotional turmoil from the day before. Reuben realized he'd been staring at the Englischer and headed back toward one of the cows that was milked and ready to be released.

The work went quickly with Trevor's help. As they neared the last of the cows, Rose said she was going into the house to get supper on the table. "We'll just have sandwiches—I didn't have time for anything more, but I do have a chocolate shoofly pie for dessert," she said. "Both of you should come in and eat."

Reuben wasn't sure about Rose inviting a stranger in when her father was gone. He cleared his throat.

"Don't worry," Trevor said, his voice low. "I told Joel I'd eat over at their house."

Reuben simply nodded. At least the man had some common sense.

"Come on, Trudy," Rose called out to her little sister, who had been playing with a kitten for the last half hour.

After Rose and Trudy left, it took another half hour for Reuben and Trevor to clean up. When they'd finished, Reuben shook Trevor's hand. "Thank you," he said.

"What about in the morning? Who'll do the milking then?"

"Tim and Rose," Reuben said, sure Tim wouldn't spend the night at the hospital. Zane might—but Tim would come home.

"All right," Trevor said. "I'm staying with the Becks for a few more days. I'll check in with Tim and see if there's anything

44

I can do to help. Zane's been a good friend to me—I'd like to be able to help out any way I can."

"I think Tim will be all right doing his own chores." Reuben didn't care if he sounded defensive. He didn't like the thought of an Englisch man hanging around the Lehman farm. "On the other hand," Reuben said, adjusting his voice to a kinder tone, "I really needed your help tonight. I appreciate it."

"Grateful I could help." Trevor started toward the door. Reuben followed him out of the barn and called out a good-bye as Trevor headed toward the gate to the field. He seemed to know his way around awfully well already.

Reuben watched as Trevor disappeared. Reuben felt his father, as the bishop, had been too lenient about the influence the Becks had had on the Lehman family all these years. It seemed as if it had been one thing after another. Reuben's father was a good man, but he tended to give people the benefit of the doubt more often than he should. Tim's friendship with Beth was simply another example of his father's leniency.

By the time Reuben reached the house, Trudy had the table set and Rose was heating up a pot of soup and finishing making sandwiches. Rose looked enchanting by the light of the lamp hanging above the sink that cast a soft glow over her face.

"I'm going to go check the answering machine," Rose said. "I should have done that before I came in. Maybe Dat left a message about Lila." She dried her hands on her apron. "Wash up," she called out as she hurried out the back door. "We'll eat as soon as I get back."

After he washed, Reuben headed back to the kitchen. Trudy sat at the table, looking a little lost. Reuben wasn't sure what to do and hoped Rose would return soon—it shouldn't take long to listen to the messages. A knock on the back door startled him.

Before he could react, Trudy scampered to the mud porch. "Beth," she said, her voice full of relief.

Trudy pulled her teacher into the room.

"Hello," the woman said. She wore her cape and bonnet. "I thought perhaps Rose and Trudy could use some company. I didn't realize you'd be here, Reuben."

"I helped with the milking." He hoped it didn't seem inappropriate for him to be in the house. He stepped toward the back door. "Rose went to check the answering machine. I'll go tell her you're here."

"I already said hello to her." Beth took her bonnet off. "She told me to come on in."

"Oh?"

Beth nodded. "She's talking to an Englischer out there. I think she said his name is Trevor."

Reuben nodded and tried to sound calm even though he was alarmed Trevor had returned. "He helped us with the milking."

"So he said." Beth slipped out of her cape and headed back to the mud porch, most likely to hang up her things. She returned with a container that she must have left on the shelf when she first came in.

"I brought lemon bars," she said. "I'm guessing Rose already has dessert made, so these can be for tomorrow." She put the pan on the counter and then placed her arm around Trudy. "How are you doing, sweetie?"

Trudy grew sniffly. Reuben pointed toward the door and said, "I'll go check on Rose." As he trudged down the steps, Trevor headed toward the lane.

Rose must have already gone to the barn, and Reuben decided to sit down on the steps and wait for her. The sun set as he waited, and immediately a chill filled the air.

When Rose returned, her face was pale, and she pulled her cloak tight around herself.

Reuben stood. "Was there a message?"

Rose nodded. "Lila's badly hurt. Internal injuries. Something about her spleen rupturing. Something's broken—I can't remember exactly what. And a concussion, like Simon had when he was young."

Reuben put his arm around her.

"Dat said he would come home tonight. Shani will bring him. But he'll go back after the milking's done in the morning."

"I can help as needed," Reuben said. Tim was supposed to work at the lumberyard the next day, but he wouldn't be able to do that.

"Denki," Rose said. "And I'm guessing Trevor will help as needed too. And Joel and Adam. I'll call over there after supper."

Reuben cleared his throat, wanting to warn her about Trevor.

"What?" she asked.

"Nothing," he said, changing his mind. If Trevor's motivation really was to help, Reuben didn't want to put any ideas in Rose's head.

She leaned against Reuben. "I can't believe this happened to Lila." Rose shook a little, maybe from the cold but more likely from the shock of Lila's injuries.

Reuben knew that in the past the sisters hadn't always gotten along, but in the last couple of years that had changed. Emotion welled inside of Reuben. It was for Lila, jah, but more for what Rose was feeling. "Don't you think she'll be all right?" he asked. Hopefully they got her to the hospital in time.

Rose exhaled. "I hope so. She's already had one surgery and it sounds as if she may need another."

He squeezed her shoulder, and Rose turned her doe-like eyes toward him. He sensed a hunger in her, or perhaps more accurately a desire. It was something he'd never seen in Lila, at least not directed toward him. He would have liked to kiss Rose then, but it hardly seemed appropriate with her sister in the hospital.

"Are you worried about Lila?" he asked.

"Jah," she answered. "Are you?"

47

"Of course," he answered. But his thoughts weren't on Lila. They were on Rose, on the fullness of her lips, on the look in her eyes, on the way she tilted her head toward him.

"Let's go eat," he said. "Beth and Trudy are waiting for us."

⸻

By the time he reached his dark house, Reuben felt nearly overcome with loneliness. Not many Amish people lived alone, but he had since his sister married and moved out. Before that their father lived with them, until he married Monika and moved into her large home.

Before that, their mother lived with them, until she died. Before that his two brothers lived with them too. But they'd both moved out and married years ago.

Reuben was the only one left in the old house by the lumberyard. He stopped the buggy by his barn, unhitched his horse, led her into her stall, brushed her down, and fed her.

He entered his house through the back door, went into the kitchen, and leaned across the first table he'd made with the help of his Dat. He pulled his battery-operated lantern closer and turned it on. He was grateful he'd already eaten at the Lehmans' place. There was nothing worse than sitting at his kitchen table by himself. He looked forward to Rose cooking for him. He enjoyed the food she made, more than he'd let on. He didn't want to praise her too much, to make her prideful, but no one made a better lemon pie than she did. Or a better pecan one. Or a better peach cream pie. And the chocolate shoofly pie she'd made for tonight had been delicious.

He picked up the lantern. The kitchen hadn't changed in the thirteen years since his mother died. A home needed a woman. He never thought he'd be twenty-six and without a wife. He'd waited for years for Lila, only to have her reject him. He wouldn't be so foolish as to wait so long for Rose.

Reuben walked through the kitchen, into the empty living room. His sister had taken most of the furniture when she moved out. Sometime before he and Rose married, he'd need to buy some more.

He headed on up the stairs to the landing and stared out the window overlooking the lumberyard. He'd lived in the house his entire life and worked in his father's business for as long as he could remember. His father said he would sign the house over when Reuben married, and in time the business would belong solely to him too.

There were three bedrooms and a bathroom upstairs. It wasn't a big house, but it was large enough. He'd shared a bedroom with his brothers while their sister had one to herself.

Reuben thought four children would be a good amount. No doubt Rose would be a good mother. She was good with Trudy, and she seemed to do well as a mother's helper.

She wasn't as serious as Lila, and Reuben appreciated that. He didn't see any reason to be overly concerned about world events or what happened outside their district. There was little to be done about it anyway. He liked that about Rose, that she didn't dwell on things that didn't impact their Plain world the way Lila had. That had been Zane's influence, Reuben was sure, but also Lila's disposition.

The truth was, he'd been devastated when Lila broke things off with him. She said it wasn't because of Zane, but Reuben wasn't surprised when a few months later they began seeing each other.

Reuben knew Lila and Zane had always been friends, but he never guessed she would choose an Englischer. He was even more surprised that Zane became Amish. He hadn't expected that at all. Oddly, Reuben's father seemed to have influenced Zane's decision.

He sighed and headed down the hall, stopping at what used to be his parents' room and opening the door. He held the lantern high. Their old bed, with a quilt his mother made, and a bureau were all that was left in the room. He hoped Rose would like it.

He imagined coming home to her, to her laughter, her teasing, and her wide smile. He imagined kissing those lips of hers every day. Several times a day. Just the thought made his heart race.

She was the life of the party at every singing. Sunday he hadn't wanted to stay and play volleyball because he hated the way the boys watched her. Even the men. He didn't like the jealousy he felt over it, and he would never tell her how he felt. It wasn't her fault.

Many outsiders believed Amish women to be quiet and passive. That wasn't true. Most of the Amish women he knew were quite assertive within the community, making their opinions known, and sharing in the decision making. Rose very much enjoyed interacting with others in their district, but she was friendly with everyone, Amish and Englisch alike. He'd never seen her shy away from anyone.

Lila had insinuated a few times that Rose was lazy, but that was a side Reuben had never seen. She would make a wonderful wife, homemaker, and mother. She had a playfulness to her that he appreciated, that made him smile.

He closed the bedroom door firmly and continued on down the hall. One single bed, a small chest of drawers, a small table, and pegs along the far wall were all that were in his room. He lived a sparse life—that was for certain.

The evening had grown chilly, so Reuben undressed quickly and slid under the quilt on his bed. He picked up a library book on different kinds of wood from his bedside table and began to read. Soon his eyes grew heavy and he put the book down and turned off the lantern.

Jah, it was time for the house to have a woman in it again. As soon as Lila was stable, Reuben would talk with Rose. They didn't have to wait until Lila and Zane could marry, especially if Lila's recovery took a while, which it probably would from the sound of her injuries. True, it might be seen as insensitive, but he couldn't put his life on hold because of Lila again. He needed to take charge and make sure his plan worked out this time. The sooner the better.

5

Rose rubbed her hands together, trying to warm them up in the early-morning chill, as she spoke to Dat. "I need to get breakfast started and wake up Trudy for school."

"Go ahead," he said. "I can manage."

"Trevor would—" He'd given her his cell-phone number the evening before.

Her father shook his head.

"But he's staying with the Becks. He helped Reuben and me last night. He used to work on a dairy."

Dat shook his head. "I'll finish up just fine. You go on ahead."

Shani had dropped Dat off long after Reuben and Beth had left the night before. Rose had stayed up as late as she could and was just heading to bed when she heard Shani's van outside. Dat hadn't said much, just that Lila was on a lot of pain medication and was out of sorts. Rose hoped she could go see her soon.

"I'll have breakfast ready when you come in," Rose said.

Dat nodded.

"Then will you go back to the hospital?"

"Jah," he said. "I have a driver coming soon."

"What about Shani?" Rose said.

"She has some sort of early meeting at work—she was going to leave about now."

Rose wrinkled her nose. "I'd like to see Lila sometime too."

"Jah," Dat said. "That would be *gut*."

Rose wasn't so sure he would make it a priority for her to get to the hospital. She'd ask Shani, once she was back from her meeting, if she could get a ride with her.

By the time Rose returned from taking Trudy to school, Dat had left. She poured herself another cup of coffee and then tackled washing the frying pans. Once she finished, she decided to walk up the lane and see if Shani had come home.

The morning fog had burned off, and the sunshine was beginning to warm the world. Along the lane, the changing leaves of the maple trees fluttered, and the boughs of the cedar tree swayed in the breeze. Rose quickened her step. She was worried about Lila, but her thoughts went to Reuben. It was like him to put Lila and Zane first. Rose admired his unselfishness, but she couldn't help but resent it also.

Lila wouldn't care if Rose and Reuben married first. Rose wished he'd lighten up a little. Play a game of volleyball. Laugh a little more. Touch her more. She longed to have his arms tightly around her—not just around her shoulder like last night. And she longed to have his lips on hers. She sighed. What was taking him so long?

She knew she shouldn't be thinking about Reuben when Lila was so horribly injured, but she couldn't help it. Their relationship wasn't turning out the way she expected. And now, with Lila's accident, everything would be delayed further.

She stepped around the bend in the lane and the Becks' house came into view. Shani's van wasn't anywhere in sight. Either she wasn't home yet, or she'd parked it in the shed or by the barn. She continued on. Joel would be at work and Adam at school. Maybe Shani had stayed up at the hospital to see Lila. There weren't any other cars around, so that meant Trevor had already left for the day. She wasn't sure what he would be doing though. Maybe he'd gone up to the hospital to be with Zane.

She might as well knock on the door and see if anyone answered. Some of the leaves of the geraniums that filled Shani's pots on her porch had turned yellow, but the flowers continued to put off big red blooms. Rose hurried up the steps and knocked lightly at first and then a little harder. When no one answered, she turned to go. When she reached the bottom step the door opened.

As she turned back around, Trevor said, "Rose? Is that you?"

He stood barefoot, wearing shorts and an Army T-shirt.

Rose's face grew warm. "I was looking for Shani."

"She's not here."

"Oh." Rose felt foolish for coming over. Of course she'd stay at the hospital to be with Lila. "I'll leave a message on her cell phone," Rose said. Maybe Shani would take her up to the hospital that evening.

Trevor yawned and stretched his arms.

Rose's face grew even warmer.

"Do you want a ride up to the hospital?" he asked.

"I was hoping I could catch one with Shani, but I could call a driver." She wasn't sure why she said that except to be on her way as soon as possible.

He stepped out onto the porch. "Driver?"

"Jah," she said. "We hire Englischers to drive us around."

"Englischers?"

Her face was hot now. She nodded.

He took a step forward. "Like me?"

She nodded again, feeling even more self-conscious. "I need

to get going. Thank you." It unnerved her to be alone with a half-dressed man. She hurried down the last step.

"I can give you a ride," he said.

"Oh, no. That's too much," she responded, catching her foot on a flagstone on the walkway. She tripped a little but caught herself.

"It's no problem," Trevor said. "I'm going that way anyway." He glanced down at his shirt. "I just need to get a shower."

Surely it wouldn't hurt to get a ride with him. Hopefully Dat would understand, under the circumstances.

She turned back around. "Could you stop by and pick me up on your way?"

He nodded. "Give me twenty minutes."

"See you then," she said. His car must have been in the shed or parked over by the barn or maybe even by the little house. She hurried back down the lane, put away the breakfast dishes that had dried in the rack, left a note for Dat in case their paths didn't cross, and grabbed her purse.

She had no idea what she'd cook for supper that night, but she'd figure it out. She took her lip balm out of her purse, ran it over her lips, and then headed to the back door, locking it behind her with her key. By the time she reached the driveway, Trevor's car was coming toward her. She squinted into the morning sun, shading her eyes as she walked toward it.

By the time she met the car, Trevor had stopped and opened the passenger door from the inside. She climbed in and fumbled for the seat belt as he turned the car around. He wore some sort of fragrance, aftershave probably, and his hair was still wet.

His car was a little messy inside. She'd noticed some paper bags in the back seat when she'd turned to fasten her seat belt. And there was a pile of receipts in the cubby under the stereo. She'd expected that a soldier would keep things tidier.

"I'm glad you stopped by," Trevor said. "I wanted to get up to the hospital today too."

"Thank you," she said as he turned sharply onto the lane. "I appreciate the ride."

"No problem," he answered, shifting gears as he did. She pulled her legs to the side, close to her door, away from his hand. The interior of the car was all black except for the panel of instruments. It looked pretty fancy. So did the radio.

"Poor Zane. Must be a bummer to be planning to get married in a month and then have this happen." Trevor frowned. "I think that sounded wrong. Poor *Lila*. She's the one going through all the pain."

Rose smiled a little. "I know what you mean. Besides, Zane is your friend—of course you'd be sympathetic toward him."

Trevor smiled again. "Thanks," he said. "For giving me a pass."

She didn't respond. What he'd said hadn't been that big of a deal. He seemed to be a thoughtful person.

Once they were on the highway, he shifted again and the vehicle practically flew. A field of sunflowers zoomed by in a yellow blur. She leaned back against the seat, sure Trevor was speeding.

She steadied her voice. "You must have grown up in a small town to have worked in a dairy."

"That's right. We don't have any Amish though." He flashed her a grin.

Rose smiled back instead of saying that there were Amish in Delaware. She couldn't remember exactly where though. "Did you join the Army right out of school?"

"No," he answered. "I took classes at the local community college, although I didn't do very well." He chuckled. "And worked in the dairy. Then I joined the Army."

"So you were in Afghanistan with Zane?"

Trevor nodded and said, "Yep." There was no hint of the emotions he had displayed on Sunday, but still she gathered he had deep feelings about the topic. She couldn't help but feel concerned for him.

Ahead was a buggy with the morning sun reflecting off the orange triangle on the back. At first she wondered if Trevor was going to slow down, but then he did.

"I can't get over how beautiful the horses around here are," he said. "And I really like the sound of the hooves on the pavement." Trevor shifted again and then glanced toward her. "I like it here."

Rose wasn't sure how to respond. She'd never been anywhere besides Lancaster County. Not even to Maryland or Ohio, like some of her friends had. Not even to the next county, truth be told.

The highway turned into four lanes and Trevor accelerated. Rose sank back against the seat, feeling like a child. She really hadn't done much of anything in her life. Courting Reuben was the most exciting thing that had happened, and truth be doubly told, it hadn't been all that exciting. At least not yet. And the way things were progressing, it wasn't going to be for a while.

When they reached the outskirts of Lancaster, Trevor shifted down again. This time Rose didn't move her legs and his hand bumped against her knee. Instead of apologizing, he smiled at her.

She smiled back and then kept her eyes straight ahead. She'd only been into town a few times. She loved watching the big brick houses with their expansive lawns on the outside of town. Soon the large houses gave way to rows of houses with just a sidewalk out front. A few older people were shuffling along, and several stood outside a small store. The neighborhood, so close to home but so different than anything she knew, fascinated her.

"How much older are you than Lila?" Trevor stopped at a traffic light.

"Pardon?" Rose asked.

"Your little sister. How old is she?"

Her face grew warm again. "I'm younger than Lila."

"Oh, really," Trevor said. "I thought you were the older sister. So how young are you?" he teased.

She squared her shoulders. "Eighteen."

"Which makes Lila how old?"

"Twenty-two."

"So a year younger than Zane?"

Rose nodded. "How old are you?"

"Twenty-three also."

Three years younger than Reuben. Five years older than she was.

The light turned green, and Trevor turned right. A few minutes later they passed the main entrance of the hospital and then turned into a parking garage. All these years Rose had imagined the hospital—the one where her mother had died. Where Simon had gone when he was kicked in the head by the horse. Where Shani worked.

She opened the door and climbed out.

"Which way do we go?"

"I'm not sure," Rose said. "I've never been here."

"Really?" Before she could answer, Trevor said, "Well, that's not a bad thing, right? It means you and your family haven't had to come here."

She shook her head. "Others have."

"Like who?" he asked, leading the way around to the entrance.

"My mother."

"Oh," he said, seeming a little confused. "I didn't see her yesterday, right?"

Rose shook her head. "She passed away a little over eleven years ago."

Trevor stopped and turned toward her, looking down. "I'm sorry."

She blinked. "It was a long time ago. It's fine."

The double doors opened and Trevor stepped aside, letting Rose pass through first. He took the lead though and headed toward the lobby desk. Rose stayed back, feeling self-conscious about being with an Englisch man.

The woman at the desk said something and then pointed toward a hallway. Trevor thanked her and then said to Rose, "Lila's in critical care. Let's go up to the waiting room and see if we can find Zane."

She followed him to the elevator as several other people stepped onto it. An Englisch man. A doctor, she thought. And a woman wearing a skirt and jacket. Trevor motioned for Rose to go first and she found a spot on the side. No one spoke as the elevator ascended. Rose held onto the railing on the side, until she noticed no one else was. She let go and leaned against the wall.

When the elevator stopped, Trevor nodded toward the door and she followed him into a hallway. He paused for a moment and then pointed to the right. Zane wasn't in the waiting room. "Stay here," Trevor said. "I'll ask someone to find him."

Rose sank down onto a sofa, grateful Trevor was with her. She picked up a magazine with a group of children on the front and leafed through it as she waited. The articles were about activities to do with kids in the Lancaster area. Museums and petting zoos. The train out in Strasburg, near their farm. A pumpkin patch to go to. She put the magazine down as Trevor approached.

"He'll be right out." Trevor sat down beside her.

Wanting to make conversation, she asked, "What was it like serving in Afghanistan with Zane?"

Trevor leaned forward, his hands on his knees. "It's not like I hung out with him that much or even really noticed him at first, but he was always a good guy. Really decent. Then he got shot, which was scary. Of course I noticed him a little more when he came back." He turned his head toward Rose and smiled a little. "I was driving the MRAPs by then, and he probably saved my life." Trevor's gaze shifted to the windows, where sunlight streamed through. "I got a Purple Heart—Zane got his earlier, when he was almost killed."

Rose didn't know what a Purple Heart was, but it sounded important and she guessed it was some sort of Army award. She'd never heard Zane mention it.

"Out of all of us—besides Casey, who's still in the Army . . ."

Rose nodded.

"That's right. She's dating one of your brothers, correct?"

Rose nodded again.

"Anyway," Trevor said, "my point is that Zane's doing better than most of us. Grant got out and moved to Michigan, but he's not doing too hot. His wife is a saint. She pretty much does everything as far as their two kids. Wade is still in the Army and in Texas but seems kind of messed up. Parties a lot. Can't seem to commit to one girl. Most of the other guys who got out haven't found decent jobs yet."

"How about you?" Rose asked.

He looked at her blankly.

"Do you have a girlfriend?"

A frown crept across his face. "It seems I may have more in common with Wade than I thought, as far as committing."

Rose wasn't sure what to say, but once again she felt sad for Trevor.

"That's why I came here," he said. "I thought maybe Zane could help me—the whole 'never leave a fallen soldier' thing. But he obviously . . . ." Zane came through the doors and Trevor's voice trailed off.

"Hey," Zane said.

"How's she doing?" Trevor asked.

"A little better. The surgeon still needs to operate on her pelvis but wants to wait until some of the swelling goes down from the other injuries and from the surgery yesterday." Zane turned to Rose. "Would you like to see her?"

"Jah, very much." Rose did want to see Lila, but she suddenly felt hesitant.

Zane must have sensed her hesitation. "I'll go with you," he said.

"All right." Rose stood.

"I'll wait here," Trevor said.

Zane nodded. "We'll have time to talk soon."

Rose asked if her Dat was with Lila as she followed Zane down the hall. "No, he's filling out paper work. My mom's with him."

"Oh? I thought she had a meeting this morning."

"She did, but it's been over for a while."

"Oh." As Rose followed Zane through a door, she began to feel a little sick to her stomach. She looked up to see Lila propped up a little in a bed. Her face was cut and starting to bruise, and her blond hair was braided and draped over one shoulder. She wasn't wearing a Kapp or a scarf. A tube ran under the skin of her arm, and something poked into her finger. Rose felt a little light-headed.

Lila opened her eyes and smiled—or maybe grimaced. Rose stepped to her side, and Lila reached out her hand. As Rose took it, tears welled in her eyes. Her usually capable sister was so small and helpless in the hospital bed. Besides the wounds on her face, cuts covered her arms too. One place was stitched. Rose had never seen her big sister so vulnerable. She'd always been so strong.

"How are you?" Rose asked.

"All right," Lila answered, her face contorting some. Her blue eyes were bloodshot and heavy. She looked past Rose.

"I'm right here, baby," Zane said, stepping to Lila's other side.

Lila seemed to relax a little as Zane held her hand, and she focused on Rose again. "How did you get here?" she asked.

"Trevor gave me a ride."

Lila frowned and looked at Zane. "Do you think that's all right?"

Zane shrugged.

Rose bristled. "It was fine. He's very nice."

A machine started making a weird noise. Rose stepped back, feeling light-headed again.

"It's just the blood-pressure cuff," Zane said, pointing at Lila's arm. Then Rose noticed the other machines.

A nurse came into the room, asked Lila how she was feeling, and then stood at a computer Rose hadn't noticed and started typing. "How's your pain?" the nurse asked.

Lila answered, "Maybe an eight."

"Time for more meds, then," the nurse said.

Rose concentrated on her sister. Something dripped from the bag and down through the tube into Lila's arm. There was a second bag at the end of the bed. Rose turned, thinking maybe she should leave the room and go sit in the waiting room with Trevor.

She swayed a little.

Zane grabbed her arm. "Are you all right?"

Everything went black before she could tell him she wasn't.

When she came to, she was propped on a chair, with Zane holding her in place.

"I thought someone was getting restless," the nurse said. "Put her head between her knees."

"No, I'm all right," Rose replied, embarrassed. She tried to see the situation from Lila's angle and feared her sister would think she was being overly dramatic, the way she used to act when she was younger.

"Let's get you out to the waiting room." Zane helped Rose stand.

"I'm sorry," Rose said.

Lila frowned. "It's disturbing, I know."

Mortified, Rose leaned against Zane as they shuffled along to the waiting room. Trevor stood when he saw them coming. "Are you all right?" he asked.

Rose nodded. But she wasn't. She began to cry as Trevor reached out to take her arm. She should have been strong for Lila—instead her sister was still the strong and capable one, even when she'd been horribly injured.

A half hour later, without seeing Dat or Shani, they were on their way home. Rose started crying again. She wasn't sure if it was a reaction to the fainting or the shock of seeing Lila so hurt.

"There are napkins in the glove box," Trevor said. "Help yourself."

Feeling foolish, Rose opened it and grabbed one, noticing the fast-food restaurant logo on the tissue. It looked as if Trevor ate in his car a lot. She wiped her eyes, disappointed in herself. She'd been so sure she'd grown up these last couple of years and learned to put others before herself, but maybe she hadn't as much as she thought. She'd been eager to see Lila and encourage her, but instead she'd made a scene and only made things harder.

"How about if we go to Strasburg?" Trevor asked. "I drove through there the other day. It's charming."

Rose smiled at his choice of words, not expecting a soldier to care about a historic village. But she agreed; it was charming. Her grandmother had a quilt shop, which Rose never spent much time at in the little town. Unlike Lila, she didn't like to quilt. She'd rather cook.

"Sure," Rose answered.

As they drove through town, Rose hunched down a little, especially past the quilt shop, not wanting her grandmother to see her riding with an Englischer in his red sports car. But there was no sign of her *Mammi* through the shop window.

A couple of minutes later, Trevor found a place to park on the street. "How about some food?" he asked. "You'll feel better."

Her head was pounding, and she thought a cup of coffee might help. "Sure," she answered. She had some money in her purse to pay. "The Strasburg Creamery has a deli too—you could get a sandwich."

Trevor hurried around to her door and helped her out.

"I'm all right." She still clutched the napkin. "Just embarrassed. Really embarrassed." And not just from fainting—she'd never done that before—but from the crying too.

"You don't need to be," Trevor said. "It could happen to anyone."

Rose knew he was just being nice. Neither he nor Zane would ever faint in a hospital. Neither would Lila. She'd taken care of their grandmother after her cancer surgery, changing her dressings and everything. Just the thought made Rose feel lightheaded again. She needed to get over this. When Lila came home, Rose would be the one caring for her, most likely.

Trevor opened the door to the Creamery and directed Rose to the first booth. "I'm buying," he said as they sat down.

"You don't need to," Rose answered.

His face lit up. "It's the least I can do."

Rose only ordered coffee and a cinnamon roll while Trevor ordered a Reuben sandwich, which made Rose wince. *Reuben.* What would he think of her with the Englischer?

The Creamery served the best ice cream around, and the production of waffle cones filled the entire building with a sweet scent. Shani had brought all the kids into Strasburg for ice cream several times when they were little, which were fond memories now.

Once they settled into a booth with their coffee and food, Trevor asked how Lila was doing.

Rose's eyes filled with tears again. "I've never seen her like that." She inhaled sharply. "I'm so embarrassed I fainted. She used to think I was overly dramatic—and I was. I didn't mean to be so today." She dabbed at her eyes.

"You? A drama queen?" Trevor shook his head. "I don't see that in you at all."

Rose tried to smile. "Well, I do have it in me." She'd never been as bad as Lila thought, but she'd definitely been more dramatic than Lila ever was. She supposed she could still be.

"She wouldn't think you fainted on purpose," Trevor said.

Rose wrapped both hands around her coffee cup. She didn't really think that—at least she hoped Lila wouldn't go that far. "That would make me quite the actress, right?"

"Yes, an Academy Award-winning one." He smiled again.

Rose had read about those awards in the magazines she sometimes bought, although none of it really made sense to her.

Trevor told Rose about the first time he'd heard about Lila. "I didn't find out about this until we were in Afghanistan, but one of the other soldiers saw a photo of her on Zane's phone. He teased him about it relentlessly."

"Oh?" Rose didn't know anything about a photo of Lila.

Trevor nodded. "We all thought it was pretty weird he had an Amish girlfriend." He grinned. "I still think it's weird, but I kind of get it now. I can tell they really love each other."

Rose nodded and then said, "She wasn't really his girlfriend back then. She was courting Reuben."

"Oh." Trevor tilted his head. "The guy who helped with the milking yesterday?"

Rose nodded and then, not wanting the conversation to stay on Reuben, asked, "Do you know how long you plan to stay in Lancaster?"

He shook his head. "Joel said I could stay for a few days. I'm hoping maybe I can help, considering everything that's going on with Lila." He seemed so caring and confident, nothing like the out-of-sorts man he appeared to be on Sunday.

Rose leaned back against the booth as Trevor continued to talk, saying he found Lancaster County fascinating. He went on to say that he'd grown up with just his dad. "My mom left when I was ten. She'd had a few affairs, and the whole town knew. She abruptly changed my world, stole my innocence, really. I ended up figuring out a lot about life at a pretty young age." The guy liked to talk. He'd played sports in high school—football, basketball, and baseball.

"I found that same camaraderie in the Army," he said. "Plus, chicks like guys in a uniform." He smiled. "Just sayin'."

Rose guessed Trevor looked pretty good in a uniform.

He kept talking. His dad had treated him more like a friend from early high school on, and they got along fine. Not that they talked a lot or anything, but Trevor said he knew he always had a place to stay with his father.

Jah, Rose was embarrassed she'd fainted, but now the day was going better. She liked Trevor. He was so open and honest. She felt a sense of freedom with him, as if she didn't have to be careful about what she said and did. An entirely different feeling than when she was with Reuben.

Trevor paused a moment and took a drink of coffee. As he put his cup back down, he smiled at her again. She returned the smile, this time without her face growing warm.

She'd never had a running-around time. If Reuben wanted to postpone getting married because he cared more about others than about her, then maybe she should have a little fun while she waited. Nothing life-changing—just a few conversations with Trevor. A few smiles. A tiny bit of flirting. Just enough to distract her from thinking about Lila's injuries and Reuben's unselfish ways.

6

Lila knew they were all talking about her out in the hall— her doctor, Dat, and Zane. After two surgeries and over a week in the hospital, it was time for her next move. She hoped to go home. She realized it would be hard to get her in the house, but once she was inside she wouldn't need to go back out. She knew it would be a stretch for Rose to care for her, and she'd definitely need Shani's help, but Lila would certainly care for Rose if their roles were reversed. It would be good for Rose to step up and take more responsibility. She'd figure things out.

The nurse came in and checked her vitals. "How are you getting used to that thing?" the woman asked as she pointed to Lila's hips.

Lila tried to smile, hoping she wouldn't cry again. Maybe it was the pain pills. Or how broken she was. Or how uncomfortable. Anyway, she'd been crying a lot lately.

"Did you ever play with an Erector set when you were little?"

Lila shook her head. Zane had mentioned the same toy when he first saw the apparatus—it was bolted to both sides of her pelvis and was called a fixator. She had to wear it for six weeks, but it would keep her pelvis in place and allow the crushed bones to grow back together.

She wore a loose gown that rode up over the metal, and a pair of pajama bottoms that rode low on her hips. Shani had brought the bottoms for her, thankfully. Lila hadn't worn her Kapp at all in the hospital, although Shani had brought her a kerchief to wear over her long hair. There was no use putting it in a bun when she was in bed all the time so Shani had been braiding it for her. That worked best.

Besides commenting on the fixator, Zane and others had compared her to Frankenstein. She didn't really understand the similarities, even though Zane had tried to explain it, but it seemed they had to do with stitches on her face and arms, along with the bruises that had turned a yellowish purple.

The nurse handed her a pain pill, which Lila accepted with gratitude. She didn't like taking them, but she couldn't imagine surviving without them. She'd never experienced such excruciating pain. The swelling was finally going down in her abdomen, but between her internal injuries and her crushed pelvis, she was in constant pain.

The nurse watched her swallow the pill and then left. Lila prayed she could go home. Rose could care for her. A couple of years ago, Rose couldn't have handled it, but even though her sister had fainted when she'd come to visit, Lila was sure she could handle it now. Fainting was a reaction to being in the hospital, not to Lila's condition. At least she hoped so. Rose had definitely matured over the years. And she'd grown since she started courting Reuben.

The bulk of figuring out what to do had fallen to Zane, with Shani's help. Dat didn't seem to want to be involved.

Zane stepped back into the room. "Your Dat, the doctor, and I want to speak with you."

Lila nodded. She'd be brave. She'd do what was needed. The worst was over.

But for a moment she was back in the buggy, going through the windshield, over the top of Billie.

"Lila?" Zane said.

She blinked and refocused. Sometimes it was hard to follow a conversation.

The doctor and Dat had stepped into the room.

"Go ahead," Dat said, deferring to Zane.

His gaze fell back on her as he said, "We have a couple of options. A rehab center . . ."

Lila nodded.

"Or our house."

She turned her head toward him. "Our house?"

"Getting you in and out of the front door won't be a problem. We'll move a bed into the living room—and a recliner, so you can be up part of the time. I'll finish the downstairs bathroom, starting tomorrow. Not having a shower won't matter. You'll have to keep taking sponge baths until the fixator comes off, and by then you'll be able to move back home. Anyway, I'll move in with my folks. Gideon says that's all right under the circumstances, and Mom and Rose will take turns caring for you."

"Can I go home instead?" Lila asked.

Dat shook his head. "We'd have to carry you into the house, and that wouldn't be safe with your injuries, not so soon anyway."

"Can't you build a ramp?" Lila asked. Dat and Charlie had built a ramp for Joel when he was in a wheelchair.

"The incline is too steep," Zane answered.

Dat said, "Besides, it will be easier for Shani to care for you in the little house. It will be closer for her."

"Rose could care for me at home."

Dat shook his head. "She can help in the little house, but it would be too much for her to do all of it."

Lila frowned. If Rose was injured, Dat wouldn't be sending her off somewhere else. But maybe it was more than that— maybe he didn't want Lila in the house. Maybe he thought it would be too much for all of them. She blinked back her tears. Maybe if she were his biological daughter, like Rose was, Dat would feel differently.

"We need to decide tonight," Zane said.

"I'll go do some paper work," the doctor said. "Send one of the nurses for me once you've made up your mind. Then I'll write the needed orders."

Lila and Zane both thanked the doctor at the same time. As he left, Shani stepped into the room. "What's the matter?"

"Has anyone asked Rose? Maybe she would be fine caring for me at our house. It wouldn't be too hard to carry me in, just once. Right?" Then again, even though the nurses were trained and had experience, they still jostled her in ways that made the pain worse. Getting carried into the house and having Rose care for her might mean more pain. Still, she wondered what Rose was willing to do. "We could call the barn phone," she said. "And hope she's still out there and answers."

"She should be done with the milking by now," Dat answered.

"Trevor said he planned to help today." Zane looked at his mom. "You could call his cell—he could go tell Rose to call."

"Who else was helping with the milking, besides Trudy?" Shani asked.

Zane's face reddened. "I didn't ask."

Dat crossed his arms. "Maybe Reuben."

Shani took out her cell phone. "I'll call the barn first." When no one answered, she dialed the second number, stepping to the corner of the room. Lila overheard her say, "Okay. We'll see you soon."

As she hung up, Shani said, "They're on their way here."

Lila shifted her focus to Dat. His arms were still crossed, and his lips turned down into a frown. "Where's Trudy?" Lila asked.

Dat stayed silent, but Shani answered, "Trevor said Beth brought supper over. She's staying with her."

"Oh," Lila said. She hadn't thought about Beth and her ill ex-husband since the accident. She glanced at Dat. He shrugged and then asked, "Why is Rose getting a ride with the Englischer?"

Shani slipped her phone into her purse. "Trevor said she's been wanting to see Lila again, before she went to rehab."

Dat didn't respond, but he didn't look happy.

Shani had a concerned look on her face but didn't say anything more about Rose. "I'm going to go get a coffee. Anyone else want one?"

Dat said he'd go with her.

Once they left, Lila patted the side of the bed and Zane sat down next to her, careful not to bump her or the fixator. "Don't you think it would be best if you were in our house? That way it would be easier for me to see you every day. For Trudy too. For everyone, really."

Lila agreed, resigning herself to the idea. "I can see the little house would work, but home is still my first choice."

Zane's face fell. She hadn't meant to hurt his feelings.

Tears filled Lila's eyes.

"Baby," he said.

She leaned toward him.

"What is it?"

"Everything. My injuries." There was no telling how bad the damage was. When she asked if she'd be able to carry a Bobbli someday, the doctor told her she should discuss that with an obstetrics doctor in a couple of months. "Having to depend on other people. I don't want your mom to miss work."

"She'd do anything for you," Zane said. "You know that."

Lila blinked back tears. She did know that.

"It will all work out," Zane said.

A sob caught Lila off guard.

Zane put his face next to hers.

"I'm sorry," she said. "This has affected your work. And now you have more to do on the house, if I go there." Another sob shook her, pulling against the fixator. She took a deep breath. "Maybe I should just go to the rehab place. It'll be easier on everyone." Especially Dat.

"But it won't be," Zane said. "All of us will have to travel to see you. The one that would work best is farther away than the hospital." He stroked her forehead. "And it will be more expensive. This way will be more economical."

"Really?" She hadn't thought of the money involved. "But won't the insurance have to pay?"

Zane didn't respond.

"What is it?"

"It's probably not a big deal, but the guy who hit you is saying Billie veered out in front of him and pulled the buggy into the middle of the road."

That wasn't how she remembered it. She heard someone behind her, then felt the impact. The next thing she could recall was flying through the windshield and over the top of Billie. She couldn't imagine she would have allowed the horse to step to the left. "Billie was doing such a good job that day. He didn't spook once."

"I'm guessing a deputy will ask you some questions about the accident, sometime soon. Just tell them what happened."

She nodded. "How is Billie?" She'd been afraid to ask until now, afraid he'd died or had been put down and no one wanted to tell her.

"He's at your place. All things considered, he's doing pretty well. Your Dat's concerned about his right foreleg, but there's no verdict yet. It's not broken, just sprained."

Lila knew a lame horse wasn't worth anything, but she couldn't bear the thought of Billie being put down. Zane would be the one to make the decision though—not Dat. Hopefully it wouldn't come to that.

She closed her eyes, feeling sick that perhaps she was in some way responsible for the accident, that she'd done that to Billie. To herself. And she guessed her medical bills could deplete the church's mutual aid fund in no time.

Each year, Dat paid money into a fund that included Amish families from districts throughout the county to cover any accident expenses. If it did turn out to be her fault, the fund would pay for whatever damage was done to the driver's SUV—but not for Zane's buggy. She closed her eyes.

Why would the man say Billie pulled out in front of him if he hadn't? Could she have forgotten what happened before the accident, due to her injuries? Or maybe because of her concussion. Or even from the trauma of everything that happened.

She must have fallen asleep, because the next thing she knew Rose was in the room, saying, "How is she?"

"Better." Zane sounded groggy. Perhaps he'd dozed too. "We need to talk about her going home."

"She's coming home?" Rose asked.

"We're trying to figure it out," Zane answered.

"But Dat said she couldn't come home."

"We're thinking about the little house," Zane said. "We'll set things up in the living room. I'll put a toilet and sink in the half bath."

Lila opened her eyes and nudged Zane with her elbow. She didn't want him to say any more without knowing she was awake. "Hi, Rose," she said, looking up at her sister.

Trevor stood against the wall. He waved his hand in greeting but didn't say anything.

Lila shifted her gaze back to Rose. "Dat went to get coffee, but when he comes back he wants to talk with you about helping Shani take care of me."

Rose took a step backward. "Already?" Rose shot Trevor a helpless look. He shrugged. She turned her attention back to Lila. "I thought you were going to a rehab place."

"That was a possibility," Lila said. "But there seems to be a consensus that closer to home is preferable for several reasons, including financial."

Zane explained his mom would do as much of the caregiving as possible. "But she'd need help."

Rose wrinkled her nose as Dat came back into the room with Shani, both holding cups of coffee. Without Dat saying anything, Rose took the defense. "I wanted to see Lila. I thought she was going to a rehab place, and I wouldn't see her for a while."

"Jah, that's what I wanted to talk with you about," Dat said.

"Lila told me. You want her to come home to Juneberry Lane."

"To the house Zane built," Dat said. "I think that would be better than our house. Don't you think?"

Rose nodded.

"Lila wants to make sure you're in agreement to help care for her though, either way."

Lila sank into the bed. That wasn't exactly what she'd wanted to know—she'd hoped Rose would care for her at home.

"I could help more with the chores," Trevor said.

"But you won't be around." Shani stepped to the end of the bed. "You'll be staying at Charlie and Eve's, starting tomorrow night."

Lila hadn't heard that, and she wondered at it. Perhaps Shani was worried about Trevor spending too much time with Rose. Charlie and Eve had a lot going on with the baby, but maybe everyone felt it would be better for Trevor to stay there anyway.

"I can drive over to help with the milking," Trevor said. "Until I find a job."

Lila hadn't realized he planned to stay in the area. She thought he was just passing through.

"The issue at hand is whether Rose can help care for Lila. We need to decide now, so the doctor can write the orders if, in fact, she goes to the rehab place," Zane said.

A look of panic passed over Rose's face but then she said, "Of course I can help. And I expected to, though not this soon. But if Shani shows me what to do, I'll do it."

"It's settled, then," Dat said. "Lila will come home tomorrow, to the new house. I'll go find the doctor to tell him."

Lila closed her eyes. Dat didn't want her home. Maybe the stress of her being injured was getting to be too much for him.

The next day, Zane wheeled Lila through the front door of their house in a special tilted chair the doctor had ordered to accommodate the fixator. In front of them, on top of the braided rug, was a single bed with a sort of adjustable backrest on it, covered with the quilt her Mamm had made. Next to it was a high table on wheels, like in the hospital, and Joel's recliner. Zane either moved everything the night before or early that morning. But she doubted he'd started the fire that crackled in the wood stove.

"Oh, isn't it cozy in here?" Shani entered after Lila and Zane.

A giggle almost escaped from Lila. Not only was Zane not carrying her over the threshold, but his mother was with them. And besides that, they weren't even married. It wasn't at all what they'd planned.

She thought of the addressed wedding invitations, probably still on her dresser. Everything had changed.

"I bet you're tired," Shani said, stepping to the side of the wheelchair, the bag from the hospital, filled with bedpans and warm socks, and a plastic pitcher in her hands. "Let's get you to bed."

Lila squinted in the dim light. The sheets were turned back over the shadow quilt. She guessed Zane had brought it down from the bedroom, but he wouldn't have turned the bedding back like that.

She'd thought perhaps her Dat had made the fire, but there was no way he'd turned the bedding back. She doubted Rose had either.

"Who got everything ready?" Lila asked as Zane transferred her from the chair into the bed, and then tucked pillows behind her back.

"Eve," Shani answered. "She left food too."

"I'm not hungry," Lila said.

"You still have to eat," Shani answered. "Oh, and my freezer is full too, from all the women in your district dropping off bread, soups, and casseroles. They're amazing."

Lila's eyes filled with tears again, this time from gratitude, as a knock fell on the door. Zane stepped toward it as Shani tucked a pillow under Lila's knees, to take pressure off her pelvis, making the fixator stick up even more under the quilt. It looked as if a small table had been placed on top of her, under the bedding.

A draft of cold air swept into the house as Rose said, "Is she here?"

Lila turned her head toward her sister. She wasn't removing her bonnet. It didn't look as if she planned to stay.

"I was hoping you'd come by," Shani said, stepping away from the bed. "I wanted to work out a schedule. Come on into the kitchen."

As Zane sat down on the edge of the bed, another knock sounded, and then the door came open. Lila expected her Dat. Instead it was Trevor.

"Ready?" he asked.

"Yep," Zane answered, turning to Lila. "Trevor's giving me a ride to the job site so I can get a half day in."

She nodded. He needed to work, not just for the money but to keep his job too.

"I'll stop by as soon as I'm home. I hooked up the toilet, but not the sink yet. I'll work on that." He must have bought the toilet on his way home from the hospital last night and then installed it this morning.

Lila nodded again. He took her hand and squeezed it, and then started toward the door. Rose had stepped from the kitchen and gave Trevor a smile. Lila couldn't see how the man reacted.

Another draft of cold air swept through the room, and then the door closed.

"Rose?" Shani said.

"Coming." Rose turned back toward the kitchen.

Lila closed her eyes. Never would she have guessed she'd spend her first day—who was she kidding? Six weeks at least—in her new house in a single bed in the living room. She wished she could curl up into a ball, but that was out of the question. She couldn't move to her side either. All she could do was stay on her back. Instead she clutched the extra pillow to her chest. This time she didn't stop the tears. They seeped out of her closed eyes and trickled down the sides of her face.

She woke to Rose telling Shani, "I'll come back before you pick up Trudy and Adam."

"Perfect," Shani said. "Joel will bring the cot over this evening. If you can spend tonight then I'll spend the next two."

"All right," Rose said. "There's a barn raising on Saturday at Daniel and Jenny's. The weather is supposed to be nice. I'd like to go to that—with Reuben."

"Of course," Shani said. "Zane will be here to help then."

Lila closed her eyes again. She'd forgotten all about the barn raising. Daniel had been up to the hospital two days ago but hadn't mentioned it.

She must have fallen asleep again, because the next thing she knew, Shani was waking her, asking her about her pain levels.

She must have slept for quite a while because the light in the house had faded, and she was in a lot of pain. "Pretty bad," she said.

"I probably should have woken you earlier." Shani had her medicine ready and a bowl of soup too. "Rose will be here any minute, and then I'll leave to get the kids."

Lila took the medicine and a few bites of the soup. She noticed Shani looking at her watch and said, "You should go ahead and go. I'll be fine. I'm not going anywhere." After a few more minutes, Shani agreed.

Lila rested again, and about ten minutes after Shani left, Rose came in the door. Her cheeks were pink, and she was out of breath. This time she took off her bonnet and cape, but she didn't say anything about being late.

She didn't ask how Lila was either.

"So what do I do?" she asked. "Just sit with you?"

"Sure," Lila said, having no idea what Shani would want Rose to do. "Pull the recliner around."

Once Rose did, Lila asked her how things were going with Reuben.

"Good," she answered, blushing.

Maybe Reuben had been over at the house and that's why she was late. "Is he working today?" Lila asked.

"Jah, just like every day. Dat's at the lumberyard too. I forgot to tell you earlier that he said he'd come over this evening."

"What have you been doing?"

Rose blushed again. "You know. The usual. Cleaning. Getting supper started. That sort of thing."

Lila nodded. She did know. She just couldn't figure out why Rose kept blushing.

It was a relief when Shani returned with Adam and Trudy. Lila hadn't seen her baby sister since before the accident. It seemed that Shani had prepared her, because she didn't seem nervous and came right up to the bed. Lila motioned for her to climb up and then told her to stretch out beside her, without bumping the fixator. She did.

Adam had a concerned look on his face, while Rose seemed restless. "You can go back to the house," Lila said. "I bet Adam will walk Trudy home later."

"Perfect," Rose replied. "I need to get supper started."

"I thought you already had," Lila answered.

Rose blushed again. "Well, you know, I need to get it on the stove."

Lila was tempted to press her sister more, but she didn't have the energy. "See you tonight," she said. For a moment she feared perhaps Rose had spent time with Trevor earlier and that's why she was late, but surely she wouldn't be foolish enough to do that.

Rose grabbed her bonnet and cape and headed out the door without saying another word.

7

I'll walk you back over," Dat said to Rose as she headed toward the mud porch. "I want to say hello to Lila on her first day back." He hadn't gone over when he said he would. Rose felt bad she'd told Lila that he would, but now wasn't a good time.

She shook her head. "Trudy hates to be alone. I think she'd be frightened if you weren't here." She was in bed but not asleep. "I'll be fine," Rose said. "I'll take a flashlight and go down the lane."

"I wanted to see Lila today."

Rose shrugged. "She'll understand. Besides, she's probably already asleep."

Dat tugged on his beard and then said, "All right. Tell her I'll stop by tomorrow."

"I'll see you in the morning." Rose would help him with the milking, get breakfast made, and then get ready for the barn raising. A couple of years ago, Reuben came to help with the milking every morning so Lila could take care of their grandmother after her surgery. Rose wished he'd have offered to help regularly now, while she was caring for Lila. But he hadn't said a thing. Everyone always seemed more willing to help Lila than to help Rose.

Rose turned away from Dat, quickly put on her cape and bonnet, and then grabbed a flashlight and her bag. She called out a good-bye to Dat, which he answered, and headed out the door into the drizzly fall night.

She breathed in the acrid smell of smoke from the wood stove and hurried down the driveway, pulling the hood of her cape over her bonnet. When she reached the lane she turned left and waved the flashlight in front of her, dodging the potholes filled with rainwater as she walked. She stayed close to the edge of the lane, under the row of trees.

When she reached the cedar at the halfway point, headlights came around the curve. She stepped closer to the tree, hoping it was Trevor. It was. She returned to the lane and waved, glad their plan had worked out. They were both right on time.

The car stopped when it reached her, and the passenger window slid down a little. "How about a ride?" he asked playfully.

"Jah." She stepped closer. "I'd appreciate it."

He smiled as he leaned across and opened the door for her. As she climbed in, he pushed a button to make the window go up. The windshield wipers were on a low setting, mixing a rhythmic swish in with the low hum of the engine. She settled into the seat and fastened her seat belt as Trevor turned the car around in the lane.

He'd been down by the creek when she walked through the field on her way to sit with Lila. They'd had a pleasant conversation, which had made her late. That was when they made the plan to see each other now. "How was the rest of your day?" she asked.

"Good," he answered. "I was just helping Zane with the

bathroom. The toilet and sink are both in now, but there's still quite a bit to do. Joel's going to buy handrails, but we'll have to put plasterboard up before they can be installed." He slowed for a pothole. "And I got a job." He smiled.

So he planned to stay. "Where?"

"With the same construction company Zane is working for. I talked to his boss when I picked him up. I'm going to be doing cleanup, to start with. I've had some construction experience in the past, so hopefully I'll be doing more soon."

Rose felt conflicted. She enjoyed talking with Trevor, even flirting, just a little, but she thought he'd only be around a short time. That had made interacting with him feel safer. "So you're going to stay?" she asked.

He nodded. "At least for a while, but over at Charlie and Eve's. Shani, in particular, seems to think that will be best. I'll stay there tonight." He paused for a moment and then added, "This will work out well. I can give Zane rides to and from the job site, and that will make his life a little easier."

She nodded. Sometimes Zane worked on the other side of the county, which made for a long commute.

Trevor shook his head. "I still can't figure out why he'd give up his truck. I mean, I get that he's in love with Lila and pretty much a pacifist, and that he likes your lifestyle. Honestly, I admire that. But I can't imagine not being able to drive." He patted the steering wheel with both hands as he spoke.

Rose didn't blame him for not being able to understand. Englisch people loved their vehicles.

He pulled around in front of Shani and Joel's house and then continued along the side of the barn. But instead of driving on to the little house, he stopped and put the car into Park. Rose's heart began to race. What was he doing?

He turned toward her. "I just wanted to let you know how much I've appreciated getting to know you."

Rose's face grew warm. She didn't want to have a serious talk.

"You've been kind to me—when I've needed it." He glanced at her, a pained expression on his face, and then shrugged. "I'm grateful."

"You're welcome," Rose whispered, hoping he wouldn't start crying again.

He didn't. Instead he shifted the car back into Drive and then crept forward. "Sheesh," he said. "I hope I didn't make you uncomfortable just now."

"No," she said. "It's fine."

"I wasn't thinking."

Her face grew warmer, embarrassed that she'd thought he might have ulterior motives. Of course he didn't think about her in a romantic way. She was a young Amish woman. A relationship with her was the last thing he'd be considering. For some reason he enjoyed talking with her—flirting, just a little. But that was all.

Trevor stopped the car in front of the little house, and Rose thanked him. As she climbed out he said, "I hope to see you soon."

She nodded, her heart racing. He had that effect on her. She hurried through the drizzle, reached the front door, and turned back to the car. The passenger-side window was down again, and Trevor was smiling at her. She liked that. She waved and opened the door, feeling giddy as she stepped into the house.

A battery-powered lamp cast a bit of light from the table beside Lila's bed. She appeared to be asleep. There was a cot in the room now, against the far wall.

A knocking noise in the back of the house startled Rose at first, but then she started toward it, going through the kitchen. Zane, with his profile toward her, was standing in the little bathroom, wearing a headlamp that illuminated the entire room and banging a hammer against a two-by-four.

"Hello," she said.

He kept banging.

She said it louder.

He turned around quickly, the hammer held high. "Oh, Rose. You startled me."

"Sorry." She stepped back a little. "Did your Mamm go home already?"

Zane nodded. "She wanted to tell Adam good-night before he fell asleep." He leaned against the doorway that had the frame torn from it. He was probably planning to enlarge it.

He inhaled, as if catching his breath, and said, "She left some instructions for you." He pointed toward the counter. In the dim light, Rose could make out a piece of paper. She wished Shani had stayed to tell her.

"There's a walkie-talkie on the table beside Lila. I'll have the other one with me. If anything happens, call me immediately."

Rose nodded. He didn't need to worry. She'd call in a heartbeat.

"I'll go ahead and clean up now," he said. "And get out of your way."

Rose picked up the sheet of paper and headed toward the lamp in the living room. Shani had left instructions about pain meds and positioning Lila. She wrote that she'd be over at five a.m. so Rose could help with the milking. Rose said a silent prayer that Lila wouldn't need anything before then.

Once Zane left, Rose put on her nightgown and brushed her teeth. She checked on Lila one more time. She was sleeping soundly, probably from the pain meds. Rose placed the lamp beside her cot, turned it off, and climbed under the blankets.

She intended to say her prayers, but instead her thoughts drifted to Trevor.

The next morning, Rose leaned back against the buggy seat as she rode with Reuben to the barn raising. The cold morning air helped perk her up a little, but a second cup of coffee would probably help more. Surely Jenny would have a pot brewing. Staying with Lila, doing the milking and all of her chores, and fixing breakfast had resulted in a nonstop morning.

"How is Lila doing?" Reuben pulled to the edge of the road to let a vehicle pass.

"All right," Rose answered, but she wasn't really sure. She'd given her pain meds during the middle of the night, but Lila hadn't woken up by the time Rose left. She turned her head to the right. An Englischer farmer harvested silage, sending up a cloud of dust that made her sneeze.

"Are you looking forward to the day?" Reuben asked.

"Jah," she answered. There was nothing better than a barn raising—it was even more fun than a singing. The weather had turned sunny and warm, which wasn't unusual for late September. She looked forward to a day spent with the women while the men put up the barn.

Daniel and Jenny had moved to a little farm about a year ago. The old barn wasn't worth saving, and Daniel had torn it down. Thankfully the foundation was good, and it wouldn't take long for the men to put up a new one.

"Rose?" Reuben was staring at her.

"Jah?"

"I asked how you are doing. If you're able to keep up with everything."

"Oh," she said and then yawned. "I didn't sleep well," she said. "Lila needed pain meds in the middle of the night, and then I was up early to do the milking."

"Jah," Reuben said. "But it's temporary, right? And you know Lila would do the same for you."

"Of course." She tried to keep her voice light. "That's what I keep telling myself."

Reuben reached over and patted her hand, and they rode in silence after that. She couldn't help but feel as if he had just scolded her.

She thought of Trevor stopping his car on the other side of the barn the evening before, and her heart raced again.

"You're quieter than usual," Reuben said.

Rose smiled a little. "You should welcome the silence," she teased. "Because I'm sure it's temporary."

He patted her hand again but didn't say anything more. A few minutes later, he turned down the road to Daniel and Jenny's house.

Several people had already arrived, including Dat. Trudy had decided to stay with Shani and Lila for the day instead of coming to the barn raising.

Dat headed toward the lumber that had been unloaded out in the field, not far from the foundation of the barn. Rose asked Reuben if it had come from his lumberyard.

"Jah," he said. "I hired a truck to deliver all the sawed logs and the beam earlier this week. Daniel spent a few days making the peg holes."

Rose knew he would have used a hammer and chisel to do that.

Reuben stopped near the old farmhouse, and Rose jumped down. "Have fun," she said, giving him what was probably a sassy look. Even though she hadn't intended to.

He smiled. "I'm sure I will. You too."

The farm belonged to Jenny's uncle, who Daniel worked for. When his previous renters left, leaving the place a mess, he asked Daniel to clean up the property and work on the old house for free lodging. It was a good situation for Daniel and Jenny both. Daniel enjoyed restoring old houses, and Jenny had a knack for decorating—in a Plain way, of course. The home was two stories with a wide porch and an oak tree on either side of it.

Rose hurried toward the steps, eager to see Jenny. She had more in common with her sister-in-law than she did with Lila. Jenny always had the latest information about people in the district or a new recipe to share or a housekeeping tip or an idea about decorating. As opposed to Lila, who only liked to talk about books and current events and the latest quilt she was making.

Rose knew she wouldn't see Jenny much once her Bobbli arrived, so she was especially looking forward to spending time with her today. The front door was open, and Rose entered, greeted by the smell of coffee.

The living room was small and cozy. Wainscoting lined the walls and bookcases flanked the fireplace. No fire burned, but the house would soon be warm with so many people arriving.

Rose called out a hello.

"We're back here!" Monika responded. Rose hurried through the dining room into the kitchen. Monika stood at the stove, while Jenny sat in a chair in the eating nook, her legs up on another chair.

Rose stopped abruptly. "Are you all right?"

"Jah," Jenny said. "Just tired."

"It's only eight o'clock."

Monika laughed. "Most women are constantly tired the last month of pregnancy. You'll understand someday."

Jenny put her feet down on the floor, and pushed herself up from the chair. "How's Lila doing?"

"As well as can be expected," Rose said, realizing that's what everyone would be asking her today. She turned her attention toward the coffeepot on the stove. "Mind if I help myself?"

"Go ahead." Jenny placed her hand on her lower back. She'd

really gotten bigger in the last few weeks. Rose didn't mention it though. Instead she grabbed a cup from the cupboard and filled it with coffee. After she took her first sip, she asked, "What do you want me to do?"

"You can make the hot cider," Jenny said. "We'll serve it with the sweet rolls when the men are ready to take a break."

Rose got to work dumping cider from the glass jugs on the counter into the large pot on the back of the stove. As she added cinnamon sticks and then cloves, more women arrived. Most of them were young and friends of Jenny. Two of her sisters came, bringing their children.

"Add a little of this," Monika whispered, handing her a bottle of maple syrup.

Rose did as she was told. She learned something new from Monika nearly every time she saw her.

"Who's the Englischer out there?" Jenny asked her mother, after coming back to the kitchen from the front porch.

"I don't know," Monika answered, peering out the window over the sink.

"He's handsome," Jenny said. "Short sandy hair. Square jaw. He's working with Reuben."

Rose's face grew warm as she guessed Trevor had shown up.

Monika stepped to the window. "Rose," she said. "Is that Zane's friend? Gideon mentioned him the other night."

Rose stepped to Monika's side. Reuben held one end of a board and someone dressed in jeans and a green jacket held the other. She couldn't see his face, but she recognized him nevertheless. "I believe it is," Rose said, doing her best to keep her voice even.

"What's his name?"

"Trevor. Trevor Anderson." She stepped back to the stove and the hot cider. He hadn't said a thing about coming today; Rose had no idea how he even knew about the barn raising.

She smiled a little to herself. Perhaps Zane had told him about it. She'd find out during the snack break.

Two hours later, as she set up a piece of plywood over two sawhorses with Jenny's oldest sister, Trevor noticed her and grinned. Rose waved, trying not to smile. But by the expression on Reuben's face, she wondered if she had without meaning to. She stood for a moment, watching the men working. There were at least thirty of them, and they nearly had the entire barn framed.

When it was time for the snack, Trevor approached her. "What are you doing here?" she asked, shading her eyes from the morning sun.

"Zane felt bad he couldn't help out. I said I'd do it for him."

"What's he doing?"

"Picking up plasterboard with his dad." Trevor unzipped his jacket and then pushed up the sleeves. "Did you make the cinnamon rolls?"

Rose shook her head. "I fixed the cider."

He smiled, his eyes twinkling. "I'll think of you when I drink it, then." As he stepped toward the table, Rose quickly looked for Reuben. He was still nailing a board into place.

Rose started his way, waving at Dat and Bishop Byler as they headed toward the snacks. She was determined to show her interest in Reuben. She didn't want anyone to get any ideas about her talking with Trevor. No good would come from that.

"Come get a snack," she called out to Reuben.

He looked up and shook his head. "I'm not hungry," he said. "We have a lot of work to do if we're going to finish today."

Rose stopped a few feet from him. "I'll bring you a cup of cider. I made—"

"I'm fine." He smiled a little. Still, her feelings were hurt at his abruptness. It felt like rejection.

"All right." She watched for a moment as he pounded more

nails but then turned and headed back to the others. Trevor was introducing himself to Monika. Then he turned and talked with Dat and Bishop Byler.

Daniel stood at Jenny's side. Rose's heart swelled at the beauty of the little family. Wasn't that what she hoped for? A loving husband. A home. And children.

She headed toward the piece of plywood and poured herself some cider. As she did, Trevor stepped beside her, saying, "That's really good. I think I'll get a second helping of it."

Rose smiled at him over the rim of her cup.

He lowered his voice. "What's with Reuben?"

Rose wrapped both of her hands around the cup. "He's worried the work isn't going to get done on time."

Trevor raised his eyebrows. "Is he always so responsible?"

"Jah," Rose answered. He was the most responsible person she knew, and the most dependable too. But responsibility in one area could feel like negligence in another.

"Well," Trevor said, "I should probably get back to work." He drained his cup and then held it up. "What do I do with this?"

"I'll take it," Rose said.

His hand brushed against hers, sending a tingle up her arm. "Thank you so much for helping out. I know it means a lot to Daniel and Jenny," she quickly said.

His eyes twinkled. "Does it mean anything to you?"

"Of course," she said. "I'm very grateful."

"Good," he responded, "because I keep thinking about our rides together and conversations. I look forward to more of the same."

Before she could respond, he headed back toward Reuben. Rose watched him go.

Jenny stepped to Rose's side. "Which one are you watching?"

Rose smiled.

Jenny chuckled. "Both?"

Rose shook her head and said, "I only have eyes for Reuben."

"Well, it doesn't hurt to look—as long as you don't touch."

"Jenny," Rose said, her face growing warm again.

"Just kidding," she said, her hand falling to her belly. "I was just being silly."

Rose put her arm around her sister-in-law and whispered, "I won't tell Daniel if you don't tell Reuben." They both laughed and then gathered up the empty cups left on the end of the makeshift table and headed back to the house. Jah, Rose would have a little fun while she could. Soon life would be all responsibility and seriousness, being married to Reuben. She was still sure she wanted to marry him—ninety percent sure, at least—but she'd have her own secret time of running around with Trevor. The Englischer would move on, and there would be no harm done.

8

Reuben stood surveying the barn. All that was left was the roof, and he wanted to finish it as quickly as possible so he'd have some time with Rose. He feared, if it was already dark out, Tim would expect her to ride home with him. Or worse yet, what if she caught a ride with Trevor?

Reuben heard the Englischer had given her a ride to the hospital twice. He couldn't help but feel concerned. He'd lost one Lehman sister to an Englischer. He didn't want that to happen again.

He'd taken a short break at noon to eat, but other than that he'd been working nonstop all day. When Daniel had asked him to design the barn, Reuben had relied on some plans he came across, modifying them as needed. He felt responsible to make sure everything fit the way it should. Thankfully it had. Now they just needed to finish the roof.

Reuben scrambled back up the ladder. As his head came up over the roofline, he could see Trevor on top of the beam, pounding nails at the peak.

Reuben climbed back on top of the beam, too, and pulled his hammer back out of his tool belt. As he did, he started to lose his balance but caught himself before he fell backward.

"You okay?" Trevor called out.

"Jah," Reuben responded as he started to nail.

"I'm coming toward you," Trevor said. Reuben nodded. He was impressed with what a hard worker the Englischer was and how knowledgeable too. Not only did he know his way around a dairy, but he was also familiar with construction.

Reuben looked past the other men toward the house. The women would have a meal ready to eat by the time the sun set. A couple of women stood in the yard, but Reuben didn't see Rose. He knew she relished being with the other women. Reuben enjoyed the work, but he didn't crave interaction with others the way Rose did.

Trevor walked along the beam, with quite a bit of agility, and then squatted not too far from Reuben and began pounding again. A few times Reuben glanced toward the house. Finally Rose came out with Jenny, laughing. He couldn't help but wonder what they were talking about. Did Rose gossip about him with her friends? Reuben had never wondered about that with Lila. She was so serious. He couldn't imagine her talking about anyone.

He welcomed Rose's constant chatter—all about happenings in the district, not issues half a world away. She didn't seem to mind if he didn't answer her, not the way Lila did. She'd wanted to hear his opinion on everything. The truth was, he didn't have an opinion on much, especially things that didn't immediately impact him. He had the feeling Rose might gossip though. Not to him, necessarily, but to other people.

As he edged down the beam to where Trevor worked, he glanced toward Rose every once in a while. One time she waved at him and he smiled back. But when he realized Trevor had held up his hammer, Reuben wasn't sure she'd been waving at him at all.

He wondered what Rose thought of him, compared with Trevor. He sighed and kept on going. He wasn't sure why he cared, but maybe it was because of being dumped by Lila. Jah, he needed to speak with Rose soon about his plan. There was no need for them to wait to marry. Lila's recovery could take months.

He finished the section and stepped over a bundle of roofing, losing his balance a little again. He must have been more fatigued than he'd thought. Trevor called out, "Are you doing all right?"

"Just fine," Reuben replied, but as he spoke his foot slipped again. He must have gasped because Trevor whirled toward him. It wasn't as if he would have fallen off the beam, Reuben was sure, probably just straddled it. At least he hoped. But Trevor grabbed his arm and held on to him, keeping him from doing either.

Reuben wondered if they had some sort of agility training in the Army. The man was like a tightrope walker.

"Denki." Reuben exhaled.

Down below a couple of men clapped. Reuben glanced toward the house. Rose stood at the makeshift table, her hand covering her mouth. Obviously she'd seen what had just happened. Reuben wished she hadn't.

"Are you steady now?" Trevor asked. His voice and words were kind. He wasn't being condescending, not in any way.

"Jah," Reuben said.

Trevor let go of him slowly. Reuben squatted down and began nailing again. He was sweating now, even though the day had grown chilly as the sun had fallen to just above the treetops. He drew in a deep breath and pounded as hard as he could.

By the time they finished the last of the roof, the sun was

setting, leaving streaks of pink and orange in the western sky. Reuben stood for a moment, taking in the scene. Trevor stepped to his side.

"Beautiful, isn't it?" Reuben asked.

"Yep," Trevor answered.

Reuben glanced his way. The man wasn't watching the sunset. He was glancing down toward the house. The yard was in the shadows, growing darker with each moment. Lanterns had been lit and placed along the table and the porch railing. Reuben squinted, scanning the area. Sure enough, Rose stood on the porch.

Trevor left before supper, saying he needed to get back to help Zane. Reuben was happy to have him leave.

Reuben sat beside Rose on the porch as they ate casseroles, broccoli salad, and bread. "Are you cold?" he asked Rose.

"A little," she answered.

Reuben quickly took off his jacket, which he'd put on after coming down from the roof, and gave it to her. He was still warm from feeling shamed up on the beam.

"Denki," Rose said. They ate the rest of their food in silence. Once they were done, Rose took his plate and disappeared into the house. At the end of the porch, Reuben's father and Tim were deep in conversation. Reuben stood, not wanting to eavesdrop as his father said, "We can talk more about this later."

"All right," Tim said. Reuben wondered why Beth hadn't come to help today. Perhaps she was keeping her distance.

Reuben hitched his horse and drove his buggy around to the front of the house. Rose stood on the porch, laughing with Jenny again. She waved to him as she hurried down the steps, a playful expression on her face.

For a moment he felt like the most fortunate man in the

district. He'd bring up the topic of them marrying before they reached Juneberry Lane.

As he pulled onto the highway, Rose asked, "What happened up there on the beam?"

"When?"

"When Trevor saved you."

"Saved me?"

"You were falling. He grabbed your arm."

"I did slip a little." Reuben smiled at her, hoping to make light of the situation.

"I thought you were going to fall to your death," Rose said.

Reuben chuckled. "It wasn't that serious."

"It looked that way from where I stood." Rose's eyes grew large by the light of the lantern. "I was grateful Trevor was so close to you."

Reuben didn't answer, urging the horse to go faster instead. Did everyone see it the way Rose had? That the Englischer saved him?

Not only had Reuben's father not dealt with Tim and his friendship with Beth, but he'd never dealt with the Lehman family's Englisch neighbors either. If his father had forbade them from befriending the Becks all those years ago, Lila never would have fallen for Zane. And Trevor wouldn't have been at the barn raising.

He wrinkled his nose. Then again, Reuben wouldn't be with Rose either.

"What are you thinking about?" she asked.

"Nothing," Reuben muttered. A sliver of a moon rose over the horizon, and a few stars started to shine. He'd talk to her about getting married tomorrow night, after the singing. As he turned onto Juneberry Lane, he asked, "Who did the milking tonight?"

"Joel and Adam."

Reuben shivered a little in the cool air. It wasn't that the Becks hadn't been good friends to the Lehmans. They had. It hadn't been a one-way street. The Lehmans had been good friends to them too.

He slowed the horse as he turned down the Lehmans' driveway.

"Want to come in?" Rose asked as Reuben pulled the horse to a stop.

The house was dark. "No one's home, right?"

She shrugged, a smile on her face.

When he didn't respond, Rose said, "I guess I should go pick up Trudy. She's with Lila."

"I'll give you a ride." Reuben pulled the buggy around, back down the driveway, and onto Juneberry Lane. They rode in silence until they reached the Becks' house. It was pitch-dark.

"They all must be over at Lila and Zane's," Rose said.

That seemed odd that she referred to it as Lila and Zane's home when they weren't married yet. A lot of things seemed odd on Juneberry Lane.

The sooner he married Rose, the better. He just needed to find the right time to talk with her about it. When he wasn't around her family.

"Go around the side of the barn," Rose said.

Reuben followed her directions even though he knew. After all, he'd helped Zane frame the house. As they reached the end of the barn, he could see the place, lit up with lanterns on the porch and lamps in the windows. Shani's van was parked out front, and also Joel's pickup. On the other side of those two vehicles, Reuben could make out Trevor's sports car. He suppressed a groan.

"Would you wait and give Trudy and me a ride back?" Rose reached for the door handle.

"Of course," Reuben answered. He wouldn't leave them to

walk home in the dark, and he certainly didn't want Trevor giving them a ride.

"How about if you just come in?" Rose's voice had a bit of a teasing tone to it. "I'm sure everyone would like to see you, including Lila."

Rose never seemed bothered that Reuben and Lila had courted. Reuben hopped down, tied his horse to the hitching post, and followed Rose to the front door. She knocked rapidly and then opened the door before anyone answered it. Reuben followed her onto a shiny hardwood floor. As he closed the door behind him, Reuben took a deep breath.

It was as if a party was going on. Trudy and Adam both slid by in their socks, waving their arms as they did. Someone who was out of sight yelled, "Hand me the mallet." It could have been Zane.

Shani leaned over a recliner, blocking Reuben's view. When she stood up straight, he saw Lila. She looked surprised, but then she called out a soft hello. She wasn't wearing a Kapp but did have a scarf on her head. Her blond hair hung in a long braid over her shoulder. She wore an oversized long-sleeved T-shirt and was covered with a quilt. But it was elevated in an odd way, as if something was underneath it.

Rose started toward her. "How are you doing?"

"All right." Her voice was weak. "How was the barn raising?"

"Good," Rose answered. "Did Trevor tell you what happened?"

Lila shook her head.

Reuben pointed toward the other side of the house. "Is Zane back there?"

"Jah," Lila said. "They're having troubles with the plumbing."

Reuben stepped toward the kitchen as Rose said, "Reuben was up on the beam . . ."

The last thing he wanted to hear was the story of Trevor "saving" him. Trudy and Adam were in the kitchen, each grabbing pizza from a cardboard box on the counter. Reuben turned to his right. Joel stood in the doorway of the bathroom, leaning on his cane. "It has to work," he said. "Keep trying."

A bang startled Reuben.

"Easy," Joel said.

"Someone's at the door." Trudy put her pizza back on the counter and ran out of the kitchen. Reuben stepped to the archway as the girl flung open the front door.

"Simon!" She threw herself into her brother's arms. "Casey!"

Reuben crossed his arms as Adam yelled to his father, "Simon's here! And Casey." Both were in the Army, but they were now dressed in civilian clothes—jeans and jackets. Casey had her long dark hair pulled back in a bun, much like the Amish women wore, but of course her head wasn't covered.

Joel started across the kitchen, his cane thumping against the wood floor. Trevor came out of the bathroom next, followed by Zane. Both shook Reuben's hand as they passed by, but they were on their way to see Simon. At least Zane was. And Casey. Reuben didn't think Trevor had ever met Simon, but he'd served in Afghanistan with Casey.

Zane wrapped his arms around Simon and lifted him in a bear hug. Simon let out a whoop and hugged Zane back, slapping him on the back. "How was it?" Zane asked.

"Boring compared to your tour," Simon answered. "We played a lot of *Call of Duty*—on a buddy's Xbox. Not a lot going on."

"Thank goodness," Zane said. "That's exactly what I prayed for. Minus the *Call of Duty*." He smiled.

Simon's face grew serious. "And I saw Jaalal."

Zane stopped smiling. "You did? Where?"

"His village. I asked to go on a special assignment. He sent his greetings to you." Simon smiled a little. "And to Lila."

Reuben wasn't certain exactly who Simon was referring to, but he suspected Jaalal was the translator Zane had worked with in Afghanistan.

"He and his wife are doing well. He's not translating anymore. Troops don't go through that area much, and he didn't offer any information about what's going on as far as the Taliban there. We were trying to make contact with a specific tribal leader, but we didn't end up finding him."

Reuben crossed his arms again as he listened. A part of him couldn't help but envy all Simon had seen, but it was foolish of him to join the Army and be part of such a destructive force.

When Simon and Zane paused, Rose hurried over and hugged Simon and then Casey. Trevor watched her as she did, a smile on his face. Reuben shifted from one foot to the other, puzzled again that his father had let the Lehman family get so out of hand.

Finally Simon saw Reuben and smiled. "Ru," he said, stepping forward. Reuben stuck out his hand, but Simon stepped forward and embraced him instead, slapping his back. For a moment Reuben forgave Simon—all the Lehmans really. But then Simon released him and said, "Anything new? Or are things still the same old, same old?"

Reuben must have bristled because Simon said, "Just kidding!" as he turned toward Rose, grinned, and nudged her with his elbow. Before either could respond, Simon asked Zane, "Where's Lila?"

Zane pointed toward the recliner. Simon grinned and started that way, followed by Casey.

Rose stepped to Reuben's side. "You don't need to stay. Simon can give us a ride home."

Simon was hugging Joel and then Shani. Finally he made it to Lila's side. The prodigal son—but not really. They all adored Simon.

"Where's everyone going to stay?" Reuben asked. He couldn't imagine Tim letting Simon's girlfriend stay at his house.

"Casey is staying here with Lila," Rose said. "She told Shani she'd take a turn. And Simon is staying at our house." She sighed. "Hopefully he'll help with the milking in the morning."

She turned toward Reuben and looked him in the eye. Her voice was kind, but he didn't sense the enthusiasm in her that he had before. Perhaps it was just because she was tired. It had been a long day. "Thank you for the ride. See you tomorrow," she said.

"Jah," he said. "I'm looking forward to the singing. I hope we'll have time to talk."

"That would be good," she said, but she didn't sound as if she meant it. "See you then." She gave him a playful shove. "Go on now. I know you hate these messy family moments."

He stood his ground. "What do you mean?"

"All the noise. Simon yelling. So many people." She nudged him again.

"No," he said. "I don't mind. . . ." He just found it confusing. His mother had insisted on keeping their house quiet—always. His older brothers roughhoused outside some, but they all toed the line inside. But everyone in his family, except for their Dat, was pretty quiet. Nothing like the Lehmans.

"Really," Rose said. "Go ahead and go. I know you're tired. We might be a while."

"I don't know if I should," Reuben said. "I'm worried about you, and Trudy too, hanging out with Englischers like this. Let me take you home."

"Come on, Ru," Rose teased. "You know we've been friends with the Becks forever. Nothing is going to happen."

"Where's your Dat?" Reuben asked. "Shouldn't he be here?"

"He was staying to help Daniel. He said he'd be a while." Rose crossed her arms. "Zane and Lila are Plain. We're well supervised."

But the majority of people in the room were Englisch—and one, Reuben was certain, had his eye on Rose.

"Don't be such a fuddy-duddy." Rose's voice had turned a little sharp. "This is my family. They're not bad people."

"The Becks aren't your family." Reuben's face grew warm as he spoke. Perhaps once Lila and Zane married, she could claim their neighbors as family, but they weren't married—yet. Reuben pressed again. "I don't think your father would approve of you and Trudy being here. Let me take you home."

Rose smiled, but as if she was annoyed. "We're fine. See you tomorrow."

Everyone in the house except Reuben and Rose had gathered around Lila in the recliner. It was like some sort of family reunion. Trevor glanced over his shoulder, directly at Rose. It was impossible to miss. Reuben waited a long moment and then said, "I guess I'll see you tomorrow, then."

"Jah," she said. "Have a good rest of the evening."

⤙⤚

Instead of going home, Reuben headed over to his Dat's. It was Monika's place, really. His Dat had remarried nine years ago, almost two years after Reuben's Mamm had died. He'd been happy his father found another wife, and Monika was a good match for him. It took Reuben several years to admit that Monika was probably a better match than his mother had been. Monika was warm and caring. She didn't mind if her house was a mess or not, or how noisy it got—as long as it was filled with people. She'd successfully blended the two families: her five girls and their growing families with Reuben and his two brothers and sister and their families.

Since her youngest, Jenny, had married Daniel, Monika had poured her attention into Reuben, wanting him to settle down soon, encouraging him when he began courting Lila, consoling him when Lila broke off their relationship, and then encouraging him to court Rose. She did have a bit of advice as far as Rose though—don't court too long, she'd said, even though she's younger. She's a girl who is easily distracted.

Perhaps that was what was going on now. She was distracted. But a conversation about a wedding date would get her refocused, he was sure.

He smiled a little.

The house by the lumberyard would never be as big and fancy as Monika's house, but Reuben could see Rose turning it into a home—a much warmer home than it had been when his mother was alive. He could see Rose behaving much like Monika in a few years, filling his house with people and fun. Rose truly seemed to care about others, although she did still cater to herself at times. But she'd learn with time to always put others first.

Reuben slowed his horse as he turned the corner and then pulled up the driveway. Monika's first husband, a building contractor, had built her house. Through the kitchen window he saw two men sitting at the kitchen table. Reuben hitched the horse and walked up the steps to the back door. No one answered. He almost let himself in but stopped. Perhaps his Dat wouldn't want him to know who was over. Perhaps it was church business. His father tried to be discreet—Reuben appreciated that.

Finally Monika came to the door, a lamp in her hand. "Reuben!" Her eyes shone.

"I just stopped by to see Dat."

"He's busy," Monika answered.

"I thought so," Reuben said.

"Want to visit with me?" Monika asked. "We can sit in my sewing room. We won't disturb your Dat."

Reuben was tempted to. He could tell Monika all about Rose and her distance. About the way Trevor looked at her. At his frustration that his Dat had never put his foot down with the Lehmans. But he shook his head. "No, that's all right. Tell Dat I stopped by."

As he left in the moonlight, swinging his buggy wide, he noticed the buggy parked by the barn. It was an old one with a tattered caution sign on the back that needed to be replaced.

It was Tim's buggy, he was sure.

It looked as if his Dat really was doing the right thing when it came to the Lehmans. Better now than never—he just hoped it wasn't too late.

9

Lila stirred in the middle of the night, ready for her pain meds. Lying flat on her back with the fixator jutting out of her middle made it hard to sleep, and the pain meds were the only thing that helped. When she was wide-awake and in pain, her mind tended to race. She worried about the future. Would she be able to have a baby? Would Zane get fed up with how dependent she was? Would he become frustrated with how hard it was to be Amish?

Jah, he was her person, the one she most wanted to be with, to spend her life with. What she feared had happened. God did have another lesson for her to learn to teach her to trust him more and Zane less.

The thought brought her no comfort, only panic. And the only thing that numbed both her thoughts and her pain was another pill. She turned her head toward the cot where Casey was sleeping. Lila was completely helpless. She couldn't move at all, not even to get her own meds and water bottle off the table.

The sound of the door opening startled her. But then Zane

stepped to the end of the bed. "Are you awake?" He spoke in a normal voice.

"Jah," she whispered. "What are you doing here?"

"I couldn't sleep." He had a flashlight in his hand, pointed at the floor. He wore a jacket and stocking cap. When he came around the side of the bed, she could see that he wore a pair of sweatpants instead of Amish trousers. "Do you need your pain meds?" he asked, this time his voice lower.

She nodded.

He took the pillbox off the bedside table, popped out the middle-of-the-night dose, and handed her the pill and then the water bottle. After she swallowed, she said, "You should go back to bed—you can't keep going like this, without getting any rest."

"I woke up worried about you," he said.

"I'm all right."

"I had a dream. . . ."

"A nightmare?"

He nodded. "But it wasn't about Afghanistan."

"What was it about?"

"You going over the top of Billie and into the creek."

"Zane." Lila reached for his hand, her sense of panic building. "I'm going to be fine." She hoped so anyway.

"But you could have been killed." He'd said the same thing a few times before. It wasn't helpful to her. He sat down on the edge of the bed. "I keep thinking about you going through the windshield and about the man who hit you. I want to know exactly what happened."

Lila didn't answer.

"Was he texting?" Zane asked. "Or blind to buggies? Didn't he see the caution sign? Because I know you wouldn't let Billie pull out in front of the vehicle."

"Zane," she said. "Stop."

He shook his head and then said, "I'm sorry. I didn't mean to wake you up."

"You didn't." The pain had. "But you should go back home."

He ignored her. "It's good to see Simon, isn't it?"

"Jah," she said, lowering her voice even more, "and Casey too." She didn't want to wake up their friend.

Zane nodded, a faraway look in his eyes.

"Do you miss all of it?" Lila asked. "The Army? The other soldiers?"

He paused for a moment. Then he said, "No."

Lila closed her eyes. He'd paused. They'd been all set before the accident. Marriage was a month away. Zane was adapting to living Plain. They had the support of her Dat and of Zane's parents, and Gideon too, of course. But maybe now Zane was second-guessing everything. Transitioning to a horse and buggy was hard enough for everyday life, but throw in a catastrophe and she could see why he felt overwhelmed. He didn't know how to cope with tragedy in the Amish way. He was used to doing something about it, fixing everything. He was wearing her out.

"I'll leave you be," Zane said, using an expression she was sure he'd picked up from her.

Lila nodded without opening her eyes. The numbness had started to settle in, masking the pain and slowing her thoughts. They both needed to rest. She sensed him stepping to the side of the bed and then leaning down, careful not to bump the fixator. When he kissed her forehead, she opened her eyes and said, "We'll get through this." She hoped it was true.

He nodded. "I know. I just wish I could have protected you."

She tried to smile as she reached for his hand. "Think about everything you're doing. Where would I be without your help?"

Zane looked pathetically sad. "I just wish I could fix it now."

She squeezed his hand. "Go back to bed."

He yawned. "See you tomorrow." He stopped at the wood

stove and stoked the fire. A minute later the front door closed behind him.

"Everything all right?" It was Casey's voice from across the room.

"Fine," Lila answered. "Sorry we woke you."

"No worries." By the sound of it, Casey had flopped over to her side.

There were many times Lila wished the accident had happened after the wedding. Then Zane could have taken care of her. Then they'd be together all night long, not just for a quick visit when Zane couldn't sleep. But then, if he changed his mind about staying Amish, it was a blessing they hadn't married yet. She had to trust God—and trust his timing.

◦◦◦◦

Lila woke the next morning to a clatter in the kitchen and the smell of bacon frying. She couldn't imagine that Casey was much of a cook. Maybe Shani had arrived already.

"Shoot!" It was Casey all right, probably doing her best to control her language.

"What happened?" Lila called out.

"Nothing." There was another clatter. Then silence.

"Do you need anything?" Lila asked.

"No," Casey said, her voice sharp.

Lila adjusted the backrest until she could see the counter left of the sink through the kitchen doorway. A wooden spoon sat in a mixing bowl. There was a mug next to it. Lila breathed in the smell of bacon mixed with coffee.

Her stomach began to growl for the first time since the accident. "How about a cup of that coffee?" Lila called out.

"Coming right up." Casey poked her head around the corner. "With cream?"

"Black," Lila said.

108

A minute later Casey appeared with a mug in her hand. Her dark hair was pulled back in a ponytail, and she was wearing a pair of Army sweats. Even in the drab gray, she looked beautiful.

"Here you go." She put the mug on the table beside the bed. "Do you need your meds?"

Lila nodded. It had definitely been four hours since her last pill—both the pain and anxiety had returned. "Thanks." Once she'd swallowed the medicine, using the coffee to wash it down, she asked, "What are you making in there?"

Casey smiled. "You'll see."

"I didn't take you for much of a cook."

Casey stopped smiling.

"What's the matter? Did I say something wrong?"

Casey shook her head. "No one seems to think I'll be able to run a house, including Simon."

Lila couldn't help but laugh. "What does Simon care? He's the biggest slob—" She stopped, realizing she shouldn't have said that.

"Right?" Casey responded. "But he still seems to think I should be able to cook."

"Wait," Lila said. "What are you two planning?"

"Well, we're not exactly planning anything yet. But we're talking."

"M-marriage?" Lila stammered.

Casey nodded, a smile spreading across her face. "Is that all right with you?"

"Of course," Lila said. It meant Simon really wouldn't come home and join the church, but she hadn't expected he would. She inhaled. But she hoped he wouldn't stay in the military much longer. "Is Simon planning to make a career out of the Army?"

"Perhaps," Casey said.

"And what about you?"

"We'll see," she answered. "I don't want to be one of those

couples where both parents get deployed and the kids end up going to stay with grandparents." She paused a moment and then said, "I'm going to admit that I snooped, but here goes. I'm curious is all. I opened the door to the room upstairs after my shower, the one at the top of the landing."

"Oh?" Lila said, shifting a little in the bed.

"Yeah, I shouldn't have. I know." Casey wrinkled her nose. "So do all Amish couples furnish a nursery before they get married?"

Lila gasped. "The room's furnished?"

Casey nodded, a confused look on her face. "Crib. Bureau. Rocking chair."

Lila shook her head. "No, it's not normal. Zane did all of that."

"Oh, sorry," Casey said. "I shouldn't have snooped. I shouldn't have brought it up."

"No," Lila said. "It's fine. Don't worry about it."

Casey nodded toward the kitchen. "Simon and Rose will be here soon, so I need to get back to work. I want things to be ready when they get here."

Casey headed back to the kitchen, while Lila contemplated what she'd said. Zane wouldn't understand, but what he'd done was prideful. She knew he did it as a gift to her, but it was far too early. Far too soon. Tears flooded her eyes, and she swallowed hard. Not only had she loved Zane too much and put too much of her trust in him, but he was already counting that God would bless them with children before they'd even married.

They'd both been foolish.

She dabbed at her tears. She wasn't going to spend the day crying. Not again.

A hint of smoke came from the kitchen, overpowering the scent of bacon. Lila took a sip of her coffee. The smoke got worse. "Everything all right?" she called out to Casey.

"Fine," she answered. "I'm just trying to get used to this stove."

Smoke started to billow out of the kitchen just as Simon came through the front door, followed by Rose. Then the smoke alarm started wailing.

"Whoa!" Simon called out, dashing into the kitchen. "What's going on?"

Lila couldn't hear Casey's answer. Rose headed toward the kitchen and then back toward Lila, a smile on her face. "She burned the hotcakes."

"Poor Casey," Lila said.

Rose sat down on the side of Lila's bed.

"Is Reuben coming over later?" Lila asked.

Rose shook her head again.

"But you're going to the singing with him. Right?" It was an off Sunday as far as church, but a singing had been planned for the evening.

"Maybe I'll go . . ." Rose answered.

"Maybe?"

She shrugged. "I think I'd rather hang out here, see more of Simon before he leaves."

"But you told Reuben you'd go?"

"Jah, but I'm not sure he cares that much."

"What do you mean?" Lila wrapped her hands around her mug and held it close.

Rose shrugged again.

Lila cocked her head. Rose wasn't being honest. "Come on, Rose. What's going on with you and Reuben?"

"Nothing."

"Relationships don't just happen. You have to work at them. Nurture them. Put the other person first."

Rose frowned. "Like you did with Reuben?"

"I never loved Reuben," Lila answered. "But I thought you did. That's what you said. Did that change?"

Rose frowned. "Of course not." She stood. "We need a little break is all. He was all uptight yesterday. First at the barn raising and then over here."

"He didn't seem uptight."

"He was—believe me." She smiled then, flashing her dimples. "It's no big deal, really. I just think he needs some time to sort things through." Rose started toward the kitchen. Obviously she didn't want to talk about Reuben anymore.

As she reached the doorway she barked, "Knock it off."

Simon growled, in a teasing way, "Get out of here."

Lila could imagine Simon sneaking a kiss in the kitchen.

"When's breakfast?" Rose asked.

"As soon as I make the hotcakes," Simon answered. Lila could also imagine the teasing grin he'd probably just shot Casey.

Rose stepped back into the living room.

"Who's making breakfast for Dat?" Lila asked.

"He already ate," Rose said. "It's almost eight, you lazy girl."

"Where's Trudy?"

"With Dat. He didn't say what they're doing today." Beth and Dat usually visited when it was an off Sunday. Lila couldn't help but wonder if there was any news about Beth's ex-husband. No one had said anything.

"How about if you transfer me to the wheelchair?" Lila didn't particularly like the tilt of the chair, but that way she could be in the kitchen with everyone else. Her pain had started to ease and so had her worries.

Rose made a face but wheeled the chair over. She transferred Lila, tucked a blanket around her, and then pushed her into the kitchen. Simon stood at the stove making hotcakes, while Casey took a bottle of orange juice out of the refrigerator. The back door was open to air out the kitchen, and the room was soon cold. "See," Lila said to Casey. "You don't need to learn a thing about cooking. Simon can do it."

Simon grinned and flipped a hotcake high into the air. It twirled back down, and instead of landing on the griddle—or even on the stove—it hit the floor. Simon laughed as he bent to pick it up.

"Never mind," Lila said. As Rose pushed Lila toward the table, Zane and Trevor came through the front door. Rose left the chair and hurried into the living room. But then Zane appeared at Lila's side and pushed her up to the table.

"I'll need help eating," she said. She couldn't reach her plate with the wheelchair tilted back.

"I know," he answered, grabbing a plate and spearing two hotcakes.

"Just one," she said.

He put one back. Zane had fed her half of the hotcake and a piece of bacon by the time Rose and Trevor sauntered in. Rose's face was flushed and Trevor's eyes bright. Lila tried to catch Zane's gaze and express her concern, but he was distracted by Simon's antics as he flipped another hotcake.

When he finished, Simon said he had an announcement to make. Lila braced herself, expecting it was either about marrying Casey or another deployment. It was the latter.

"I'm going to Iraq," Simon said.

"I thought all of our soldiers had come home from there," Lila said.

"It's not about Iraq," Zane said. "It's about Syria."

Simon nodded. "They need snipers in the area, near the border."

"That sounds horrible." Lila glanced at Casey.

She nodded and said, "Not many are being sent. No one from our unit. But they need Simon."

"For how long?" Lila asked.

"Six months or so," Simon answered. "Maybe longer."

Lila felt as if she couldn't breathe. Not Simon. Not again.

Worse than how badly she felt was how excited Simon seemed to be about going. She glanced at Casey again. She seemed subdued but not worried. Lila would never understand the lives of soldiers.

Zane offered her another bite, but she shook her head. She felt too sick at her stomach to eat any more. Maybe it was the pain meds. Or Simon's announcement. But she felt awful. The anxiety was back.

A half hour later, Simon and Casey decided to go into Lancaster to look around, and Trevor said he'd give Rose a ride back to the house. Lila didn't think that was a good idea, but she didn't say anything. After they all left, once Zane had Lila back in her bed, a knock fell on the door.

"Were you expecting anyone?" Zane asked.

Lila shook her head as Zane turned to open the door.

"I'm Deputy Howell," a deep voice said. "Is Lila Lehman here? Her father directed me this way."

"Yes, she's here," Zane answered. "Come on in, Officer." Zane held the door open wider, and the deputy stepped through. He was young, maybe in his mid-twenties. Officers sometimes ate at the Plain Buffet, but Lila didn't recognize him.

Zane introduced Lila and then pulled up a chair for the officer. He took out a little notebook and then said, "I'm sorry about your injuries."

Lila thanked him.

"I was in the neighborhood and had a few extra minutes, but I'm sorry to come by on a Sunday."

"I'm not going anywhere," Lila said, meaning it as a joke, but the officer didn't seem to take it that way.

He sat even straighter. "I stopped by the hospital soon after the accident, but you weren't in any shape to talk with me."

Lila had no memory of him.

"Can you tell me what you remember from the accident?"

114

Lila explained she was driving the horse and buggy to pick up her little sister, that the dog along the fence line was barking, and she suspected someone was coming up behind her. At that moment, just as she started to look in the mirror, she was rear-ended.

"Tell me about the horse. Any problems with him?"

"Not that day," Lila said.

"She's good with horses," Zane said. "She's been driving buggies since she was a little kid." That might have been a little bit of an exaggeration. But she had been driving since she was twelve.

"Any chance you might not remember exactly what happened?"

Lila wasn't sure how to answer that.

The officer paused and then said, "Tell me about your injuries. You were in pretty bad shape when I saw you before."

She rattled off the crushed pelvis, ruptured spleen, bruised bladder and liver. She didn't mention any of the possible long-term damage.

"How about a concussion?"

"Jah," Lila said. "A slight one." It had been the least of her worries. Sleeping the first four days after the accident had helped it heal, mostly.

"Could that have affected your memory of the accident?"

"Hold on," Zane said. "What are you implying?"

The officer closed his notebook. "She went through a traumatic event and had a brain injury. She wouldn't be the first person not to remember an accident correctly." He stood. "And I took a look at the horse. He seems pretty skittish."

"He was traumatized too," Zane said.

Lila tried to get his attention with her eyes, but he was staring the officer down.

"Look," the deputy said. "I'm just doing my job."

Zane crossed his arms. "Sounds like a he-said-she-said situation."

"Exactly," the deputy said.

"Unless there were other witnesses."

"That doesn't appear to be the case." The man stood. "I got the information I needed. I'll see myself out."

Lila's stomach clenched as he headed toward the front door.

After the door clicked shut, Lila tried to keep her voice calm. "How odd."

"Intimidating is more like it." Zane stared at the door. "We need to find you a lawyer."

At first she thought he was joking. "Zane?"

He turned around, an angry expression on his face.

"We're Amish, remember? We don't 'find a lawyer.' And we certainly don't sue."

Zane's stubborn look, the one that was so familiar from their childhood, settled on his face. "Yeah, but this is about justice. Plus medical bills that could easily top a hundred fifty thousand dollars."

She knew the bills would be expensive, but she wouldn't have guessed that much. That could wipe out the district's mutual aid fund, the collection of money they all contributed to in case of emergencies. "Let's see what happens," she said. "We can get advice from Gideon. Surely he's dealt with this before."

Zane didn't reply—instead he said he was going to finish the sanding in the bathroom.

"Wait," Lila said. "What's going on with Trevor and Rose?"

"Nothing," Zane said. "Rose is courting Reuben."

"She seems awfully taken with Trevor. They took their time coming into the kitchen today."

"Oh," Zane said. "I didn't notice. There's no way Trevor would let anything happen. I'm sure of it, but I'll ask him."

She settled down into the bed. At least Trevor was staying

at Eve and Charlie's now—he wouldn't be around as much as he had been.

"Anything else?" Zane asked.

She shook her head. Working on a house project wasn't usually what one did on a Sunday, not even a non-church one, but the toilet was leaking.

When she woke up a couple of hours later, Shani sat beside her reading a book but looked up as soon as Lila stirred. "How are you, sweetie?"

Lila took a moment before she spoke. Shani stood and handed Lila her water bottle. After Lila took a long drink she asked where Zane was.

"Trevor took him into town," Shani said. "He needed a part for the toilet."

"Oh," Lila said, sinking back against the bed. She couldn't expect Zane to be at her side all the time, not when he needed to work, sleep, and get the plumbing working. He frustrated her when he was nearby, but she felt panicked when he was away.

Zane had been right about the little house being the best place for her though. Dat hadn't been over to see her at all—clearly he hadn't wanted her at his house. She felt a stab of homesickness. She was thankful for Shani, she really was, but at the moment she felt a little lost.

10

That evening, while Rose helped with the milking, Dat asked her what time Reuben was coming by.

"He's not," she answered.

He stood with the feed shovel in midair. "You're not going to the singing?"

"No," she answered. "I left him a message a couple of hours ago. I'm going to stay with Lila tonight." Simon and Casey had headed back to Maryland, where she was stationed, an hour ago. Leave it to Simon not to stay and help with the milking.

Dat gave her a questioning look, but she turned back to the cow. The less she said to Dat, the better. Maybe it would work for her to have a couple of weeks of running around, but that didn't mean she had to tell her Dat what she was doing. A little bit of a break from Reuben would do her good.

She knew he had been judgmental and critical of her family the evening before. True, they weren't a typical Amish family, and she knew their chaos made him uncomfortable. But it was her family, and she loved them all dearly. His criticalness, combined with his high standards for himself, was beginning to rile her. It wasn't that she didn't think they had a future together. She did. But she was a hundred percent sure a break would do her good.

After a supper of navy-bean soup and biscuits, Rose read to Trudy and then started a game of Scrabble with her. As they played, Rose thought of the ride home with Trevor from the little house that morning. He'd stopped the car at the end of the drive, where Dat couldn't see them, and let the engine idle while they talked. He shared more about Afghanistan, about the day that Zane was injured and then later, after Zane had returned to the base, when their vehicle detonated the IED. *Improvised explosive device*, Trevor had to explain. A bomb. He'd been driving and took, along with their sergeant, the worst of the explosion.

She listened and listened, but finally she said she needed to get going. She didn't want Dat to come down the lane in the buggy and find her with Trevor. But when she reached the house, Dat was napping in his chair. As it turned out, he and Trudy didn't go visiting at all.

Dat simply said he needed a day of rest. Rose had noticed Dat was slowing down some, but he always seemed to perk up when he was around Beth. She was good for Dat—she kept him calm and centered and noticing what was going on around him in a way he'd never been capable of before. It really was a pity they couldn't marry.

"Rose?" Trudy had one hand in the air.

"What?" Rose shifted in her chair, wondering how long she'd been daydreaming.

Trudy exhaled as her hands fell to her lap. "Like I've said three times, it's your turn."

"Oh," Rose responded, looking at her tiles as Dat passed through the kitchen.

"*Guder Nacht,*" he said as he reached the hall. "See you tomorrow."

Thankfully Joel would help him with the milking in the morning. And Trudy was going to make breakfast. It would be the first day Shani worked since Lila's accident. Rose would care for Lila in the morning and then take Trudy to school. Then she'd return to Lila. It was a crazy schedule. Thankfully Shani had the rest of the week off.

"Maybe I'll make Dutch babies," Trudy said.

"Stick with scrambled eggs and ham slices," Rose said. "That's easy and it will fill Dat up."

After a couple more turns, Rose told Trudy it was time for bed. "I need to get over to help get Lila to bed."

Trudy's lip turned down. She didn't like sleeping in their room by herself. She'd shared it her entire life with both Lila and Rose.

"I'll see you in the morning," Rose said. She already had her bag packed and by the back door.

"Can't I go with you?"

Rose shook her head. "There's only one cot." There were other reasons too, but those didn't concern Trudy. "Brush your teeth," Rose said. "And don't forget to say your prayers." Trudy only had three years of school left, and then she'd be running the household for Dat. It was good for her to start taking more responsibility. They'd all spoiled her.

As Rose walked down the lane under the light of a nearly full moon, she couldn't help but hope Trevor would come along and give her a ride. Just the thought of him gave her a jolt as she passed the cedar tree and approached Shani and Joel's house. Trevor's car sat in the driveway. Maybe she would see him.

The evening had grown crisp and cold, and she pulled her cape tighter as she walked slowly by the Becks' home. When no one came out, she stepped around the side of the barn. A single lamp burned in the kitchen window of the little house. Perhaps Shani had already helped Lila get ready for bed.

As she hurried onto the porch, the door swung open and Trevor stepped into the near darkness. "I was waiting for you," he said. "To say good-night."

Rose smiled and stepped closer.

He gazed down.

"Who all is here?" she asked.

"Just Zane and me. We're ready to leave though." He stayed in the doorway. "So did you go to the singing tonight?"

She shook her head. "I played games with Trudy instead."

He smiled.

"Ready?" Zane asked, coming up behind Trevor.

"Yep," he answered, stepping aside so Rose could enter the house.

Zane wore an Englisch jacket over his Amish shirt. "Lila just had her pain meds."

Rose told the boys good-night, shut the door, and then took off her cape and hung it on a peg by the front door. The fire was roaring, and it was too warm in the little house. She approached Lila and after saying hello added, "Did Shani already get you ready for bed?"

Lila nodded. Rose tucked the quilt around her sister, feeling she should do something, and then she moved the lamp and sat down in the recliner, pulling the latest copy of the *Budget* from her bag.

When she was certain Lila had fallen asleep, she put her cape back on and tiptoed to the front door.

Lila stirred. "Where are you going?"

"To get some fresh air. It's burning up in here."

"Rose . . ."

"Honestly, Lila. I'm just going to stand on the porch for a minute and then change into my nightgown and get some sleep before you need your next pill." She turned the doorknob. When Lila didn't respond, she went ahead and stepped onto the porch, breathing in the cool air as she pulled the door closed. She could see a sliver of light coming through the apple trees from the Becks' house. She continued on, knowing exactly what she was hoping for. She was sure it wouldn't happen though. Trevor had probably gone over to Eve and Charlie's as soon as he left.

She walked along the barn and then stopped at the corner, craning her neck to see if Trevor's car was still there. It was.

"Hey."

She gasped and then giggled. It was Trevor, at the other corner of the barn. "Hey, yourself," she said and then giggled again at the risk she was taking. But she wasn't going to feel guilty about it. She should have spent some time running around two years ago. That was the mistake she'd made.

"What are you doing?" He slipped something into his pocket.

"Getting some fresh air," she answered. "It's a hothouse in there."

"Yeah," he said. "Well, Lila was cold, and Zane kept stoking the fire. I told him we were all going to die from heatstroke, but he wouldn't listen."

Rose smiled and then said, "I thought you would have left by now. What are you doing out here?"

"I was hoping you'd come out to say good-night."

Her heart skipped a beat. "I already said good-night," she teased.

He stepped closer. "A second good-night, then." His breath smelled a little sweet and a little peppery at the same time. He turned on the flashlight on his phone and nodded his head toward the barn. "We could sit in there."

"All right," she said, leading the way, following the beam of light as Trevor pushed the door open. The Becks' barn was mostly empty. Rose knew Lila and Zane wanted to raise a couple of calves and some chickens, but currently the family had no animals. There were a few bales of hay, probably from when Zane kept Billie there for a short time.

There was a bench in front of one of the stalls. Trevor pointed toward it. Rose sat down, and Trevor sat next to her, on the far side of the bench. She scooted a little closer to him before she considered what she was doing. She stopped. It was one thing to flirt with him but another to be too forward. She'd never acted so un-Plain in all of her life.

"Do you think Zane is doing all right?" Trevor asked. "I'm worried about him."

"Oh?" Rose hadn't really given Zane much thought.

"He's upset about the other driver. And the deputy that questioned Lila. He's afraid the insurance company is going to get out of paying."

"Doesn't it take a while for those things to get settled?"

"Sure," Trevor said.

"It hasn't been very long."

"True." Trevor placed his cell phone, the flashlight beam shooting upward, between them. "Zane always seemed so calm and level-headed in the Army. He seems like a loose cannon now."

"What do you mean?"

Trevor shook his head. "I probably shouldn't say anything. . . ."

Rose leaned a little closer. "What happened?"

Trevor didn't answer right away, but then he said, "I think he feels helpless. Like there's not a lot he can do to help Lila."

"Oh," Rose answered. There really wasn't much he could do. He couldn't dress her or sponge bathe her or spend the night with her. She didn't want to talk about Lila and Zane, but she wasn't going to tell Trevor that.

He sighed. "I can understand being frustrated about not being able to help someone you really care about."

"Oh?" Rose said again, but this time in a teasing way.

He turned toward her, his eyes serious. "I'd care about you in a split second, if you weren't Amish. As it is I can't risk the wrath of your father. He seems pretty formidable."

Rose wasn't sure what to say. Dat wasn't anyone to make mad—that was for sure. Trevor picked up his phone and held it in his hand, partially blocking the light. Rose placed her hands in her lap and stared at him. His face was in the shadows, but he was still looking at her.

"Jah," she finally said. "We definitely come from different worlds." And that was fine. She certainly didn't want anything from him, except some fun.

As he turned his body toward her, she leaned forward. He put his hand on her shoulder gently, then scooted closer. When his lips met hers, she wondered if perhaps she was only fooling herself. Perhaps she did want more. It was as if something was exploding deep within her. She couldn't help but think that Reuben kissing her would never feel like this.

She scooted closer to Trevor until they were hugging as they kissed, each pulling the other closer. His mouth was warm and then open and tasted both sweet and spicy, just like his breath smelled. He'd been drinking something by the barn. He held her tighter and kissed her harder. But then he pulled away suddenly.

"Wow," he said, standing quickly. She looked up at him, afraid she'd offended him somehow. "Look," he said. "I didn't mean for that to happen." He inhaled deeply and then exhaled, shining the light toward the door. "I'll walk you back."

Confused, she followed him out the door.

"You okay?" he asked as he walked with her around the barn.

"Jah," she answered. "I can walk the rest of the way alone."

"No," he said. "I'll see you safely there." When they reached the porch, he put his hand on her shoulder.

She turned her face up toward his, longing for him to kiss her again.

Instead of guessing at her wish he said, "Look, I shouldn't have kissed you like that. I'm sorry."

"Don't be," she said. "I didn't mind. Not one bit." She smiled up at him. None of her kisses with boys she went to school with had been like that. She hadn't known a kiss could be so passionate. That she could feel so—

"No, I am sorry," he said. "I don't want to take advantage of you. Of your innocence."

She shook her head, feeling a frown spread across her face. She'd rather have him kiss her than talk down to her. "Good night," she said and then hurried to the door, her heart aching.

As she entered the house, Lila called out her name.

"Jah," she said. "I'm here."

"*Gut,*" her sister answered. "I can sleep now." Rose wasn't used to Lila being dependent on her. That in itself was unsettling.

But what was most unsettling was the way Trevor's kiss had made her feel. For a moment, she thought of Reuben and a wave of guilt washed over her. No, she'd ignore that. Trevor wouldn't kiss her again. She'd pretend it never happened. Nothing would change between her and Reuben. The only thing that had changed was that she'd caught a glimpse of what she'd wanted before she'd set her sights on Reuben, before she'd joined the church. Jah, it had probably been a mistake to do both so young. She definitely should have done a little more running around before it was too late.

<hr/>

Rose didn't see Trevor for the next couple of days. She knew he picked Zane up and then dropped him off after work, but he wasn't coming into the little house. He was probably avoiding her on purpose. She didn't blame him. He was probably afraid

Rose had fallen for him. She wouldn't embarrass herself. She'd play it cool when she did see him, wouldn't give it away that she was thinking about him every waking moment.

Finally, on the third day, as Rose helped Lila from the recliner to the bed, she asked her sister what she knew about Trevor.

"He's from Delaware," she said.

Rose knew that.

"It seems he had a girlfriend."

Rose nodded. He'd told her that.

"Zane thinks he regrets breaking up with her—or maybe that they're not entirely broken up."

Rose hadn't gathered that from what Trevor had said before. Her face grew warm. No wonder he'd immediately regretted kissing her. She should have gone to the singing with Reuben on Sunday evening instead of sneaking out to see Trevor.

"It's time for me to go get Trudy," Rose said. "Are you all right? Or should I go get Shani?"

"I'm fine," Lila said. "I'll sleep while you're gone."

Rose had parked the buggy outside Joel and Shani's barn after she took Trudy to school that morning and had put the horse in a stall. She'd brought over a bale of hay and spread it on the floor. As she led the horse out, past the bench she and Trevor had sat on, she couldn't help but remember their kiss.

He'd been apologetic. Obviously he wasn't that interested in her.

The clear skies had held, and the day was warm. She had the horse hitched in no time and headed down the lane. By the time she reached the school, it seemed that she'd seen at least ten red sports cars. None of them was Trevor's though. Thinking about him so much alarmed her. Was this how Dat felt about Beth? Was Rose accidentally falling in love with Trevor? She couldn't let that happen, and yet she could feel her certainty about marrying Reuben diminishing each day.

Perhaps she was only seventy percent sure now. The thought troubled her.

She tied the horse to the hitching post and started toward the building. "You're late." Trudy stood on the top step.

Behind her, Beth waited in the open doorway of the school. She waved at Rose and called out, "How is Lila doing?"

"*Gut*," Rose answered. Actually Lila seemed to be in a lot of pain still. It didn't seem to be getting better, and she was taking as many pain pills as always. She said she couldn't sleep without them.

"How are you doing?" Rose asked the woman.

"Fine," Beth said, but she didn't seem fine.

Rose stepped onto the first stair and shot Trudy a questioning look, but her little sister just shrugged her shoulders.

After stepping up another level, Rose asked, "What happened?"

Beth shook her head.

Rose raised her eyebrows.

Beth paused a minute and then said to Trudy, "Go get your book to take home. You should be able to finish it tonight."

Once Trudy slipped back into the school, Beth said, her voice low, "A few weeks ago Gideon cautioned your Dat and I from spending so much time together."

"Oh." It was as Rose suspected, but she was surprised that Beth and Dat would be caught off guard by Gideon's warning. "I'm sorry," Rose said. "I know how much you two . . ." She wasn't sure how to finish her sentence.

But Beth nodded.

Again Rose wondered if Reuben had said something to his Dat. Sure, it would be perfectly acceptable within their community to be concerned. Dat worked for Reuben, and they were friends besides. If anyone should say something, it should be Reuben. But the thought of him doing so still troubled Rose.

127

What was the harm? Dat and Beth knew they couldn't marry. It was like Reuben to put his principles before people.

"Is your Dat doing all right?" Beth asked.

"A little quiet." Rose wrinkled her nose. She'd noticed but hadn't been paying a lot of attention to him.

Trudy bounded back onto the porch, a book in her hand. She gave Beth a hug and then hurried down the stairs. Rose waved to Beth and followed Trudy to the buggy. Once she'd unhitched the horse and climbed up, Trudy asked her, "What's wrong with Beth?"

"She's a little sad."

"Why?"

"Well, you know how she and Dat have been friends for a while?"

Trudy nodded.

"Gideon—Bishop Byler—doesn't want them to spend so much time together."

"Why not?"

"Because they can't marry."

"Do they want to marry?"

Rose wasn't sure. Perhaps, if Beth could, they might. But then again, she couldn't imagine Dat marrying again. Almost all Amish widows and widowers remarried, and soon after their spouses died, but Dat had never seemed interested. Finally, Rose said, "I don't know."

"Well," Trudy said, "if they wanted to why couldn't they?"

"Because Beth was married before, and her husband is still alive."

"Oh." Trudy bit her lower lip. Obviously all of them had failed to explain that to her, which wasn't surprising. Sometimes Rose felt as if there were all sorts of things they hadn't told Trudy that she might need to know someday. Information about their mother and her illness and why Simon joined the

Army and why Lila didn't marry Reuben. But all of that could wait until another time. Sometimes it felt like a relief to have one person in the family still innocent.

Instead Rose said, "In the eyes of the church she's still married to her first husband until he dies."

Trudy shifted on the bench. "So he didn't marry anyone else?"

"I don't know for sure." She had the impression he had. "But I know he left the church."

"Oh," Trudy said, taking it in. "Did Beth want to leave the church?"

Rose shook her head. "No, she didn't." Rose didn't know that Beth's ex-husband wanted her to leave though. She had the idea he left both the church *and* Beth.

"Did you think maybe Dat and Beth would get married someday?" Rose asked, motioning for Trudy to scoot closer.

Her sister nodded as she snuggled up against Rose. She hiccupped. Rose realized she was crying. "I'm sorry," she said.

Trudy continued to cry. Rose wanted to also. Beth would add so much to all of their lives. Then she realized Dat probably felt the same. Did his heart ache for Beth the way Rose's was beginning to for Trevor?

11

Zane stood beside Tim and held a lantern high as the veterinarian examined Billie's foreleg. "The swelling has gone down. I'd say he's going to make it."

"But will he be able to pull a buggy?" Tim asked. "Or will he be prone to reinjure it?"

"Another injury will be a little more likely, sure," the vet said, "but I think he'll do all right. He should have several more good years."

Tim wouldn't want Zane to keep the horse if it couldn't pull a buggy. As gentle as he was with his cows, Tim was still practical when it came to animals. He wouldn't condone keeping one around just to feed.

"All right," Tim finally said. "We'll give it another week or so and see how he's doing."

Lila would be heartbroken if Tim thought Billie should be put down. So would Zane and his budget. He already had to buy a new buggy—and perhaps with no insurance money to help.

Zane continued to hold the lantern up as they all left the

barn. "Thank you," Zane said as they reached the door. "How much do I owe you?"

"Ach," Tim said. "I'll cover it." He turned toward the vet. "Put it on my bill."

"I will," the vet said. He'd checked on one of the dairy cows too.

Tim turned toward Zane. "Thank you for helping with the milking."

"Sure." Zane had gotten off work early and knew Rose could use a break.

"Could you listen to a message on the machine before you go?" Tim asked. "It's about the accident."

"Oh?" Zane thought he'd given everyone his parents' phone number, hoping they'd call there.

"From the insurance company, I think," Tim said. "Go listen to it."

Zane stepped into Tim's office, wishing he'd told him earlier about the call. The agent had most likely left by now. Zane clicked the button on the machine. A man's voice came on, identifying himself and the insurance company he worked with. Zane grabbed a pen. The man said, "After gathering more information from Mr. Addison, the driver of the SUV, and reading the police report filed by a Deputy Howell, I wanted to give you an update. Please call me back at your convenience." He rattled off his phone number twice and then said good-bye.

Zane scribbled down the number and quickly called the insurance agent back. He let it ring several times, expecting a voice message after each ring. He wanted to at least leave a message. He didn't want to have to call back the next day.

Just as he wondered if he should hang up, the insurance agent picked up and said hello.

"Zane Beck, here. Calling back on behalf of Lila Lehman."

"Thank you," the man said. "May I speak to Ms. Lehman?"

"No," Zane said. "I'm in her father's barn, using the phone in his office. She's in a house without a phone."

"I see," the man said. "And you are?"

"Her fiancé."

"I see," he said again. "You'll still need to have her call me back. I can't divulge any private information to you."

Zane exhaled sharply. None of this was easy. "How long will you be in your office?"

"I'm on my cell. Call me any time."

"I should be able to get a phone to her within a half hour, at least."

"Perfect," the man answered.

Zane hustled out of the barn and jogged across the field. When he reached the little house, Rose and Reuben stood on the porch. At first, Zane felt relieved to see them together. He'd been worried by the way Trevor was looking at Rose the evening Simon and Casey showed up. After he called out a hello, he realized they were deep in conversation. It looked pretty serious. Reuben had his hat in his hands and Rose had her arms crossed.

Reuben said a quick hello, but Rose didn't say anything.

"Sorry to interrupt," Zane said as he approached. "Is my mom around?"

Rose shook her head. "She went home about twenty minutes ago. She was going to heat up supper and bring some over."

"Denki." Not wanting to intrude, Zane started toward his parents' place. "Tell Lila I'll be over in just a minute," he called over his shoulder.

Rose sighed. "All right. And then I'm going home to get supper on the table for Dat and Trudy."

Zane waved to let her know he'd heard her, tipped his hat to Reuben, who nodded in reply, and then hurried over to his parents' house. He opened the door, stepped inside, and found

Trevor sprawled the length of the sofa, asleep, and Adam sitting in a chair, reading a book.

"Mom," Zane called out, veering off toward the kitchen. She stood at the stove stirring a pot of something. "I need to borrow your cell phone."

"What for?" Mom let go of the spoon and reached into her apron pocket.

"So Lila can talk to the insurance agent."

She handed the phone to Zane. "Tell Rose I'll bring supper over soon."

Zane nodded toward the living room. "What's Trevor doing?"

"Sleeping," Mom answered. "And soundly. I dropped a cookie sheet and he didn't even stir."

"But why is he here? Why didn't he go over to Eve and Charlie's?"

Mom shrugged. "Ask him when he wakes up, but he probably feels more comfortable here, rather than hanging out with Eve until Charlie gets home."

That made sense. It also reminded Zane he needed to call Charlie and tell him he needed more time off from volunteering at the station. He wasn't sure when he'd go back—it might be a long time. "Thanks," he said, holding up the phone as he headed for the front door.

⁓

He had to wake Lila up, which wasn't easy. "How many pills did you have?" Zane asked as Lila rubbed her eyes.

She shrugged. "Just one. The usual."

Zane held up the bottle. There were only a few left. He'd talk to his mom about renewing the prescription.

"Babe," Zane said, his frustration growing. "I need you to talk to the insurance agent. I'll put the phone on speaker and take notes so we don't miss anything."

133

"All right," she said. "Help me with the backrest."

He adjusted it so she was reclining at an angle, the fixator jutting out in front of her.

Zane pulled the slip of paper with the phone number on it from his pocket, dialed, and then put the phone on speaker. It rang twice and then the agent picked it up. Zane told him hello and then nodded at Lila.

"Hello," she said.

"How are you doing?" the man asked.

"Fine," she answered.

"Oh, good," the man said.

Zane winced. He'd believed her. "Actually, she's not fine," Zane said. "She has a crushed pelvis with a fixator bolted to her hip bones. Have you seen one of those before? It's like a Frankenstein contraption. She can't sit up straight. She can't walk more than a few feet. No one would even use it as a torture device." Zane's frustration turned on the man. "Plus, she's recovering from a ruptured spleen, a bruised bladder, a bruised liver, and a concussion."

"Oh, well," the agent said. "I'm so sorry to hear that." He paused for a moment and then said, "I wanted to give you our update after interviewing Mr. Addison and examining his vehicle. And reading the deputy's report."

Lila didn't respond.

"Are you there, Ms. Lehman?"

"Jah," she answered. "I'm just a little sleepy."

"Is this an all right time to talk?"

"I think so," she said.

"Yes or no?"

"Jah," she answered. Zane wished she'd stop saying *jah*. It sounded so lackadaisical. *Yes* sounded much more precise.

"Okay, then listen carefully," he said. "We've come to the conclusion that your buggy veered out in front of Mr. Addison's

SUV, causing him to hit the back of your buggy. There was no way for him to avoid the collision."

"Pardon?"

"You heard me."

Zane bristled again, his frustration turning to anger.

"No," Lila said. "I don't think that's what happened."

"Mr. Addison hasn't changed his story, beginning with the 9-1-1 call. We have it as evidence."

"I'm pretty sure that's not what happened," Lila said, her voice soft and calm.

"Pretty sure or sure? The police report indicated you were uncertain," the man said. "And the report indicated"—there was the rustling of paper—"that you had a head injury from the accident, perhaps contributing to a cognitive issue."

"It was a mild concussion," Zane corrected.

"But can Ms. Lehman be certain she can remember the moments right before the accident? To know the horse didn't cut in front of the vehicle."

"I remember being over as far as I could be on the road and then being hit from behind, and I remember going through the windshield, over the top—"

"The police report corroborates Mr. Addison's story."

"No," Zane said. "It doesn't."

"Pardon?" the man said.

"The deputy believed the driver over Lila. That's all." Zane stood but leaned toward the phone on the table. "I think your client is trying to take advantage of Lila being Amish. And I'm guessing you are too."

"No, no, no, that couldn't be further from the truth," the man said. "And we could counter you're trying to take advantage of a driver who happens to have accident insurance as opposed to the driver of the buggy who obviously does not." Zane bristled. Was that how insurance companies worked?

"We'll be sending Ms. Lehman the cost of the repairs to Mr. Addison's vehicle."

"That's ridiculous," Zane said.

"No, that's the law."

"We'll be contacting an attorney," Zane said.

The voice grew deeper. "I thought you just said Ms. Lehman is Amish."

"And that's why you thought you could bully her?"

"Of course not," the man said. "But we won't be paying for her medical bills or for the buggy. Like I said, she'll need to pay for the repairs to Mr. Addison's vehicle."

"Good-bye," Zane said, hitting the End button and picking up the phone. "They're bluffing," he said, before Lila could respond. She appeared shell-shocked.

"I can't call an attorney," she said. "That's not what we do."

"I'll talk to one and get some ideas." Zane wondered where he'd come up with the money.

Tears filled Lila's eyes.

"Don't think about it," Zane said. "I'll figure it out."

"I don't want the mutual fund to have to pay for it," Lila said. "Not when I'm the one who was hit."

"I know." Zane didn't really understand the fund, except that everyone contributed to it to pay for medical expenses of people in the district. Lila's accident certainly qualified, but the man's insurance should have to pay for her medical care. And the buggy.

Zane stumbled to his feet.

"Are you mad?" Lila asked.

"Of course not." Zane stopped beside the bed even though he felt like running. He exhaled. It wasn't her fault.

"I'm sure I was over as far as I could be, that Billie didn't pull to the left. There's no way he could have. But the way the agent was talking, it makes me question myself."

"You're a good driver," Zane said. "I believe you. Keep believing yourself."

"Denki," she said.

"Dad has a lawyer acquaintance. He's across the street from the Veterans Center—he's a vet and helps other vets. I'll see about talking to him." He patted her arm and then put the phone on the table. "Don't worry. Try to rest some more, until Mom comes over with supper."

She nodded.

"I'm going to go work on the bathroom until then."

Lila already had her eyes closed as he walked away.

As he sanded by hand, his frustration grew. He'd felt such harmony a year ago when he joined the church, standing in front of the congregation as he proclaimed, *I am a seeker desiring to be part of this church of God.* He knew seeking after God and Christian community were both lifelong endeavors. He knew life had its ups and downs. He just expected the downs to come a little later.

He embraced the Amish, he really did, and he'd never felt such peace as the day he joined, such confidence that it was what God wanted him to do. But maybe the whole lifestyle thing wasn't as doable as he thought.

Lila's injuries were worse than his had been when he'd been shot in Afghanistan, and her recovery would take much longer. He remembered the pain he'd been in and the meds he'd taken to get through it. He knew she had to be in horrible agony, probably far worse than she let on. Her body had been tossed from the buggy, then flung through the air, and landed in the creek with the horse on top of her. He shuddered. He hated to even think of it, to replay it in his head.

If Lila had been in a car or pickup she wouldn't have been hurt so badly. And if the Amish sued, the insurance agent wouldn't be trying to bully Lila.

He threw the sandpaper on the floor. And if he could use an electric sander, he wouldn't be rubbing off his fingertips.

"Zane?" It was Mom, standing in the middle of the kitchen, staring at him, her coat still on and holding a pot with oven mitts.

Mom's eyes were full of concern. "Are you all right?"

"Yeah," he said. "I'm fine."

"What's going on?"

"Lots." Where would he start? He'd tell her about the conversation with the insurance agent later. He jerked his head toward the living room. "What's with Lila? Is she taking too many pain meds?"

"No," Mom said. "We've been regulating them carefully."

"She's all wiped out—like she can't stay awake."

"Her pain is still really bad. Plus she needs to sleep to heal."

"Is there another bottle of pain meds? Because she's almost out."

"There's one in the cupboard in the kitchen. She usually only takes half the prescribed dose—the whole dose is sometimes too much."

"Okay," Zane said. At least she wasn't taking as much as he feared.

Mom said the soup was from one of the Amish ladies and then put the pot on the stove. Zane picked up the sandpaper and started sanding the molding along the door, thinking about what he wouldn't give for a Shop-Vac to clean everything up.

❧

Lila slept for the rest of the evening and only woke enough to eat some soup. Finally, around eight, Zane headed back over to his parents' house to eat there, leaving Mom with Lila.

Trevor was still asleep on the sofa when he arrived. Dad was sitting with Adam at the kitchen table, helping him with his homework. Without saying hello, he nodded toward Trevor and then asked his dad what was going on.

"I don't know," Dad said. "I'm guessing he's tired."

Adam closed his math book.

"Sorry, Bub," Zane said. "Were you done?"

"Yep. I just have my reading. I'll do that upstairs."

Once Adam left the room, Zane sat down and told Dad about the conversation with the insurance agent.

"Is Lila sure she didn't pull to the left?"

"Yes," Zane answered. "And I believe her. She's cautious and methodical when she drives. But she's doubted herself some, because of what the other driver said." Zane shook his head. "She's really not herself."

"Give her time," Dad said. "And space. That's what I needed after my injury. It's what you needed too."

Zane exhaled. His dad was right. Lila had encouraged him through that time. He needed to do his best to encourage her now.

Dad grabbed his cane from where it hung on the table edge and stood. "But it sounds as if the insurance company might be trying to take advantage of her, maybe even manipulate her memory."

"That's what I'm afraid of," Zane answered. "I thought maybe I could talk with that lawyer who does pro bono work sometimes."

"Brad Garrett?"

Zane nodded, remembering when he'd met the man a couple of years ago. He'd been impressed with him then.

Dad smiled a little as he leaned on the cane and pushed himself up out of the chair. "Yeah, I'm sure he'd be happy to give you some advice. Do you think Tim would be all right with that?"

Zane shrugged.

"Don't go behind Tim's back," Dad said.

"I want justice for Lila."

Dad cocked his head. "That's not really the Amish way though, is it? They'd probably rather pay her expenses out of the mutual aid fund than get involved in any lawsuit."

Zane shrugged again. When he'd wrangled with whether he could live as a pacifist or not, he'd thought through the fighting part of it. He hadn't thought through a case like this, through the legal side of it.

"I know you've always held yourself and others to a high standard as far as doing the right thing, but you're living under different rules now." Dad took a step toward the kitchen doorway. "You should probably talk with Gideon or someone else in the church before you talk with Brad."

Zane didn't respond to his father. Instead he stared at his chapped and scraped hands for a long moment. Construction work was taking its toll. He should wear his gloves more often. Finally he stood and dished up some soup—beef barley—from the pot Mom had left on her stove and sat back down at the table. As he shoveled the food into his mouth, Trevor wandered into the kitchen, bleary eyed.

"What's for supper?" he asked.

Zane tilted his nearly empty bowl so Trevor could see. "Soup. It's on the stove."

Trevor retrieved a bowl from the cupboard, filled it, and sat across from Zane. "Who's hanging out with Lila tonight?"

"Mom."

"Is Rose there?"

Zane wrinkled his nose. "Why do you ask?"

"Just wondered."

After Lila mentioned her concern about Trevor and Rose on Sunday, Zane had brought up the topic with Trevor on the way to work on Monday. Trevor had assured Zane he had no interest in her.

One of the reasons Mom thought Trevor should stay at Eve and Charlie's was so he'd be away from Rose, saying Tim wouldn't feel comfortable having a stranger staying so close. Zane thought she was being paranoid, but he had to admit now she'd probably been wise in her judgment. And maybe he'd been too quick to believe Trevor on Monday morning.

Zane put his spoon in the bowl and pushed back a little from the table. "What's going on with you?"

Trevor blushed, which he didn't do very often.

Zane exhaled. "Don't tell me you're falling for Rose." What a nightmare that would be. "You said you wouldn't."

Trevor shook his head. "Of course not. She's beautiful though. And her innocence is appealing."

Zane crossed his arms, alarmed, and cleared his throat.

"Don't worry—I didn't mean it that way. I meant she's spunky and fun. Not the way I imagined an Amish girl to be—not at all." He blushed again. "No offense."

"None taken."

"I always thought you were crazy to fall for an Amish girl, but now I get it."

Zane shook his head. "No, you don't get it. Leave Rose alone. She and Reuben are courting." He wouldn't mention that they seemed to be stressed. "Hopefully they'll marry soon. You'd only hurt her."

"I won't. I promise." Trevor took a bite of the soup and then said, "Maybe I'll head back home sooner than I thought."

"You said you planned to stay."

Trevor held his spoon in midair. "I appreciate Charlie and Eve's hospitality, but it's awkward staying there. I don't know them, and their baby cries a lot." He paused for a moment and then said, "Being here has made me feel more isolated—not less."

"Isolated?" He was around people all the time.

"Yeah, I'm the outsider. I see what you have with Lila. I see your family. I see you with your dad, something I never really had—I mean, he was there . . . but not really. I see Rose's family. The other Amish people who have brought meals over." He shrugged. "I've never seen anything like it."

"And it makes you feel isolated?"

He nodded. "And it's not just that I'll never have anything like this. It's that you all dress the same. Drive the same buggy. Live in white houses with flowers planted all around. You really know how to make a guy feel like an outsider." He took another spoonful of soup.

Zane thought about what Trevor said. He wasn't sure how to explain it but he had to try. "We appear the same for the sake of modesty."

"Yeah, I get that. The women hide behind those dresses."

"No, that's not it," Zane said. "We all aim to practice modesty. It shows we identify with each other, that we've chosen to be part of a Plain community. That's why our buggies look alike too—no one can flaunt their money by having something much nicer. Same with the houses. We don't want to call attention to ourselves, to insinuate one person is better than another. We all have value in God's eyes. We're all equal to him."

Trevor shook his head a little and then said, "Yeah, whatever. I'll stick with my car—red and fast." He smiled.

Zane shrugged. In all of his frustration lately, he was still grateful he'd chosen to identify with the Amish. He appreciated both the outward and inward commitment to God, family, and community, instead of to individualism. Sure, competition was normal between people, but there wasn't the same sort of everyone-for-himself competition he'd experienced as an Englischer. He appreciated the way they took care of each other through life's trials.

Trevor swallowed another spoonful of soup and said, "I'll go back home in a month or so. Maybe I'll find a job in construction. Sit around and drink on the weekends."

Zane raised his eyebrows. "I thought you'd stopped drinking."

"Yeah, well. I have. Mostly."

"It's not anything to mess with."

Trevor shrugged. "What can I say? I'm pathetic."

"Have you been drinking recently?"

Trevor pushed his chair back. "I was just joking—don't get all righteous with me." He leaned back in the chair. "I should probably get over my fear of commitment and try to work things out with Sierra. Maybe we can get back together, get married, start a family. Maybe she'll back off and stop nagging me all the time. Maybe I can have a little bit of what you have. Except I won't have everyone in the county helping me like you do. I'll barely have my dad's help."

"What about going back to school? With the G.I. Bill."

Trevor brought the chair back down. "I've never liked school."

"You could use it for a vocational program. There are all sorts of possibilities. You can talk to one of the counselors at the Veterans Center."

Trevor shrugged. "I guess I'm in a funk is all." He held up his spoon. "I'll finish this and get out of your way."

"Take your time." Zane stood and took his empty bowl to the sink. "I'm going to get to bed." Maybe a good sleep would help him feel better.

Zane started to head up the stairs but realized he hadn't asked Trevor what time he'd come by to pick him up in the morning. He backtracked, stepping back into the kitchen. Trevor's back was to him, but he held a flask.

Zane exhaled. "You weren't joking."

Trevor turned around, putting the cap back on the flask as he did. "Looks like you caught me."

"You promised not to drink here."

He slipped the flask into his pocket. "I didn't. Not until today."

"How much have you had?" Zane asked.

"Not much." He patted his pocket.

Zane wasn't sure what to do.

"Look," Trevor said. "I really am sorry. I'll work for another couple of weeks and then give my notice. I'd leave sooner, but I'm going to need the reference."

Zane nodded. "We need to talk with Dad about the drinking."

Trevor frowned. "I'll talk with Charlie tonight and ask him to hold me accountable. You and your dad have enough to deal with right now."

Zane hesitated and then said, "Talk with Charlie." He held out his hand. "But give me the flask."

"Good idea," Trevor said, handing it over.

For half a second Zane thought maybe he understood the appeal. He could use some numbing himself at the moment. Instead he poured the alcohol—whiskey—down the sink and dropped the flask into the garbage.

"I'm just going to go over and tell your mom thanks for supper," Trevor said. "Then I'll get going. I'll pick you up at six thirty."

"Thanks," Zane said. "I appreciate it. But don't bother going over to tell Mom thanks. She probably already has Lila down for the night. She might be getting ready for bed. Besides, one of the Amish ladies made it anyway."

"All right," Trevor answered. "See you tomorrow. And listen, I'm sorry. Really."

Zane nodded, walked Trevor to the door, and then waited on the porch as his friend drove away. Trevor would go back to Delaware. Marry Sierra. And maybe he would be a father in a year or so, if he straightened up.

A *father*. As much as it would hurt Zane not to be a father, he knew not being a mother would hurt Lila even more, but he wasn't going to give up on them being able to have children.

But maybe Lila had, from that one ambiguous conversation with the doctor. Maybe that was why it seemed she was so distant. That or the pain pills. Or maybe she was trying to numb herself from the uncertainty that the future held. Or perhaps his mom was right, and she needed the meds to get through her pain.

He felt as if he was failing her, day by day. He couldn't take care of her. He couldn't take her pain away. He didn't understand what this new level of being Amish meant for him. This level of not fighting for justice. Of trusting God and the district to provide over a hundred fifty thousand dollars when the insurance company should be responsible for paying.

He'd use the rest of his savings to buy a new buggy. He wasn't going to dwell on the injustice of that. It didn't matter.

But he would talk to the lawyer. If the insurance company didn't pay, he'd accept whatever help the mutual aid fund could offer. And then he'd contribute as much as he could to it every month for the rest of his life.

12

A draft of cold air in the little house awakened Lila. She opened her eyes, expecting Zane. Instead Trevor was closing the front door. She raised the backrest a little. "What are you doing here?"

He spun around. "Good morning," he said. "I'm looking for Shani."

"She might be in the kitchen."

"I'll check." He disappeared through the archway to the kitchen and then returned a couple of minutes later. "She must be upstairs," he said. "Listen, I can't stick around. I'm picking up Zane for work. Would you tell Shani thanks for the soup last night? It was delicious."

"Sure." Lila was beginning to feel annoyed with Trevor, except that his giving Zane rides was a big help. She was grateful for that. "Tell Zane hello." He usually came over every morning before work, but maybe he was still out of sorts from their conversation with the insurance agent.

Trevor said that he would and then asked, "Is Rose helping today?"

"Jah." Sometimes it was hard to keep track of everyone's schedule. Shani was going to work. Joel was already helping with the milking. Rose would be over within the hour, after she cleaned up from breakfast. Dat would take Trudy to school today.

"Tell her hello." Trevor waved and then hurried out the door.

A few minutes later, the door flew open, allowing another cold draft of air to pierce the cozy house, and Zane hurried toward her.

"I thought you weren't coming," Lila said.

"I overslept," he answered. "Trevor's waiting with his car running so I only have a minute." He stopped at the side of the bed and took her hand. His was warm even though it was cold outside. "I want to talk with you sometime soon," he said.

Her stomach sank. He sounded so serious. "All right," she answered.

"It's important." He had that intense look he used to have a lot, but hadn't as much in the last year.

She nodded. "I'll be here." The joke was getting old.

"I'll see you then." He hurried out the door.

After Shani helped Lila dress for the day, she took the pillbox into the kitchen to fill it for the day. A minute later she came back in. "Where's your other bottle of pain meds?"

"You said they are in the kitchen cupboard."

"They're not there," Shani said. "Did Rose move them?"

"She didn't say anything," Lila said.

"We need to find the bottle." Shani appeared concerned. "I can get another refill at the pharmacy, since you haven't been taking the full dose, but this isn't good."

"I'm sure they were just misplaced," Lila answered. "I'll ask Rose." She wanted to be done with the pain meds, but she couldn't sleep without them, and her pain levels were high during the day too. The doctor said she'd heal faster if she wasn't fighting the pain all day long, but Lila still wanted to stop taking the meds soon.

Soon after Shani left for work, Rose arrived. Lila told her about the missing pain meds.

"I haven't seen them," Rose said. "Shani must have misplaced them."

Lila doubted that. "Could you get me a couple ibuprofen?" Hopefully they would be enough to help her tolerate the pain.

Rose complied. When she returned, after Lila swallowed the two pills, Rose asked, "Have you seen Trevor this morning?"

"Jah, he stopped by. And he was in the kitchen by himself."

"You're not insinuating he took the meds, are you?" Rose's face grew red as she spoke.

"I'm just saying he was in the kitchen." Lila raised her gaze to meet Rose's.

Her sister put her hands on her hips. "Maybe the meds are making you paranoid."

Lila doubted that. She wouldn't bother to tell Rose that Trevor had said to tell her hello. Lila asked about how Trudy was that morning.

"A little out of sorts," Rose said. "I told her she could come visit after school."

"And how is Dat?"

"Missing Beth," Rose answered. "He's been really quiet."

"He hasn't been over," Lila said. "Not once. I think he's avoiding me."

"No, not on purpose." Rose sank down into the recliner. "He's just . . . a little lost." Rose looked a little lost herself as she spoke, her eyes taking on a faraway look.

Lila couldn't imagine Dat staying away if Rose or Trudy were injured. He'd provided for her all these years, that was true, and she was very grateful. But there had always been something missing. He had come to see her in the hospital, but now he'd disappeared.

She pulled her mother's quilt up to her chin as best she could, without tugging on the fixator.

"Do you need anything?" Rose asked.

Lila shook her head, but then she said, "Do you think it's normal for me to wonder about my and Daniel's biological father?"

Rose seemed puzzled. Lila didn't blame her. It wasn't as if anyone in the family ever mentioned him, ever even acknowledged such a person existed.

"Never mind," Lila said.

"No." Rose leaned forward. "I don't think it's abnormal. You've just never brought him up before. I was surprised to have you mention him. I didn't think you ever even thought about him."

Lila shook her head. She wouldn't tell Rose how much.

"Have you ever thought about trying to find him?" Rose asked.

Lila shrugged. "Not really." Aenti Eve had told her the name— Butch Wilson. Zane told her she could look online and see if she could figure out who he was with the information she had. She'd never done it though.

"Jah." Rose stood. "It's probably for the best not to try to find him. You have so much going on as it is. And I think it would upset Dat. It would probably upset a lot of people." She pushed herself out of the recliner. "I'll go make some tea." She headed to the kitchen.

Rose was right. It would upset Dat. And most everyone in the district. They'd all see her as ungrateful, as putting her nose in business she had no right to, even though it was her business. Daniel would probably be upset too.

Tears stung Lila's eyes. She pulled the quilt up to her cheeks and let the soft fabric soak up her tears. She wasn't sure how to make up for the emptiness that was growing inside of her.

〜〜〜

Lila was wide-awake when Rose and Trudy came through the door after school. Trudy crawled up on the bed, but without her pain meds the pressure of having Trudy so close was too much for Lila. "You'll have to sit in the chair," she said.

As Trudy told Lila that Beth had asked after her and sent her greetings, Lila shifted in the bed, as much as she could, trying to get comfortable. Then Trudy said that Beth had a visitor at school the day before, an Englisch man wearing a suit.

"Oh?" Lila managed to say.

"They spoke out in the entryway. She didn't tell us what it was about."

"It must have been private," Lila said.

Trudy nodded and prattled on about playing softball at recess. Finally Lila interrupted her little sister and called out to Rose in the kitchen for more ibuprofen, but it did nothing to cut the pain.

"Would you look for the pain meds again?" Lila asked. "They have to be here somewhere."

Rose said she'd searched all the cupboards and drawers.

Gritting her teeth and wondering how in the old days anyone survived, Lila asked, "Would you look again anyway?" In the old days she wouldn't have survived the accident, especially not with her spleen ruptured. Of course, an SUV would not have rear-ended her in the old days either.

Rose didn't answer but retreated to the kitchen. Lila doubted she actually searched again, but a few minutes later she came back in with her hands in the air in a hopeless gesture.

"What time is it?" Lila asked.

"Four fifteen," Rose answered.

It would still be a while before Shani returned. "Would you read to me?" Lila asked Trudy.

"Jah," Trudy said, her eyes lighting up. "I'm reading *Pippi Longstocking* right now. I can start over at the beginning."

"No," Lila said. "Just read from wherever you're at." She needed something to distract her.

Trudy read for the next hour, not stopping until Shani came through the door. For a moment Lila feared she'd forgotten the pain meds, but as she took off her coat she pulled a small bag from her pocket. "How's your pain?" she asked.

"Bad," Lila said.

"So Rose didn't find the bottle?"

"No," Lila answered.

As Shani approached the bed, she told Trudy that Adam was raking leaves. "Do you want to help him?" Shani asked.

"Sure." Trudy put her book on the table and hurried out the door.

Shani opened the bottle, took out a pill, put it in Lila's hand, and then handed her the water bottle. "I'm going to keep these with me. I don't want any more to go missing. And I'll ask everyone who has been in this house if they saw or took the bottle."

Lila nodded her head and then swallowed the pill. She wondered for a moment if she should tell Shani about Trevor being in the kitchen but decided not to. Maybe the meds were making her paranoid. Chances were the bottle had fallen behind the refrigerator or something.

Trudy returned with Adam, but Lila was too sleepy to speak with them. After a while Shani said she was going to go get Adam started on his homework. Lila nodded and went back to sleep. Rose woke Lila up to tell her that she and Trudy were going to help Dat with the milking, but that she'd be back after supper to spend the night. Lila nodded but didn't answer.

The next time she woke up the room was dark and cold. Trevor stood at the end of the bed and Zane was at her side.

"Where is everyone?" Zane asked.

Lila shrugged and went back to sleep. When she awoke again the lamp was on and the fire was roaring. Rose was back. Lila could hear her sister talking with Trevor in the kitchen. Lila wondered where Zane was, but then went back to sleep.

When she awoke again, Zane sat at her side, the lamp was dimmed, and she couldn't hear anyone else.

"Are you hungry?" Zane asked.

Lila shook her head.

"You need to eat," Zane said. "Rose has potato soup and bread."

"All right." Lila raised the backrest some. "I'll try some." She hoped Zane had forgotten that he wanted to talk with her. She wasn't up to it.

As he walked toward the kitchen, Lila heard another voice besides Rose's. Trevor was still in the house. Zane returned with a tray of food. She raised the backrest to a semi-sitting position, and he swung the table around, careful not to bump the hip fixator.

As she ate, Trevor and Rose put on their coats.

"Where are you going?" Lila asked her sister.

"Over to Shani's. To get your pain meds."

As the door closed, Zane said, "I've talked with Trevor twice now. He swears he's not interested in Rose."

"Well, Rose didn't go with Reuben to the singing on Sunday. She won't admit it, but I think she's smitten with Trevor."

Zane nodded. "I understand your concern, but I don't think he'll encourage her," Zane said. "He's just walking with her, so she doesn't have to go by herself."

"She doesn't need an escort. This is Juneberry Lane," Lila said and then took another bite of soup.

Zane nodded. "I'll talk with him again, tomorrow, on the way to work."

"Denki," Lila said.

Zane smiled a little. "I've found a buggy to buy."

"Oh? How is Billie doing?"

"He seems fine. Your Dat even thinks so. I'll buy the buggy tomorrow, and then they'll deliver it. I'll go up and down the lane with Billie to start with, to see how he's doing. We'll take it a step at a time."

Lila nodded. Zane had an easier time becoming Amish than anyone else she could imagine, but it still wasn't easy, not even for him.

Lila couldn't finish all of her soup so Zane gobbled the rest and then took the bowl back to the kitchen. Lila thought Rose and Trevor should have returned by now, but perhaps Shani offered them supper over there.

"I've been thinking," Zane said.

Here came whatever he wanted to talk about—she hoped it wasn't that he wanted to leave the Amish.

He reached for her hand. "That we should go ahead and get married right away."

Lila inhaled sharply. That wasn't what she'd expected.

"That way I could stay here with you at night." His eyes grew more intense with each word. "I could give you your pain meds instead of relying on other people."

Lila shook her head. "What good would that do? You'd be too exhausted to work."

"My mom works after she's stayed with you."

He was right, but it was easier for Shani. She was a nurse and a mom. She was used to taking care of people—Zane wasn't. "I can't plan a wedding now," she said.

"It's all planned," Zane said.

"But I haven't been working. My wages were going to help

153

pay for everything." Of course she still had her savings, but she was counting on that last month of work too.

"We can cut down on the invitation list. In fact, we could just have family attend," Zane said.

She stared at the ceiling.

"Lila?" He stood.

"I can't think about getting married right now." She kept staring upward. "I barely have the energy to concentrate on healing. I can't imagine sitting through a service."

"Gideon would keep it short."

She shook her head. Short was relative. Two hours instead of three, maybe. "Besides," she said, "we still don't know what my internal injuries are and what long-term damage there is." If she couldn't have children someday, she wanted him to know that before he married her. He might not think it mattered now, but it could someday.

And there was the matter of his frustration of the limits of living Plain. Insurance. Suing. Justice. Talking with lawyers. Perhaps it was all too much for him. If he changed his mind, she'd rather he do it before they married than after. "Did you contact the lawyer your father knows?" she asked.

"I left him a message but haven't heard back from him yet. Dad says he's been out of town, working on a case in D.C."

Lila closed her eyes.

"So is that it?" he asked. "End of the marriage discussion?"

"Jah," she answered. "It is." She kept her eyes closed. "Would you go check on Rose? She's been gone too long."

Zane didn't answer. She knew he was frustrated. He headed toward the door.

Rose was the one who needed to be getting married. To Reuben. And the sooner the better.

Zane wasn't being practical. Not at all.

A few minutes after Zane left, the front door opened again. "Hallo?" It was Dat's voice.

Lila opened her eyes and called out, "Come in."

Dat appeared, his hat in his hand. He smiled and then turned his head. Beth stepped to his side as she closed the door.

Lila pointed to the pegs on the wall. "It's warm in here. You can hang up your coats."

"We won't be long," Dat said. He cleared his throat, but Beth spoke.

"How are you feeling?" she asked.

"Better," Lila answered. And she finally was—the medication had dulled her pain. She could concentrate on talking now. And her Dat had finally come to see her.

He pointed to the upraised blanket. "How much longer do you have to have that contraption on?"

"Four more weeks."

"And then you'll start physical therapy?"

Lila nodded. "Why are you two out and about? And where's Trudy?"

Beth glanced at Dat. "She stayed back at the house, doing homework."

Trudy was gaining independence with Lila not around. She was the age Lila had been when their Mamm died. Three years later, Lila started running the household.

"We wanted to talk with you," Dat said. "Before we tell anyone else."

Lila shifted her weight a little, trying to get comfortable. "What's going on?"

"We're going to get married," Dat said.

"What?"

Beth nodded.

"But what about—" Lila paused.

Beth raised her eyebrows. "Mr. Yoder?"

"Jah," Lila said.

Beth glanced at Dat. "He passed away three days ago."

"Oh." Lila wasn't sure how to respond. Saying she was sorry didn't make any sense.

"We want to be clear," Beth said, "that we don't take joy in his passing in any way, even though it opens the door for us to marry. These are two separate issues."

Lila nodded. Yet the two issues were very much connected. "When will you marry?"

Again Beth glanced at Dat.

He clung to his hat a little tighter. "As soon as possible. I spoke with Gideon, and he's speaking with the deacons tonight. We applied for a marriage license today."

"Really? It seems so soon," Lila said. "Aren't you worried about what everyone will say?"

Dat shook his head. "I don't care about appearances."

"You don't?" Lila was dumbfounded. "You used to." She thought about when they were young, after their Mamm died, and how hard he tried to give the impression that the family was doing well.

Dat shrugged. "I suppose I did. But you kids cured me of that." He smiled a little, and she guessed he was thinking about Daniel's Rumschpringe, Simon joining the Army, and her breaking up with Reuben. She didn't smile back.

"What about you?" she asked Beth. "Are you concerned about what people will say?" Lila knew some gossip had been going around already. It would only get worse.

Beth looked misty-eyed, but then she glanced at Dat and her expression turned to one of resolve. "I don't want to wait another day."

Lila tried to shift in the bed a little, partly to get more comfortable, partly to stall. Finally she asked, "Why did you want to tell me first?"

Beth stepped closer to the bed. "Because we should be planning your Hochzeit right now. Not ours."

Lila's eyes filled with tears. "Zane wants to go ahead and get married."

Beth took Lila's hand. "You could."

Lila shook her head. "It's too much right now." She appreciated Zane's optimism—but there were times when he was simply unrealistic. "I'm really happy for the two of you though—honestly. And I know everyone else will be too." Except those intent on gossiping about them, but in time they would come around too.

Dat cleared his throat again. "There's more I need to say."

Lila tried to smile, to encourage him.

"I never intended to care for Beth the way I've come to. I never guessed I'd care enough about someone to marry again. I loved your Mamm, truly, but I wasn't the best husband to her."

Lila shook her head. "You don't need to say this."

Dat sighed. "No, it's true. I didn't feel I deserved another wife, but then as I spent more time with Beth and got to know her more . . ." He shrugged. "Well, Gideon probably should have stopped us from spending time together, but the truth is, I should have. I knew how I felt. I just couldn't do it on my own."

Beth reached for his hand and in a soft—but also teasing—voice said, "Tim, you're making this sound worse than it was."

Dat smiled a little. "I don't mean to." He shook his head. "I shouldn't have let myself have feelings for someone I couldn't marry."

Beth didn't respond.

Lila raised her eyebrows.

"Jah," Beth said. "Well . . ." She shrugged. "Things have worked out."

Feeling uncomfortable, Lila scrambled to change the subject. "Did your ex-husband remarry?" she asked Beth. "Did he have any children?"

"He did remarry, but then divorced, again. And no, he didn't have any children."

"Oh," Lila said, feeling a little foolish for having asked. It really didn't matter.

Beth glanced at Dat. He tugged on his beard and looked around, clearly done with the conversation. "Where's Rose?"

Lila's face grew even warmer. "Over at Shani's. Getting my medicine."

"All right," Dat said. "We'll head that way. We wanted to speak with her too."

Before Dat and Beth got to the front door, Lila heard voices on the front porch. Then laughter. Rose, her face flushed, tumbled through the door, followed by Trevor. Dat cleared his throat.

"Oh, hello," Rose said, her eyes downcast.

Trevor's smile faded. He quickly greeted Dat and Beth and then said he needed to get going. "Good-bye," he said to Rose and then waved toward Lila as he headed out the door.

"We went over to Shani's," Rose said. "To get Lila's medicine."

"Where's Zane?" Lila asked.

Rose shrugged. "We didn't see him."

"He went over to find you."

She shrugged again. "He must have gone behind the barn, then."

Lila was sure her sister was lying.

"You should load up my pillbox and then take the bottle back to Shani."

"Oh, dear," Rose said. "Trevor put the bottle in his pocket." She stepped toward the door. "I'll catch him before he drives away. Be right back."

Dat directed his gaze toward Lila and shook his head.

It was Lila's turn to shrug. "I have no idea what's going on," she said. Being injured was hard enough, but keeping track of Rose was impossible.

Beth and Dat said good-bye again and then headed out the door. Jah, Dat had finally come but to share his big news—not to see how Lila was doing. She was happy for him—she really was—but the emptiness inside her expanded a little bit more. Perhaps he was simply doing the best he could. She wished it felt like enough.

13

As Rose reached Shani and Joel's yard, the taillights of a car disappeared down Juneberry Lane. It had to be Trevor. She couldn't knock on their door and ask to use their phone and reveal Trevor had the pills in his pocket. Shani had been very direct in telling Rose to take good care of the meds, and she'd even asked Trevor if he knew anything about the missing bottle.

Of course he didn't, and Rose had been uncomfortable when Shani asked him. Most likely, Shani had misplaced the bottle and it would turn up soon. Then, to make things even worse, Shani had also directly asked Trevor why he was with Rose. Shani put her hand on her hip and shook a finger at him, saying, "Trevor Anderson, you're staying at Charlie and Eve's. You shouldn't be on Juneberry Lane this late in the evening again." Rose had never seen Shani so cranky.

Trevor just laughed though and said he'd mind his manners better. "I'm not here to stir up trouble," he'd said. "I promise." Rose wasn't sure if Shani believed him or not, but the annoyed look on her face said she probably didn't. Surely Trevor wouldn't take Lila's pain meds.

Jah, Rose couldn't knock on the Becks' door—that was for sure. She had only one choice—run to Dat's office and call Trevor from there. He'd given her his number when Lila was still in the hospital, and Rose had quickly memorized it. As she turned toward the field, the Becks' front door swung open. It was Zane, calling out, "Hello! I'm headed back to see Lila."

That complicated things. She couldn't have him going back over to the little house with Dat and Beth heading toward the lane. He was sure to bump into them, and then when Zane arrived he'd find Rose wasn't there. Once he told Lila he'd seen Rose a few minutes earlier, they'd all wonder where she'd gone.

She started to speak before she thought everything through. "Dat's over with Lila. This is the first time he's been to see her since she got out of the hospital—I think it would be good for them to have some time. . . ."

"Did Lila send you over to tell me that?"

Rose nodded, trying to ignore the guilt welling up inside of her.

"All right." Zane seemed resigned to do what he thought Lila wanted. "How long should I wait?"

Rose shrugged. "Thirty minutes, maybe." She waved and hurried away, dashing in back of the hedge before he could say anything more or before Dat and Beth walked around the barn. Once she reached the field, she stayed close to the poplars.

She'd literally run into Trevor going around the barn on her way over to Shani's earlier. He'd grabbed her by the shoulders to keep her from falling, and then said he needed to speak with her. At first she was reluctant to follow him into the barn again, feeling the shame of being rejected by him after their kiss.

But then he'd said, "I need to talk with you about what happened." She couldn't resist wanting to know what he had to say. What if he didn't regret kissing her after all? She followed him into the barn.

"You're courting Reuben, right?" he'd said. "And I have an ex-girlfriend back home, one I've had on and off since high school. I broke up with her, but I'm, well, I'm still sad about all of that. So we're kind of in the same boat, right?"

Rose had nodded, surprised at her relief that he was no longer with his girlfriend.

"So let's just have some fun," he'd said. "Talk and things like that."

Standing in the Becks' barn, Rose decided she liked that idea. She didn't tell Trevor that. She'd simply said, "We'll see."

But now, as she reached her Dat's barn, she realized what Trevor was proposing was exactly what she'd hoped for in the first place. A little fun until Reuben got over his taking the high road in deciding not to marry her until Lila and Zane could marry each other.

She opened Dat's office door and stepped to the phone on the desk, breathing hard as she dialed Trevor's cell phone. He didn't answer so she left a message, asking him to return the medication immediately. Then she hurried back to the little house.

She stopped for a moment before she reached the porch, breathing deeply. There would be no point rushing inside, panting. That would only make Lila suspicious.

A moment later, she slowly opened the front door and stepped inside. "Sorry it took so long. Shani ran an errand—I waited, thinking she'd be right back." Rose couldn't believe how easy it was to spin one lie after another. "I'll go back over in a few minutes."

Lila gave her a puzzled look. Rose hoped she'd fall asleep, and that Trevor would return before Zane arrived.

Lila did fall asleep, which was a blessing. Zane arrived before Trevor and sat by her side, even though he should have been finishing the bathroom. The door still didn't close properly. He just sat there, staring at Lila.

Finally Rose said, "Aren't you tired?" She was considering dashing back over to the barn and calling Trevor again.

Zane shook his head but then yawned. He put his hand to his mouth. "Maybe a little."

"She's fine," Rose said.

"It sounds as if she had a rough day," Zane said.

"It wasn't too bad." Rose returned to the kitchen to scrub the sink.

Finally Zane left, and just as Rose swung her cape on to dash back to her Dat's barn, there was a light tapping on the door. It had to be Trevor. She opened the door a crack. He stood in front of her with an impish grin on his face. Relieved, she put her finger to her mouth.

Trevor motioned for her to step outside, which she did, closing the door behind her. She held out her hand.

"Sorry about that." He pulled the bottle from his jacket pocket and handed it to her. "I parked by the cedar tree—so the Becks wouldn't know I'm around. Want to go back to the barn?"

Rose hesitated, squeezing the bottle in her fist, wondering how much longer Lila would sleep. "I'll go check on her," she said. "And load her pillbox." She knew going to the barn wasn't a good idea. "Then you can walk me back over to Shani's."

"Sure." His voice had a hint of teasing to it.

Rose filled the pillbox and then led the way to Shani's, telling Trevor to wait when they reached the edge of the lawn. She dashed up the steps and knocked softly on the door. Zane answered. "I'm returning these to your mom," she said.

He held out his hand.

Rose held onto the bottle. "I told your mom I'd give them to her."

Zane gave her an odd look, shook his head, and then said, "She's in the kitchen."

"Denki." Rose hurried past him, noticing he had sweats on instead of his Amish pants. Perhaps he was growing lazy living with his parents. The house was warm. The lights were on.

Shani was starting the dishwasher. "Oh, hi," she said.

Rose handed her the bottle.

"Thanks so much," she said.

"Lila's asleep, but I better get back," Rose said.

"See you in the morning," Shani answered.

Rose waved at Zane, who sat on the sofa with a book in his hand. At least he didn't have the TV on. He waved back and said, "I'll do the milking for you in the morning."

"Denki," she answered as she opened the door. "I appreciate that." She truly did. It was a pain to spend the night with Lila and then trudge across the field before dawn. "Tell your mom she doesn't need to come over early, then."

Trevor wasn't waiting where she'd left him. She heard a horrible imitation of the hoot of an owl coming from the barn, so she started that way and saw a beam of light from the doorway.

"Whew," she said as she approached Trevor. "I was afraid we were going to get caught."

"Caught?"

"Shani told me to keep the pills with me—and you took them." She giggled. "I had to be *creative* with Dat and Lila—and then Zane too. But it all worked out."

"Why is Shani so uptight about the pills?" Trevor asked.

"She's afraid someone took the missing bottle. I don't think it's a biggie. . . . It probably just got misplaced."

Trevor had a sweet smile on his face, as if he'd stopped listening. He nodded toward the bench. "Can you sit, for just a minute?"

She nodded and followed him. As they sat, he reached into

his pocket and took out a small metal container and unscrewed the lid. "Want a drink?" he asked.

"What is it?"

He smiled. "Nothing much. Cheap whiskey."

She shook her head.

"Come on," he said. "Just taste it."

Simon and Daniel used to drink, and Simon probably still did. She never had, not even the one time when one of the boys her age passed her a bottle behind a shed after a singing. It wouldn't hurt to try it—just once.

She reached out her hand. Trevor smiled and passed it to her.

She took a taste, swallowing quickly. It burned going down, and she started to cough. She swallowed again.

"Try it again," Trevor said.

She did. This time she felt the burning deep in her body. She handed the flask back, quickly, a little alarmed by how it made her feel.

Trevor took a drink, left the lid off, and then handed it back to her. She took another drink and then one more. When she returned it, he twisted the lid on and slipped the container back into his pocket. He put his arm around her.

She scooted close. "You didn't take the pills, right?"

"Of course not." He didn't seem offended that she'd asked. "I had to take that stuff for pain, after I got injured. No fun at all. At first it dulls the pain and numbs your mind. It starts as a nice escape, but then I ended up getting anxious when I wasn't on the meds and had this weird feeling of impending doom, which ended up feeling like a panic attack. So that was no fun. It took me a while to get off the stuff." He shook his head. "So, yeah, I wouldn't touch those ever again."

Rose leaned back a little, alarmed. "Do you think Lila's going to have a problem?"

Trevor smiled. "Not with Shani controlling the meds." He laughed.

Rose didn't think it was funny. She nodded to the flask in his pocket. "Do you drink much?"

"Wow," he said. "Innocent Rose is asking all sorts of questions tonight."

She wrinkled her nose. "Sorry."

"No, don't be. It's fine." He patted the flask. "No, I don't drink much. I did. Now I take a few sips in the evening is all. Right? I only took one just now." He smiled again. "You had four." He laughed again.

She shot back, "At your urging."

"I was just teasing you," he said. "I know you're not a drinker."

Rose smiled, just a little. He hadn't gotten defensive at either of her questions. She believed he was telling the truth. She wouldn't drink again, and she'd encourage him not to either.

She appreciated his honesty. She'd found Reuben annoying when her family and the Becks were crowded in the little house, when he seemed judgmental but wouldn't say anything outright. And him not wanting to get married right away felt like a rejection. He'd always been so dependable, but now she wasn't so sure. Reuben seemed to put others before her, over and over. And he beat around the bush instead of being honest, including the last time he stopped by.

Rose and Trevor sat silently for a while. She assumed he was lost in his thoughts too. Then just as she was about to say she needed to get back to Lila, he tilted his head toward her.

She looked up at him, her eyes searching his. He kissed her, first gently but then passionately, pressing his body against hers. She responded, relieved he was kissing her again. She'd wanted it all along, even though she'd tried to convince herself she hadn't.

Trevor's hand fell to the small of her back, pressing her even closer. Maybe he was sad about another girl. Maybe she was courting Reuben. But at that moment she'd didn't care. All she wanted was to kiss Trevor.

⁘

Rose couldn't sleep. All of her being longed for Trevor. Tonight in the barn, for the second time, he was the one who pulled away, but he'd waited much longer this time.

She shifted on the cot. For a moment she thought of Reuben. She cared for him, but how could she possibly be content with him now? Her certainty about marrying him was still above fifty percent, just barely. If only she'd met Trevor a couple of years ago, before she'd joined the church. Everything was much more complicated now.

She should have been willing to listen to Reuben when he'd stopped by. After he'd talked about behaving in a way that benefited the community, he said he had something serious he needed to discuss. But she'd been too distracted by Zane and then by Lila needing her water bottle filled. If only Reuben had gotten to his point sooner. She flopped over to her side on the narrow cot, her thoughts returning to Trevor as an intense loneliness swept over her.

Finally she slept . . . and then awoke to Lila calling for her. The room was pitch-dark. Rose, thinking she was home in the bedroom she shared with Lila and Trudy, stirred. Lila's voice was faraway and soft. Was it time to do the milking?

Rose sat up.

"I need my pain medication," Lila said.

"Oh," Rose said, as it came back to her. Lila's injury. The little house.

Trevor.

What would Dat think of her? Worse, what would Reuben think? A month ago, she would have judged any girl who acted the way she had. But a month ago, she didn't know Trevor.

She wiggled into the sleeves of her robe, tied it, and shuffled over to Lila. She squinted at the clock. Four thirty. Dat would be up, ready to go milk. At least Zane was helping him today.

Rose opened the box and handed the pill to Lila. Her sister swallowed it and then said, "Denki. For everything. I know this is a really big inconvenience."

"No, it's fine," Rose said.

"You sleep on a cot. You don't have any time with Reuben. You have to give me meds. I wouldn't say that's fine."

Rose shook her head. "You're my sister. Of course it's fine." Rose headed back to her cot. She hoped to get another hour of rest, but she couldn't fall back to sleep. Her thoughts turned to the night before.

Rose regretted all of her tiny lies. A month ago she never would have guessed she could be so deceitful. Sure, she'd told a white lie now and then growing up, but this was getting out of hand.

She flung her covers off, stoked the fire, and then made coffee. From there she headed into the bathroom and turned on the battery-powered lamp. She looked into the mirror at the dark circles under her eyes. She'd get more sleep tonight, at home.

She pulled her braid over the front of her shoulder, undid the fastener, and loosened it. Her hair fell halfway down her back. She ventured back out to the kitchen, poured herself a cup of coffee, and then returned to the bathroom to fix her bun. All she could think about was Trevor.

At six thirty Zane stopped by straight from milking, bringing in a rush of cold air with him. "How is she?" he asked.

"Sleeping," Rose answered. Zane stepped to Lila's side and whispered, "*Guder Mariye.*"

She opened her eyes and smiled a little but then tilted her face away from Zane.

Rose watched, half hoping Trevor would stop by, regardless of her earlier resolve.

"I need to get going," Zane said to Lila. Then to Rose he said, "Mom will be over soon."

"*Gut*," Rose answered.

Shani came over a few minutes later and Rose headed home through the field. The sun rose over the poplar trees, revealing a cold, cloudless sky. On the far side of the field, crimson leaves crowned the maple trees. The breeze picked up a little, sending a shower of leaves to the ground.

When she reached the house, Trudy was making coffee.

She immediately hugged Rose around the waist. "We're going to have Beth as our Mamm after all," Trudy squealed. "Isn't it great news?"

"What?" Rose asked, stepping backward. "Remember what I told you? Dat and Beth can't marry."

Trudy shook her head, sending her Kapp ties bobbing along her neck. "No, they can. Beth's husband died."

Rose's hand flew to her neck. "Ex-husband. And are you certain?"

This time Trudy nodded vehemently. "Jah, they told me last night. After they got back from telling Lila." Rose had assumed Dat felt it was about time he made the trip across the field to visit Lila, not to tell her life-changing news. Why hadn't they told her at the same time? She sighed. Perhaps her giggling on the front porch had made Dat decide to wait. She hugged her little sister back, wishing she could match Trudy's enthusiasm. Now she and Reuben would have to wait even longer to marry. Her face grew warm at the hypocrisy of kissing Trevor—and then lamenting the delay in marrying Reuben. She was shameless.

A half hour later, Dat whistled as he came in for breakfast.

"I hear congratulations are in order," Rose said.

"Jah." He glanced at Trudy. "So you heard the news."

Rose nodded and Trudy squirmed a little in her chair.

"It's all right," Dat said. "I'm happy to have it shared."

"What does Bishop Byler have to say about all of this?" Rose asked as she dished up the eggs.

"He spoke with the deacons last night and then left a message. None of them have a problem with it."

"Oh," Rose said. "What about the rest of the congregation? Didn't someone talk with Gideon about how much time you and Beth were spending together, before Lila's accident?"

"Jah," Dat said. "Someone did. It was me."

"You?"

He nodded. "A couple of times, in fact. I realized I'd come to care for Beth too much. My feelings concerned me, and I needed someone to hold me accountable. I was honest with Beth that I'd spoken with Gideon, but everyone assumed someone else had brought it up."

Rose's face grew warm. "Oh," she managed to say, surprised Dat had tattled on himself. Here she thought it had been Reuben. Then again, Dat had always been forthright and honest. A wave of conviction swept through her. Maybe she should talk with someone about Trevor.

No. That would be ridiculous. If she did, what she'd done would get back to Reuben in no time. Dat didn't have anything to lose by asking someone to hold him accountable, but she did.

Dat ate his eggs and ham quickly and then thanked Rose for preparing breakfast. It probably wouldn't have mattered if she'd served him dry toast, not today. He retrieved his Bible from the side table, read the Scripture for the day out loud, and whistled his way back outside.

Dat was as happy as she'd ever seen him. He was still whistling, this time from the chicken coop, as she hitched the horse to the buggy to take Trudy to school. By the time she returned from school, the day was warming. She started on the laundry and then, while it dried on the line, prepared a dinner of meat-loaf and baked potatoes for Dat, along with an apple crisp for dessert. When he came in at noon from harvesting the corn in the far field, he asked when she planned to see Reuben next.

"I'm not sure." She dreaded their next encounter.

"He seems quiet lately," Dat responded. "Is everything all right?"

"Jah." She quickly changed the subject, asking if he and Beth had come up with a guest list for the wedding.

"Just family," he answered. "And Gideon and Monika. And the Becks."

"Do you have a list of what needs to be done?"

Dat shook his head and then smiled. "But Beth does."

What a relief it would be for Dat to have someone to partner with in life. Guilt washed over her. There was no doubt Reuben would be a good husband, much better than Trevor. How could she have been so foolish? She wouldn't see Trevor anymore—she had no future with him.

After she'd cleaned up from dinner and did the dishes, she ran a load of sheets through the wash and hung them on the line before going to pick up Trudy. Once she reached the school, she parked and went inside to say hello to Beth. She was radiant.

As Trudy told her teacher good-bye, Beth leaned down and gave her a hug. There was both a peace and an excitement in Beth that Rose hadn't seen before. She would be a mother—something she'd surely longed for her entire life. Rose thought of Reuben again, and then of Trevor. It was also obvious who would make the better father. She must, when it came to Trevor, follow her head and not her heart. Thankfully, as long as Trevor didn't tell anyone, Reuben would never know that she'd kissed the Englischer—twice. She wouldn't do it again.

The next time Reuben came by, she'd take the time to listen to him. She'd had her fun.

171

When they returned home, Rose pulled the laundry off the line, folded it and put it away, and then changed into her milking dress to help Dat. Trudy asked to go see Lila, but Rose said she needed to stay home. "Do your homework," she said. "Then put the pot of soup on the stove."

Weariness was catching up with Rose.

As she headed to the barn, the sound of a horse and buggy stopped her. She turned. It was Reuben. He waved and smiled slightly, as much as he ever did.

She waved back.

As he approached he called out, "I'll help with the milking."

She could have hugged him. "Denki," she answered. Relieved, she headed back to the house and changed into her regular clothes. She'd rest for a half hour and then make biscuits and potato cakes to go with the soup.

After settling into Dat's chair, the next thing she knew Trudy was shaking her arm. "The soup is hot," her little sister said.

Rose rubbed her eyes. "What time is it?"

"Five forty-five."

"Oh, no." Rose struggled to her feet. "Is Dat done with the milking?"

"He's just finishing up."

"What about Reuben?"

"He went on home."

Rose headed to the kitchen, calling over her shoulder, "Why didn't you wake me?"

"Reuben didn't want me to," Trudy said. "He said he needed to talk with you but he'd do it the next time he saw you."

Rose wished he hadn't left. What if he could sense what she'd done? Or worse yet, what if some sort of gossip had already started?

She turned on the heat to the oven and then quickly mixed the flour, baking powder, and salt, and cut in the butter and added the milk to the dough. Instead of rolling it, she dropped spoonfuls onto a cookie sheet. As she pulled the handful of left-over baked potatoes from lunch out of the refrigerator, Trudy announced that someone was coming up the driveway.

Standing at the window, her little sister turned toward Rose. "It's Trevor."

"Oh, dear." Rose hoped Dat was still busy in the barn. At least Reuben had gone home. She hurried out the back door as Trevor climbed out of the car.

He grinned as he saw her. "Where's the fire?" he asked.

"Right here if my Dat sees you." She tried to keep her voice playful even though she was serious.

He stepped closer, and she stepped back.

He cocked his head, a sad expression on his face. "You're not happy to see me?"

"That's not it," Rose said. "I'm cooking supper. Dat will be coming in from the barn any minute."

He grinned again. "So bad timing on my part?"

She nodded.

"I can come back. . . . I really hoped we could talk." He smiled down at her. "We need to talk."

She didn't answer.

"Say, around nine? Could you meet me in the Becks' barn?"

She shook her head and said softly, "How about our barn? But don't park here."

He nodded. "See you then." He stepped closer and put his hand on her shoulder, making her whole body tingle. He whispered, "I want to kiss you, right now."

"You can't," she whispered back, ducking away from his hand. "Go."

He pouted a little, but in a teasing way, as he retreated to his car while her heart raced. She couldn't help but compare Reuben's lack of pursuit of her today to Trevor's.

After supper, Dat said he was going to Gideon's for a short while. He told Trudy to get to bed on time and told Rose he should be home by nine.

She yawned. "I'll be in bed by then. I got up extra early with Lila today." Rose cringed inside. She'd tell Trevor tonight that she couldn't see him anymore—that she wouldn't. The thought made her sad, but it was her only choice. She couldn't have any sort of relationship with Trevor Anderson.

Trudy was in bed by eight thirty. Rose kissed her little sister on the forehead and said, "I'll be in soon."

She peeked in on Trudy at 8:50. Thankfully she was asleep. Now to get out to the barn before Dat arrived home. She grabbed the flashlight from the back porch, swung her cape over her shoulders, and hurried out the door. She wouldn't even hug Trevor. And she certainly wouldn't kiss him. She'd tell him she couldn't see him again. Sure, he might be hurt, but not any more than she would be. The alternative would be far worse.

As she approached the barn she heard the hoot of an owl again—another bad impression. She had the flashlight in her hand and swung it in a sweeping motion as she opened the door and stepped inside. Another hoot, this one from the hay stacked along the far wall. Dat wouldn't see them there or hear them when he led his horse into its stall on the other side of the barn—not that she'd stay that long.

A beam of light appeared and Trevor called out, "Rose! I'm over here."

The now-familiar longing shot through her. One kiss wouldn't hurt. A good-bye kiss. The last one ever. She hurried toward him, her resolve one hundred percent abandoned.

14

Three weeks later, Reuben stood outside the Lehmans' barn with Tim and Daniel. "We need help with the benches is all," Tim said. "It's going to be a small gathering."

Daniel nodded. "Hopefully I'll be here. Jenny's been having contractions."

"Aren't first babies usually late?" Dat asked.

Daniel shrugged. "I don't think that's anything to count on."

"I'll be here for sure," Reuben said. The wedding was the next day, Thursday, and he'd planned to close down the lumberyard altogether. It wouldn't hurt to lose a day of business. Tim was his friend, and he wanted to support him, but he hoped to have a chance to finally spend time with Rose too and talk with her about setting a wedding date. It seemed it might be quite a while until Lila and Zane married, and although Tim had been busy getting ready for his own wedding, Reuben had never seen Tim happier and more congenial. He was grateful for how things worked out and thankful he hadn't been the one to have to say something to his Dat about Tim and Beth's relationship.

Rose had been distant and withdrawn the last several weeks. He'd been anxious about it and had even gone so far as to ask Zane if she was interested in his friend Trevor. Zane had said that Trevor wasn't spending any time on Juneberry Lane anymore, so he didn't think so. He added that he'd been concerned for a short time about Trevor, but the Englischer had promised Zane he wasn't interested in Rose and wouldn't pursue even a friendship with her.

Reuben didn't ask Zane if Rose had been interested in Trevor. Clearly, if she had been, the man hadn't returned her feelings. Reuben could live with that—as long as she was over it. She was young. It was understandable that she might be interested in a handsome Englischer with a red sports car and war stories. Hopefully no harm was done, but it would be good to speak with Rose and know for sure what her thoughts were on the matter. If only he'd had a chance to speak with her about marriage all those weeks ago.

"I need to get going," Daniel said. "See you in the morning."

"See you then." Reuben couldn't help but wonder if Jenny resented Tim and Beth scheduling their wedding at the time her Bobbli was due. Tim probably hadn't thought about it, and Beth must have decided it was worth the risk.

Reuben asked Tim if there was anything else he needed help with.

"Jah, do you have an idea of how we can get Lila into the house? The stairs are too steep for a ramp. We could carry her up in her wheelchair, but it leans back at a funny angle."

Reuben rubbed his chin. "We could make a chair with our hands and carry her up. Does she still have that contraption on?"

"Jah," Tim answered. "She gets it off Monday. Then she can walk up the steps. Carrying her like that might work. I should have thought about that before." He tugged at his beard.

Reuben followed Tim back around toward the back door. "Come on in for some supper," Tim said. "I don't know what Rose fixed—but she has something for us to eat."

The curtain over the dining room fluttered a little. Either Trudy or Rose was peeking.

Reuben hesitated, not sure if he should go on in. Tim assumed he would though and led the way. Rose wasn't in the kitchen, but the table was set. Reuben headed to the bathroom and washed his hands. When he came back, Trudy was putting a basket of bread on the table. The table was set for four people, but Rose still wasn't around.

Reuben took the place at the end of the table, where he usually sat when he visited.

Tim joined them a minute later, his sleeves still rolled to his elbows after washing. "Where's your sister?" he asked Trudy as he sat down.

"She's not feeling well."

Tim frowned but then bowed his head. After the prayer, Trudy retrieved a pot from the stove and put it in the middle of the table. It smelled good. She took the lid off to reveal a pot roast and vegetables.

"Hmmm," Reuben said. "Did you fix that?"

Trudy shook her head. "It's leftover from dinner. Right, Dat?"

Tim nodded. "I thought Rose had something else up her sleeve for our supper, but I guess not. She's probably been busy making preparations for tomorrow."

Reuben hoped so, but he didn't see any sign of it except for a large pan of rolls on the counter. Perhaps she had some pies cooling in a cupboard. If so, the scent of baking had dissipated. Thankfully the gathering would be small. "Will Simon be able to come home?"

"No," Tim said. "He shipped out to Iraq last week."

Trudy appeared downcast.

Tim patted her shoulder. "He'll be back by summer." He turned toward Reuben. "Hopefully it will just be a six-month deployment."

Reuben wondered how all of it worked. Did Simon leave messages on Tim's message machine in the barn? *Hello, Dat, I'm shipping out to Iraq. See you when I get back.* Reuben couldn't fathom all that Tim went through as an Amish father. Reuben hoped he'd never have to suffer the same someday.

Trudy began talking about what she did at school that day. Reuben half listened as he thought about Rose. She never did come out of her room. After he finished eating he left, saying he'd be back in the morning to help with the chores.

The next morning, as the sun rose, Reuben approached the house with Daniel after helping with the milking just as Beth arrived. Reuben hurried to her buggy, taking the reins from her. "I'll take care of the horse," he said.

"Denki." She climbed down. "I need help carrying everything in first."

Daniel went around the back and grabbed a box. Reuben followed and grabbed a second one. He smelled chicken. Beth must have gotten up in the middle of the night to fix them.

"Just put the boxes on the table," she said. "I'll take care of everything."

Daniel led the way, followed by Reuben and Beth. When they entered, Rose stood at the stove stirring hot cereal. Without looking up, she said, "We're having a simple breakfast. I still need to peel the potatoes."

She wore a work dress, and a scarf instead of her Kapp, and she looked as if she'd hardly slept. Reuben slid the box on the table and went back out to the buggy, leading the horse toward

178

the barn. Maybe Rose really was ill. Maybe that was why she seemed so out of sorts.

He hoped she'd feel better later and he'd have a chance to speak with her.

Shani's van arrived as Reuben returned to the house with another box. Shani stepped down, a bag in her hand, and Zane jumped out of the passenger seat and stepped to the back and pulled out a wheelchair. It did tilt backward, just like Tim had said. Zane rolled it around to the side of the van and opened the sliding door.

"May I help?" Reuben asked.

"Ach, I think we're good," Zane answered, reaching into the van. He transferred Lila to the chair. Her cape was pushed up over the apparatus around her middle, and she seemed to be wearing some sort of skirt and top. She wore a black bonnet over her Kapp.

"I'll walk with you to the front," Reuben said. "And then I can help you carry her up."

"Denki," Zane said.

As they walked along, Reuben asked Lila how she was doing.

"All right," she said. "And I'll be doing even better once I get this fixator off." She glanced up at Zane. "Then I can start rehab."

Charlie and Eve's car came down the driveway as Reuben and Zane lifted Lila out of the chair and carried her in the sling of their joined hands up to the porch and into the house. They placed her in Tim's chair in the living room, and then Zane hurried back out for her wheelchair.

Reuben stood in the archway to the kitchen as Charlie, Eve, and their foster baby came through the back door. Beth had taken charge, and Rose had disappeared. By the time Reuben finished breakfast, his Dat and Monika had arrived too, along with Jenny. She immediately sat down in a chair at the table. She was as big as any pregnant woman he'd ever seen. Of course he didn't say that.

"Let's clear the living room and then set up the benches," Daniel said to Reuben. Charlie volunteered to help. They left the women peeling potatoes, while Trudy held Eve's foster baby. Rose hadn't returned. Reuben guessed she was getting dressed, but she seemed to be taking her own sweet time—that was for sure.

Zane had transferred Lila back into her wheelchair, and Reuben overheard her ask Trudy to go tell Rose they needed her help. The truth was they didn't, but Trudy obeyed her oldest sister. She returned a few minutes later and said, "She'll be right out."

Rose finally appeared right before the nine o'clock service started. She'd changed into a good dress and wore her Kapp and apron. It seemed to Reuben that she avoided looking at him. Zane parked Lila's chair on the women's side and then joined the men's side. Reuben settled down next to Charlie. Tim and Beth came down the middle of the living room and sat on the two folding chairs in the front, facing each other, smiling as they did.

After leading the small group in a song, Reuben's Dat read the Scripture from Colossians about putting on charity and letting God rule in your hearts, and then about wives submitting to their husbands and husbands loving their wives.

Next he preached a sermon, one Reuben had never heard before, about God's love for the church and how the Lord called for the same sort of love in families—both unconditional and sacrificial. Reuben thought of his parents and how gentle his father had been even when his mother was harsh and judgmental. He was certain he took after his mother more than his father and for a moment feared he wouldn't love Rose the way he should. But he put that thought aside as his Dat continued

on, quoting Ecclesiastes 4:9, 11-12: "'Two are better than one
. . . if two lie together, they have heat: but how can one be warm
alone? And if one prevail against him, two shall withstand him;
and a threefold cord is not quickly broken.'"

Reuben glanced over at the women's side. Rose had her head
down as if praying. Reuben couldn't help but hope she was
praying about their relationship.

After the sermon, Gideon instructed Tim and Beth to stand.
Then he asked them if they would remain together until death.

Both answered, "Jah."

"And will you care for each other during sickness, weakness,
adversity, and affliction?" he asked.

Again they answered, in unison. "Jah."

He took their hands in his and said, "Go forth in the Lord's
name. I now pronounce you man and wife." Tim beamed down
at Beth, pure joy on his face. She returned the expression.

That was what Reuben wanted with Rose. That moment.
That commitment. He had to speak with her.

After the service, the women retreated to the kitchen while
the men turned the benches into tables for the meal. It was by
far the smallest wedding Reuben had ever been to—there were
fewer than twenty people.

When the tables were set up, Reuben peeked into the kitchen.
Rose stood with her back to the refrigerator, her arms crossed.
Beth was clearly in charge, arranging the food on the table. Lila
sat in her wheelchair, tilted back, watching Rose, while Trudy
did her best to help Beth.

Reuben stepped back into the living room. Charlie held their
foster boy, Jackson, and Zane and Joel both stood beside him,
trying to make the little one laugh. Reuben appreciated Eve and
Charlie caring for an orphan, but he was surprised they wanted
to adopt the boy. Reuben wasn't sure he'd be able to accept a
child he had no biological connection to.

From the joy on Charlie's face though, it looked as if he wouldn't have a problem claiming the child as his own.

By the time dinner was over, Jenny seemed to be uncomfortable and retreated to the kitchen. Daniel asked Shani if she'd check on her.

"I'm not a maternity nurse," Shani said.

"I know," Daniel said. "But maybe you can give us an idea of whether we need to head to the hospital."

"Probably not yet," Shani said.

Reuben moved to the archway between the two rooms. Jenny leaned against the counter while her mother rubbed her back.

"Are you having contractions?" Shani asked.

"Maybe," Jenny answered, standing up straight.

"Are you using a midwife or a doctor?"

"Doctor. My blood pressure has been high."

"How long have you been having pains?"

"On and off since I got up this morning."

"Let's time them." Shani lifted her wrist. "Tell me when the pain starts."

A minute later, Jenny leaned against the counter again and said, "Now."

Shani kept her eyes on her watch. "Tell me when it ends."

Jenny nodded as her face contorted. She turned toward the counter, and Monika dried her hands on another towel and then put her hand on Jenny's back. Finally, Jenny said, "It stopped."

"Ninety seconds. That's nice and strong. Let's see how far apart they are." Shani glanced at her watch again and then back up at Jenny. "Tell me when it starts again."

Jenny started to smile but stopped. She definitely appeared uncomfortable.

Rose moved through the archway and bumped against Reuben, her unfinished plate of food in her hand. "Excuse me," she said quickly. As she raised her head she asked, "What's going on?"

"Shani's seeing if Jenny is in labor."

Rose sighed. "That's all we need today."

Reuben ignored her comment and asked, "Are you feeling better?"

"No," Rose said, squeezing past him and into the kitchen. She scraped her plate into the scrap pail, completely ignoring both Jenny and Monika.

Jenny held up her hand. "It's starting again."

"Three minutes," Shani said, searching for Daniel. He stood by the back door. "We need to get her to the hospital. Want me to drive?"

"Jah," he said, stepping to Jenny's side.

She was breathing heavily.

"Come on, Grandma," Shani said to Monika. "Let's get these kids to Lancaster General."

"I expect Gideon, Tim, and Beth want to go too." Shani pulled her keys from the pocket of her sweater. "I have room."

"We'll stay and clean up," Eve said. "Unless Rose and Trudy want to go. Then Charlie can drive them."

Trudy clapped her hands together, but Rose appeared even more pale than she had before and shook her head.

Eve turned to Shani. "Call Charlie's cell phone once there's news. If it's not too late, we can bring Trudy up then."

Shani agreed.

"Can we stop by our place and grab my bag?" Jenny asked. "It's already packed."

"Of course," Shani said. "But only because it's on the way."

As Shani and her crew hurried out the door, Reuben and Zane, with Adam's help, folded up the benches and carried them out to the church wagon. Trudy played with the baby while Eve washed the dishes, Joel and Charlie dried, and Rose put everything away.

When everything was cleaned up, Lila said she was weary. Joel volunteered to take her back in his pickup, but it was decided she'd be able to more easily get into Eve and Charlie's sedan.

"We'll stop back by on our way home and see if you and Trudy want to go to the hospital," Eve said.

"It could be hours before the baby is born," Rose replied. "There's no reason to go this soon."

Reuben helped Zane carry Lila down the steps, and soon everyone but Trudy, Rose, and Reuben had left. "I should get going," Reuben said.

"Jah," Rose answered. "I need to rest."

"Would you walk with me out to my buggy?" Reuben asked.

Rose shook her head. "I'd rather not, to be honest. I'm really not feeling well."

"Could we talk in the living room?"

She shrugged. "For a few minutes."

"May I go over to Lila's?" Trudy asked.

"No," Rose answered. "But you can go check the answering machine and see if Dat has left a message."

Trudy pouted. "He wouldn't have yet. They wouldn't have been at the hospital for long."

"Go check," Rose said.

Trudy complied, although reluctantly.

"Sorry you couldn't be at the hospital with everyone," Reuben said once they were alone, sitting on opposite ends of the sofa.

"No, it's fine." Rose crossed her arms over her chest. "I really didn't want to go."

She seemed so testy and—even a little rude. What had happened to his fun-loving Rose?

"What did you want to talk about?" she asked.

"Us," he answered.

She stood. "I don't feel well enough to think about that."

"Rose . . ."

She walked away.

"Rose!" he said again, following her through the kitchen to the hall. She hurried into her bedroom and slammed the door. Reuben froze, not sure what to do, but when he heard sobs coming from the room he knocked on the door.

The sobbing stopped.

"Rose?"

"I'm sorry," she said. "I'm really not well. Let's talk later."

"All right," he said.

"And could you walk Trudy over to Lila? Ask Eve and Charlie if they can take her up to the hospital. She'll be better off with Beth than me."

"All right," Reuben said again. He paused, not sure what to say next. Finally he said, "I'll see you soon."

When she didn't answer, he left the house and started toward the barn.

Trudy came skipping toward him. "No message," she called out.

"Rose wants me to walk you over to Lila's so Eve and Charlie can give you a ride to the hospital."

Trudy clapped her hands together.

"You should probably get a book to read though, in case it takes a while. And your cape." There was a chill in the air that indicated the weather was changing. A cold snap was predicted, the first so far.

He waited outside. Trudy didn't take long, holding a book in one hand and her cape in the other when she returned.

"How was Rose doing?" Reuben asked.

"She was asleep," Trudy answered.

"Oh."

They walked down the lane just in case Eve and Charlie

would be driving back up, but they didn't meet anyone. The bare branches of the maple trees creaked in the wind above their heads. Reuben always hated this time of year, when the world seemed bleak, between the glorious changing of the leaves and the first snow.

Charlie and Eve's car was parked by the Becks' house. They stopped there first and knocked on the door, but no one answered.

"Follow me," Trudy said, leading Reuben around the side of the barn and back to the little house.

As they approached the front door, laughter practically rocked the house. Reuben was ready to knock, but Trudy went ahead and opened the door and stepped in. "Hi, everyone!" she called out.

"Trudy!" Adam yelled, rushing toward her.

Joel held the foster baby while Eve made coffee in the kitchen. Lila was back in her bed, leaning against the backrest, a smile on her face. Charlie and Zane stood face-to-face, as if they were in some sort of contest. But both now had their eyes on Reuben.

He waved and said, "Rose was hoping Eve and Charlie could take Trudy up to the hospital. Rose isn't feeling well—she thought Trudy should be with Beth."

Lila frowned.

Eve stepped from the kitchen. "Of course. We'd be happy to." She glanced at Charlie. He nodded.

"Denki," Reuben said. "See all of you later." He waved, a little awkwardly, patted Trudy on the head, and retreated.

As he closed the door, he could hear Charlie say, "Where were we?"

"You claimed you could flip me," Zane answered. "But that sounds a little violent and may go against my faith."

"Ach, I don't believe that's true," Charlie answered, laughing.

Reuben stepped away from the house, disturbed by how much

of an outsider he'd felt. He took his hat off and ran his hand through his hair. As he headed up the field, he was tempted to go try to get Rose to talk again, but he knew it would be useless.

He was happy for Tim and Beth, for their marriage. And for Daniel and Jenny, for their baby. But he couldn't help but feel out of sorts. His life wasn't going as he'd planned, not at all.

15

At 6:00 a.m., on the next Monday, Lila struggled to relax on the day-surgery gurney, breathing in the crisp odor of disinfectant. She felt sick to her stomach—hopefully she wasn't coming down with Rose's flu—and the smells were making it worse.

Zane couldn't take the time off work. And Dat didn't. He would have had to find someone to do the milking, such as Reuben or Joel, but Lila knew he could have if he'd wanted to.

Instead, Shani, along with the doctor, stood by her side.

"It will take more time for the anesthesiologist to do her work than for the surgeon to remove the fixator," Shani said.

"Or I could take it out without any anesthesia," the doctor said. "I did that one time. You could hear the guy screaming in the next county."

Lila politely declined, too out of sorts to try to joke.

"I'll see you in recovery." Shani patted her arm and then stepped away.

"And I'll see you in surgery," the doctor said, heading down the hall.

Everyone said her recovery from the surgery would go quickly. Lila hoped that it would, and that they could go up and see Jenny and her Bobbli afterward. Jenny had ended up with a hard labor and then a C-section, so they were still in the hospital.

Beth said the Bobbli was beautiful, that Daniel was as proud as could be, and that Jenny seemed to be recovering well. Trudy had seen the Bobbli a couple of times too, and wouldn't stop talking about her.

As the two nurses pushed Lila down the hall, she waved at Shani. She was only awake for a couple of minutes in the operating room. The next thing she knew she was in recovery with Shani at her side.

Lila reached down to her hips. The fixator was gone. She exhaled in relief.

"How do you feel?" Shani asked.

"Pretty good," Lila answered, sitting up straight for the first time in eight weeks. "May we go see Jenny and the Bobbli?"

Shani smiled. "Let's see how you're feeling in a half hour or so."

Lila drank some juice and ate a few salty crackers, and kept both down. After a while, Shani helped her get dressed and then the nurse came in with the discharge papers.

"What do you think?" Shani asked.

"I'd really like to see Jenny—and my niece," Lila answered.

"Let's go get some breakfast first," Shani said. "And see if you still feel strong enough after that." She adjusted the back to the wheelchair and moved it into place. It was the last time Lila would use the chair.

Rose had promised to pack Lila's things while they were at the hospital, and then help Shani load them into her van. Lila would spend the night at home for the first time since the accident. She'd sleep better in her own room with Rose and Trudy.

Once she moved out of the little house, Zane would move in. Gideon said he'd been living with electricity long enough and it was time for him to start living Plain again.

Lila did her best to eat a bowl of oatmeal in the hospital cafeteria but mostly she nursed a cup of coffee. Shani seemed satisfied with her effort and wheeled her toward the elevator. In no time they were on the maternity ward.

"Jenny's down this way," Shani said. Monika was in the room, and Lila guessed she'd spent the night. That didn't surprise her, not one bit. Every girl longed to have a mother like Monika. Tears filled Lila's eyes but she blinked them away. She had Shani—look at everything the woman had done for her the last eight weeks. And now she had Beth too.

"Look at you," Monika said. "You finally got that contraption off."

Lila nodded.

"She's straight out of surgery," Shani said, "but insisted on coming up here."

"I have to see my niece," Lila said. As Shani pushed her closer to the bed, she could see the little one tucked into the crook of Jenny's arm. They'd named her Brook—which wasn't a common name for an Amish baby, but many of the younger parents were choosing uncommon names.

"Ah, she's beautiful," Lila said, overcome with emotion for the little one.

Jenny smiled. "Daniel named her. Would you like to hold her?"

"Of course." Lila held out her arms. Monika stepped closer, scooped the Bobbli up, and then handed her to Lila, who held her high, breathing in her sweet smell. Brook's fine blond hair was fuzzy on top. The Bobbli shifted a little, frowned, and then relaxed against Lila.

"Oh, she's wonderful." Lila had expected to feel jealous, but she didn't. Not at all. Maybe that would come later.

Her sister-in-law beamed.

Monika put her hand on Lila's shoulder. "You're recovering so well. You and Zane will soon marry, and you'll have one of your own in no time."

Lila tried to take a deep breath, but it turned raggedy, and then a sob escaped.

"What's the matter?" Monika asked, her hand falling from Lila's shoulder.

"Oh, nothing. I'm just emotional." It wasn't jealousy. It all just hurt so badly. She and Zane should have been adjusting to married life by now. Maybe she would have already been pregnant. The accident had taken so much from her.

"You've been through a lot," Monika said.

Jenny nodded.

"I should probably go home. I may have pushed too hard today."

Lila held onto Brook a moment longer though, taking in her sweet face. She reminded her of Trudy as a Bobbli. Their mother had still been alive, barely. She was terribly ill—dying, in fact. This Bobbli carried Lila and Daniel's DNA, both their mother's and their biological father's, whoever he was.

Lila looked from the Bobbli's face to Shani's, and then relinquished the little girl. Shani held her for a long moment and then handed her back to Jenny.

"I'm so happy for you," Lila said to her sister-in-law. "Really."

"I know," Jenny answered. "I'll tell Daniel you stopped by. Come see us in a few days, once you're feeling better."

"I will," Lila answered, embarrassed for her tears. She hoped Monika and Jenny would keep her behavior to themselves. No one would understand why she reacted the way she did. She barely understood herself.

In the car on the way home, she couldn't stop her tears. They matched the icy, pouring rain.

Shani reached over and patted her arm. "Want to talk about it?"

"No," Lila managed to say.

"Anything in particular or everything?"

Lila tried to smile at Shani, but another sob escaped. "Both," she stammered.

"What is it?" Shani glanced toward her, a sympathetic look on her face. "Does it have to do with the uncertainty around your internal injuries? As far as getting pregnant and carrying a baby someday?" Shani never was one to beat around the bush.

"Probably," Lila answered.

"When do you go to the gynecologist?"

"Friday."

"Try not to worry until then. They'll do an ultrasound to see how much scar tissue there is. They'll soon have an idea." Shani hesitated. "There's no way to know for sure though."

Lila nodded. Eve hadn't had any injuries, and she still couldn't have children.

"But even if you can't have a baby, you know there are other ways to have a family, right? Look at Eve and Charlie."

Lila nodded but didn't answer. Lila expected it would be hard for an Amish young couple to qualify to foster. And Eve and Charlie were older. Eve was a teacher and Charlie an EMT. They were perfectly qualified to care for children.

If they hadn't been able to foster Jackson, Eve still had her teaching. What would Lila have?

She didn't say any of that to Shani though. Nor did she bring up how she feared Zane might react to not being a father someday. He'd talked about having children more than anyone she knew, more than she did. Goodness, he already had the baby's room furnished. He longed to re-create their childhood on Juneberry Lane for their own children. How would he react if the doctor said she'd never be able to have a Bobbli?

Lila put her head back and pretended to doze the rest of the way home. She couldn't explain how badly she wanted a child of her own. Her Mamm was gone. She didn't know her biological father. Daniel was the person most connected to her, as far as DNA. It wasn't that she didn't feel connected to her other three siblings. She did. But she longed to hold a baby that she'd carried, that she and Zane made together.

When they reached Juneberry Lane, Shani said, "I have your crutches in the back. I'll help you up the stairs."

"We should go to the front door." It wasn't as steep as the back.

Shani agreed and pulled the van around. With Shani's help Lila made it into the house, collapsing in Dat's chair. "Rose must still be over at the little house," Shani said. "Do you need anything before I head over?"

Lila shook her head. "Tell Rose to hurry. It's almost time for Dat's dinner."

As Shani headed for the door, footsteps fell in the kitchen.

"Rose?" Lila called out.

"Oh, hello." She stepped into the living room.

"Oh, good." Lila craned her neck to look at her sister. "You finished packing everything already?"

Rose blushed. "No, I was just going to go do it now." She appeared disheveled, as if she'd been resting.

"But it's time to get dinner for Dat."

Rose shook her head. "He ended up going to the lumberyard today." She started back for the kitchen. "I'll just grab my cape and go with Shani right now. It won't take me any time."

Lila bit her tongue from saying anything more. Rose seemed less dependable lately, as if she'd reverted back to the way she had been a couple of years ago. And she felt bad that Dat was off at the lumberyard today, and Beth was back teaching at school. It was pretty much business as usual for them, except for Beth moving into the house. She still had to clean the little cottage she'd been living in though. Lila sighed, wishing she could help. She doubted Rose had thought of it.

⁓

When Lila awoke, two plastic crates were stacked by the front door, and the house was still. And there was no scent of bread baking or soup simmering. Perhaps Rose was doing some outside chores. Lila shifted in the chair and went back to sleep.

The next time Lila awoke, the sun was low. "Rose?" she called out, reaching for her crutches. She hadn't realized how tired she'd been.

No one answered. She called out again.

Finally her sister came into the room. "Have you started supper?" Lila asked.

"No," her sister said. "I thought Beth might have an idea."

Lila shook her head. "She's taught all day, and she still has to clean her cottage. You need to cook supper."

Rose's eyes grew teary. Lila ignored her sister. She didn't have patience for her drama.

"Are you picking up Trudy?"

Rose shook her head. "She's waiting at school and coming home with Beth." She swiped at her eyes. "You're right. I need to make supper. I'll get started now."

Lila braced herself with the crutches, pulled up to a standing position, and made her way to the hallway and the bedroom she shared with Rose and Trudy. Her bed, the one Rose had most likely been sleeping in, wasn't made. It would have been thoughtful of Rose to put clean sheets on it. Perhaps she still planned to.

Lila shuffled back and forth between the boxes by the front door and the bedroom, tucking nightclothes and toiletries under her arm to transport them. After a few trips she stopped. She'd wait and ask Rose to carry the boxes in.

By the time Trudy and Beth arrived home, Rose had a pot of stew simmering on the stove and biscuits baking in the oven. Beth greeted everyone warmly and then said she'd go out and help Dat finish up with the milking.

When they all came in the house a half hour later, Zane was with them. "We got off work early," he said. "A building permit didn't come through."

Lila appreciated him helping Dat.

Beth was all smiles as she asked Zane to stay for supper and then headed down the hall to wash up. Trudy finished setting the table and started filling the glasses with water without being told. By the time they sat down at the table, Lila felt weary but grateful. The house felt alive again. Rose still seemed down in the dumps, but the atmosphere had changed.

After Dat led them in prayer, Beth said she had an announcement to make. "It seems the board has found a teacher to take my place after Christmas vacation."

Lila was surprised. She'd assumed Beth would keep teaching.

"*Wunderbar*," Dat said. "That is good news."

"Who is it?" Trudy asked.

"A niece of Monika's," Beth replied. "She lives in the next district over. She's nineteen and has been hoping for a teaching position."

"All the scholars will be sad to see you go," Trudy said.

"And I'll be sad too," Beth answered. "But I have a husband to take care of. And a home. And daughters." She looked straight at Trudy. "And with Lila and Rose both getting married soon, there's even more reason for me to be home."

Zane reached under the table and squeezed Lila's hand. She appreciated his kind gesture. Rose buttered her biscuit, keeping her eyes down.

Beth smiled again. "I'm very aware of how blessed I am," she said. "To become a wife and mother and grandmother—all in one day. It's more than I could have ever dreamed of. Moving to Lancaster County turned out to be the best decision of my life."

Lila smiled back at her, trying to formulate something to say in return. Before she could though, Dat surprised her by saying, "It's me who's blessed. Having you in my life, in my home, a part of my family—well, it's more than I ever hoped for too."

Lila was dumbfounded. She'd never heard Dat speak from his heart like that.

There was a moment of silence before Beth said, "Denki, Tim." She swiped at her eyes quickly and then said, "Rose, the stew is delicious. And the biscuits smell heavenly." She took one from the basket.

The conversation shifted to a cow that was near giving birth, and a calf that was slow to take the bottle. Trudy said she'd feed it in the morning, that the little ones did better with her.

Everyone laughed, but she was probably right.

Lila took a few bites of the stew. It was good. Rose was a good cook. Lila buttered half of a biscuit and took a few bites of it too, wishing she were hungrier. She didn't burn enough calories to need to eat much though. She was sure her appetite would return once she was doing more.

⌇∽⌇

The next morning the physical therapist came to the house and worked with Lila for an hour, teaching her exercises to strengthen her core and legs, and stretch out her pelvic area. She hadn't slept well, and she'd been anxious most of the night.

After the therapy ended, Lila decided to take a pain pill and nap.

Zane got off work early again, in midafternoon. He came by in his buggy and asked Lila if she wanted to go visit Jenny

196

and the Bobbli. He'd been running Billie up and down the lane and then out on the highway for the last couple of weeks, and he'd been doing fine. When Rose chirped up that she would like to go, Lila could hardly refuse to, even though she still felt groggy from the meds. It would be her first buggy ride since the accident.

Lila retrieved the Bobbli quilt, made from yellow-and-green scraps, she'd stitched last summer in anticipation of Jenny and Daniel's baby.

Rose carried Lila's crutches down the stairs while Zane carried Lila. She giggled a little as he did.

"You're too light," he whispered as they reached the buggy. "You should work on gaining back the weight you lost."

She shrugged, not wanting to talk about it.

Zane drove extra cautiously and asked Lila several times if she was doing all right.

"I'm fine," she answered each time, but she caught herself glancing in the rearview mirror several times and bracing herself when Zane stopped at an intersection and a car came up behind them. She held her breath as Billie sidestepped one time, but then he stayed still. Zane drove cautiously and seemed to be in control of the horse.

When they reached Jenny and Daniel's house, Lila breathed a sigh of relief and resolved to be as cheerful as she could. And it worked. This time it was much easier to see the Bobbli. Jenny had just finished feeding her, and once Lila was seated, she handed Brook to her to burp.

"Rose," Lila said. "You should take her. You haven't had a chance yet."

"I'll hold her next," Rose said.

Daniel hadn't gotten home from work yet, but Monika was helping Jenny out, getting supper started in the kitchen. Rose wandered in to talk with her.

When Rose returned, Lila told her to take the Bobbli.

Rose seemed a little reluctant, but finally she took her. She sat down on the sofa beside Lila.

"What's wrong?" Jenny asked.

Lila glanced at Rose. She was crying. Confused, Lila tried to make light of it. "I guess our little niece has a strange effect on us Lehman girls."

Rose turned toward Zane, shielding her face. "How about if you have a turn?"

"I thought I'd never get the chance." He stood and scooped Brook into his arms, ignoring Rose, which was probably for the best. He held the baby with ease, making eye contact and then making a funny face. "I'm so pleased to meet you, Brook," he said. "I'm Zane. Soon I'll be your Uncle Zane. Someday Lila and I'll have cousins for you to play with."

It was Lila's turn to brush at her eyes, and not just out of sadness. Under the best of circumstances, Zane would have sounded prideful to assume they'd be able to have a Bobbli of their own. Under the present circumstances, he sounded foolish.

Lila reached for her crutches, wanting to escape. She'd go down to the kitchen and talk to Monika.

But Rose beat her to it. With tears rolling down her face, she hurried down the hall, either to the bathroom or back to the kitchen. Lila couldn't be sure.

～⁓～

Friday morning, just before the driver arrived to take Lila to the doctor, she took a pain pill and then put the bottle on the counter. She only had a half bottle left, and she'd save those just in case she needed them to get through appointments and the very worst nights. She wouldn't refill the prescription once it ran out—she'd already told Shani she didn't want to—and she'd honestly do her best not to take any more at all.

She made her way toward the front door, hoping to get down the steps and wait for the driver outside, instead of making him wait for her when he arrived.

But as she made her way past the table, the sound of a car surprised her. The driver was early. She stepped to the window and looked out. It wasn't the driver. It was Trevor's red sports car. Zane climbed out and hurried up the back stairs, knocking on the door.

Lila crutched her way to the door and opened it. "What are you doing here?" she asked.

"Mom said I should go to the doctor with you," he said. "I took the day off work. Trevor said he could give us a ride."

Lila shook her head, as Trevor came up the steps behind Zane. "You shouldn't have taken time off. A driver is coming any minute. It's too late to cancel." The last thing she wanted was for Trevor to hang around at the doctor's office with them.

Zane smiled. "Well, I want to go, but I guess we don't need you to drive. Thanks for offering, though."

Trevor shrugged. "I'll go ahead and go to work, for just the morning." He shoved his hands into his pockets. "Is Rose around?"

"Somewhere . . . She'd mentioned doing the laundry." She'd gotten behind earlier in the week.

"I just wanted to say hello," Trevor said. "Mind if I check down in the basement?"

Lila didn't think there was any harm in Trevor saying hello, although she thought it was odd. "Call down the stairs first," Lila said. "Don't surprise her. It's kind of creepy down there."

Once he disappeared, Lila whispered, "I was thinking I'd wait outside for the driver. But I don't want to go outside if Trevor is in the house with Rose."

Zane glanced toward the end of the kitchen where the basement door was. "I don't have any idea what he's up to—I don't think they've seen each other in weeks. I'll help you outside and then go check on them."

Lila nodded. Maybe Trevor was just being friendly, but she appreciated that Zane shared her concern. "Denki," Lila said. "Let's go down the front steps." By the time she reached the bottom one, the driver was in sight. "Go check," Lila said. "Tell Trevor he needs to leave and hurry back."

She shivered in the frigid air as Zane bounded back up the steps. The sky was an angry gray with storm clouds gathering in the distance. Once the car parked, Lila slipped into the back seat, asked the driver to wait, and positioned her crutches along the floor of the car. She was thankful the heat in the car was on, nearly full blast.

A minute later, both Zane and Trevor came down the back steps. Trevor waved and Lila waved back. Once Zane was settled in the back seat beside her, she asked in a whisper if Trevor thought it was weird that Zane had gone in after him.

"He was back in the kitchen," Zane said. "He said he just told Rose a quick hello."

"Weird," Lila said.

Zane exhaled. "Yeah, Trevor can be a little sneaky, but there wasn't enough time for anything to happen, not even a conversation."

Lila's thoughts soon fell to the doctor's appointment ahead of her, and she didn't give Trevor or Rose another thought.

The driver stopped at the front door of the clinic, and Zane grabbed Lila's crutches. He hurried around to her side of the car and then stayed by her side as she shuffled into the building and on down to the office at the end of the hall. After filling out the paper work, Lila was called back into an examination room for a test. Zane stayed in the waiting room while Lila made her way down the hall on her crutches, annoyed by the pain under her arms. First she changed into a gown and then carefully climbed onto the table. When the technician returned she explained that she would be doing an ultrasound and that they had waited until now to do it because they needed the swelling in her abdomen to go down. "That way we can get an idea of how much scar tissue there is," she said.

Lila closed her eyes during the test, not wanting to look at her ovaries and uterus and try to guess at the damage. When the technician finished, she told Lila to get dressed and go back out into the waiting room until the doctor was ready to see her.

They waited over an hour, and when they were finally called back it was to the doctor's actual office, not a clinical room. Framed certificates lined two of the walls and books filled a case behind his desk.

He looked up from his computer as they entered and then stood, reaching out to shake Zane's hand. Once Lila sat down, he shook hers.

The doctor was probably around Dat's age, with short graying hair.

"I'm sorry about your accident." He looked Lila in the eyes as he sat down.

She nodded, and he turned back to the computer screen. "I have the results of the ultrasound here." He glanced her way as he spoke.

"Your left ovary is damaged by scar tissue," the doctor said. "Your right one appears to have some damage, but not as much. As far as your pelvis, it definitely has been compromised. If you can get pregnant, you'll probably have to be on bed rest and then have a C-section. It would probably be too much pressure on your pelvis to deliver vaginally."

Lila sat perfectly still, unable to respond, although her face grew warm. She wasn't accustomed to such frank talk.

"Any questions?" the doctor asked.

Lila shook her head.

Zane cleared his throat. "What's the probability of pregnancy?"

"There's no way to know for sure," the doctor answered.

"Is there a chance that more scar tissue will develop?"

"Yes, there's always that chance. Harvesting eggs is definitely something you should consider."

Lila tried to catch Zane's attention, but he continued on with his questions. "How much does that procedure cost?"

The doctor frowned. "A lot. You'd have to ask our business department for the exact numbers."

It didn't matter how much it cost—it wouldn't be allowed. She didn't know of any Amish women who had gone through fertility treatment. If a woman couldn't get pregnant, it was God's will. Not something to be fixed by expensive treatments.

Zane leaned forward. "Would you say that the sooner natural pregnancy is attempted, the better the chances?"

Lila wanted to cover her face with her hands. She was sure her cheeks were red by now.

The doctor smiled a little. "Yes, if scar tissue is a concern, then trying to get pregnant soon makes sense." The doctor rubbed the back of his neck. "My Amish patients don't usually have so many questions."

Zane was quiet for a moment, but then he cleared his throat and finally met Lila's gaze.

Stop, she mouthed.

He shook his head. "How soon can—"

Lila eased herself out of her chair, grabbed her cape and then her crutches.

"Sexual relations be continued?" the doctor asked.

Zane shook his head. "Started. We're not married."

"Oh," the doctor said, glancing at the chart.

"But we will be. As soon as—"

Lila turned her head toward the door. She'd never felt such a gap between Zane and herself in all of her life.

When Zane didn't finish his sentence, the doctor said, "I don't see any physical reason to wait, but it's up to the patient of course. Discomfort can't be gauged by an ultrasound or any other test. It varies from patient to patient."

Why couldn't Zane take her feelings into consideration? These were answers she could get another way, she was sure. Or at another appointment, without Zane.

Lila swung her cape over her shoulders and positioned her crutches under her arms. "Thank you," she said to the doctor. Then she headed out the door. She was in the hall before she realized Zane hadn't followed her. She kept on going.

She waited in the lobby. She'd signed a release allowing Zane to speak with the doctor, but she hadn't expected he'd go on and on with his questions.

The receptionist asked if she could help her.

Lila shook her head, afraid that if she spoke she'd cry. She wasn't sure what was worse—the uncertain news or Zane not cooperating with her. She understood it was his concern too, but he wasn't being sensitive to what she needed.

She lowered her head, concentrating on composing herself, her thoughts drifting to baby Brook, to the baby's DNA, some of which was her biological father's. *Butch Wilson.* Did he still live in Virginia? If he knew what she was going through—about the accident, the medical bills, the repercussions—would he have come to see her?

She shook her head at her own foolishness. There was no point in tormenting herself. Dat might not verbalize his care, but he'd certainly shown it by providing for her all of these years. She had no right to dig up the past. It would only cause hurt and conflict.

Finally Zane started down the hall, carrying her purse. She'd forgotten all about it. "Why did you leave like that?" he whispered when he reached her.

"Because I didn't want to talk about all of that with him."

"But he's the doctor. If you couldn't talk with him, where will we get our answers?" His voice was quiet but firm.

"You weren't listening to me," she said.

"You weren't talking."

"Maybe not, but I was communicating."

He gave her an exasperated look.

"With my eyes. With my expression. And by not saying anything."

He pushed open the front door, still holding her purse. "I'm supposed to understand what you don't say?"

"Jah," she answered, stepping into the wintery day. She was glad she'd taken a pill before she left the house. The pain was bad enough as it was.

"If getting married sooner rather than later would help us have a Bobbli, we should do that. Or if you decide to have eggs harvested, you should do that right away."

"Zane." She kept her eyes on the parking lot pavement. "Have you ever heard of an Amish woman who has done that?"

"Well, no," he said. "But someone has to be the first."

She shook her head. "Not me. Besides, who would pay for it? We have enough to worry about as it is."

They reached the car and the driver hopped out, but Zane had already opened Lila's door. "We'll talk about your bills more when we get home."

She looked up at him. "Did you hear from the lawyer?"

Zane nodded. "We have an appointment to talk with him this afternoon. That's another reason I took the day off. We'll finally figure this out."

— 16 —

After Zane helped Lila up the front steps and into the Lehmans' house, she collapsed into her Dat's chair. He kneeled by her side, wishing he could make everything easier for her.

"Do you want to talk more?" he asked.

"No." Her answer was short and abrupt.

"Did you take a pain pill today?"

Her eyes flashed, in anger it seemed. "Jah," she answered. "And lucky for you I did. Otherwise I'd be yelling."

Zane felt his own emotions rise.

"You keep going on and on about things," she hissed. "First talking to a lawyer. Then quizzing the doctor. Now talking to the lawyer again. You're trying to do all of this your way. The Englisch-Zane way. Not Lila's way. Or the Amish way."

He raised his head. "But it's wrong for this guy to lie about what happened to get out of having his insurance cover your bills. It's unfair to you—and it's just not right. If we don't do anything, he'll get away with it."

"What if I did pull out in front of him?"

"But you said you didn't. And you wouldn't have. From the beginning you said you pulled to the side and that Billie didn't shift to the left."

She shrugged. "I really think that's what happened, but how can I be sure? The buggy was all in pieces, right?"

"Yep," Zane answered. In so many pieces he could see it would have been hard for the deputy to figure out exactly what happened. But that was no excuse to blindly believe the driver.

"Please don't make me anxious with this talk about lawyers and suing and insurance companies and who's responsible. And I don't want to go talk to the attorney today either."

Zane swallowed hard, not sure what to say. He'd never been so frustrated with her—and befuddled, all at the same time. She couldn't keep denying what was going on. "I get that it's upsetting for you," he answered, "but it's the way things are. It's the way the world works."

"Not our world," she said, her eyes narrow.

Zane exhaled. They'd had an argument now and then, but never a fight like this—thanks to Lila. She was the peacemaker between the two of them. Regardless of how angry they both were, he didn't want to have a fight now either. Not when she was so fragile. And not when he was so frustrated.

"Sorry," she said. "I'm tired." She pulled the afghan from the back of the chair and spread it over her lap. "I'm going to rest for a while. Would you tell Rose we're back?"

He nodded and stood, tucking the afghan around her, taking a breath and exhaling slowly as he did. "Do you care if I speak with the lawyer anyway? Just to get his advice."

She yawned. "I'm not going to tell you not to, but I won't necessarily do what he recommends."

Zane nodded. She could be so stubborn—but so could he. If the church fund didn't cover all the expenses, the debt would impact them as a young couple just starting out. They might never be able to buy their own farm or start a business. He kissed Lila's forehead and then left in search of Rose.

When he reached the kitchen, she was coming up the stairs, a full laundry basket on her hip. Her face was red and blotchy and for a minute he wondered if she'd had some sort of allergic reaction, but then he realized she'd been crying.

"Are you doing all right?" he asked.

She nodded but didn't answer.

Puzzled, he said, "Lila is back."

"Jah, I gathered that." She went on outside.

It was eleven thirty, time for Tim to come in for dinner and there didn't appear to be anything cooking, but Zane wasn't going to remind Rose of that. Instead Zane went back in the living room and sat on the sofa, watching Lila sleep. Her face was relaxed. It had been a long time since he'd seen her at peace—since before the accident. He was afraid, in his determination to fix everything, that he sometimes overlooked how much pain she was in. He could see that healing was taking all of her energy and that to have to deal with the turmoil surrounding the accident was too much for her. He thought of what his healing process was like after he was wounded in Afghanistan. He was out of sorts much of the time. Irritable. Uncertain of what he needed to do next.

The back door opened. Zane stood and stepped into the kitchen. "Hello," Zane said. "Lila and I just got back. She's asleep in your chair."

"How's she doing?" Tim asked.

"All right." Zane certainly didn't want to elaborate. He doubted Lila would say more than that to him.

"Is Rose around?"

"She's hanging the wash."

Tim glanced at the stove, and then went to the refrigerator

and took out a plastic container full of roast beef and a jar of mustard.

"Want a sandwich?" Tim asked.

"Sure," Zane answered.

"*Gut*," Tim said. "I can have some company while I eat mine." When he finished making his, he motioned to Zane while he pulled a gallon of milk from the refrigerator and poured two glasses.

As they sat down at the table, Rose came in, carrying the empty basket and a stack of mail. "Sorry, Dat," she said, putting the envelopes on the table. "I got behind on my chores. I would have made your sandwich."

Tim shrugged. "Make one for yourself," he said. "And perhaps for Lila."

Zane shook his head, eyeing the mail. "She'll probably sleep for a while." The return address on the top envelope was from Lila's surgeon. More bills.

"And I'm not hungry," Rose said, heading for the basement.

Tim shook his head. "I can't figure out these girls, not for the life of me. I'm hoping maybe Beth can." He smiled and then led the two of them in a silent prayer.

Zane bowed his head and prayed for Lila and for wisdom and that God would provide a way to pay her medical bills. And that he'd be able to contain his frustration.

～⌣～

After finishing his sandwich, Zane headed back through the field. First, he stopped by his parents' and left a message for the lawyer, saying he'd be coming without Lila.

Next he went to the little house. It seemed so empty. He'd moved the single bed up to the Bobbli's room and pushed the recliner back to the far corner. Mom had returned Lila's wheelchair the day after the fixator had been removed. He'd need to look for a sofa soon, probably at a secondhand store. Buying the buggy had wiped out his savings.

He'd slept upstairs in their bedroom the night before, but he'd tossed and turned all night. He'd rather stay at his parents' house, but he understood Gideon's concern about relying too much on Englisch ways. And it made more sense for him to stay in the little house than go back to Gideon and Monika's Dawdi Haus.

He headed to the bathroom and picked up the tape measure off the toilet seat. The downstairs bathroom had been functional for almost two months now, but he needed more molding to finish the trim work. He hoped Trevor would take him to the lumberyard on their way home from Lancaster. He quickly measured the spaces along the floorboards, committing the numbers to memory.

Then he returned to the living room and wandered up the stairs, running his hand up the smooth railing that he'd worked so hard to fashion, taking each step slowly. The sun must have been trying to poke through the storm clouds gathering on the horizon because a shaft of light streamed through the landing window. He started toward his room—his and Lila's—but then stopped and turned toward the closed door.

He opened it slowly. He'd found the pale yellow curtains at a secondhand store. And the crib and bureau. The single bed had come from his parents' house, but he'd bought the platform rocking chair new. The quilt hanging over the back was one that the women at Lila's grandmother's quilt shop had sent for him to give away in Afghanistan. This one had ended up in his trunk and was sent back home after he was injured. He liked the fact that his and Lila's Bobbli would have it someday.

He closed the door. At least Lila hadn't seen the room and didn't know he'd furnished it. He'd box up everything except the twin bed. Maybe after they were married, Trudy would want to spend the night sometimes. Or maybe Simon when he came home from Iraq.

He stopped on the landing, looking over to his parents' house as Trevor drove up Juneberry Lane. Zane headed back down the stairs, out the door, and around the barn. Trevor sat in his car, texting on his phone. As Zane approached he looked up, waved, and rolled down the window. "Ready?"

Zane nodded and climbed in on the passenger side. "How was work?"

"Short." Trevor smiled and slipped his phone into his jacket, backed his car around, and headed back up Juneberry Lane to the highway.

A half hour later Trevor pulled into the parking lot of the Veterans Center. Zane had been visiting the facility since he was a boy, after his dad started working there as a technology support specialist not long after he was discharged from the Army. When Zane was a soldier, he visited the place a few times, including when he was home on furlough from Afghanistan, but he hadn't stopped by since. Every once in a while Dad would tell him about a group that was being held that he thought might interest Zane. His only remaining connection to the Army was his dad and his relationship with Charlie—and Trevor, of course, but Zane expected he would be leaving soon. He didn't keep in touch with any of his fellow soldiers—except Casey, and that was through Simon. It had been a fluke that Trevor had written him and then shown up. They hadn't been in touch since Zane gave up his phone.

"Want to come in?" Zane asked. "You can wait in Dad's office after I head across the street to the attorney's."

Trevor shook his head. "I'll wait here."

Zane stepped into the building, said hello to the receptionist, and then headed back to his dad's office. Dad was on the phone but when he hung up he said, "Brad is expecting you."

"Thanks," Zane said. He'd met Brad Garrett one time before.

"What did Tim say about you talking with a lawyer?"

Zane's face grew warm.

Dad caught on pretty quickly. "You didn't say anything to him?"

"Not yet." Zane should have earlier that day, but it didn't seem to be the right time. "I will, depending on what Brad says."

Zane told his dad good-bye and made his way across the street and up the steps to the brick building, pushing open the heavy door. Then he headed up the staircase, stopped at the first door, and knocked.

Finally, someone called out, "Come in."

Zane opened the door to the small office. Behind a desk stacked with files sat the lawyer, his reading glasses perched on the end of his nose. He took them off and stood as Zane entered.

"Ah," he said. "It's good to see you." He nodded toward Zane and then stared for a moment. "Your father told me you'd converted." The man's gray eyes twinkled. "For a girl, I heard."

Zane smiled. "Is that what Dad said?"

The man cocked his head. "Well, maybe not in so many words."

"It's a little more complex than that," Zane said, although chances were he never would have joined if he didn't love Lila. He wasn't entirely sure though.

Zane continued, "But she's the girl I came to talk with you about. She was in a bad accident, almost two months ago."

Brad nodded. Dad had probably explained what had happened. Zane went ahead and told him the story from the beginning, just so he'd have all the details straight. The man took notes as Zane spoke. When Zane finished, Brad asked, "How much are the medical bills?"

"I don't have the exact number. They keep trickling in. But at last count they were over a hundred and fifty thousand dollars."

"And how about lasting damage? What's the long-term prognosis?"

He explained that Lila had just started doing PT. "We'll have a better idea as far as her mobility in time," he said. "Right now she's walking with crutches." Then he took a deep breath and said, "She saw a gynecologist today. Both ovaries have been compromised by scar tissue, one worse than the other. If she can get pregnant, she'll probably have to be on bed rest and then have a C-section."

"No children so far?"

Zane nodded. "We were planning to marry—" he exhaled— "last month. But we had to postpone it because of the accident."

"It sounds like a clear-cut case. Why is the insurance company denying payment?"

"Because the driver of the SUV says Lila swerved in front of him—and he said that in the 9-1-1 call."

"Did she?"

Zane shook his head. "At first she said she didn't. Now, I think because of the conflict around all of this, she's questioning what she remembers. She's afraid that she might not remember the last seconds before the accident correctly, but I think the insurance agent planted that idea." Zane leaned forward. "She's a good buggy driver. Cautious. Firm with the horse. Lots of experience. By the time she was twelve she was driving her younger siblings to school every day. But she expects the best of people, and I don't think she can fathom that someone would lie about this sort of thing."

Brad pushed back in his chair. "Why do you think this person would lie?"

Zane shrugged. "Because he doesn't want his insurance rates to go up? Because he doesn't think an Amish person would sue him?"

The man nodded as he spoke. "Or maybe he's about ready

to lose his insurance. Have you Googled him? To see if he's been in other accidents."

Zane shook his head.

"What's his name?"

"Donald Addison," Zane said. "I'd say he was in his thirties."

"You've met him?"

"No, but I saw him at the accident site. The agent called him Mr. Addison, but I remember him being called Donald when I saw him. It's one of those things that stuck in my head." Actually, every detail of that day was stuck in his head.

Brad turned to his keyboard and began typing. "We'll see what we can do." He read the screen for a moment and then said, "Here's a Donald Addison. His address is listed as in Ephrata. He's thirty-seven . . . and he was in an accident last January where a child was injured." He looked up. "What was the date of Lila's accident?"

"September seventeenth."

"All right," the man said. "So that would be two bad accidents pretty close together." Brad kept his eyes on the screen. "Here's another one, just over three years ago." He turned toward Zane. "As far as his saying she'd pulled out in front of him in the 9-1-1 call, well, that just indicates he thinks on his feet. And the stakes were certainly high enough for him to come up with a quick lie." Brad steepled his fingers. "So why would Lila want to sue? When the Amish don't."

"They usually don't," Zane clarified. "Sometimes they do."

The man smiled, just a little. "Really?"

"I heard of a case in Indiana." Zane's face grew warm. It was actually the only case he'd ever heard of where an Amish person sued after a traffic accident. "I don't know that she would sue. In fact, she very well might not. But I don't think she understands how much the bills are going to add up to. Or that the driver could be lying about what happened to avoid responsibility."

"But it will be up to her to make a decision on this," Brad said. "Right?"

Zane nodded. He knew that.

"And you're Amish too."

Zane nodded again. "That's right."

"But you think suing would be the right thing to do?"

"Maybe," Zane said. "At this point I just want to explore our options." He cleared his throat. "I mean her options."

❧

On the way home, once they were out of Lancaster, Zane asked Trevor if he would take him by the lumberyard. "I need some more molding to finish the bathroom."

"It won't fit in my car," Trevor responded.

Zane kept his eyes on a farmer harvesting silage. "I'll get Reuben to cut it."

Trevor nodded but didn't say any more. When they reached the lumberyard, he parked in the middle of the lot, even though there wasn't another car, truck, or buggy in sight. When he didn't turn off the motor, Zane climbed out and walked by himself toward the building.

Reuben stood at the counter doing paper work. It took him a long moment to look up and acknowledge Zane.

Finally he said, "Oh, hello there."

Zane teased. "Absorbed in your work?"

"Jah." Reuben smiled. "A bit, I guess. What can I do for you?"

"I need some molding cut."

Reuben closed his notebook and followed Zane to the molding section.

"I thought you were done with your house," Reuben said.

"Oh, you know how it goes. There's always that last bit that gets put off. I'd stopped noticing it—until this morning." Zane picked out the molding and followed Reuben back to the saw.

214

Reuben donned his protective eyewear, Zane gave him the measurements, and Reuben quickly made the cuts, sending up quick puffs of sawdust.

In another couple of minutes they were back in the front, where Reuben rang up the purchase. As Zane counted his money, Reuben looked out into the lot and asked, "Why didn't Trevor come in?"

Zane shrugged. He wanted to tell Reuben how odd everyone was acting. Rose. Lila. Trevor. But he didn't dare.

He could tell him about one thing though. "Do you have an extra minute?" he asked.

Reuben smiled warily. "It's not like I'm flooded with business right now."

Zane told him about the driver saying Lila pulled out in front of him, and that his insurance company was now claiming they weren't responsible for any of the medical bills.

"Didn't Lila end up in the ditch?" Reuben asked.

Zane nodded.

"Wouldn't she have ended up in the road if she'd pulled in front of him? The front of the buggy would have been pointed to the south, not the north."

"But she could have pulled in front of him and then corrected herself."

"Possibly," Reuben said. "Check to see if there are any skid marks at the scene of the accident. A copy of the police report would help—hopefully they took measurements where the bulk of the buggy ended up. And where Lila landed." He took his hat off and rubbed his hand through his hair. "The sheriff comes in here pretty often. I could ask him about it."

Zane nodded. "Denki, Reuben. I really appreciate it."

"Any time," he answered. "And would you do me a favor?"

"Sure. Anything."

"Tell Rose hello." Reuben put his hat back on. His voice sounded a little raw. "And that I miss her."

"Will do." Zane grabbed the molding from the counter. "See you soon," he said. As he hurried across the parking lot, the rain began to fall. It was cold enough that Zane was sure it would soon turn to snow.

When Zane approached the car, Trevor was texting on his phone again. "What's up?" Zane asked as he settled into the passenger seat.

"It's Sierra," Trevor said.

"Oh," Zane said.

"She keeps asking when I'm coming home. So does my dad."

"So when are you going home?"

Trevor shifted into drive. "I'm not sure. I should have given notice at work. I'm just not thinking very clearly."

"Are you still drinking?"

"No," Trevor said. "It's not that."

Zane wasn't so sure.

"I'll talk with the boss tomorrow. I'll give my two weeks' notice and then be on my way after that," Trevor said. "Like I should have been a few weeks ago."

Zane wanted to sigh in relief but stopped himself. Maybe, someday, things would return to normal on Juneberry Lane. One step at a time.

17

Rose headed toward the chicken coop, her arm looped through the egg basket. The first dusting of snow had fallen the night before, and the farm appeared as if powdered sugar had been sifted over it. If she hadn't been so out of sorts, she'd have marveled at the beauty of it.

Trudy was ill with a bad cold—hopefully not the flu—and Lila had told Rose to tend to the chickens.

Beyond the coop, Dat hitched Beth's horse to her buggy, just as he did every morning. It was a lot to teach school, and Rose could tell Beth was doing all she could to help with meals and clean up and chores, in addition to her teaching responsibilities.

When she reached the coop, Rose opened the door quickly and stepped inside, squinting in the dim light. The hens stirred and then began to cluck. Rose opened the bin, scooped up the feed, and stepped to the little door that led to the chicken yard. The rooster was already out there, strutting around. Rose flung the grain on top of the thin layer of snow. Most of the hens flew down and headed out the door to the yard.

Rose turned her attention to their nests and began gathering the eggs as quickly as she could, the shells warm against her bare hands.

She hadn't been sick yet this morning. That was a good sign. She sighed. It really wasn't. It was irrelevant. At first she hoped she had the flu, but it had gone on for weeks. Not even she could be in denial that long.

She hadn't taken a test yet. She would, even though she didn't need to. She was one hundred percent sure—and absolutely positive she'd made the worst mistake of her life.

Tears blurred her vision, but as Beth called out her name she blinked quickly. Her stepmother—how odd that word still sounded—stood in the doorway to the coop, carrying a book bag stuffed with binders and papers.

She was a little out of breath as she said, "I just wanted to check on you to see how you're feeling."

"I'm fine," Rose answered.

"All right. Trudy is still in bed. I just gave her medicine for her fever. Make sure and check in a couple of hours, but don't give her any more medicine for another four."

Rose nodded, wondering how Beth thought they'd managed without her.

"Lila said the physical therapist is coming at ten. Keep Trudy in your room—we don't want her to expose the poor soul."

Rose nodded again. She might not have thought of that.

Beth reached for her arm. "Are you sure you're doing all right? You seem so unsettled lately."

"I'm fine," Rose answered. "Really."

"Is it adjusting to me being here? Is it . . . difficult?"

"No, no," Rose said. "I'm so happy you're here. Honestly." She truly was.

"Then is it Reuben? Because he hasn't been around, not at all. Your Dat hasn't noticed as much because . . . well, he's

LESLIE GOULD

just not thinking about those sorts of things right now. But
I'm worried—"

"Ach, no. I'm fine," Rose said.

"Would you tell me if you need my help? Because I'd do anything I could. Listen. Help come up with a solution. Anything."

Dat called out, "Beth?"

"In here," she called back.

"Denki," Rose said. "You should get going. We can talk later."

"All right," Beth said. "Tonight when I get home." She stepped
back out the door. "Have a good day."

"You too." Rose picked up another egg. It was cracked and
broke in her hand. She flung it to the floor and burst into tears.

She'd seen Reuben at church last week. He'd said he'd pick
her up for the singing that night, but she declined, saying she
needed to help with Lila. He hadn't pressed her, but the moment felt awkward, and she feared he could see right through
her. She hadn't seen Trevor. He'd come by that one day when
she was doing laundry and tried to talk, but all she could do
was cry. He'd grown frustrated with her and said to call when
she was ready to talk.

She'd been so taken with him, until the morning after that
night in Dat's barn. Then it hit her what she'd done. To Reuben.
To herself. Even to Trevor.

Immediately, she'd been convicted. Verses she'd hardly listened to came back to her, including, "*Whoever walks in integrity walks securely, but he who makes his ways crooked will
be found out.*"

Yes, she would be found out. There was no stopping it. Until
now she'd had no idea how deceitful she could be. How lack-
ing in integrity.

She had no idea how hard it could be, in the face of tempta-
tion, to follow Christ's teaching, to adhere to what her community required. There was a reason for those teachings—to

219

protect her from herself. From deception. From evil. From being utterly alone in the hardest thing she'd ever faced.

She didn't feel any worse when she missed her period. It didn't make what she'd done any more dreadful. It just meant everyone would soon see right through her. She felt no more shame at knowing what she'd helped create than in knowing what she'd done.

She'd confessed her sin to God. Now it was time to confess it to others. But first she needed to talk with Trevor. She wiped her tears and headed out of the barn as Dat's buggy passed by. "I'm taking Beth to school," he called out. "Just in case the roads are bad."

Beth smiled and waved. Rose waved back, but she couldn't manage to smile. Dat would be so disappointed in her, but at least he'd have Beth to help him cope.

The buggy wheels left two crisp lines in the snow. Rose watched the buggy until it turned right onto the lane and disappeared.

With Dat gone, this was her chance to call Trevor—or to at least leave a message. She'd ask him to come talk with her as soon as he could. She never thought she'd consider leaving the Amish, but she needed to know his response before she could be sure.

If she'd learned one thing growing up, it was that a child should be with both of its biological parents. It was obvious, even to her, that Dat favored Simon, her, and Trudy over Lila and Daniel. She would never expect Reuben to accept her Bobbli with another man. She wouldn't want him to. She'd seen what it had been like for Lila and Daniel. She didn't want that for her child.

She headed into the barn and Dat's office, putting the basket on the desk and picking up the phone, dialing Trevor's number. He didn't pick up, so she left a message, saying she needed to speak with him as soon as possible.

She hung up the phone, waited a minute just in case he would call back, and picked up the eggs. As she reached the door, the phone rang. She rushed back to answer it, hoping it was Trevor, but she said, "Hello, this is the Lehman Dairy," as if it might be a business call.

It was Trevor. After he greeted her she asked if he had listened to her voicemail.

"No," he answered. "I just saw that you called."

"I need to speak with you, in person."

"What about?"

"I'd rather say face-to-face."

"I'm pretty busy."

"It's important."

He didn't answer.

"Trevor."

"I'm thinking. Look, if it's about what happened, I'm really sorry. I tried to tell you that when you were doing your laundry, when I stopped by that day."

"Jah," she said. "I should have talked with you then." She would have, if she'd been sure she didn't have the flu, that it was more than that.

"You seemed willing enough that night, in the barn."

She paused, not sure what to say. Finally she decided to be honest. "I was."

"Then what's the problem?"

"We need to talk."

"Can you come over to Eve and Charlie's tomorrow? Mid-afternoon? Eve won't be home yet."

"All right," she answered. "I'll see you then."

"Yeah," he answered. "Bye." The line went dead before she could say any more. His tone stung. It was far from that of the friendly, confident man he'd been before. She walked back to the house with her free hand against her abdomen. She feared he wasn't who she'd thought he was, not at all, but no matter what, he was the father of her child.

Trudy didn't go to school the next day either, but Lila was fine being in charge. Early in the afternoon, Rose told her she needed to run an errand. More snow had fallen, and the trip to Eve's was cold, with gusts of wind rocking the buggy from time to time. Rose usually loved winter. Sledding and skating. Snowball fights after the singings. But this year nothing about winter appealed to her. The icy wind seemed to go straight to her bones.

When Rose arrived at Charlie and Eve's house, Trevor's car wasn't parked in front of the garage. Instead Eve and Charlie's black sedan was. Maybe Trevor had parked in the shed, but that didn't explain why Eve's car was at the house. She should have been at school, teaching her kindergartners. Rose hitched her horse to the post along the side of the garage and headed toward Eve's front door, pulling her scarf tight around her neck against the wind.

She opened the screen door and knocked a couple of times, hoping Trevor would quickly open the door, but no one came. She knocked again, a little louder, and then took a step backward. Icicles hung from the eaves of the house, and snow was starting to blow across the yard. Jah, winter had arrived with a vengeance.

Finally footsteps fell across the floor, and then the door swung open, but it was Aenti Eve not Trevor. Eve wore jeans, a sweatshirt, and a pair of fleece-lined slippers. She looked as if she hadn't slept in a week.

"Oh, hello," Eve said. "Come on in."

"I didn't expect you to be home," Rose said.

"Jackson is sick with a bad cold. Maybe the flu. He has a fever. I have a call in to the doctor."

"Trudy's ill too. She's home with Lila."

Eve looked exhausted. "There's definitely a lot of illness going around. I've been missing a lot of work to stay home with Jackson. I didn't want to resign from my job until we knew whether we'd be able to adopt him for sure or not, but I think I'm going to have to soon."

Rose hoped her expression was sympathetic. Dat didn't think Eve should have gone to college, let alone taken a teaching job. He believed only unmarried women should work. Dat had even implied that the reason Eve wasn't able to get pregnant was that she'd been prideful and had gone to college. And then even worse, sought a job. But Rose suspected that Eve had been trying to get pregnant since she got married. A wave of guilt washed through Rose.

"What brings you here?" Eve asked.

Rose squared her shoulders. "I was hoping to speak with Trevor."

Eve had a confused expression on her face as she said, "He's not here. In fact, I'm not sure he'll be back. He said he was going to spend the night at Zane's, before he leaves in the morning."

Rose put her hand against the doorjamb. "He's leaving?"

Eve nodded.

"Where's he going?"

"Back home, is what I understand. But he hasn't been very forthcoming." She motioned for Rose to come in. "You need to get out of the cold."

Rose stepped inside, and Eve closed the door. She pointed toward the sofa. "Sit down." Then she asked, "Do you have time for me to make some tea?"

Rose nodded.

"Let me take your cape."

Rose slipped out of it and handed it to Eve and then stepped into the living room. Why had Trevor told her to meet him here?

She started to sit down, but a fussing noise caught her attention from down the hall. She headed toward the noise. The door to the baby's room was open, and the little boy was on his back in his crib, waving his arms and legs, screaming. Rose stepped to the side and lifted him out. He stopped crying for a moment, looking into her face. But then he started to scream again. She put him to her shoulder and began patting his back.

He began to calm down. Even though he felt warm, she grabbed a blanket from the top of the bureau and wrapped it around him.

As she headed back out to the living room, he hiccupped a couple of times but stayed calm.

Eve poked her head out from the kitchen. "Oh, thanks," she said, glancing at the clock. "He didn't sleep long."

The kettle began to whistle and Rose stepped into the kitchen as Eve poured hot water into the teapot. "I don't want you to get sick. Are you okay holding him?" she asked.

Rose nodded. She'd probably already been exposed from Trudy, but she honestly felt conflicted holding the little one. In another year she'd have a Bobbli his size. And she might be far away from Lancaster County. She swallowed hard, trying not to choke up.

Eve turned toward her and crossed her arms. "So what's going on? Why do you want to speak with Trevor?"

Rose's face grew warm. She'd never been as close to her Aenti as Lila had been. Sure, she knew Eve cared about her, but she'd never confided in her about anything. Rose had been a little girl—only eight—when Eve and Charlie had married, forcing Eve to leave the church. But she'd always had the impression that at one time in her life, before she joined the church, Eve had a wild side. No one ever talked about it, but it seemed that was part of Dat's criticism of Eve all these years.

"Rose," Eve said, her voice kind, "what's going on?"

Rose took a deep breath. She really needed to speak with Trevor—not anyone else.

"I didn't realize you and Trevor knew each other, not really," Eve said. "But maybe I've been so wrapped up in other things I didn't notice."

Rose shifted the baby to her other shoulder, between her and Eve, and said, "Trevor and I spent some time together."

"What kind of time?"

"Talking time." Rose shrugged. "He'd hang around after Lila fell asleep. I'd meet him in the Becks' barn. And ours . . . one time." It felt as if her face was on fire.

"What about Reuben?"

"Well . . . " Rose wasn't sure what to say. She exhaled. "I convinced myself that I hadn't had a Rumschpringe, that I deserved a little fun. And Reuben was all concerned about others—instead of about me." She wrinkled her nose, aware of how stupid that sounded. "I was being awful—I admit it. I told myself that Reuben was boring, that he didn't even seem that interested in me, in that way, if you know what I mean."

Eve cocked her head. "And Trevor was interested in you . . . in that way?"

Rose nodded.

Eve took two mugs out of the cupboard and asked, "What happened?"

Rose met her Aenti's eyes. "I didn't mean for it to happen. But I didn't stop it."

Obviously Eve knew what Rose was insinuating. "And?" her Aenti asked slowly as she poured the tea into the mugs.

"I think I'm pregnant."

"Oh, Rose," Eve said, carefully putting the kettle down. She made eye contact and then said, "I need to ask a difficult question."

Rose nodded.

"Was your . . . contact with Trevor consensual?"

"Jah," Rose answered. "I wanted it, at least I thought I did, until it happened. Then I regretted it, especially by the next day. Then I saw it for what it was."

"Which was?"

She frowned. "It didn't seem to be about love, or really even caring about each other all that much." Tears welled up in her eyes. "I was so caught up in how I felt, how my body felt, that I didn't think of any of that."

Eve wrapped her arm around Rose. "Was it just one time?" Rose nodded.

"You set a boundary, then. That's good."

Rose shook her head. "But it didn't matter. Once was enough."

The baby reached for Eve, and she took him, leaving Rose feeling empty and awkward and completely unsettled.

"What do you plan to do?" Eve asked over the baby's head.

Tears filled her eyes again. "Tell Trevor. I hope he'll want to get married and be a father to our Bobbli."

"Would you be willing to go to Delaware?" Eve asked.

Rose wrapped her arms around herself. "I hope he'll want to stay here. I don't want to leave everyone. What would I do all alone, without my family?"

"You'd have a new family."

Tears flooded over the rims of Rose's eyes.

"Do you know Trevor well enough to commit your life to his?"

"I think so." Rose exhaled again. "I know it won't be easy. But I think it's what's best. I think we can come to love each other, to learn to."

Eve cocked her head. "Marriage is hard, under the best of circumstances."

"I know," Rose said. At least she had some idea it was hard. It wasn't as if she wanted to marry Trevor, but she was over fifty percent sure, just barely, it would be the right thing to do. "I should get over to Zane's. So I can talk to Trevor." She couldn't believe he planned to move back home, not now.

"You need someone to go with you," Eve said. "Like Shani. Or Beth."

Rose shook her head. "I don't want to tell them."

"Then wait until Charlie gets home, and I'll go with you."

Rose shook her head. She didn't want that.

Eve frowned. "You should know we've had some concerns about Trevor. I wouldn't say anything except for your circumstances. He's moody. And he had a couple of outbursts when Charlie asked him pointed questions."

They'd probably been too nosy. Before she could say anything, the phone rang.

"That's probably the doctor." Eve stepped toward the landline. Rose nodded.

Eve answered the phone, replied to a few questions, and then said, "We'll be right in." When she hung up, she said, "I've got to go."

"Of course," Rose said. "I appreciate you listening."

"I'll buy a pregnancy test at the pharmacy," Eve said. "Come back tomorrow and take it. Then you'll know for sure. You can stay here if you need to, until you decide—until you figure things out, as far as your future."

"Denki," Rose said, stepping into the entryway and retrieving her cape from the coat-tree. "I'll take you up on the pregnancy test offer. I'll see you tomorrow."

Eve gave her a half hug, said good-bye, and hurried down the hall. Rose let herself out, leaving the hot tea behind, facing the icy cold and the task of tracking down Trevor on her own.

❧

When Rose reached the end of Juneberry Lane, Trevor's car was parked in front of the Becks' home, but she turned around and drove back home, telling herself she didn't want to leave her buggy at the neighbors'. She parked and unhitched the horse, getting her into her stall in the barn. Dat was gone—he'd probably gone to get Beth. After she brushed, watered, and fed her horse she sat down on a hay bale outside of the stall and put her head in her hands and tried to pray. But absolutely nothing came.

Finally she stood, gathered her courage, and started through the field. A layer of ice covered the snow, causing her to slip several times as she shuffled along. Already the sun was lowering behind the line of poplars. She could make out the melody of the creek, beyond the trees, but she couldn't enjoy it. She pressed forward, walking as fast as she could in the ice and snow.

When she reached the hedge, she veered toward the left, toward the little house. Smoke swirled out of the chimney. She hoped Trevor was there alone.

After knocking a couple of times and not getting an answer, she peered through the front window. There weren't any lamps lit. Perhaps Trevor had gone with Zane to his folks' house—or maybe they'd left in Trevor's car.

She knocked a third time. "Hey," said a voice from behind her. It was Trevor. She turned, slowly, her knees weak. She dreaded speaking with him more than anything in her entire life.

"Hey, yourself," she said. "Why did you stand me up?"

A confused expression passed over his face, and then he said, "Oh, no."

She raised her eyebrows.

"I forgot all about it," he said. "I packed all my things from Eve and Charlie's this morning. I'm staying here tonight."

"Because?"

"I'm going home tomorrow."

Rose wrapped her arms around herself. "Were you going to tell me?"

He shrugged. "I didn't think you'd care."

The truth was, she wouldn't have a couple of weeks ago. She would have been happy to have him leave. But now everything had changed.

"Where's Zane?" she asked.

"Over at his parents'. Playing a game of Scrabble with Adam." Trevor held up his phone. "I was just charging this." He sighed. "What did you need to talk about?"

Rose exhaled slowly, holding on to her forearms under her cape as she did.

He stepped closer, towering over her. "Look," he said, "like I told you, I didn't intend for that to happen. I knew it was a bad idea as soon . . ."

Tears started to sting her eyes.

"Will this make things difficult with Reuben? Will he break up with you, if he finds out? Because I haven't told anyone. There's no way he'll know, as long as you haven't said anything." He glanced over his shoulder and then back at Rose, his voice lower. "Have you told anyone?"

She nodded.

He groaned. "Who?"

"Eve."

"Okay," he said. "She can be trusted. She would never tell Reuben, right?"

Rose shook her head. "That's not the problem."

"What's the problem?"

"I'm pregnant."

"No," he whispered. "Are you sure?"

"Jah."

"You mean, you took a test and it was positive. That kind of sure?"

"I'll take the test tomorrow. But I'm sure." She was never late and everything felt different. The never-ending morning sickness. The fatigue. Her body.

"Look," he said. "I'm going home. I quit my job here. I have a lead on another one there—I've been planning this for the last month."

Rose put her hand on the rail, to steady herself. "Are you getting back together with your girlfriend?"

He shrugged. "She knows I'm coming home, but we haven't really talked things through." He ran his hand through his hair. "I don't think you and I should even talk about this until you've taken a test, right? Because how can you know for sure?"

"I do," Rose said.

"No!" He stormed past her. Reaching the door, he grasped the knob and said, "Take the test. Then call me. There's no reason to get all worked up until we know for sure."

A tear spilled from her eye and then another one. "I'll call you tomorrow." She turned back toward the field, slipping as she did.

He must have turned to watch her go, because he called out, "Wait. I'll walk with you."

Rose kept on going, but she sensed him coming up behind her, and then he grabbed her elbow. At first she wanted to fling her arm away from him, but she didn't. Instead she stopped and looked up into his eyes.

"I'm sorry," he said. "We'll figure this out."

"All right." She swallowed hard, not wanting to cry in front of him.

He bent down and hugged her, first just a friendly hug but as she responded he held her tighter. Jah, the passion was still there. She forced herself away from him and started across the field again. Sure, a marriage with Trevor might be a lot of work, like Eve said—more than she could imagine, she was sure—but she would do it for her Bobbli. She'd become Englisch if she needed to. She didn't blame him for wanting her to take a test to make sure. They'd figure things out after it was definite.

If things didn't work out with Trevor, she wouldn't marry Reuben. She wouldn't do that to her child. Who was she kidding? Reuben wouldn't want to marry her. Not after what she'd done.

As she continued on, she ached for Trevor. Hopefully they'd figure everything out sooner rather than later.

❦

The next afternoon Rose stood in Eve's black-and-white-tiled bathroom and watched a pink dot appear on the end of the plastic stick in her hand. It only confirmed what she already knew. She headed out to the living room and held it up for Eve.

Her aunt's eyes were kind. "Did you talk with Trevor yesterday?"

"Jah," Rose said.

Eve held up her cell phone. "Would you like to call him now?"

Rose shook her head. She'd call him later.

"What will you do after you talk with Trevor?" Eve asked.

"I'll tell Reuben. And Dat. Although maybe not tomorrow—I might need some time to work up my courage."

"Are you seeing Reuben at all?"

Rose shook her head. "Only at church."

"Well, it's good you plan to tell him. He deserves to know what's going on, to hear it from you."

Rose didn't reply.

"What if Trevor doesn't step up, but Reuben wants to court you again, regardless of what's happened?"

Rose shook her head. "I don't want that."

"What will you do? Never marry?"

Rose shrugged. "I don't know what I'll do. I just don't believe Reuben would ever truly accept my child."

"But look at your Dat. He—"

Rose shook her head again. "He didn't. He never treated Lila and Daniel the way he did the rest of us."

"Rose . . ."

"You know it's true."

"But he got over it eventually, right?"

"No, not really. If I were in an accident like Lila was, do you think he would have sent me off to live in a house over by the neighbors? No. He would have built a ramp to our house. He would have put a bed in the living room, if needed."

"It was easier to have Lila stay over there. That's all. And besides, it will be her home soon."

Rose wrinkled her nose. "She was hurt that Dat didn't care more. She would never admit it, true, but it still hurt her. She was talking about her real father not too long ago—"

"*Biological* father. Tim is her *real* father."

"Oh," Rose said.

"Families get formed in all sorts of ways," Eve said. "Charlie and I both feel absolutely committed to Jackson."

"Jah," Rose said. "It appears that way. But you'll never have other children to compare how you feel, you'll never know if you'd favor a biological child."

"We wouldn't," Eve said.

"But my point is, Dat did. You can't deny it. And Reuben is a whole lot more like Dat than like you and Charlie."

Eve started to say something but then stopped. Finally she said, "But you're going to need a husband. And your baby is going to need a father."

"Jah," Rose said. "And I am hoping Trevor will step up." She held out her hand, changing her mind about calling Trevor. "I guess I better give him a call. He's not going to have a chance to do the right thing until he knows what's going on."

She dialed and then stepped into the kitchen to leave a message. She simply said the test had been positive. "Call me back on

Eve's phone as soon as possible. If I'm already gone, let her know when I can call you back. We need to figure out what to do."

She finished the call and returned to the living room, handing Eve the phone. Then she rested her head on her Aenti's shoulder. Eve patted her shoulder. "Remember, this baby is the consequence of your sin not the punishment. This baby will be a blessing."

Rose nodded. She didn't feel that in her soul, but she knew it was true. In time she hoped she'd feel it, for the Bobbli's sake.

"You can come live with us," Eve said. "You could be Jackson's caregiver. That will give you a break from home and give your Dat and Beth more time together."

"Lila still needs a lot of care."

"Beth will be finished working soon." Eve's voice was so soft and gentle that for a moment Rose almost believed everything would work out.

"I'll talk to Dat about all of this and let you know," Rose finally said. But first she'd practice on Reuben. She might be Dat's biological child and have his unconditional love, but she was still afraid of him. Even if he had Beth by his side. He'd survived Daniel running around. Simon joining the Army. Lila jilting Reuben.

But she couldn't imagine how he'd survive her being pregnant.

18

Reuben was surprised when Rose drove her buggy through the parking lot and up to the hitching post. He stood at the counter watching her, wondering if he should go out and greet her or wait for her to come inside. He'd only seen her at church since Tim and Beth's wedding. She'd claimed caring for Lila was taking all of her extra time, but he wasn't sure he believed her. He feared something else was going on.

He'd heard through his father that Trevor had left Lancaster County and gone back to Delaware. At least Reuben didn't have to worry about his influence on Rose anymore.

She tied the horse and turned toward the building, her face red from the cold. His heart raced at the sight of her walking toward him, and he stepped through the door of the warehouse, toward her. "Rose," he called out.

She waved, slightly, and started toward him. The wind whipped at her skirt, and he held the door wide, motioning her inside.

Once she was in the building, she undid her black bonnet and swung it from her head.

"Would you like a cup of coffee?" Reuben asked. "I just brewed a pot."

She shook her head and then asked, "Is anyone else here?"

"No, it's a slow day." Business had been down, and Tim hadn't been coming in for the last couple of weeks.

Rose glanced around, as if making sure.

"What's the matter?" Reuben asked.

"I have a confession to make," she said. "I need to speak with my father and your father too, but first I wanted to tell you. I didn't want you to hear it from anyone else."

His hands and feet grew cold and his face warm, all at the same time. He didn't want to hear a confession, not from Rose.

By the devastated look on her face and then the motion of her hand across her cape, he was certain she was pregnant. Tears filled her eyes.

"Whose is it?" he asked. For a moment he thought maybe he was wrong and was ashamed that he could be so cruel. But when she bowed her head, he knew he'd guessed correctly.

"Is it Trevor's?"

She nodded.

He braced himself against the counter. "Why?"

"It's the stupidest thing I've ever done. It just . . . happened."

He doubted that was true. It had been impossible to miss the way she and Trevor had looked at each other—both at the barn raising and that night in the little house. Those were just the times he'd witnessed what passed between the two of them. It hadn't just happened.

But maybe Trevor had forced her. "Have you spoken with anyone else about this?"

"Eve."

"Did she ask you about . . . what happened?" It wouldn't be proper for him to bring it up.

"Jah," Rose said, her face growing even redder. "It wasn't like that. Honest."

For a minute Reuben felt it would be easier on him if she had been forced, but then he felt ashamed for thinking that way. That meant Rose would have been abused. He didn't want that.

He had loved her. He had trusted her. He had wanted to marry her. His throat burned as he spoke. "Does Trevor know about the baby?"

"I told him I suspected. . . . And then I left him a message, but I haven't heard back."

"Did you keep seeing him up until the time he left?" Reuben asked.

"No, not at all . . . after . . . after what happened. But I did see him the day before he left."

"To tell him?"

She nodded.

"What do you plan to do now?"

She shrugged. "Tell my Dat. And your Dat. Confess before the congregation."

"And then?"

She looked away from him and whispered, "I don't know."

"What about Trevor?"

She shrugged again.

"Would you follow him to Delaware? To his home?"

She met his gaze. "I have no idea what I'll do. I won't know until I have a chance to talk with him."

He nodded then. That was all he could ask of her.

"I really am sorry," she said.

He nodded. Of course she was. Her sin had found her out.

"Please forgive me," she said.

He nodded. He had no choice but to forgive her, although

that didn't mean he wouldn't feel the pain of what she'd done. For a long time. Maybe forever. But she didn't owe him a debt, and he wouldn't hold it over her.

"Do you need anything from me?" Reuben finally asked. "I could go with you to tell your Dat—and my Dat too."

Rose shook her head. "That's too much."

He didn't want her to have to go alone. "I'll go if it would help."

"It would . . ." Her voice trailed off as if she wasn't sure of what she'd just said.

"I can come over right after supper. Then we can go from your place to my Dat's."

"Denki," Rose said. "I appreciate it."

⌣⌒⌒⌒⌣

After she left, Reuben flipped the sign to Closed and shuffled over to his house, feeling like an old man. He'd been burned twice by the Lehman girls, but this hurt far worse than the first time. He needed something to numb the pain, so he veered off to the side yard, picked up his axe, and began splitting wood. He did that for the next hour. In that time, not one customer stopped by. After he'd finished, sweaty and tired, he took the wood into the house, load by load, filling the box by the stove. Then he went to the warehouse and finished up the accounts for the day.

Next, he washed up, made himself a sandwich for his supper, and ate it standing at the counter. Perhaps his old house would never have the touch of a wife or the laughter of children in it again.

A half hour later, the smell of coffee greeted Reuben as Tim welcomed him into the warmth of the kitchen. A peach cream pie, the sauce still bubbling, sat in the middle of the table, and Rose and Beth were wiping the last of the supper dishes.

Rose gave him a little wave, followed by a pained look. Then she bent down to put a frying pan in the drawer under the stove. Reuben turned away, not wanting to hurt himself more by watching her.

"What brings you here?" Tim slapped Reuben on the back. Beth smiled at him as she hung her towel.

Tim and Beth both seemed so happy. He hated to think of the disappointment they would soon feel.

Before Reuben could answer, Beth asked, "How about a cup of decaf? And some pie. Rose made it."

"Denki," Reuben answered. "I'll take you up on both the decaf and the pie."

In no time they were settled around the table. Reuben could make out Trudy's voice in the living room and every once in a while Lila's soft murmur.

"So what does bring you out tonight?" Tim grinned, first at Reuben and then at Rose. "Are we to have another wedding in the family soon?"

"Ach, Dat," Rose said. "It's not that. I'm afraid I have news that won't make you very happy."

"Oh . . ." Tim's face fell.

Rose tried to speak again, but no words came out. Reuben wrapped his hands around his mug of coffee.

Gently, Beth asked, "Does this have to do with the two of you?"

"It has to do with me," Rose answered. "Reuben is just here to support me."

Tim's eyes narrowed. "What's going on?"

"I'm going to have a Bobbli," Rose said.

Tim exhaled, as if the air had been kicked out of him. "And the father isn't Reuben?"

Rose shook her head. Reuben felt as if he couldn't move.

He was doing nothing to support Rose, except sitting beside her, paralyzed.

"Who is the father?" Tim's voice grew louder. "Not that Englisch boy who was hanging around here, I hope."

Beth put her hand on Tim's shoulder. For a moment Reuben thought he might shrug it off. But he didn't. Instead he reached up with his hand and covered hers.

"Rose?" Tim said, this time quietly.

"Jah, that's right," she answered. "Trevor is the father."

"Does he know?"

Reuben followed Rose's eyes toward the archway to the living room. Lila stood there, leaning on her crutches. "I left him a message." Rose pulled her eyes away from her sister.

"But you haven't heard back from him?" Tim asked.

Rose shook her head.

Tim exhaled again. "I wish you hadn't told him."

"Why?" Rose sputtered.

"He might want parental rights. Shared custody. That sort of thing. It might make things more difficult, in the long run." Tim tugged on his beard. "We can pray he doesn't contact you. That might be best for all involved."

Reuben couldn't help but notice the frown on Lila's face. And then the confusion on Rose's.

"Trust me, Rose," Tim said.

Now Tim was looking at Reuben. "I'm guessing you're here because you plan to stand by Rose."

Reuben cleared his throat, aiming to choose his words carefully. "I want to support her, jah. As far as standing by her . . . what exactly do you mean?"

"Going through with your commitment to her."

Reuben's mouth went dry. Tim had married Lila and Daniel's mother—and he wasn't their biological father. But Reuben couldn't imagine that Rose actually wanted him, not after being with Trevor, and if Trevor called her back or returned to Lancaster County, Reuben wouldn't have a chance.

"Dat . . ." Rose said.

Tim leaned forward, away from Beth's steady hand. "Reuben, why else would you be here?"

"Because he's kind," Rose said. "I don't want him to sacrifice for me."

Tim's eyes narrowed. "I'd like to hear what Reuben has to say."

"Dat," Rose said. "We haven't talked—"

"What do you have to say, son?"

Son. Everyone knew Tim cared for Reuben as much as he did his own sons. And Reuben cared for Tim the way he did his own father. In many ways, he understood Tim better than he did his own father.

Reuben glanced at Rose. She frowned.

Finally Reuben said, "To be honest, I don't know what I plan to do. I think there's time to figure that out." Then he turned to Rose and said, "Are you ready to go speak with my Dat?"

Beth, her expression tense, stood. "How about some more coffee first?"

Tim pushed back his chair. "I think we're done with dessert." He fixed his gaze on Rose. "I'll take you over to Gideon's. You should have your Dat with you at a time like this." Tim didn't look at Reuben.

Beth stopped in the middle of the kitchen and turned back toward her husband. "Tim . . ."

"I know what I'm doing," Tim said. "Let's go, Rose."

Beth didn't budge.

Reuben stayed put as well while Rose whispered "Denki" to him and then stood. Tim led the way to the back porch. Rose followed. A moment later the back door slammed.

Beth turned toward Reuben. "I'm so sorry," she said. "Are you all right?"

Reuben couldn't reply, but tears stung his eyes—as Lila's crutch hit the floor.

~~~~~

Fifteen minutes later, Reuben hurried to the Lehman barn and called Shani Beck. Lila had made him wait until Tim and Rose left before calling. The phone rang and rang, and he was just about ready to hang up when Joel answered. Shani was over at Zane's little house.

"Could you tell her Lila fell?" Reuben asked. "She says she's fine, but Beth wants Shani to come take a look at her."

"I'll go get her," Joel said. "And Zane too."

"Or I could go tell them," Reuben said, wondering how hard it was for Joel to get around with his cane in the dark.

"No, stay there. I'll go get them."

Reuben thanked Joel, hung up the phone, and leaned against the wall of Tim's office. How many times had he been overwhelmed by the chaos of the Lehman family? How many times had he felt the need to distance himself? And yet he'd loved Lila. And he had loved Rose too. *Had?* Was his love gone, just like that?

Reuben was tempted to go on home. Shani and Zane were on their way. There was no reason to stay. He sighed and lingered longer even though he needed to go in and tell Beth and Lila good-bye. And Trudy too. He wasn't sure if she was upset solely because Lila had fallen or if she'd overheard the conversation, but she was out of sorts. Poor girl. She'd gone through so much in her short life.

Finally Reuben slipped through the office door, out into the barn. Maybe in time he'd come to care for Rose in the same sisterly way he did for Lila now. He cared for their Dat too. He never had to guess what he was thinking, and he always worked hard, harder than anyone else Reuben knew. Tim and Reuben did have a lot in common as far as their personalities—and they'd always gotten along well—although Tim clearly wasn't pleased with Reuben now.

He left the warmth of the barn for the cold night. Stars glimmered overhead, and a nearly full moon rose above the poplar trees. He stepped into the driveway, staring at the sky, mourning what he'd lost. A wife. A family. In-laws.

He stood longer than he'd meant to, until headlights turned toward him. Shani's van, most likely. He hurried toward the house, but Zane beat him to the back door. Reuben waited on the top step for Shani and opened the door for her.

"Thank you for letting us know," she said.

By the time they reached the living room, Zane was kneeling on the floor beside Lila, who reclined on the sofa. Beth hovered at the end of the sofa, and Trudy sat in Tim's chair, staring at her sister.

Shani said hello and then asked, "Did you twist anything when you fell?"

"I don't think so," Lila said.

Shani stepped closer and asked her to move each foot and then each leg. She was able. Then she had her sit and then stand, pushing up with one crutch.

"Hand her the other crutch," Shani said to Zane.

"Mom," he replied. "Don't push her."

"No, it's best to get up and move around."

Zane handed Lila the crutch, and she took a couple of steps.

"I think you're okay," Shani said. "Take some ibuprofen. Keep moving. If you're worse in the morning, call the doctor."

Beth thanked Shani. She simply nodded, said, "Of course," and gave Lila a hug and then Trudy one too.

She turned to Zane. "I'm going to get home so I can read Adam a bedtime story. Want to come with me?"

"I'll be by later," Zane said.

As Beth walked with Shani to the back door, Lila told Trudy she needed to get her pajamas on.

"Is Rose really going to have a Bobbli?" Trudy asked.

Zane spun toward Lila. "What?"

"Jah," Lila said. Then she turned to Trudy. "Go get ready for bed, and then either Beth or I will come talk with you. And plan to go to school tomorrow. You haven't had a fever today, and your cough is much better."

Trudy nodded, as compliant as ever. After she left the room, Zane asked, "What's going on?" This time looking at Reuben.

"It's not what you think." Lila collapsed into her father's chair.

"I should get going," Reuben said.

"No, please stay," Lila responded.

Reuben couldn't guess why Lila wanted him to. Beth stepped from the kitchen to the hallway and then into the girls' room.

When the door clicked shut, Zane glanced from Lila to Reuben and then asked, "Who's the father?"

Lila answered, "Trevor."

Zane groaned and turned toward Reuben, his expression pained. But he didn't say anything.

There were all sorts of things Reuben wanted Zane to say. That he was sorry that he hadn't watched his friend better. That Rose getting pregnant was the culmination of all the years of influence the Beck family had on the Lehmans. Jah, there were all sorts of things Reuben wished Zane would say.

Instead he said, "I don't understand. Trevor said he wouldn't pursue Rose, not even as a friend."

"Apparently they were sneaking around," Lila said. "Which makes sense now. There were times Rose left the little house after she thought I was asleep. I thought Trevor was over at Eve and Charlie's though, so I assumed she was seeing Reuben. Maybe." Lila shook her head. "Actually things were pretty foggy for me."

Reuben couldn't hold Lila accountable for what Rose had done. And, as much as he wanted to, he couldn't hold Zane directly accountable for Trevor either. It sounded as if he'd tried to address what he saw as a potential situation. But the decade-long relationship between the two families really was the foundation for Trevor getting to know Rose at all.

Zane raked his fingers through his hair. "What's going to happen now?"

"She's with Dat over at Gideon's," Lila said. "Then she'll have to confess to the church. She'll be banned, then reinstated. Then she'll have the Bobbli and . . ." Lila's voice trailed off.

Reuben guessed they both expected him to say something, but he had no idea what.

Lila shifted her gaze to Zane. "Did Trevor say anything about Rose?"

"No," Zane answered. "Not in particular anyway. Not about them." He dragged his hand over his face. "He told me he'd leave her alone, and foolishly, I believed him." Zane shook his head. "There was that morning when we were going to the doctor. That seemed a little odd. And before he left for home, Rose stopped by the little house. At least I think she did. I saw her heading toward the field that day." Zane paused for a moment as if thinking and then asked, "What was Trevor's response to the news?"

"Rose left a message for him," Lila said, "but he hasn't gotten back to her."

Zane grimaced. "One of the reasons he went back home was because of his girlfriend."

It was Lila's turn to groan.

Reuben turned toward Zane. "Do you know for sure that he got back together with his girlfriend?"

"No."

"Then I think we should wait to tell Rose." Reuben doubted

Trevor was out of the picture for good. He'd seen the way the Englischer looked at Rose. He'd be back.

"All right, but I don't think it's best for Trevor to be in the picture." Zane turned toward Reuben. "He's not reliable. Not good husband or father material. Rose would end up leaving the church, possibly moving to Delaware. It would be horrible for her, of all people, to be so far from home."

Lila shook her head. "If Trevor will take responsibility for this Bobbli, I think that would be best."

"He can barely take responsibility for himself. Besides," Zane said, "you weren't raised by your biological father. Things turned out all right."

She wrinkled her nose, glanced toward the hall, and then said in a low voice, "Jah, perhaps so . . ."

"Your Dat loves you," Zane said.

Lila sighed. "Of course he does, but would he have ever done for me what he did for Rose tonight? Going over to Gideon's like that?" She shook her head. "No, I would have been on my own."

Zane reached for her hand. "I don't think that's true. I think he would have." When Lila didn't respond, Zane glanced Reuben's way again. "You're awfully quiet."

Reuben just nodded. He couldn't get past Lila not feeling as loved as Tim's biological children or the fact that Rose saw the situation in the same light. He'd always admired what a good father Tim had been to Daniel and Lila. True, he seemed to have higher expectations for them, but they were the oldest. That wasn't uncommon. He knew his parents had been more lenient with him than they'd been with his older brothers. But perhaps, for as much time as he spent with the Lehman family, he didn't know them as well as he thought.

If Tim Lehman hadn't loved Daniel and Lila like he did his other children, then Reuben was pretty sure he'd never love Trevor Anderson's Bobbli as his own. He felt too much anger.

Too much betrayal. Tim had the advantage of not being betrayed by Abra. And as far as he knew, Tim never met Lila and Daniel's biological father, not even later. Reuben could never get the image of the way Trevor looked at Rose out of his head. Nor the way Trevor humiliated him at the barn raising.

"I'm going to look for my biological father," Lila announced.

"Babe," Zane said. "Why?"

"I need to know who he is. I know his name, and I'll ask Eve if she has any more information. I want to know what I missed."

Stunned, Reuben managed to say, "But that'll hurt your Dat."

"I'm not doing it to hurt him," Lila answered. "I'm doing it because I've wanted to for years. And now that it seems I might not be able to have children—" Her voice caught.

Reuben tried not to react but guessed the accident had done some sort of damage.

"I want even more to know the person who's always been missing from my life."

"Babe," Zane said again. Reuben's heart fluttered at the way Zane talked to Lila. His love for her was so obvious, in a way Reuben—as an Amish man—wasn't accustomed to witnessing. Zane took Lila's hand. "We don't know about the Bobbli part," he said. "For sure."

She swiped at a tear. "It doesn't matter. I still want to find my father."

Reuben cleared his throat, feeling uncomfortable. He'd stayed too long. "I need to get going."

Zane stood and shook Reuben's hand. "I'm sorry," he said. "Really."

Reuben swallowed hard and said, "It's not your fault." It was Rose's fault. And Trevor's. "I'll let myself out."

Zane followed him to the kitchen. Reuben stopped a moment and faced him. Zane took a step backward.

"Don't worry about all of this," Reuben said. "In time, it will work out. Like all things do." He believed that—he just couldn't feel it right now. He continued on to the mud porch, grabbed his overcoat, and hurried out the back door. Thankfully Zane didn't follow him. Otherwise he would have seen him swiping at his eyes as he jogged toward his buggy.

It wasn't as if he was fleeing a burning building. It was more like he was fleeing the charred remains of the life he'd hoped to have. First with Lila. Then with Rose.

He was out of options.

19

The next morning Lila got out of bed not long after Rose, took her turn in the bathroom, and then managed to dress by herself. She was sore from her fall the night before and decided to take a pain pill, even though she hadn't had one since the morning of her ob-gyn appointment. But the bottle wasn't where it belonged. She looked through all the cupboards but didn't find it anywhere. Perhaps Rose had put the bottle away somewhere different.

Lila woke Trudy and told her she needed to get dressed. "Rose is helping Dat with the milking, so you need to feed the chickens." Trudy yawned and snuggled under her quilt for another minute but then slipped out of bed and dressed quickly. She wasn't one to chat much in the morning, which was fine with Lila. She hoped Beth had talked with her about Rose the night before because, honestly, Lila wasn't sure what to tell her.

As Lila pinned her Kapp in place, instead of the scarf she'd been wearing for the last few weeks except when she left the house, she realized how focused she'd been on herself. True, right after the accident she had to concentrate on her healing. She had no energy for anything else. But it was time for her to start putting others before herself again.

She crutched her way to the kitchen, cheered by the thought of a mug of coffee. As she poured, Beth stepped into the kitchen, ready for the day. "My, you're up early," she said. She seemed a little too chipper considering what was going on in the family. "What shall we fix for breakfast?"

Lila shrugged. She wasn't sure what was on hand.

"How about a haystack?"

Just the thought of it made Lila's mouth water—for the first time in months. Biscuits on the bottom, diced ham, eggs, cheese, and then gravy. Dat would be in heaven.

"Sounds good," Lila said. "I can chop the ham and grate the cheese."

"Great idea," Beth said. In no time she had Lila set up at the table while she mixed up the biscuits.

"Have you seen my bottle of pills? They were in the cupboard next to the refrigerator."

"No," Beth said, opening up the cupboard. "I don't know where else they would be."

"I'll ask Rose," Lila said.

Trudy came in, gave Beth a hug, and headed to the bathroom to wash.

Beth hummed "Amazing Grace" as she cooked. Perhaps Dat had stoked the fire more than usual, or perhaps it was Beth's goodness that warmed the house. She popped the biscuits into the oven and then traipsed over to the refrigerator, pulling out the gravy from the night before. She dumped it into a pan and lit the burner. Then she opened the carton of eggs on the counter.

"Life was so easy for you before," Lila said. "You probably ate an apple and cheese for breakfast."

Beth stopped for a moment. "A banana and peanut butter was actually my favorite."

Lila shook her head. "Try feeding that to Dat."

Beth smiled back and then said, "I'm so thankful I'll never eat breakfast by myself again, Lord willing." She turned back to cooking the eggs. "It's a privilege to be part of a family again."

Family. Tears filled Lila's eyes. She was grateful for their family too. Yet she longed for something more, for a deeper connection. Trudy interrupted Lila's thoughts, asking Beth if she should go help Dat and Rose.

"No," Beth said. "Please set the table."

As Trudy worked, she asked, "Will Rose keep living here?"

Beth turned toward her. "What do you mean?"

Trudy positioned Dat's plate. "Well, since Trevor is the father of her Bobbli, shouldn't she marry him?"

"Possibly not," Beth said. "There are a lot of issues to take into account. Remember how we talked in class about gathering all the evidence before making a decision? Rose needs to do that."

Lila's heart contracted. None of it felt fair. She had a man who loved her, a house . . . and a body that might not be able to get pregnant, that wouldn't be able to carry a Bobbli in a normal way.

Rose had the Bobbli but no husband or home.

<hr />

Dat was thrilled with breakfast. In light of the news from the night before, everyone was on their best behavior, until Rose turned to Dat and said, "I will take Eve up on her offer to be Jackson's caregiver. That will be better for everyone."

Dat pushed back in his chair. "Could we discuss this later?"

"Sure," Rose said, "but I'm going to go over and talk with Eve this afternoon."

After breakfast, Dat drove Beth and Trudy to school and Rose started to clean up. Lila sat at the table and asked, "How did things go last night over at Gideon's?"

"Fine," Rose answered.

"What did he say?"

"That I'll need to confess in front of the congregation. Then be under the *Bann*. The usual stuff." Rose shrugged.

It was all expected. "Did he say anything about Reuben?"

Rose shook her head and started washing the dishes.

An hour later the physical therapist arrived. Day by day, all of it was getting easier for Lila. But still, by the time the woman left, Lila was exhausted.

❧

When Dat came in for dinner—pork loin with applesauce—he told Rose that he had a message that Reuben had a big delivery to make and he needed Dat to work at the lumberyard. Then he said, "I'll need you to pick up Beth and Trudy."

"All right," Rose said. "I'll do it after I go by Eve's."

Dat shook his head. "I wish you wouldn't do that."

Rose shrugged.

Lila watched the two. Something was changing in both of them. Beth had definitely mellowed Dat, but it was more than that. He seemed more settled as a parent. Much more than he had been with Daniel's Rumschpringe, Simon joining the Army, or with her decision not to court Reuben.

But she knew Rose's news was still hard on Dat. He pushed back his chair, thanked Rose for dinner, and left for the lumberyard. He didn't tell Lila good-bye.

While Rose scrubbed the dishes, Lila said, "I'll go with you. I want to talk to Eve too."

"All right," Rose answered, but she didn't ask about what and Lila didn't offer her any information.

251

Lila was still in pain though. "Have you seen my meds? They were in the kitchen cupboard."

Rose sighed. "Not this again. When was the last time you saw them?"

"That last doctor's appointment."

Rose shook her head. "I haven't seen them."

Lila searched the bathroom and, not finding the bottle, took two ibuprofen.

They arrived at Eve's just after four. She'd just gotten home from her teaching job and hadn't taken Jackson's coat off of him yet. Rose took the baby from her and pulled his arms out from each sleeve, and then bounced him gently while Eve put her book bag away and took off her coat. She wore pants and a cardigan over a long-sleeved cotton shirt. It was still hard for Lila, even though it had been over ten years, to get used to her Aenti dressing Englisch.

Lila managed to plant herself on the sofa. Eve offered them tea, but first Lila and then Rose declined. "Sit down," Lila said. "We both want to talk with you."

"All right," Eve said, a concerned look on her face. She sat on the other end of the sofa.

"You go first," Lila said to Rose.

Rose turned toward Eve as she patted the baby's back. "I'd like to be Jackson's caregiver and live here. I think it would be good for me—I'd get more experience with an infant, more than just being a mother's helper. And I think it would be good for Dat and Beth too—even Trudy—not to have me around." Her eyes grew a little misty, but her voice was strong.

"Rose," Lila said. "That's not how anyone feels."

"I know," Rose said. "Dat's responded much better than I expected, but it would be easier for them. Dat and Beth don't deserve to have to deal with me right now."

Eve exhaled. "I would be glad to have you care for Jackson."

Rose nodded.

"Have you spoken with Trevor?" Eve asked.

Rose shook her head. "He never returned my call."

"Do you want Charlie to call him?"

Rose shook her head again. "No. I want to let it be, for now."

"All right," Eve said.

When neither said any more, Lila cleared her throat. "Speaking of birth fathers."

Rose rolled her eyes. Lila smiled. That was more like the sister she knew.

"Yes," Eve said.

"I'd like to find mine, and I wondered if you have any more information on him."

Eve stood. "Did you speak with your Dat about this?"

"I'm an adult. I don't need his permission." Lila felt a little foolish. She was totally dependent on her father.

"Have you thought it through? What if you can't find him? Or what if he doesn't want to meet? What if he does agree to meet, and you don't like him?"

"Why?" Lila asked. "Was he not very likable?"

Eve smiled. "No, that's not it. He was very likable. But that was a long time ago, and I honestly didn't know him very well."

Lila shrugged. "At least I'd know who he is."

Eve hesitated. Finally she said, "I really don't know any more than that his name is Butch Wilson. And that he was from Virginia."

"Do you know what city?"

Eve shook her head.

"How old do you think he was? You know. Back then."

"Twenty. Maybe. Not more than twenty-one."

"So he'd be forty-three or so?"

Eve nodded.

Lila's mother would only be forty if she'd lived.

Eve leaned forward a little. "How do you plan to find him?"

"I'll ask Shani if I can use her computer."

"Use mine," Eve said. "Now, if you want to."

"Really?" Lila struggled to her feet but before she could make her way around the coffee table, Rose cleared her throat.

"We need to get going. Remember? Dat asked us to pick up Beth and Trudy."

"Oh, that's right," Lila said, disappointed. "But we still have some time. Could you just give me a few minutes?" It would be a while until she'd have much time over at Shani's.

Rose nodded, but she didn't look happy.

"Sit back down," Eve said. "I'll bring you my laptop."

It didn't take long, with Eve's help, and there were only eight Butch Wilsons listed in all of Virginia.

"How will you call the numbers?" Eve asked. "You probably don't want them leaving messages on your Dat's machine."

Probably not. She'd need to ask Shani. "Do you have a piece of paper and pen? I'll write down the numbers and call later."

Eve produced both. As Lila recorded the numbers, Eve told Rose she should move in and start her caretaking at the beginning of the new year, once Beth had quit her teaching job.

Lila felt a pang of loss. Rose would soon be gone. Life was constantly changing.

⁓

Lila sat in the buggy, a wool blanket wrapped around her legs, and stared out the window as Rose drove toward the school. A ribbon of fog hung low across the field. They passed two boys wearing black coats and straw hats racing their scooters along the narrow shoulder. Then a farmer dragging his field. Vapor curled up from the noses of his workhorses. As they neared the

254

site of the accident, Lila began to tense. She hadn't been back since that fateful day.

"Is that Reuben's wagon?" Rose asked.

Lila shifted her eyes from the side window to the windshield. Someone had stopped in the road. Most likely Reuben.

"What in the world is he doing?" Rose slowed the wagon. "Would it be rude not to stop and say hello?"

"No, I think it would be fine to keep going." Lila craned her neck. It was definitely Reuben's wagon—and he was standing on the right-hand side. After last night, he probably wouldn't want to see them anyway.

He started to wave and then motioned for them to stop. Rose groaned and slowed the buggy. Reuben wore his work coat and leather gloves.

"Hey!" he called out. Maybe he had an axle break or something.

"You'd better stop," Lila said.

Rose pulled the buggy behind the wagon.

"No," Lila said, glancing over her shoulder and making sure there wasn't anyone behind them. "Pull over farther."

Reuben came around to Lila's door and opened it once the buggy stopped. "Zane and I were talking about your accident a while back—about the driver claiming Billie veered off into the road. I mentioned his concerns to the sheriff, but I've been thinking about it more."

Lila wrinkled her nose.

"Billie wasn't hit, right, by the SUV?"

"No," Lila said. "The impact pushed him into the ditch, on top of me, but the SUV didn't hit him."

"Can you come look at what I've re-created?"

Lila glanced at Rose. She wasn't sure if she had the energy.

"I'll help you get down." Rose set the brake and then hurried around the buggy.

Reuben nodded to Rose, and he didn't seem upset. It was as if the night before hadn't happened.

Once Lila was safely on the ground, her crutches in place, she asked Reuben, "Where are you delivering the lumber?"

"Just past the school," he said, pointing.

Reuben grasped a tape measure in his hands as he asked Lila, "Where did you and Billie end up?"

"In the creek," she said. "I lost consciousness, but I remember coming to. I could see the maple there—some of the leaves were still green but some were turning red. It was really beautiful." Now the branches were completely bare.

"You went over the top of Billie, right?"

"Jah," Lila said. "The impact launched me off the bench and through the windshield, on to Billie. By the time we reached the ditch, I must have gone over the top of him and then he landed on me."

"But he wasn't hit?"

Lila shook her head. "No. Just the back of the buggy was." She leaned against the crutch. "What are you thinking?"

"That if Billie had veered out in front of the SUV, you would have ended up in the middle of the road, not the creek."

"But wouldn't the police have figured that out?"

Reuben shrugged. "I think once the driver said that the horse had stepped in front of him, that's what the police officer had in mind and that's what got written down in the report."

"Oh." It was kind of Reuben to research the accident on her behalf, but she doubted the police would believe him. As they walked back toward the buggy, she fell behind Rose. Reuben stayed at Lila's side. He seemed so calm. Perhaps he hadn't cared as much for Rose as she thought he had.

"You seem to be doing all right," she said quietly.

He nodded but when she glanced toward him his eyes were watery. Perhaps it was the cold air. Or the wind.

Rose helped her back up into the buggy, and they both told Reuben good-bye. Then he shut the door firmly, pressing his hand against it as he did.

Lila waved, a lump forming in her throat.

"That was awkward," Rose said.

Lila swallowed, not sure what to say. Finally she said, "He's a good man."

Rose's voice wavered as she said, "I know."

Lila turned her attention toward her sister. Rose swiped a tear away. Surprised, Lila placed her hand on her sister's arm. "What are you feeling?"

"Regret. Shame. Disappointment in myself for what I've done. For hurting Reuben. For changing the entire course of my life."

It wasn't like Rose to feel shame. Lila inhaled and kept holding on to Rose. "Do you love him?"

Rose pressed her lips together. Finally she turned toward Lila. "I thought I did—but obviously I didn't or I wouldn't have treated him the way I did. In the midst of our time in the barn, I told myself I loved Trevor, until . . . Then it was so clear that I didn't, and that he didn't love me either."

Reuben's wagon began to roll forward.

Rose watched it go but didn't release the brake. "I guess I'm not sure what love is at this point. I respect Reuben. And I admire him even more for how he's dealing with this."

Lila continued to hold on to her sister's arm until a vehicle passing them on the left startled her. It was a black SUV. It passed Reuben's wagon too and then turned right. "Would you follow it?" Lila asked, wondering if the man who hit her lived close by. Was he preparing to turn when he plowed into the back of her buggy?

Rose complied, but by the time they turned, the vehicle was out of sight. Perhaps it had turned into the driveway of one of the three houses along the lane.

"Denki," Lila said. "There's no reason to keep going."

"I'll just go as far as the last house. Perhaps we'll see the SUV in one of the driveways."

"Chances are it's not the same SUV that hit me."

"It could be though," Rose said. "It's worth investigating."

The vehicle was parked in the driveway of the second house. No one was in sight, but there was a pink bike propped up against the garage and a green turtle sandbox with a missing eye in the yard.

"Want me to go knock on the door and ask?"

"No." But Lila appreciated Rose's courage. She'd talk to Zane about it. "Let's go get Beth and Trudy. They probably wonder what's taking us so long." They'd have to light the lantern when they got to the school. Dusk was already falling and the caution sign on the back of the buggy wouldn't be enough. Lila shivered, anxious to get home.

When they reached the school, Beth and Trudy stood on the porch waiting for them, holding hands. Jah, everything was changing. Trudy wouldn't need Lila the way she had all these years. It was a blessing, but it didn't feel that way to Lila. She wasn't sure what her role in her family was anymore. She had little to offer right now. To her family and to Zane.

20

Zane stood against the half wall of concrete blocks on the construction site, waiting for Mom to pick him up. Hopefully they'd get to the lawyer's office before it closed. His boss waved as he headed to his truck. "Need a ride?"

Zane shook his head. "Thanks anyway." He kicked against the blocks to knock the snow and mud from his boots, buttoned his coat, and clapped his gloved hands together. Dusk fell early now that winter had arrived.

Mom's van came around the corner. He could have called someone else for a ride—like most Amish, he had several drivers he could rely on—but it was easier to ask Mom. As she pulled up beside him, Adam climbed into the back seat, and Zane hopped into the front. He couldn't help but feel like a kid again. Sometimes those years of driving seemed like a dream.

He had to admit his pickup was what he missed the most, more than a phone, more than the Internet, more than continuing his education. And it wasn't just the act of driving. It was not being dependent on someone else.

"What time is your appointment?" Mom asked.

"I told him I couldn't get there until five fifteen or so."

"How long will it take?"

"Probably not long. Maybe a half hour. I'll get a ride home with Dad." He knew his joining the Amish hadn't been easy on his parents. He'd expected his father, especially, to give him grief about his decision. But he hadn't. Zane's situation was definitely an easier transition than that of others who'd joined the Amish—and he only knew of a few—but still it was a big change.

Traffic slowed as they reached Lancaster, but then Mom turned onto a side street and zigzagged her way through town, probably a route she took when she was running late to the hospital. She stopped across the street from the center.

"Thanks," Zane said, jumping down. He couldn't imagine how he would have survived the last two months without his parents. He stopped on the top step of the old brick building and checked his boots for mud again. They weren't bad. He pushed open the heavy wooden door, let it swing shut behind him, and hurried up the narrow staircase. It turned out Brad was still with another client. Zane sat down and waited, thumbing through a news magazine as he did. He read through the current events— more fighting in the Middle East, both in Iraq and Syria. He said a prayer for Simon. Thankfully Casey was back in Texas.

Then he flipped to the back of the magazine to the movie reviews. He hadn't heard of any of them. He tuned out when the Englisch guys at work talked about what they'd seen over the weekend. It didn't interest Zane anymore. He flipped back to the book reviews—he hadn't heard of any of them either. He hadn't been to the library since Lila's accident, and probably wouldn't be any time soon. He doubted he'd get back to volunteering at the fire station for a while either. He knew Charlie understood.

The truth was, everything had changed because of Lila's accident. He wondered if the man who hit her had any idea what the consequences had been.

A few minutes later, a middle-aged woman with red eyes came through the waiting room and went out the door. Zane didn't want to speculate what her worries might be. Everyone had a sad story. Usually more than one. He knew that.

Zane still hadn't said anything to Tim—or Gideon—about talking with the lawyer. He figured they both had plenty to deal with right now. He'd broach the subject soon though.

A few minutes later Brad appeared. "Come on back," he said.

Zane followed him and sat down. The shades over the windows were up, showing the dark sky behind them. Zane took off his gloves and wiggled out of his coat.

Brad smiled. "I still can't get used to you dressed that way."

Zane nodded. "It's a little hard for me at times too." He hoped his voice sounded light and jokey, but he doubted it.

"How is Lila?" Brad asked.

"Good. She's getting around on crutches. Doing therapy. She's moving along."

"Anything new from the doctor?"

Zane shook his head.

Brad opened a file and put on his reading glasses. "The sheriff reopened the case. The new investigation shows that it's unlikely, based on where the buggy ended up, that the horse veered to the left."

"Great." Reuben had told Zane at church on Sunday that he'd done some measurements, ran some numbers, and then talked with the sheriff again. "Lila found out something that might help too." He told Brad about the SUV that appeared to be the same type that hit Lila being down the next road, to the right, from the accident. "Perhaps the driver was getting ready to turn right and then got distracted."

"Or maybe he was on a call. Or texting." Brad sighed. "I'll ask for his phone records."

"Good idea," Zane said. "Can you get his address? Just in case it's the same SUV?"

Brad flipped a few pages back in the file. "What road did you say it was?"

"Derry Road."

Brad looked up. "Bingo." He twirled his pen around his finger.

"Maybe he'd just moved there, from Ephrata." That was the address listed before.

"Probably," Brad said. "This is coming together. If the driver hadn't told 9-1-1 and others at the accident scene that the horse had pulled in front of him, none of this would have happened. He'd told enough people that they were repeating it by the time the police arrived."

Zane asked, "So the insurance company will go ahead and pay the medical bills?"

Brad wrinkled his nose. "I wish it were that easy. The insurance company will open a new investigation. Mr. Addison will be interviewed again and so will Lila."

"Then what?"

"Depending on what they find, we may be able to arbitrate. Normally, both parties would have insurance companies representing them. In this case, Lila could have me. If she chooses."

"But if she doesn't win, then we'd need to pay you, right?"

Brad shook his head. "Not necessarily. Let's see what the other investigator comes up with and go from there. I won't do anything you'd have to pay me for without running it by you and Lila first."

"She won't like any of this. Another investigation. Negotiating. Any of it."

"It's part of life." Brad tapped his desk with the pencil. "The investigation won't be a big deal. She'll be questioned at home. If it goes to trial, it will be at the courthouse. That might feel like a big deal."

Zane leaned forward. "Trial? Why would it go to trial? The evidence seems solid."

"Well, if the police actually charge the driver with negligence, that will help, but there's no indication they plan to. His insurance can still claim Lila was at fault, if that's what their investigation shows. They might be hoping that her church or fund or whatever will just pay the bills to keep her from having to sue the driver."

"She'd be suing the driver—not the insurance company?"

"Yes," Brad answered. "The insurance company represents the driver."

"But the company would pay, if Lila won?" His heart sank as he asked the question. No one would agree to this. Not Lila. Not Tim. Not Gideon.

"Yes, the company is the one who pays."

Zane thought of Lila's description of the man's home, of the bicycle and sandbox. It sounded as if he had quite a bit of responsibility.

Brad turned back toward Zane. "We'll just take it a step at a time and see what happens. I need to meet Lila soon though—to see if she actually wants me to take her case."

"All right," Zane said. "I'll talk with her." He thanked Brad and said he'd be in touch soon. As he left the office he wiggled back into his coat and then hurried down the stairs and out into the cold. Lila had been so quiet lately. Most likely she was depressed. He didn't blame her, but it was hard to get her to talk about how she felt. She seemed worse in the evening, probably because she was fatigued.

He crossed the street and entered the Veterans Center, taking a deep breath as he hurried down the hall toward Dad's office.

He'd thought becoming Amish would make life less complicated, not more.

⌇⌇

As Dad's pickup came around the curve on Juneberry Lane and the house came into view, it looked like all the lights were on, welcoming them home. Then he noticed the buggy. He squinted in the dark, sure the horse was Billie. Dad parked and Zane jumped down, going over to the horse to say hello. Billie had a blanket on his back and nickered and rubbed his head against Zane's shoulder. Zane scratched his ears and then his neck. He'd been boarding Billie over at the Lehmans' barn as much as possible so that he'd be with the other horses.

"Who brought you over?" he asked. "Rose?" Maybe she had some questions for his mom. She must not have planned to stay long since she hadn't put Billie in the barn.

Dad was already at the front door, opening it, when Zane started up the ramp. "Hi, Rose," Dad said, as Zane caught up with him. She was sitting on the sofa next to the wood stove, staring into the little door that showed the fire.

Zane stepped toward her. "Rose? Are you all right?"

"Oh fine," she said, looking up.

"What are you doing here?"

She nodded toward the kitchen. "Lila's using the phone."

"Oh?"

"Jah. She has a list of Butch Wilsons in Virginia that she's calling."

Dad gave Zane a funny look. "What's going on?"

Zane sighed. "She's trying to contact her birth father."

Dad raised his eyebrows. In a low voice he asked, "Does Tim know about this?"

"I don't think so." Zane turned toward the kitchen.

Lila sat at the table with her crutches propped against the

264

wall. She held the cordless phone to her ear. Then she said, "So sorry to bother you. Thank you for your kindness." She hung up and placed the phone on the table.

"Where did you get the numbers?" Zane asked.

"At Eve's. I used her computer. I found eight Butch Wilsons."

"Any luck?"

She shook her head. "One number has been disconnected. One rang and rang. And I've left two messages so far. That's the first person I spoke with. He sounded old." She smiled. "I hope I didn't confuse him too much."

"You did fine," Mom said from the stove, where she broke spaghetti noodles in half and dropped them in a pot of boiling water.

"I have three more to call, and then Rose will take me back home."

"I'm going to wash up," Zane said. "Don't leave."

She nodded as she dialed the next number.

By the time he returned, she was sitting in the living room on the opposite end of the sofa from Rose, holding on to her crutches.

Zane plopped down beside Lila but turned to Rose and asked quietly, "Did Trevor call you back?"

She shook her head.

He frowned and then said, "Things aren't always what they seem. It might be best if you don't hear from him."

Rose shook her head again but didn't say anything more. Zane wanted to give her a hug, but he feared that would only make things worse for her. He'd failed Rose, and he felt horrible about it.

He turned toward Lila. "I need to talk with you."

"About?"

"All sorts of things. I spoke with the lawyer again."

She wrinkled her nose.

"And other things." He smiled.

"I want to get home." Rose yawned. "I'm really tired."

"I'm pretty tired too," Lila said. "How about tomorrow?"

"All right. How about in the afternoon? I'm working half a day." His company didn't usually work on Saturday, but they were making up hours they'd missed earlier in the week. "We'll go for a ride. We can talk about Christmas—and the other stuff."

She hesitated, and for a moment he wondered if she was done with him. But then she said, "I'd like that."

"Dress warmly," he said.

"I will."

"I'll come by around three."

"See you then." Lila scooted forward on the sofa. Zane stood quickly, helped her to her feet, and handed her the crutches. She positioned them under her arms and made her way toward the door. He went ahead and took her cape from the coat-tree, draping it over her shoulders when she reached him.

Rose slipped her cape over her shoulders too and called out a good-bye.

"Bye," Mom said, stepping to the kitchen doorway, a potholder in her hand. Zane wondered if Rose had said anything to Mom about being pregnant. He hadn't told her, but Rose probably assumed he had.

He walked behind Lila down the ramp and then helped her into the buggy. "You have that intense look on your face," Lila said, looking down at him from the bench. "What's wrong?"

"Nothing," he replied. "I'll see you tomorrow." He shut the door securely.

When he reached the house, Dad, Adam, and Mom all sat at the kitchen table. "I'll get something to eat over at my place," Zane said. "I'll see you tomorrow."

"Wait," Mom said. "I need to talk with you." She and Dad

exchanged a look, but then she followed Zane toward the front door. Both put their coats on and she stepped out onto the porch with him, under the light.

"What's going on?" she asked.

"With?"

"You and Lila. And her looking for her birth father."

Zane didn't know where to start, but he had to go ahead and tell Mom about Rose. Finally he said, "I don't know what has to do with what, not exactly, but Rose is pregnant."

"Oh, no." Mom leaned against the railing.

"Yeah, but it gets worse."

"What do you mean?"

"The father probably isn't who you think."

"Not Reuben?"

"No," Zane said. "It's Trevor."

Mom's face fell. "No."

"Yes."

"How did that happen?" Mom asked. "He said he wouldn't spend time with her."

"Apparently, they were sneaking around when Rose stayed with Lila."

Mom grew pale.

"And even worse," Zane said, "he hasn't returned Rose's message. It seems he's abandoned her and the baby altogether."

"I'm not surprised." Mom crossed her arms. "How is Lila doing with all of this? The timing has to be painful."

Zane blinked quickly. "I know. But I haven't had a chance to really talk with her. I'm not sure how she's doing." He did know that she seemed to be shutting him out more and more. Hopefully the buggy ride tomorrow would give them time to talk things through.

"Give her time," Mom said. "But be persistent. And challenge her not to withdraw. I've seen her do that before, and there's more at stake now. She's stronger than she thinks. She needs to know that."

Zane nodded, but he wasn't sure she'd listen to him.

❧

The next afternoon Zane harnessed Billie to his buggy and then arrived at the Lehmans' back door. Rose answered his knock. He asked how she was doing and she answered, "Fine." But she looked pale. She didn't motion for him to come in. Instead she stayed on the stoop of the back porch and asked, "Have you heard from Trevor?"

Zane shook his head. "Do you want me to call him?"

"No," she answered. "I just wondered if he'd said anything." She stepped aside and motioned him in. "Lila's resting. I'll go tell her you're here."

"Who else is around?" he asked, stopping at the kitchen table.

"No one. Beth took Trudy over to see our grandparents, and Dat's out in the barn." Rose kept heading toward the hall. "I'll wake Lila."

Zane took off his hat and had just sat down at the table when he heard someone at the back door. He stood, expecting Beth and Trudy, but it was Tim.

"So you're taking Lila out for a ride?"

Zane nodded. "I thought some fresh air would be a good idea."

Tim nodded in return, headed to the counter, and lifted the coffeepot off the back of the stove. "There's some left," he said. "Want some coffee?"

"Sure," Zane said, thinking maybe it would take Lila a while to get ready.

Tim started opening cupboards. "I think there are some sticky buns around here too. Beth made them this morning." On the third try, he found them and then dished two onto plates.

He hesitated for a moment, smiled at Zane, and then added another sticky bun to each plate.

He handed them to Zane, grabbed two mugs, filled them, and then met Zane at the table.

The two men ate in silence at first. Tim seemed in a good mood, considering, but Zane couldn't believe the man wasn't upset with him. He thought for a moment that perhaps he should tell him about talking with the lawyer, but then decided not to. There was no reason to put him in a bad mood.

Finally Zane said, "I'm sorry about Rose. . . . I really am."

"Jah," Tim answered, "I know you are."

"I had no idea Trevor and Rose were spending time like that."

"You had a lot going on," Tim said. "Rose and Trevor are the ones who are responsible. Although I'd just as soon he didn't take responsibility."

Zane gave him an inquisitive look, and Tim kept talking.

"I always felt it a blessing that Abra never contacted the father of Lila and Daniel, after . . ." His voice trailed off. He took another bite, chewed and swallowed, and then said, "That way there was never any threat of him coming back, of him ever wanting to have a relationship with the children."

"Would that have been so bad?" Before the words were out of Zane's mouth he regretted saying them.

"Jah," Tim said. "It would have been bad. What if he'd wanted a custody agreement? Where the kids have to go back and forth? Can you imagine that happening with an Englisch family? How confusing that would be? How dangerous?"

Zane understood Tim's reasoning, but he felt Trevor had a right to be involved in his child's life. Plus, he should help support the baby. But he said, "I'm guessing Trevor will stay away. I think he would have called Rose back if he planned to take responsibility."

Tim drained his coffee mug. "You never know what people

will do, believe me." He scooted his chair back. "If Rose hadn't told Trevor, I think Reuben would be more likely to step up—like I did. But who wants the threat of a real father returning?"

Zane bristled at the word "real," especially coming from Tim. But he didn't say anything. He knew, deep down, Tim felt he was Daniel and Lila's real father, even if he didn't know "biological father" was the more accurate term.

Tim stood. "This will work out one way or another. I know Rose plans to go live with Eve and Charlie for a while, and that's fine, but she'll always have a place here, no matter what happens."

Zane nodded. He knew Tim would take care of her and the baby. But Zane still puzzled over the situation. "May I ask you a question?"

Tim smiled. "Depends . . ."

Zane frowned.

"Give it a try," Tim said.

"I thought you'd be more upset than you are. Are you not, because, you know, of what Abra went through back with Lila and Daniel?"

Tim put both hands on the back of a chair for a moment, as if he were giving the question some thought. Then he stood up straight and said, "I'm probably more upset than I'm letting on, but Beth keeps saying things will work out, to not worry. I don't feel so alone anymore. It's easier to trust God, for me, when I have someone encouraging me to do so."

Zane nodded. That's how being with Lila had always made him feel. Until now.

Tim cocked his head. "How's your job going?"

"Fine," Zane answered. "There's been a delay on some permits. We ended up working this morning, which was good. But I haven't been getting as many hours as I'd hoped."

"Oh? Are you looking to pick up some extra hours? I could really use help with the milking, especially once Rose goes to Eve's."

"Denki," Zane said. "I'll help when I can."

Tim nodded. "I won't be able to keep working like this forever. Daniel isn't interested in farming, and Simon won't be coming back. You're the most likely one to take it over." He smiled a little. "Especially when half the land I farm is owned by your family."

Zane hadn't thought much about the logistics of the farm. Technically his grandfather owned half the property that Tim farmed. Someday his parents would. And then, after they were gone, he and Adam would inherit it. But he imagined Tim leasing it, forever.

"I've always enjoyed helping you," Zane said. "And, jah, I'd like to learn more of the business." He couldn't imagine the dairy would also support him and Lila. He had the idea it barely supported the Lehmans. That was why Tim worked at the lumberyard. And Tim wasn't even fifty yet. It would be a long time until he was ready to retire.

By then, God willing, Zane and Lila would have a houseful of children, which would mean Zane would need to have a reliable vocation to support them.

Zane heard Lila's crutches before he saw her. But then there she was, in the doorway to the kitchen. She wore her lavender dress and had her Kapp on, instead of the scarves she'd been wearing recently.

"Ready?" she asked.

Saying he was going to get back to work, Tim stepped out onto the mud porch. But then he said hello to someone.

For a moment, Zane thought it was Reuben, but then the person spoke, and it was Mom.

"I have a message for Lila," she said to Tim. "Is she home?"

"Jah," Tim said. "She and Zane were getting ready to go for a ride."

"Oh, good," Mom said. "I'm glad I caught them before they left." She told Tim good-bye and stepped into the kitchen.

The back door closed, but as Mom started to speak, the door opened again. Mom must not have heard it, because she said, "One of the Butch Wilsons called back. I have his number." She extended her hand, with a note in it. "He said to call back as soon as possible."

Lila froze.

"Who's Butch Wilson?" Tim asked.

Mom turned, slowly.

Lila hesitated and looked at Zane.

"That's the name of Lila and Daniel's birth father," Zane answered.

"Oh," Tim said. He turned slowly toward Lila. "What's this all about?"

"I've wanted to find out about him. Get some information."

"Where did you get his name?"

"Eve."

"I see." Tim turned around and headed through the mud porch, closing the door firmly behind him. No one said anything for a long moment.

Finally Mom said, "I'm sorry. I thought he'd left."

"It's not your fault," Lila said. "He would have found out sooner or later."

Mom sighed. "Do you want a ride to the house?"

"We'll come over in the buggy," Lila said. "That way we can leave from there for our ride." Zane nodded in agreement. Lila could make the phone call from the Lehmans' barn, but that would be awkward with Tim around.

Mom said she'd go ahead and go to the store, then. "Joel

and Adam are running errands too." Zane guessed she wanted Lila to know that she'd have privacy.

Once they were in the buggy, they didn't talk at first. But Zane finally asked, "What are you thinking?"

"About how long I've wanted this information," she answered. "I think the accident and everything else that's happened has finally given me the courage to seek it."

Zane had a lot of other things he wanted to say to Lila but thought it best to wait until after the phone call. When they got to the house, Lila sat at the kitchen table to make the call. Zane stood in the doorway, but Lila waved him away, saying he made her self-conscious. She didn't feel totally comfortable speaking on the phone, not the way he did. He knew that.

He stepped into the living room, hoping he could still hear. He could make out Lila introducing herself and then saying, "I see," a few times. Mostly she listened.

Finally she said, "I'd like that very much."

After she said good-bye, Zane stepped back into the kitchen. "Well?" he asked. "What did you find out?"

Lila looked up at him, her face tense. "The man I talked with is only eighteen, but he—and his mother—think there's a possibility that Daniel and I could be his father's children."

"What about the father? What does he think?"

Lila exhaled. "He passed on. Two years ago. From a heart attack."

"I'm sorry." Zane stepped to her side and put his hand on her shoulder.

She squeezed his hand, and for a moment he felt a connection to her, but then she said, "I don't feel like going for a ride. I'd rather go home and rest."

"All right," he said. "But we need to talk about what the lawyer said. Sometime soon."

"I can't think about that right now," Lila said.

"You'll have to think about it sometime. The insurance company will start their own investigation soon. They'll be contacting you."

She wrinkled her nose. "Butch is going to talk with his mother and try to figure out a time when we can meet. I need to figure this stuff out first," Lila said, looking up at him. "I'd really like to meet Butch. He could be my half brother."

Zane handed Lila her crutches, chewing on his lower lip as he did. None of this would make Tim happy. Honestly, it concerned him too, but he wasn't sure exactly why. The accident had changed so much between Lila and him. *For better or worse.* It wasn't what he'd been expecting. Not at all. Especially not before they were even married.

Even though he hadn't had the chance to make the vow in front of others and to Lila, he'd made it to himself and to God. He'd do everything he could to try to figure out how to help her.

21

The weather had turned icy, and the cold wind stung Rose's cheeks as she held her cape with one hand at her neck, keeping her hood snug on her head. She carried a flashlight in her other hand as she hurried toward the barn.

She'd waited until Lila and Trudy were asleep and she could hear Dat snoring before sneaking out. She hoped Beth was asleep too, but Christmas vacation had started, and she'd been staying up later than when she was teaching. Rose couldn't wait any longer though. At first she'd been hesitant to call Trevor again—she wanted to give him some space to think things through. But she'd become more anxious with each day. She'd be moving to Eve and Charlie's in two weeks. What if Trevor planned to come back to Lancaster County before then?

She reached the barn, pushed hard against the door, and slipped inside. A cat ran in front of her and then a cow mooed, probably the heifer Dat said was in labor. Hopefully he wouldn't come check on her anytime soon.

She stepped into the office. The best thing would be if Trevor came back to Lancaster County. She'd never expect him to join the Amish as Zane had, but maybe he'd become Mennonite or maybe Baptist. She hoped he wouldn't expect her to learn to drive a car or anything like that. She wasn't as courageous as Aenti Eve was—not that Charlie had expected it, as far as Rose knew. Aenti Eve had wanted to get her GED and go to college, which she did. Rose had no such aspirations. She picked up the phone, dialed, and let it ring. She counted to eight. What if he never called her back?

It kept on ringing. Just when she expected for it to go into his voicemail, someone answered, saying, "Hello?" It wasn't Trevor though—it was a girl.

"Hello?" the voice said again.

Trevor's voice was muffled. "Give me the phone."

The girl cursed and then Trevor came on. "Hey," he said. "You're on speaker."

Rose didn't respond.

"Who is this?" the girl asked, her voice angry.

Rose hung up the phone, feeling as if she might be sick. Did Trevor get back together with his girlfriend? She thought about what Zane had said, *"Things aren't always what they seem."* Is that what he'd meant? What did he know that he hadn't told her?

It was ten thirty now. Zane would be asleep, but she didn't care. She hurried out of the office and through the barn, pulling the door tightly behind her. She'd go through the field—it would be faster. Thankfully she had the flashlight, because there was no moon, and she had to dodge the cow pies. Spreading the manure was probably on Dat's list of things to do.

She marched along the poplar trees, and when she reached the hedge she veered to the left around the Becks' barn toward the little house. All the lights were out, as she expected. Zane probably slept upstairs. Maybe he wouldn't hear her knocking on the door, and she certainly didn't want to be loud enough to wake Shani and Joel.

"Lila?"

She shone her flashlight toward the voice. Zane stood in the shadows of the house, over to the left.

"It's me, Rose."

"Oh," he said. "For a minute I thought you were Lila. What are you doing out?"

"I need to talk with you, but I thought you'd be in bed."

"So you decided to come over anyway?"

She nodded. "It's important."

He sighed. "Will it take long? I was just coming home from my folks', but I don't think I should invite you in."

Her face grew warm, even in the icy cold. "No, I just need to ask you something. I tried to call Trevor tonight."

"Oh?"

"A girl answered. And I doubt she's his sister."

"He doesn't have a sister," Zane said.

"Do you know who it might be?" she asked.

When Zane didn't answer, Rose said, "Tell me what you know. I need you to."

He nodded. "I probably should have told you earlier, but I wasn't sure what was going on. Especially after you told him about . . ."

"The Bobbli?"

He nodded. "His girlfriend—"

"Ex-girlfriend?"

"Right." Zane nodded. "She texted him and said she wanted to get back together. That's one reason he decided to go back."

"So they're back together?"

"I don't know that for sure," Zane said. "But they could be."

"Why won't he talk to me?"

"Why do you want him to talk with you? He wouldn't make a good husband or father."

She crossed her arms. "But he *is* the father. Wouldn't he want to work it out?"

"Not necessarily."

Rose didn't respond. She felt disappointed. Betrayed. Rejected. Jah, her pride was hurt. But it was more than that.

"He used you, and I'm sorry about that."

"I knew what I was getting into."

Zane shook his head. "You weren't experienced in those things."

Rose's face warmed even more. She'd felt connected to Trevor, but she hadn't truly known him.

"I'll walk you home," Zane said.

"No, I'm fine," she answered, choking back her tears.

"Rose," he said, touching her shoulder. "I'm sorry."

"You don't have anything to be sorry about."

"I'm the reason Trevor came here. I overestimated his character. I didn't protect you."

Rose swallowed hard. "You didn't know. I did. I should have protected myself." She put her hand to her stomach and then turned and hurried away.

Zane started to follow her, so she called out, "I want to be alone." He stopped.

By the time she reached the field, the snow had started to fall. Big, wet snowflakes. Each different. Each unique. Her hand went to her belly again. Her Bobbli was unique—already whomever he or she was going to be.

She wasn't the first Amish girl to get pregnant out of wedlock. Others had, including her own Mamm. For years she thought she was better than that, sure nothing like that would ever happen to her. Now she knew just how foolish she'd really been.

278

By the time she reached the house, a layer of snow had already covered the ground, transforming the night into a bright landscape. She slipped a little going up the steps but caught herself by grabbing hold of the railing. She paused to catch her breath, and then went on inside.

She'd get through Christmas and then move to Eve's. She'd concentrate on the Bobbli inside her, and on becoming a mother. She'd do her best to stop thinking about Trevor Anderson, because he obviously didn't want anything more to do with her.

⌘

On Christmas, Beth took charge of the meal. Daniel, Jenny, and Brook came over in the morning to open presents and then stayed for dinner. Beth planned the menu and did most of the cooking, telling Rose to enjoy having someone wait on her for a change.

Dat and Daniel went out to the barn, checking on a sick calf. Rose sat in the living room with Jenny, Lila, and Trudy, but after a while she realized she'd rather be spending time with Beth and headed into the kitchen. Her stepmother had everything under control, cooking for a large family with ease. She had a ham in the oven, rolls rising on the stove, potatoes boiling, a gelatin salad in the fridge, and a broccoli and cauliflower salad marinating. She had chowchow and strawberry preserves on the table, and apple, pumpkin, and chocolate pies in her old pie safe that was tucked in a corner of the room.

She had some holiday platters out on the counter to use and candles on the table. It was a lot fancier than what Rose was used to—at least at home. Monika, Eve, and her grandmother all had special holiday dishware, but the Lehman family never had.

"What can I help with?" Rose asked.

"You could set the table. Remember to add a plate for Zane."

Rose nodded. It was easier for Zane to come to their house

than for Lila to go to his folks'. As she pulled the plates from the cupboard, she asked Beth about her platters.

"Oh, I got those in Maryland," she said.

Rose knew it was a more liberal district. The bishop there had allowed Beth to teach at the school, even though she was divorced. She was still surprised at that. Even more so that Bishop Byler had allowed her to teach in their district.

"Tell me about Maryland," Rose said.

Beth explained that she had a cousin there who encouraged her to relocate. "I had no future in Ohio. I couldn't remarry. I couldn't teach, which I'd done for several years before I married. I could take care of my parents, but that was all. When they passed on, this cousin—who was also single—suggested I join her."

"And then what happened?" Rose asked as she put the last plate on the table.

"I'd been there for a while, working in farmers' markets and that sort of thing, but during the week I would volunteer at the school. No one seemed to think I would corrupt the students, which was such a relief." Beth turned the potatoes off and drained the water as she talked. "Then the teacher suddenly fell ill, and I was in the best position to help out because I was familiar with the students and the curriculum, plus I didn't have any other pressing obligations. When the teacher resigned a few months later, the school board asked me to take the job for good, and of course I said yes."

"And how long did you teach there?"

"Oh, goodness . . ." she said. "Thirteen years."

"Why did you come here?"

"Well," she said. "The bishop died and the new one thought I shouldn't be teaching, that I'd be a bad influence on the children. Gideon and I had met at the farmers' market a few years ago—he was selling his tables. This new bishop was acquainted with Gideon and tried to get his opinion, but Gideon said it wasn't his business. Once he found out I'd been let go though, he contacted me and said there was a position open here. He didn't think it was right that—as a single woman with no family to speak of—my livelihood should be taken away like that."

"Oh," Rose said, leaning against the counter.

"What's wrong?" Beth asked, turning toward her.

Rose shook her head. "I'm all right." But the severity of her own situation was sinking in. What if she didn't have Dat to watch over her and the Bobbli? Someday she wouldn't. He wouldn't live forever. How would she support the two of them then?

Beth hadn't done anything wrong, and yet she'd been shamed for years. And then again much later too, long after she probably expected those days were over. Rose had been put under the Bann the week before. It would last for six weeks, then she would be reinstated and returned to fellowship. Jah, what people thought of her would change, but she'd still be part of the community.

Now Rose wondered if there were those in the district who thought Beth had been a bad influence on the family and had affected Rose. Her face grew warm at the thought of it. Nothing could be further from the truth. Beth was one of those people who made everyone around her want to do better.

Trudy came into the kitchen and asked what she could do to help. Beth had her put the chowchow and preserves in bowls. Next, Jenny came in with the Bobbli. Then Lila hobbled in on her crutches.

"When is Zane coming over?" Beth asked.

"Any minute," Lila answered. She sat down at the table. "Anything I can do from here?" she asked.

Beth shook her head. "Just keep us all company."

Jenny sat down too, with Brook facing Lila. The little one waved her fist. Lila smiled but didn't reach out to her.

Rose couldn't believe in a year she'd have a Bobbli bigger than Brook. The little girl lunged for her. Jenny laughed. "She knows her Aenti." Rose took the little one in her arms. Standing up straight, Rose marveled at how tiny the little girl was at seven weeks.

"How was Christmas Eve at your Mamm's?" Lila asked Jenny.

Rose drifted toward Beth with the Bobbli, not wanting to think of Reuben with his Dat and Monika and their entire blended family. She held Brook closer, trying to ward off her loneliness, thinking of the horrible trade she'd made.

Jenny gushed about how lovely the evening was. Between the two families there were nine children and now eighteen grandchildren. Rose had fantasized about being part of the Byler brood, of how she would have been accepted as Reuben's wife. They were good people. She couldn't have asked for better in-laws.

Rose's family always visited Monika and Gideon the day after Christmas. No one had brought up the outing so far this year, and she doubted Reuben would be there even if they did.

Brook waved her arm, swatting at the tie to Rose's Kapp.

"Has anyone heard from Simon?" Jenny asked.

Rose turned back to the conversation.

"No," Lila said. "You know he hardly ever writes."

"How about from Casey?"

Lila shook her head.

Beth put the potato masher down and said, "We'll eat in ten minutes. Trudy, would you please go tell your Dat and Daniel?"

Lila turned toward the window, probably wondering when Zane would arrive. Rose didn't know what was going on between Lila and Zane, but it seemed things were tense. Lila definitely hadn't been herself since the accident.

Dat and Daniel returned to the house and washed up, and Beth started putting the food on the table. Lila glanced out the window again. As everyone gathered at the table to sit down there was a knock on the door. Trudy ran to it and let Zane in. It took a minute for him to take off his boots and hang up his coat, but then he stepped into the kitchen.

"Sorry I'm late," he said. "Simon called."

Rose snuck a look at Dat, wondering how it was for him to have his son call the Englisch neighbors on Christmas. He'd probably left a message on the barn phone too, but still . . . Dat's expression remained stoic.

"He said to tell all of you hello and that he misses you," Zane said. "He says not to worry, he's doing fine and he's safe." He turned to Lila. "Just after he hung up, the phone rang again. It was Butch Wilson. He asked if I'd wish you a Merry Christmas, and said he and his mother would like to meet you sometime soon, perhaps halfway."

Rose wanted to roll her eyes. Really? Didn't he get that this was a touchy subject?

"What's that all about?" Daniel asked.

Lila said, "I'll tell you later."

"Jah, let's sit down and pray," Dat said. "And get started on this wonderful meal Beth has prepared." Rose couldn't imagine what life would have been like if Beth wasn't part of their family now. Dat would be beside himself with all that was going on without Beth's steady and cheerful presence.

<hr>

After the meal was over, Rose sent Dat, Beth, and Trudy off for a sleigh ride. As Rose and Jenny did the dishes, Daniel held the Bobbli while Zane helped put the food away. He was more in the way than anything, but he seemed to want to do something.

"So who's Butch Wilson?" Daniel asked Lila.

Rose didn't need to look at her sister to know her face was growing red.

"Lila, what's going on?" Daniel asked.

"That's our birth father's name."

Jenny spun around, her hands covered with soap bubbles. "What?"

"Jah," Lila said. "But the person who called isn't our father. He may be our half brother though. And, if he is, our birth father is dead."

An expression of dismay passed over Daniel's face and then he groaned. "What have you done?"

"A little research is all."

"Lila, how could you?" he asked loudly. The baby startled. He hugged her closer and dropped his voice, but he was clearly angry. "Dat is our father. We don't need to know what's in the past."

"I've wondered about our biological father since I was little."

"Well, I haven't," Daniel said. "You could have at least asked me before digging into the past."

"Aren't you sad that he might be dead?"

Daniel shook his head. "Sorry for his family, jah. But it doesn't have anything to do with me. And if you don't know for sure, you shouldn't be making assumptions."

By the look on Jenny's face she seemed to agree. "Have you talked with Gideon about this?"

Lila shook her head, looking a little defeated.

"You should," Jenny said, turning back to the sink. "I think this family has enough problems without stirring up any more."

~⁂~

That night, after Trudy had fallen asleep, Rose whispered to Lila, "Are you still awake?"

"Jah."

284

"Are we going over to Gideon and Monika's tomorrow?"

"No," Lila said. "Dat said we needed to start new traditions. But we're still going to go over to Mammi and Dawdi's."

Rose hadn't seen her grandparents since she'd found out she was pregnant. She knew they wouldn't be judgmental, but they probably would be sad, knowing what was ahead of her.

Her thoughts fell back to Monika and Gideon. "Are they mad at me? Is it because of what I've done?"

"I don't know," Lila answered, and then it sounded as if she yawned.

"Because of Reuben, right?"

"You did betray him."

"They weren't mad at you."

Rose could hear Lila shift a little in her bed, which she knew wasn't easy for her. "Rose, I didn't do what you've done."

"You hurt him."

"Jah, but you cheated on him."

Rose didn't respond for a long minute. Finally she said, "I told him I'm sorry, which I am, and I asked for his forgiveness. He seemed all right that day we saw him on the road."

"Well, he's not all right. He cared about you. He loved you—more than he ever did me."

Rose's heart swelled. "I don't think so."

"I know so. He looked at you in a different way than he ever looked at me."

Rose swallowed hard. "I don't even know why I did it. I got so caught up in the way Trevor treated me. I could tell by the way he looked at me that . . ." She stopped, wishing she hadn't started the sentence.

Lila's voice was harsh. "That what?"

When Rose didn't answer, Lila asked, "That he wanted you? Because, jah, that wasn't the way Reuben looked at you. He looked as if he cherished you. Wanted to protect you. Wanted to spend his life with you. Wanted to have a family with you. Trevor just looked like he wanted—some excitement."

"You don't need to be so blunt," Rose said.

"Actually, I wasn't," Lila answered.

Rose bristled and stayed silent—for a couple of minutes. It wasn't like Lila to be so harsh. "What's with you?" she finally asked.

"What do you mean?"

"You're mean. And peckish. Like a cross between a bull and a hen."

Sarcasm filled Lila's voice. "Denki," she said, followed by the sound of her head shifting on her pillow, most likely away from Rose.

"I'll get out of your hair soon," Rose said. "Me being at Eve's will make it easier for everyone."

"Stop it," Lila said. Suddenly the battery-operated lamp flicked on. Trudy stirred and rolled away from it, but she didn't wake.

Rose turned toward her older sister. Tears streamed down Lila's face. "Look," she said. "Trevor took advantage of you. Zane and I both feel horrible we didn't realize what was going on." She swiped at her face. "Reuben is the victim in all of this, but he's not acting like one. You are a child of God, and God is the perfect parent—he will never abandon you. And neither will Dat. He will care for you and the Bobbli. But make it easy for him, not harder. Go to Eve's, but don't act like it's our fault you need to. It's your choice."

Your choice. All of this had been Rose's choice. She threw away a good man for a few nights of fun. She had no one to blame but herself.

Lila stared at her for a long moment and then snapped off the light.

Rose didn't say any more, but she stayed awake long into

the night. She'd thrown away the future she had absolutely wanted. Lila was right. What kind of woman did she want to be? What kind of mother? It was time for her to grow up, to humble herself.

She pulled the quilt up higher against the icy cold with one hand while her other went to her stomach. It wasn't as flat as it used to be, but it wasn't as if she was showing either. Sooner or later she would be though.

She rolled to her side. She needed to forget Trevor. And Reuben too. She had no idea what her future held, but she was sure it didn't hold either of them. The only thing she was certain of was her Bobbli. And she couldn't help but hope, as Lila said, that God loved her and would never abandon her. But that was easier to hope for than to actually feel.

Another verse came to mind. *"Therefore, brethren, stand fast, and hold the traditions which ye have been taught, whether by word, or our epistle."* That's what she would aim to do. She wouldn't call Trevor again—instead, she'd trust the Lord. That was the only thing she could be one hundred percent sure of, that would bring her any peace.

She'd also lean on her family and the community that loved her. And she'd do her best to become a good mother to her Bobbli.

22

The first Saturday of January, in the late afternoon, Lila and Zane sat on the sofa in the living room of the Lehmans' home, watching the snow out the window. Big fluffy, mesmerizing flakes were falling.

He was talking about the lawyer again, saying the man had left a message on his parents' phone yesterday. A second claims adjuster from the insurance company was investigating. "He'll come out and ask you questions on Monday," Zane said.

She leaned back against the sofa. "I told you I'd rather not talk to him."

Zane answered, "You have to."

The sound of tires over gravel caught Lila's attention.

"Are you expecting someone?" Zane asked.

"Jah, Eve and Charlie are coming for Rose."

Zane stood and went to the window. Lila leaned her head back and closed her eyes. A couple of minutes later Zane opened the door for the couple. Eve held Jackson. After they entered,

Charlie pointed to the boxes and suitcase by the door. "Are these Rose's?"

"Jah," Lila answered. While Charlie and Zane carried the items out to the sedan, Lila called out Rose's name.

"Where is she?" Eve asked. "I'll go get her."

"Try our bedroom," Lila answered.

Eve returned with Rose, who said, "I'll go tell Dat, Beth, and Trudy good-bye." All three had gone out to check on the twin calves that had been born the night before.

Jackson fussed a little, and Eve lifted him higher and then said to Lila, "I hope having Rose come stay with us won't make things harder for you."

Lila shook her head. "Not at all. Beth has everything under control. I think it will be good for Rose to be with you."

Eve glanced toward the kitchen, as if Rose might reappear. "How's she doing?"

Lila shrugged. "Sometime in the last few months she reverted back to the way she was before Reuben started courting her. I think she's trying to find her way back, but she still seems pretty self-absorbed." Lila sighed. "I keep thinking about our Mamm. She was younger than Rose when she got pregnant with Daniel and me. I can't imagine she ever acted the way Rose does."

Eve smiled, just a little.

"What?" Lila asked.

Eve shook her head. "Don't get me wrong, but your Mamm had her moments. In fact she was a lot like Rose is now."

"You're kidding." Lila pushed herself up a little straighter. "Everyone always says I remind them of Mamm."

"The way you look, yes," Eve said. "And the way you act, in some ways—but I think they're making a comparison to when your Mamm was older. Not when she was Rose's age."

Lila wrinkled her nose.

"Take that as a compliment," Eve said. "You've always been an old soul."

Lila shook her head a little. "I don't know about that."

Eve smiled and then asked, "Speaking of the other old soul I know, have you and Zane chosen a date for the wedding?"

Lila shook her head. "We haven't talked about it."

"Why not?"

Lila glanced at her crutches. "It's not like I can be much of a wife yet."

Eve gave her a sympathetic look and then said, "What does Zane say?"

Lila shrugged. She didn't want to discuss it with Eve. The truth was, Zane hadn't said much lately. "He's mostly obsessed with holding the guy who hit me accountable and getting his insurance to pay for everything."

Considering how long it was taking the men to come back in the house, Lila guessed Charlie was grilling Zane too. She appreciated their concern—she really did. But there weren't any quick and easy answers to her dilemma.

Jackson began to cry, and then a commotion at the back door distracted Eve more. Trudy came running through the kitchen into the living room, with Beth right behind her, walking quickly. After they both hugged Eve, Trudy reached for Jackson. He fell into her arms, laughing as he did. Dat came into the living room next, followed by Rose.

Lila glanced toward the front door, expecting Charlie and Zane to join the rest of them, but the door stayed closed.

"Well now," Dat said to Eve. "So you're really taking Rose away?"

Eve nodded. "She'll be a big help to us."

Dat stared at the baby for a moment. Lila could guess what he was thinking—that Eve shouldn't have taken in a foster child when she was working. It was no surprise that Beth had given up her job so soon after she married, probably under Dat's influence, although the school board probably would have required it soon enough. Then Dat turned to Rose. "Learn all you can," he said.

"Jah," Rose said. "I will."

Dat nodded. "There's a lot to learn. And about keeping a house too. Your Aenti is good at that."

Rose answered, "I'll do my best."

Lila was surprised Dat had paid Eve a compliment. It wasn't like him.

The door opened, and Charlie and Zane stepped in. After everyone hugged her, Rose stepped over to Lila and patted her shoulder. "Stop by some time."

"I will," Lila answered.

Rose smirked a little. "Keep me posted on your meeting with Butch Wilson."

Eve gave Lila a questioning look but didn't say anything.

"Jah," Dat said to his sister. "See what you've put in Lila's head? Sometimes the past should stay the past."

"Eve, don't worry. It's not him," Lila said. "Although it might be his son. We're going to try to meet sometime soon."

"Oh," Eve said. Her face reddened as she spoke. "I'm not sure what to say."

Dat harrumphed. Lila guessed Dat's frustration with Eve dated back over a couple of decades. He turned toward Lila. "What does Daniel have to say about this?"

"He doesn't want to have any part of it," Lila answered.

A hint of a smile passed over Dat's face, but then he was back to frowning. Beth stepped to his side. Trudy squealed as Jackson grabbed hold of her Kapp and pulled.

Eve came to her rescue and took the baby back.

"We should get going," Rose said. Lila thought her sister looked a little sad as she led the way out the door. This would be her first time living away from home.

After everyone left the living room, Zane said, "Speaking of Butch Wilson, I have a message for you."

Lila was glad he used enough common sense to not blurt it in front of everyone this time.

"He called earlier today. He said he and his mom want to meet you in two weeks."

"Oh," Lila said, her face growing warm.

"They suggested a place. Do you want me to call them back and tell them it will work?"

"Will you come with me?"

"Of course," he said. "And Mom already said she'd drive us."

"Denki," Lila said, her heart racing. "Jah, call him back and tell him we'll see him then."

After Zane left, Lila thought more about Rose and how self-absorbed she'd seemed. But the truth was, Lila was still acting pretty self-centered too. She wanted to put others first, including Zane, but instead she kept putting all of her thoughts and energy into finding out about her birth father. She leaned back in Dat's chair. Once she met with Butch Wilson Jr., she'd move on, sort things out with Zane, and figure out what to do next.

⁓

Monday afternoon, while Lila was resting, Beth came and told her there was an Englisch man at the door. "An insurance adjuster," Beth added.

Lila groaned.

"Do you want me to ask him to come back later?" Beth asked.

Lila shook her head as she sat up. She might as well get it over with. By the time she reached the kitchen, Beth had served the man coffee and a slice of fresh bread with butter. He seemed quite grateful. He was older, probably over sixty.

As Lila came in, he stood and introduced himself as Mr. Stark. "Owen Stark," he added. Once she sat down and propped her crutches against the table, he shook her hand. She reminded herself to look him in the eyes, which was hard for her to do with a strange man. Zane had told her it was what Englisch men expected. She was able to do it at the restaurant, but it was harder in her home. She wished Zane were with her.

"Is Dat around?" Lila asked Beth.

"He's in the barn." Beth wiped her hands on her apron. "Would you like me to go get him?"

Lila nodded her head. She didn't want the man to think that he could bully her, not the way the other insurance man had.

Mr. Stark asked her to tell him what she remembered from the day of the accident. She told him she was as far over on the shoulder of the road as she could be when she sensed a vehicle behind her, although she didn't actually see it. She described everything she could remember up until she lost consciousness.

Dat came in and introduced himself to Mr. Stark, while Beth poured a cup of coffee for him.

Mr. Stark asked Lila what she remembered when she came to. "Zane," she answered.

"Zane?"

"We were to marry in October, so a month after the accident."

"But you haven't?"

She shook her head. "I'm still healing."

"What exactly do you remember when you came to?"

"I just knew he was there, at the accident site. It gave me faith that I would make it. By the time I was in the ambulance, I was awake enough to ask for him."

Mr. Stark scribbled in his book and then asked, "Can you tell me about your injuries?"

"Jah," she said, listing them off. The crushed pelvis. The ruptured spleen. The bruised bladder and liver. The internal scarring. The concussion.

"Anything else?" he asked, lifting his eyes from his notebook and meeting hers.

"Time will tell on some of it."

"Meaning?"

"Whether I'll be able to get pregnant and then carry a child or not."

The man didn't respond but continued writing in his notebook. Both Dat and Beth were quiet for a long moment, but then Dat asked the man if he lived nearby.

The man nodded. "In Lancaster," he said. "But I grew up in the country, near Willow Street."

"So you know our ways, then?"

"Yes," Mr. Stark answered.

"Lila is a good driver," Dat said. "She read that guidebook the county put out a while back, the one on buggy driving. She's cautious and careful. She's been driving for years and never had a problem."

The man wrote down a few more things.

"Did you go to the accident site?" Dat asked. "And do the measurements?"

"I'm doing that next," the man said.

"Do you have the information on where the buggy ended up, in pieces? And where Lila ended up in the creek? With the horse on top of her?"

The man said he had the police report.

"Make sure and do the measurements," Dat said. "A friend of ours did all of that a few weeks ago. That's why the police reopened the investigation."

"I see." Mr. Stark closed his notebook and then said, "Thank you for the coffee and bread. It's been a long time since I've been in an Amish home." He smiled. "Growing up, I had neighbors who were Plain. All of us kids went to the same school, and we all rode our horses together. They were good neighbors."

"*Gut,*" Dat said. "That's what we like to hear. We aim to be the same."

Lila felt grateful that Dat had come in. He related to the man in a way she couldn't. And he'd told the man things she wouldn't have thought to.

The man rattled off Shani and Joel's number. "Is that a good number to leave a message?"

"No," Dat said. "Use ours instead." He gave the man the phone number in the barn and then shook the man's hand. "Denki," he said. "We're very appreciative."

"*Du wellkome,*" the man said and then smiled. "Denki to you too."

As Dat walked the man out, tears welled in Lila's eyes. She knew Dat cared for her. He'd just shown it. But she still didn't feel it deep inside.

⁓

Nearly two weeks later, on a Saturday, Lila, Zane, and Shani sat in a diner in Randallstown, Maryland, waiting to meet Butch and his mother.

The waitress came around and filled their coffee cups. "Do you want to go ahead and order?" she asked.

Zane and Shani both looked at Lila. "How about another ten minutes?" she asked, hoping traffic had been bad and it wasn't that they'd changed their minds. The waitress nodded and went on to her next table. They'd already been drinking coffee for thirty minutes. Lila wiped her palms on her apron. She'd started using a cane, one of Joel's, instead of the crutches, and it was propped against the table. She grabbed it and stood.

"You all right?" Zane asked.

"Jah," she said. "I just need to stretch a little." As she settled back down a young man with blond hair came through the front door along with a middle-aged woman. She knew it was Butch.

295

He looked like Daniel—not exactly but enough to be brothers. She started to wave, but they'd already started toward her. She and Zane were the only Plain folk in the restaurant.

Butch stopped and his mother took the lead. She was petite and had short dark hair with a hint of gray and big blue eyes. When she reached Lila she said, "I'm Connie Wilson. You must be Lila."

Lila extended her hand but the woman bent over some and wrapped her arm around Lila's shoulder, squeezing her a little. "It's wonderful to meet you. This is my son, Butch."

Butch stepped closer and nodded. He appeared younger than nineteen and shier than he'd sounded on the phone.

"Hello," Lila said, reaching for his hand. "This is my fiancé, Zane, and his mom, Shani."

After everyone said a greeting, Connie and Butch sat down. "I'm curious," Connie said. "How does this work?" She glanced from Shani to Zane.

"You mean how does it work that Zane is Amish and I'm not?" Shani asked.

The woman nodded and then smiled.

"I joined the Amish," Zane said. "Last year." He met Lila's eyes. "For all sorts of reasons."

She hoped he was still thankful he had.

After a couple of minutes of conversation, the waitress took their order. When she left, Connie said, "Where should we start?"

Lila cleared her throat and tried to speak but nothing came out. Zane reached for her hand and squeezed it. She tried again. "All the information I have is that my birth father's name was Butch Wilson, that he was from Virginia, and that he was in Lancaster County in the early 1990s."

She looked at Butch Jr. "You're the only person I contacted who thought you might know . . ." She looked from Butch to

Connie. "This must be hard for you. I'm really sorry for what both of you have gone through. My Mamm passed on when I was eleven. I know how hard it is to lose someone you love."

"Thank you," Connie said. "Our situation might be a little different than yours was. Butch Sr.—Butch's father—left our family almost ten years ago. We didn't have much contact with him. He traveled, down to Louisiana and then up to Alaska. He was on his way to Wyoming when he died."

Lila wasn't sure what to say.

Shani leaned forward across the table. "What happened?"

"A heart attack," Connie said. "He was only forty-one."

"So there might be some sort of genetic component."

Connie glanced at her son. "Yes," she said. "We've talked with a couple of doctors about it." She turned her gaze back to Lila. "That's one of the reasons we wanted to meet with you. So you and your brother would know."

Lila felt her legs weaken.

"I'm sure other things contributed to Butch Sr.'s health problems though. Let's just say he lived a rough life—lots of drinking, some drugs. He smoked. He worked hard, mostly manual labor." Connie took a deep breath and then continued. "He never took care of himself. He wasn't a big man, but his blood pressure was always high, even in his early thirties."

Again Lila wasn't sure what to say. None of this was what she expected.

"What was he like, as a person?" Shani asked.

Connie smiled again and glanced at her son. He shrugged. "He wasn't all bad," she said and then laughed a little. "I married him." She paused a moment. "He was a lot of fun, always ready for an adventure. He loved to travel. He hunted some. He jumped around as far as jobs, but he was a hard worker. And after he left for good, he sent money to help with support. He cared, but he just couldn't seem to stay connected."

Connie smiled, a little wryly. "All those years I left the phone in his name, not wanting to be listed as a single woman. I was thinking about getting rid of the landline when you called. I'm glad I didn't."

Lila exhaled. She might never have found them.

Connie leaned onto the table. "Can you tell me about your mom?"

Lila wasn't sure she could without crying. She wished Eve had come with them. She swallowed hard. "She was only seventeen when Daniel and I were born. She was Amish, although her parents became Mennonite later. She had us and then married Dat. Together they had three more children—Simon, Rose, and Trudy. When Mamm was pregnant with Trudy she was diagnosed with breast cancer."

"Oh dear," Connie said.

"Jah, she didn't do any chemo until after Trudy was born. By then it was too late. She died two months later."

"I'm so sorry," Connie said.

"Thank you," Lila said. She looked from Connie to Butch Jr. "I'm sorry for everything you two have been through too."

Butch Jr. stared at the table, but Connie said, "Thank you." And then she said, "What did your mother tell you about your biological father?"

"Nothing," Lila said. "I found out his name from my aunt. She knew Butch too."

"Oh? Is she also Amish?"

Lila nodded. "She used to be—she's Mennonite now. My Aenti Eve is my Dat's sister, but she was also my Mamm's best friend."

As Lila spoke, Connie opened her purse and pulled out a photograph. "This is the reason we wanted to meet with you. After he died, I found this in a box Butch Sr. left behind. I've wondered about it." She handed the photograph to Lila.

It was Aenti Eve and Mamm, looking young and sassy but wearing cape dresses and Kappa. In between them was a man with blond hair who looked a lot like Daniel.

"That's them," Lila said. "My Mamm and my Aenti."

"Then Butch is your father," Connie said. "But it sounds as if someone else has been your Dat—is that how you referred to him earlier?"

Lila nodded.

"Has he been a good father to you? Cared for you? Loved you?"

Lila swallowed hard. "Jah," she said. "He has." The tears started, and she couldn't stop them, as hard as she tried.

Zane took her hand, and Shani passed her a tissue. She kept crying. Zane scooted his chair closer and wrapped his arms around her just as the waitress arrived with their food. Lila knew she was making a spectacle of herself. She took a couple of deep breaths and then apologized.

Connie shook her head. "No need to be sorry." Then she said, "Do you pray before you eat?"

Zane nodded. "Silently though."

"We'll follow your lead," she said.

They all bowed their heads. Lila thanked God for the information, for Connie, and for Butch's willingness to meet with her, and for the truth.

"Amen," Zane said.

The women echoed him. Butch still hadn't said anything. Lila turned toward him. "What are you studying in school?"

"General studies right now," he said. His face reddened as he spoke. "But I hope to major in philosophy and then go on to graduate school."

That piqued Zane's interest, and the two began talking about different philosophers. Shani asked Connie what she did for a living.

"I'm a surgical assistant."

"Really?" Shani said. "I'm a nurse. Pediatrics."

Lila was relieved to focus on eating her food as she listened to the others talk, wondering at her public tears. It wasn't like her. She hadn't been herself since the accident.

After they'd finished eating, Shani picked up the bill, under protest from the others. "I insist," she said.

As Shani walked toward the cashier, a wave of gratitude swept over Lila as she glanced around the table. Zane was sticking by her despite his frustration. She had a new brother. And Connie was a good, kind woman. Her biological father had been loved, even if he couldn't accept it. "What was Butch Sr.'s family like?" Lila asked.

"Oh," Connie said. "That's an even sadder story. His mother died young and his father was an alcoholic. He was in and out of foster care. Later he reconciled with his father, but soon after they met his father died of a heart attack." She raised her eyebrows as she spoke. "Hard living again, but also the possibility of a genetic problem."

Lila nodded. It was good to have that information. It made her more sympathetic toward Butch Sr.

A few minutes later they all stood in the parking lot, saying good-bye. "May I hug you?" Connie asked.

Lila nodded as tears filled her eyes again. The woman patted her back as if she were a child and then stepped away.

Lila turned toward Butch Jr. "May I hug you?"

His face turned red, but he nodded. She gave him a half hug, still holding onto her cane, and said, "I always wanted another brother."

He pulled away and, looking down at her, his face even redder, said, "I always wanted a sister. And a brother too."

Lila wished Daniel was with her. She didn't expect him to

change his mind, but she believed, if he actually met Butch Jr.,
he might.

⁓

A few weeks later, after church, Lila and Zane headed back
to Juneberry Lane in his buggy. A foot of snow covered the
landscape, but the roads were all plowed. It was well below
freezing, but it had been dry the last few days. Zane turned
the buggy onto the lane and slowed. "Want to come down to
Mom and Dad's?" Zane asked

"No, I'm ready for a nap," Lila said.

Zane didn't respond but pulled into the driveway. He stopped
in front of her house but didn't hop down to help her. She opened
the door, as if she might get down by herself.

"I need to ask you something," he said.

She closed the door.

"When will you start talking with me again?"

"What do you mean?"

"You've shut me out, mostly, since the accident. I got it at
first. You were injured, badly. Then when you were recovering,
Rose revealed she was pregnant and moved out. Then you had
the stuff about your biological father. I get all that." He turned
toward her. "But do you plan to come back? Do you plan to
ever marry me? Has something changed?" He blinked quickly.
"I know I sound like a jerk. I don't mean to. I just wonder what
you're thinking. Maybe you've changed your mind, and you
just can't tell me."

"No," she said. "I haven't changed my mind. It's just . . ."

"What? What is it?"

She thought of their little house, of Zane living in it alone.
She glanced down at the cane she was still using. "I need more
time," she said. She should at least be able to get upstairs in
their house before they married.

Zane exhaled and started to say something more.

She shook her head. "I need to take a nap."

"Need to or want to?"

She swung the door open without a reply. He came around and helped her down and then up to the house, leaving her once she was inside. Dat, Beth, and Trudy probably wouldn't be home for another hour or so. Lila headed to her room and crawled into bed. She wasn't being fair to Zane. She knew it. "Lord," she prayed, "what's wrong with me?"

Her thoughts went to the day before the accident, to right before Zane showed her their house. She'd feared maybe she depended on Zane too much. She thought perhaps she had a lesson to learn, something to teach her to trust God more and Zane less. She never dreamt it would be an accident.

Tears stung her eyes. Zane was still her person, but she wasn't treating him that way. Part of her was afraid he wouldn't stick around if it turned out she couldn't have children—but she knew that was irrational. They wouldn't know until they married, and she knew Zane wouldn't leave. No matter what.

She swiped at her eyes. She hadn't learned to trust God more, despite what she'd gone through. She'd shut down. Her soul was as broken as her body.

She woke up to Trudy patting her arm. "Zane's here. He wants to speak with you." The light in the room had shifted, and Lila guessed it was four thirty or so. At first she wanted to tell Trudy to ask Zane to leave, but she didn't. She remembered her thoughts before going to sleep.

"I'll be right out," she said.

When she reached the living room, Zane sat talking with Dat. "Hello," he said.

She smiled at him.

Dat stood. "I'll go see if I can help Beth."

Lila sat down beside Zane.

"I'm sorry." Zane put his hands on his knees. "For what I said earlier."

"No, you're right. Maybe I'm a little depressed," she said.

"You have reason to be," he said. "But—"

"Did you drive your buggy over?"

He nodded. He'd been trying to take Billie out every chance he could.

"We could go for a ride," Lila said.

"All right," Zane said. "It's cold though. Will you be warm enough?"

She nodded. "We don't have to go far." She couldn't talk freely in the house.

Ten minutes later, bundled in her warm winter coat, bonnet, scarf, and mittens, she sat in the buggy with a wool blanket tucked around her. Dusk was falling and the setting sun coming through the thin gray clouds cast a bluish hue over Juneberry Lane. Perhaps it would snow again soon.

Once Billie turned onto the highway, Lila said, "I know I've been distant—I'm sorry. I think maybe I've figured some of it out."

Zane glanced toward her, his eyes heavy.

"I need to do a better job trusting God. I've been so numb since the accident."

"Are you still taking the pain pills?"

She shook her head. "I haven't, not for a long time. But I've just been going through the motions. Not opening up to you or to God or to anyone, really. I'll work on that."

"Denki," he said, turning the buggy down a country lane and parking under a willow tree. He turned toward her, his knee against hers. "Anything else?"

She smiled a little. "All these years, especially after Mamm died, I had this idea that life with my biological father would have been better than life with Dat."

Zane shook his head. "I think that's pretty normal."

"And then he turned out to be far worse. He left them. Butch Jr. seems like such a great kid, you know? But wounded."

Zane nodded.

"Even though his mom is such a great parent." Lila leaned back against the bench. "My intuition was so wrong." Lila exhaled. "I wish Mamm would have warned me."

"She wouldn't have known how Butch Sr. turned out. He was still young the last time she saw him."

"That's true," Lila said.

"But it looks like there was a reason your mom didn't tell him about being pregnant," Zane said. "Apparently she didn't think he was good father material."

"Jah, you're right," Lila said. "And I feel bad about that because maybe she did think Dat would be a good father. Maybe that's why she married him—so Daniel and I would have a father and then siblings. The truth is," she said, thinking through it as she spoke, "I truly believe Dat did favor Simon and Rose, and then Trudy too, in a way. But I don't think he did it intentionally. I don't even think he was aware of it."

Zane nodded. "Perhaps part of it was he expected more out of you and Daniel—because you were older."

Lila agreed. She'd actually wondered that before but had dismissed it. But it probably had some merit. He treated Trudy with even more leniency than he had Simon and Rose.

"Maybe you'd feel better if you said something to your Dat, thanked him for being there for you all those years."

Lila wrinkled her nose.

"Think about it," Zane said.

It was hard to imagine that sort of conversation with Dat. Maybe in time. She definitely needed to say something to Rose though. Encouraging her to hold out hope for a relationship with Trevor might not have been the right thing to do.

The blue dusk had faded to darkness, but she could see Zane's face by the light from the lantern on the side of the buggy.

She shifted toward him even more, but a jolt of pain made her shift back in a hurry.

"Are you all right?" Zane asked.

"Jah," she answered.

"Just trying to avoid talking?"

She smiled a little and then shivered.

"Are you cold?" he asked, scooting closer to her. He put his arm around her and pulled her tight. The shift caused more pain, but then it stopped. She relaxed against him, surprised at how good his touch felt.

"So what about marriage?" he asked. "Are we going to set a date?"

"Let's see how the next few months go," Lila said.

Zane paused for a long moment and then said, "All right."

"It would be better to wait until Rose has her baby." Before she even realized what was happening, a sob shook Lila.

Zane scooted even closer. "I'm sorry," he said.

She leaned her head into his chest, thinking of all the times he'd been her place of safety. She felt that now. "It just feels so unfair."

"But what she's going through doesn't have anything to do with us," Zane said. "Except for giving us a niece or nephew. It doesn't have any bearing on whether we can have children or not."

"But I feel like it does. As if her getting pregnant so easily means I won't."

"That's superstitious," Zane said.

"I know." She sighed. "She'll need me once she comes home from Eve's, and especially after the baby is born."

"Jah," Zane said, "but not for long. What are you thinking, as far as us?"

"September, maybe."

Zane's expression fell.

"I'm sorry," she said. It was more than just feeling as if she should be around for Rose and her baby. She couldn't climb up the stairs of the little house to their bedroom. She couldn't do the chores to run a house. She wouldn't be able to tend a garden. There was so much she couldn't do.

He was silent for a long moment. Finally he leaned closer. "I'll wait," he said. "I've been waiting since the first time I saw you, standing on the other side of the gate. I'll wait as long as it takes, no matter what."

"Denki." She did believe him, even though she walked with one of his father's canes. None of this was what they'd expected.

23

Rose sat on the table in the doctor's office wearing a gown. "Would you like your aunt to come back in?" the doctor asked as she typed on the laptop she'd brought in with her. She seemed young to be a doctor, probably in her early thirties.

Rose nodded. As the doctor left the room, she fixated on a photo of a newborn sitting in a bed of red tulips. The little one wore a red stocking cap and a red dress and green tights. It was a ridiculous photo—but still cute.

The clinic was near the hospital in Lancaster, the one Shani worked at. The one Lila had been in after the accident. The one Trevor had given Rose a ride to.

She hadn't heard back from him. It was the middle of March and she doubted, since he hadn't called by now, that he ever would. She'd call him when the Bobbli was born, just to let him know.

Eve had been trying to get her to go to the doctor since Rose moved in, but Rose kept saying she was young and healthy and didn't want to go yet. Finally Eve told her she couldn't keep living with them if she didn't—she needed to put her Bobbli's needs first. By the time Rose finally called the number Eve gave her, the first available appointment was a month away. Now here it was, the middle of March, and Rose was over halfway through the pregnancy.

She'd never had any type of exam before and hadn't been to the doctor at all for years. Eve told her she'd tag along if that would make it easier, and Rose was grateful for the offer. Eve had taken the afternoon off work, and Charlie was home with Jackson.

There was a quick knock on the door, and the doctor and Eve walked into the room. Once they were both seated, the doctor said she wanted Rose to have an ultrasound.

Many of the women in the district used midwives and never had ultrasounds. Rose didn't feel comfortable having a first Bobbli at home, but she'd told the doctor she didn't want to have anything that wasn't absolutely necessary. "Are you sure I need one?" Rose asked.

"Yes," the doctor replied. "You're small for twenty-two weeks—the height of your fundus should correlate with how many weeks along you are. Unless you miscalculated your date."

Rose shook her head. There wasn't any chance of that.

"There may not be anything to be concerned about, but we want to cover our bases. I can't be sure how much weight you've gained but according to what you've said it's less than ten pounds. "

Rose glanced at Eve, who had a concerned expression on her face.

"The technician will be in with the machine," the doctor said. "I'll come back in afterward."

Once the doctor left, Eve stood.

"Does she think something's wrong?" Rose asked.

"We'll know soon," Eve said.

The technician arrived, pushing a cart with the machine on it. After a couple of minutes of getting everything set up, she instructed Rose to lie back down and lift her gown. She explained that she would put gel on Rose's abdomen and then rub the wand over her belly. She pointed at the screen. "Then we'll be able to see your baby here."

Rose kept her eyes on the screen.

"Do you want to know the baby's gender?"

Rose shook her head.

"Okay, I won't say anything. You might end up being able to figure it out though."

"I doubt it," Rose said. It was all pretty blurry.

The technician kept rubbing the wand around. "There's the head," she said.

Rose's heart quickened. "Oh, goodness."

Eve stood.

"And there are the legs." The technician chuckled. "Good thing you don't want to know the sex. This one isn't cooperating." She continued with the test, saying the machine would take some measurements. After a few more minutes, she said, "I'll go get the doctor."

When she left, Rose turned to Eve. "So nothing's wrong, right? Or she would have said something."

"Not necessarily," Eve said. "The doctor explains the results."

"Oh," Rose said, and then, "How do you know?"

"I had one a few years ago."

"You were pregnant?"

Eve nodded. "I miscarried."

"I'm sorry." Rose wasn't sure what else to say.

"Thank you. It was a couple of years after we married." Eve smiled a little. "I'm so thankful we get to have Jackson in our lives now."

Rose nodded. Jackson was a sweetheart. She enjoyed caring for him, and being at Eve and Charlie's had been really good for her. At home it had been easy to rely on Lila and then Beth. At Eve's house, it was up to her to care for Jackson during the day and make sure all of the household chores got done. And nearly every evening, both Eve and Charlie said that her caring for Jackson in their home had helped make him a happier baby.

Finally the doctor arrived, carrying the laptop with her. She placed it on the tray, flipped it open, and then scanned the screen. "The baby's small for its gestational age." She turned toward Rose. "We often don't know the reason right away but in your case we do. You have placenta previa."

"What's that?" Rose asked.

"The placenta attached low in your uterus. It happens sometimes. Have you had any bleeding?"

Rose shook her head.

"Good. Sometimes, as the uterus expands, it will pull the placenta upward, but in your case it's really low, over the cervix. You're going to have to take it easy, as in bed rest. And no lifting."

"But I do childcare—for my aunt's baby." Rose nodded toward Eve.

The doctor shook her head. "You'll have to stop. This is a very serious condition. You'll have to have a C-section and your baby may come early." She went on to explain that if Rose started to spot at all, no matter what time of day or night, to call the office number. "Whoever is on call will get right back to you."

She'd need to move back home. There wouldn't be any reason for her to stay at Eve and Charlie's—she couldn't expect them to care for her.

"If you start bleeding, anything more than a spot here and there, call 9-1-1," the doctor said. "Any questions?"

Rose looked at Eve, a wave of panic rushing through her. "Can you think of anything to ask?"

"Besides bed rest, is there anything else that can be done?"

The doctor paused a moment. "Well, the usual. Take your prenatal vitamins." Rose had been—Beth had bought them for her early on. "Make sure you get plenty to eat, around 2,200 calories a day. Hopefully with the bed rest and if you eat well, you'll start gaining more weight. The bed rest really is essential though. If you don't take it seriously, you could have the baby far too early. If you do go into premature labor, we'll try to stop it. Also, do you have books about pregnancy you can read?"

"I have some," Eve said. "And we'll get more."

Both Rose and Eve stayed silent on the way home. Rose half watched the countryside zip by. A colt ran across a field. A teenage boy drove a team of workhorses. Daffodils bloomed in the flowerbeds of farmhouses, green shoots emerged out of newly planted gardens, and red geraniums bloomed from window boxes along the way.

As they turned off the highway, Eve said, "We'll figure things out. I'll talk to Charlie, but I'm thinking I'll go ahead and resign from my job. You can decide if you'd rather stay at our place or go home."

Rose inhaled sharply. "I'll think about it." She wasn't ready for her time at Eve and Charlie's to come to an end, but there really was no reason to stay.

As they neared the house, Rose noticed a buggy and horse hitched to the post by the garage. "I think it's Lila."

Once Eve had the car parked, Rose got out slowly—she was going to be fearful about everything now—and walked toward the house. Lila met her at the door with a half hug. "I'm picking up Trudy today. Beth had to go to Ohio to finish up some business." She leaned against her cane. "How are you?"

"Not good," Eve said, coming up behind her. "Lie down on the sofa for now. We can talk with Lila about what to do next."

Eve hurried down the hall, and Rose soon heard her speaking with Charlie in the baby's room. Rose eased herself down on the sofa as Lila asked, "What's going on?"

"Placenta previa," Rose answered. "The doctor said I need to be on bed rest." She explained what else the doctor had said, adding, "So I can't watch Jackson anymore."

"Oh, no." Lila leaned her cane against the wall and sat in the rocking chair.

"Do you think you could watch him?"

Lila nodded toward her cane. "It wouldn't be safe."

"Jah, I guess you're right. He's getting pretty big." It wouldn't do for Lila to be hobbling around, carrying nearly fifteen pounds.

Charlie stepped into the living room carrying the baby. "We're going to go down to the station for a little bit, and leave you ladies alone."

The baby lunged toward Rose, laughing as he did. She waved, and he waved back but began to whimper as Charlie headed out the door.

"What are you going to do?" Lila asked.

Rose shrugged. "Eve said I could stay here."

Eve stepped into the living room. "Yes," she said. "I just told Charlie I'm going to go ahead and resign. But I'll need to give them some notice. You wouldn't be able to stay here until I'm home for good. I'll put Jackson back in daycare until then."

Rose thanked her aunt and turned toward Lila. "I guess that means I'm coming home. I might as well go now." Lila would have to help take care of her after all. Even though she had resolved not to call Trevor until the baby was born, she decided he deserved to know what was going on.

While Eve and Lila went down the hall to her room to pack her things, Rose got up off the sofa and headed to the kitchen.

She dialed quickly and let it ring until it went into voicemail. Not surprising. He most likely recognized Eve and Charlie's number. She quickly explained what was going on and then said, "I've been staying at Eve and Charlie's but I'm going back home. Bye."

As much as she felt she should give up on Trevor, she couldn't help but remember Lila's pain in not ever knowing her biological father. Perhaps God still had a plan concerning Trevor.

෴

"No, I was completely wrong," Lila said. "I didn't know what I was talking about."

Rose reclined on the sofa at home, covered with the quilt from her bed. Dat had hustled Trudy out to help with the milking as soon as he saw Rose was home. She placed her hand on her abdomen. Jah, she was definitely showing now.

Lila had started the conversation in the buggy, telling her about meeting her half brother and what her birth father had been like—until they picked up Trudy. Now Trudy was out helping Dat with the milking, and Lila was at it again.

Lila shook her finger at Rose. "Are you listening to me?"

"Jah, I hear you. You were wrong." Rose turned and grinned at her sister. "I just want you to say it a couple of more times."

Lila wiggled the pillow out from under her arm in Dat's chair and threw it at Rose, hitting her in the chest.

"Ouch," she said, grabbing it and throwing it back. "Don't hurt me."

Lila caught the pillow and held it to her stomach. "It's going to be a long four months."

"Jah," Rose replied.

Lila pushed herself to her feet and grabbed her cane.

"Unless the Bobbli comes early."

Lila shuffled out of the room.

"Come back," Rose said.

"Why? You won't talk—not seriously, anyway."

"No, I will. Just come back." For as much as she used to want to sit around, she couldn't bear the thought of bed rest for the next four months. She'd never liked being by herself. "Please, Lila."

Lila stopped in the kitchen doorway and turned around. "I heard you leaving a message for Trevor today. I should have told you all of this before."

"Told her what?" It was Dat's voice from the kitchen.

Lila turned slowly, away from Rose and toward Dat. "What I discovered from meeting Butch Wilson Jr.," Lila said. "There's something I should have told you too."

"You'll have to tell me later," Dat said. "I just came in to fill my coffee cup." Beth had bought him a travel mug, which was quite a luxury for Dat. Rose could hear his footsteps across the linoleum as he called out, "We can talk later."

Lila turned back toward Rose.

"Wasn't it January when you saw Butch Jr.?"

Lila nodded.

"How come it's taken you this long to talk to me?"

"I don't know," Lila said. "I guess I was still thinking it all through. Plus, you know how much I hate conflict."

"You're acting the way you did when you loved Zane but were courting Reuben. Stop sitting around feeling sorry for yourself. When are you going to talk to Dat? Stop being so passive."

Lila stared at Rose for a few long seconds, and then retorted, "Says the unmarried pregnant girl on bed rest."

Rose felt hurt for a moment. Jah, she was on bed rest. But she wasn't being passive, at least she didn't think so. She sighed, knowing Lila had her own hurts and worries, and maybe she thought lashing out at Rose would help. Then again, maybe Rose hadn't been very understanding.

As Lila turned around and headed into the kitchen, her cane bumping along the floor, Rose called out, "I'm sorry."

The thump of the cane stopped. "What?"

"Jah, you heard me. I'm sorry."

The thumping started again but grew closer. Lila reappeared in the doorway.

Rose smiled. "Did you want me to say it a third time?"

Lila shook her head. "I just wanted to see your face."

"I'm sincere," Rose said, pushing herself up a little. "I was too harsh with you. You've gone through a lot."

"Denki," Lila said.

"And I'm sorry your birth father passed away."

Lila nodded, her eyes welling.

"And glad you have a half brother. I look forward to meeting him someday."

"Jah," Lila said. "That would be nice. I'd like that. I believe you will . . . someday." She turned again and went back into the kitchen. A cupboard opened, and there was a clatter, as if a couple of pans fell to the floor. Rose wished she could go help her sister. Instead, she pulled the quilt up to her chin and listened to the *Fogles* outside the living room window. She guessed a pair of robins were building a nest.

She was still on the sofa that evening, after Trudy had gone to bed. Dat and Lila sat at the kitchen table. If Rose listened carefully she could make out bits and pieces of what they were saying.

"I was wrong," Lila said. "I'd idealized the kind of man I thought my father was."

"So by default, I'm the better father now?"

Lila didn't answer for a long moment. Finally she said, "I guess that's the way it sounds."

Rose couldn't hear what was said next.

But then in a louder voice, Lila said, "I'm very thankful for your care."

Dat's voice was a little rough. "I know I was hard on you and Daniel. I didn't know how to show you that I loved you. But I did love you. I do love you."

"Denki," Lila said. "You don't know how long I've waited to hear that." Her voice trembled a little. "I love you too."

Rose wasn't sure what happened next. Both were silent. She thought maybe they hugged, but she couldn't be sure. Neither was very affectionate—and yet they both just had been, at least with their words.

Rose's hand went to her belly, which had just grown taut. The Bobbli kicked against it. Her eyes filled with tears. She was going to be a parent. A mother. The highest calling she could think of, but she was sure the job was much harder than she'd ever imagined.

24

Zane sat with Gideon and Lila, a piece of Monika's chocolate chess pie in front of him, in the Bylers' kitchen. It was the first Saturday in April, and the afternoon sun streamed through the windows. Zane and Lila had met with the lawyer the day before, and the meeting had been disturbing. The insurance company hadn't finalized their investigation yet, but Mr. Addison claimed he planned to sue Lila.

"All of this is hard to believe," Gideon said. The second police report faulted Mr. Addison, and Brad had found out from the man's cell phone company that he had been texting at the time of the accident, or at least right before it.

But Mr. Addison continued to claim that Lila had pulled out in front of him. Brad had explained the man had a right to sue and surmised Mr. Addison felt a jury of his peers, meaning Englischers, would sympathize with him.

"It goes against our beliefs, doesn't it? To go to court?" Lila's blue eyes lit up as she spoke. "It's the way of the world, not our way."

Gideon nodded. "That's what we believe. Has anyone suggested mediation?"

Lila wrapped her hands around her coffee cup and shook her head. Zane doubted she'd want to be in the same room with the man who'd hit her to try to mediate the conflict. But if Mr. Addison took her to court, she'd have to go, unless it could be settled beforehand.

Gideon tugged on his beard. "I never would have guessed this from the few minutes I spent with Donald Addison after the accident. He seemed pretty upset."

Zane's neck tightened. "The man called 9-1-1 and gave them false information."

"Perhaps it's what he believed though," Gideon said.

"Or what he convinced himself to believe." Zane tried to relax. "But how can he argue against the investigation? Or his cell phone record?"

Lila twisted her mouth in that endearing way she had. "I think he might live down that lane right before the school."

"On Derry Road?"

Lila nodded. "Rose and I saw a vehicle that looked like his turn down that way. We followed it to a house, but the driver had already gone inside."

"Jah, his address online indicates that he lives there now," Zane said. "Before that he lived in Ephrata."

"Perhaps he had just moved," Gideon said. "Or was looking at the house. We can't know for sure he was getting ready to turn, so we should expect the best of him, jah?"

Zane hesitated, not sure if he should speak up or not.

Lila gave him one of her looks.

Gideon sighed and said, "Go ahead, Zane. Tell me what you think."

Zane inhaled, sure they thought him too aggressive. "It's just that I don't know that we should think the best of this man.

What if he's taking advantage of Lila because he doesn't think she'll pursue justice? These medical bills are a lot of money. And now that Rose is having complications, it could put even more stress on the mutual aid fund."

"I hope you don't think any of us expect you to be responsible for Lila's medical bills," Gideon said. "Because we don't. If we can't cover it, we'll hold fundraisers. And other districts will contribute too."

"Denki," Zane said, relieved. He knew the district would do what they could, but he'd feared he and Lila would be responsible for the rest. "But this man's insurance should cover Lila's expenses—there's no way she, or the district, should have to pay for the repairs to his SUV."

Gideon tugged on his beard. "You know as well as I do that life isn't fair. That's why we leave justice to the Lord."

"I know that." Zane sighed. "I'll leave this up to Lila, with your advice."

"How about if I talk to this lawyer you know?" Gideon asked. "Would you be all right with that? And we'll pray that his insurance company's investigation agrees with the police report."

Lila nodded.

Zane tried to relax. He didn't want his anxiety to make things worse for Lila, but he did want justice. However, he might have to learn how to give up that desire, to take one more step to truly becoming Amish.

"We should talk about when you two plan to marry," Gideon said.

Zane searched Lila's face, but she wouldn't look at him.

"I'd rather not talk about that yet," Lila said.

"Why not?" Gideon asked.

Lila's face grew red.

Gideon leaned across the table. "What is it?"

Lila didn't answer, but finally she looked at Zane.

He shrugged but said, "Lila wants to wait until after Rose has her baby." He was beginning to feel that was just an excuse though.

"Lila?" Gideon asked. "Is that why you don't want to set a date?"

Her eyes welled with tears, and she glanced at her cane propped against the table. "Jah."

Gideon took another sip of coffee and then asked quietly, "Would you feel more comfortable talking to Monika?"

She shook her head. "There's really not anything to talk about."

When Gideon didn't respond, Lila said, "I'm working at healing. I'm done with the physical therapist, but I'm still doing all of my exercises. I am getting stronger." She sighed. "I feel as if everyone's trying to rush me. I love Zane. I want to marry him. But if I need a few more months to make sure Rose and the baby are settled and to be certain I'm healthier—well, then, that's what I need."

"I see." Gideon glanced at Zane.

Zane kept his eyes on Lila, not wanting to make her feel as if he were disagreeing with her by making eye contact with Gideon. She was right to say what she needed, and he shouldn't take it as a rejection. Even though he felt it was.

"How is Rose doing?" Gideon asked.

Lila sat up a little straighter. "She's feeling fine. She says she thinks the doctor made the whole bed rest thing up." Lila smiled a little. "The Bobbli's moving quite a bit. Thankfully Rose is gaining more weight."

"I see," Gideon said again, but Zane wasn't sure what he meant. Perhaps he was understanding what Lila didn't want to discuss.

On the way home, in the buggy, Zane stayed quiet. He wasn't going to force Lila to talk about anything else—or force her

320

to take action she wasn't ready to. He'd been reading 1 Corinthians 13 over and over, not in the King James Version, which their district sometimes used instead of the High German Scripture, but in his old Bible, the New International Version from when he was a boy. *"Love is patient, love is kind . . . It does not dishonor others, it is not self-seeking . . . It always protects, always trusts, always hopes, always perseveres. Love never fails."*

That was the way he wanted to love Lila. He wouldn't fail her. He'd give her the time she needed.

⤙⤚

On Monday, Zane's ride dropped him off at the intersection of Juneberry Lane and the highway in the early evening. He was thankful work hadn't slowed down much in the winter—although it hadn't picked up the way he'd hoped this spring either. His boss was waiting on a new contract while they did the finishing work on the last project.

As Zane walked the rest of the way home, he looked down the Lehman driveway just as he did every time he passed, just as he had since he was twelve. Searching for Lila. Always, searching for Lila. He wouldn't stop by today. He'd give her space. Although he would head to the barn after he put his things away and help Tim with the milking.

The trees along the lane practically glowed with new growth, all in tender shades of green that made the world seem as if it had just been reborn. Zane couldn't help but feel a sense of hope regardless of the ongoing uncertainty with Lila.

At the cedar tree he angled through the field, heading in a straight line for the little house. As he walked along briskly, Tim came up from the creek, a fence pole digger in his hand. Zane knew he'd been expanding the fence in the far field. Tim waved.

Zane picked up his pace as he made his way toward the man.

321

"Do you have a minute?" Tim called out, increasing his stride. As he walked, his beard blew in the wind. He definitely had more gray in it, but he was as big as ever, still standing tall, his shoulders broad and his back straight.

Zane had feared the man most of his life, and silently criticized him much of the time. But now watching him, Zane hoped that when he was nearing fifty he was as much a man as Tim Lehman, and not just in stature. Sure, Tim had made his mistakes, but his heart was good.

As they met in the middle of the field, Tim extended his hand and shook Zane's with vigor. "I wanted to talk with you about the dairy and your plans for your future," Tim said. "If you're still interested."

"I'm interested in listening," Zane said. Tim hadn't said any more about his idea for the last few months.

"Beth went to Ohio in March to meet with an attorney. Her first husband left her as the beneficiary of his life insurance policy and his house. It's not a large inheritance, but it's a fair amount. She'd like to invest the money into the farm."

"Really?" Zane wasn't sure how that affected him.

"I need to talk with your grandfather and your folks too, but I wanted to run my idea by you first."

Zane nodded.

"I'd like to use the money to remodel your barn into a dairy setup, which means we could double the herd. That would increase our profits, at least some." He smiled wryly.

Zane knew dairy profits weren't great. "I see," he said.

"But I need to know if you're in, if you want to partner with me." Tim swung the digger to his other hand. "I couldn't manage a bigger herd by myself."

"I don't have anything to invest in the business," Zane said. "It's not as if I could come in as a partner or anything."

"No, but your family's investment would be considerable.

322

We'd want to cultivate the south field, plant alfalfa. And of course there's the barn."

Zane nodded.

"The big question, for you, is your labor. Are you interested in becoming a farmer? In taking over the business someday when I retire?"

"I'll think about it," Zane said. He'd prefer to commit after he and Lila were actually married.

Tim frowned. "What are your concerns?"

Zane shrugged.

"Lila?"

Zane nodded, not wanting to say anything.

"This has gone on too long," Tim said. "I know she's still hurting, but she has her life. She has you. She has her family." Zane expected him to say she needed to get over it, but he didn't.

"Jah," Zane said. "She just needs some more time is all."

Tim took off his hat and rubbed his hand along his hairline. "Are you committed to her? Do you still love her—you know, as it seems you always have?"

"Of course," Zane said. "I love her more than I ever have."

"Then you two will figure it out." Tim shook Zane's hand again. "Give what I proposed some thought. Talk with your parents. There's no rush to make a decision."

Zane thanked him and said he'd be over to help with the milking soon.

Tim nodded and then headed on up the field toward his house, swinging the posthole digger as if it were a stick in his hand.

Zane continued on toward his house, skirting around the barn, imagining it outfitted with milking equipment. He couldn't help but think about how much his dad hated the smell of the Lehmans' dairy when they first moved to Juneberry Lane, but Zane hadn't heard him complain about it for years.

Zane stopped for a moment at the garden. He and his mom

were sharing the responsibility of it. He'd also bought chicks a few weeks ago and put them in his parents' coop.

"Hello!"

Zane squinted toward the porch as Gideon waved. "What are you doing here?"

"I have an update on the accident."

Zane hurried forward. "Come on in." He opened the door and stepped into the house. It was cool inside, and the light was dim. Gideon followed. "Do you want a glass of lemonade?" Zane asked.

"Water would be great," Gideon answered, looking around the inside of the house.

Zane motioned toward the kitchen, stepped through the doorway, put his lunch box on the counter, and filled two glasses from the tap. Gideon took his with a thank-you and then said, "You've done a fine job on this house."

"Denki," Zane answered. "I enjoyed the work." Because it had been for Lila.

Gideon asked, "How do you like living by yourself?"

Zane exhaled. "I don't." He nodded toward his parents' house. "It's not like I'm entirely alone, but it wouldn't be my first choice."

Gideon nodded.

"What did Brad say?" Zane asked.

"That Mr. Addison hasn't filed a suit yet, obviously, or else Lila would have been notified. He thinks the man is bluffing. Brad plans to meet with the insurance adjuster and talk things through. Hopefully they'll have completed their report by then. He thinks Mr. Addison assumes, since Lila didn't have insurance, that she doesn't have anyone to represent her. If he steps up as her representative, maybe the man won't sue."

Zane held his glass in both hands. "That sounds good," he said. "I'm grateful."

Gideon nodded. "Well, I feel partly to blame. We all assumed Donald Addison was telling the truth that day. It made this all go on a lot longer than it should have."

"I just hope the truth will prevail," Zane said. "And it would be nice if Mr. Addison would agree with it. With math. And physics and all that."

"Well," Gideon said, "we certainly don't have any control over what he'll agree with, but I don't see how he can truly challenge the police report and certainly not his own insurance company's findings. But he may still keep believing that he's right."

"Jah," Zane said.

"I have another question for you."

Zane nodded in agreement. Gideon could ask him anything.

"Are you still certain you want to live the Plain lifestyle? Has any of this changed your mind? Many people who think they want to live Plain decide they don't after a year or so—or after something challenges their core beliefs, maybe ones that are in conflict with the way we believe."

"Jah," Zane answered. "My wish is to remain Plain. Yes, I've been confronted with things that bother me more than your average Amish man." He smiled. "But it isn't all just that I was raised Englisch. Part of it is my personality." Zane shrugged. "I'm learning."

Gideon nodded. "That's all I can ask."

Zane tried to smile, but he knew it came across as more of a grimace. "How's Reuben doing?"

"He's hanging in there," Gideon said.

Zane wasn't sure why he asked. Maybe just to change the subject. He didn't expect Gideon to share anything personal about his son. Zane sighed. He felt for the guy, living alone. The idea of living without Lila for a while longer was difficult to accept—but his greater fear was that once Rose had her baby Lila would come up with another excuse not to marry.

25

Rose held on to the door handle as Eve turned her car down Juneberry Lane. The lilacs along the fence line were blooming, along with the wild irises that grew on the grassy shoulder. They were coming home from the clinic, where she'd gotten a steroid shot to help the baby's lungs develop. The doctor was certain Rose would deliver early. If the baby's lungs were more mature, it could make all the difference. "I appreciate you taking me," Rose said.

"Of course." Eve glanced toward Rose as she turned down the driveway. "Is it all a bit overwhelming?"

Rose nodded. "I'm just trying to take in everything." The doctor had said she'd have to have a C-section, for sure—the placenta hadn't budged. Thankfully the baby's size, at thirty-three weeks, was good now.

"I think we should talk with your Dat about you coming to stay with us." Eve had been home with Jackson for over a month now. "I can get you to the hospital sooner when you go into labor."

"I'll be all right," Rose said. It felt good to be home, sleeping in the same room as Trudy and Lila, and hanging out with Beth.

"It could mean calling for an ambulance," Eve answered.

Rose didn't want that. She didn't want any of it. Not a C-section. Not a hospital stay. Not her fate of being a single parent.

But she did want the Bobbli. She had a relationship with the being living inside her, kicking her ribs, throwing an elbow against her taut belly, and even hiccupping now and then. Rose couldn't marvel about it to Eve—who never carried a Bobbli to this point. Or Lila.

She had said something a few times to Beth, who shared her excitement. A couple of times Beth felt her belly and exclaimed at the movement. Rose could never tell her stepmother how much that meant to her.

It wasn't that she longed to share the experience with Trevor. After all, he hadn't tried to contact her in any way, not even after she let him know about the complications. But she longed to share it with someone. And she guessed the longing would only get worse. Sure, Beth and Dat would be kind. They'd be interested in their grandchild. They'd mark special milestones like the first tooth and all those things that Rose remembered Eve celebrating with Trudy when she cared for all of them. But it wouldn't be the same—and that wasn't anyone's fault but her own.

"Rose?" Eve had pulled to a stop by the house. "Are you sure you won't come stay with us until the baby comes?"

She shook her head. "No. I'll be all right. I'll call you as soon as I start having contractions." She wasn't sure what a *contraction* actually felt like, but she guessed she'd know when she had one. Jenny certainly knew the day of Dat and Beth's wedding. "The due date is still seven weeks away. I'm sure I still have lots of time, right?"

"Let's hope," Eve said. "But if you change your mind, let

me know." She turned the engine off. "I'll go in with you and tell everyone hello."

It was midafternoon, and Beth was in the kitchen, starting a chicken to roast. The hum of the sewing machine from the living room stopped—Lila was making a quilt of navy blue and maroon stars, for Casey and Simon. Simon would be coming home from Iraq soon. Lila wasn't entirely back to her old self, but the sewing she was doing for the family and her quilting were at least keeping her busy.

Eve told Beth hello and then headed toward the living room. The thump of Lila's cane indicated she was on her feet, probably giving Eve a hug.

"How is everything?" Beth wiped her hands on her apron and turned toward Rose.

"All right," she said and then bit her lip. She didn't want to say too much, not until they were alone.

"Can you stay for a cup of coffee, Eve?" Beth called. "I made some cookies for Trudy's after-school snack. We can have those too."

"Where is Trudy?" Rose asked as she sat down at the table. She needed to get back down on the sofa, but she'd wait a few minutes.

"Over at Shani's. She and Adam are helping Shani in their garden."

"They should work in ours." Lila followed Eve back into the kitchen.

"I'll get to it tomorrow," Beth said.

"That's not what I meant." Lila sat down at the end of the table. "You're doing everything around here."

"I'm doing fine." Beth picked up the plate of cookies from the counter and put them on the table. "I'm enjoying every bit of it."

A warm feeling startled Rose, causing her to leap to her feet.

"Sweetie," Eve said.

"Oh, no." Rose couldn't help but laugh. What was happening to her? "I think I wet myself."

"Are you sure?" Eve asked.

Rose pointed to the floor, at the puddle of water. And her underwear and skirt were soaked.

"It's probably your water," Eve said.

She gasped. "My what?" And then gasped again, clutching her belly. A pain tore through her middle.

"The amniotic fluid," Eve explained. "Are you having a contraction?"

It took a moment before she could talk. "Maybe." She'd read about the amniotic fluid. That wasn't good, she was sure. Neither was the pain.

Eve kneeled and put her finger in the liquid and smelled it. "It's not urine." She looked up at Rose. "We need to get you to the hospital."

Lila let out a yelp. "It's too early."

By the look on Eve's face, she thought it was too. "They might be able to keep the baby from coming this soon."

"I'll go pack a bag," Beth said.

"I'll help." Lila followed their stepmother. "And get a clean dress."

Eve directed Rose to sit back down. "We'll get you changed and ready to go." Eve called the doctor on her cell phone to let her know what was happening.

Fifteen minutes and two contractions later, Rose was ready. Lila gave her a hug, tears in her eyes. "Come with me," Rose said.

"What help can I be?"

"I need you." Rose choked back her tears. She needed Lila, more than anyone.

Without hesitating, Lila said, "All right."

Beth headed toward the back door. "I'll go tell your Dat. Once we finish the milking, we'll go get Trudy and ask Shani if she can give us a ride."

"Would you see if Zane's home yet?" Lila asked. "Tell him what's going on. Ask him to come up too." She turned toward Rose. "Is that all right?"

"Of course," Rose said. "Now let's go."

❧

By the time they reached the hospital, the contractions were three minutes apart. After a quick trip through the Emergency Department, Rose was in a gown and on a gurney on her way up to the labor and delivery ward. Eve stayed at her side, but Lila couldn't keep up and said she'd meet her there.

The nurses had collected some of the amniotic fluid when she first arrived and sent it to the lab to see how developed the baby's lungs were—that would help them know what to do if the contractions couldn't be stopped.

Another contraction overtook Rose, the most painful one yet. "We're almost there," the young man pushing the gurney said as Rose tried not to scream. She blew out her breath like she'd read to do in one of her books.

When they reached the floor, a nurse met them and directed the gurney into a room. She took Rose's vitals, asked a few questions, and hooked her up to a monitor. "The doctor will be right in," she said.

"It won't be your doctor," Eve explained. "She's still at her office."

Rose blinked. She hadn't thought of that.

The doctor was middle-aged and seemed kind enough. He read from the computer, "Primigravida."

"That means a woman having her first baby," Eve explained.

"Oh," Rose said.

"Placenta previa," the doctor read. "And thirty-three weeks." He looked at her again and stepped away from the computer. "I'll be right back."

Lila came in just after the doctor left. She was a little out of breath and sat down in the chair beside Rose's bed. She reached for her hand just as the nurse came in.

"I need that hand," she said, a hint of teasing in her voice. "I'm going to poke you."

Rose appreciated the lighthearted tone. It helped her not to worry as much. The doctor came back in with an ultrasound machine. Rose knew the drill and wiggled her gown up over her belly. Lila stepped toward the door.

"You should stay," Rose said, sensing her sister's discomfort. "In fact, come closer, you'll be able to see the baby." For a moment Rose was afraid she'd said the wrong thing to Lila. Her sister hesitated at the door, but then she glanced toward their Aenti. Rose couldn't see the expression on Eve's face, but Lila started back toward the bed, a look of longing on her face.

The doctor moved the wand around on Rose's belly as another contraction overtook her. The worst yet. Lila stepped to her side and offered her hand. "Squeeze it," she said.

Rose did. The doctor waited until she was done and then ran the wand over her tight belly again. The image of the Bobbli appeared on the screen.

Lila leaned closer as a little gasp escaped her mouth.

"It doesn't look good," the doctor said. "The fluid is way down." He looked Rose in the eyes. "We're going to have to go ahead and do the C-section."

Rose nodded, trying to be brave. "Can my sister come with me?" Rose wasn't going to ask if Lila wanted to or not. She needed her to. All her life, Lila had been there for her—even when Rose hadn't appreciated it.

"Yes," the doctor said. "Sit tight. We'll have you in the OR in a few minutes."

As soon as the doctor left, Lila said, "Eve should go with you. She's smarter about these things than I am."

Eve shook her head. "You go, Lila. I'm going to go call Charlie and Shani. Your Dat needs to get up here. I'll leave a message for Gideon too. And I'll call your grandparents."

"Denki," Rose said, extending her free hand to her aunt.

"And we'll all be praying. For you and the baby."

They had Rose on her way to the OR in just a few minutes. As the doctor helped push the gurney, he explained that she would be given a spinal block and that Lila would stand up by her head.

"Are you all right with that?" Rose asked, realizing she hadn't considered what it might be like for Lila.

"Of course," her sister responded. Rose could tell it was a struggle for Lila to keep up with the gurney, but she was doing well.

The doctor was speaking to Lila now. "You'll need to scrub in. We'll show you. And then wear a gown."

"May I keep my cane with me?" she asked.

"Yes," he said.

By the time Lila joined her in the OR, Rose had gone through another contraction and the anesthesiologist had given her something in the IV and then the spinal block. Everyone spoke in quiet, calm voices. Rose thought of the calves she'd seen delivered through the years. None of them had been by C-section. She'd seen a few first-time mothers that were frantic through the delivery, but their instincts usually kicked in and they knew what to do with their offspring.

She hoped she'd know what to do after the Bobbli was born. She hoped it would come naturally. She hoped she'd love the Bobbli as a mother should.

A few minutes later the doctor began to get to work. She felt a sensation on her belly—but not any pain.

"We'll have your baby here in a few minutes," the doctor said.

Rose reached for Lila's hand and searched for her sister's eyes. Lila stepped above her, squeezed her hand, and held her gaze. "You're doing great," Lila said. "I'm so proud of you."

Rose kept her eyes on Lila's, not wanting to think of what the doctor was doing. Jenny had a C-section and she did fine. Rose said a silent prayer, asking for safety for the Bobbli, asking for strength for herself, asking for peace. She thought of Trevor for a moment and again wondered if she should call him. Perhaps Eve would do it for her.

"Rose," the doctor said, "I'm reaching for the baby now."

It seemed like an eternity before the doctor said, "It's a girl. We need to get her pinked up."

Lila's eyes left Rose's.

"What are they doing?" Rose asked.

"They're listening to her lungs." Lila craned her neck. "Now they're wrapping her in warm blankets," Lila answered. "She's beautiful. Of course, she's tiny, but she has lots of dark hair."

A soft mewing reached Rose's ears. "Is that her?"

Lila nodded. "It's good she is making noises. They're bringing her this way."

A nurse held the Bobbli by Rose's head. "We're taking her to the NICU. When you're able, you can go see her."

Rose hoped it would be soon. The nurse bent down so the little one was right next to Rose's face. She was beautiful. "Hi, Bobbli," she said, letting go of Lila's hand to stroke the little one's cheek as a flood of emotions choked her.

"Do you have a name picked out?" the nurse asked.

Rose shook her head. She'd talked with Lila about, if the Bobbli was a girl, naming her after their mother. In true Lila fashion, her sister had avoided discussing the topic, and Rose surmised Lila wanted to use the name someday, if she could have children.

"Abra," Lila said.

"What?" Rose turned her head toward her sister. Had she heard right?

"We could call her Abrie," Lila said.

Rose's voice shook as she repeated the name. The baby turned toward her voice. "I'm your Mamm," Rose said.

"We'll let you know what the lab report says about her lungs," the nurse said.

"Thank you," Rose managed to say as the nurse and baby disappeared from sight.

"They're putting her in one of those warming beds," Lila said. "And pushing her out the door."

Rose felt as if her heart might break. It tore her apart to have Abrie taken from her, but she knew it was for the best.

"Denki," she said to Lila. "Abrie is perfect for her."

Lila nodded but didn't say anything more. Rose had never felt so connected to her sister, or to their mother.

Lila stayed with her as the doctor stitched her up, as they wheeled her back to her room, and as she rested in her hospital bed with a pillow against her belly. Several times she asked when she could go see Abrie. The nurse told her to rest for a while, and then she'd need to drink and eat something.

"I'll go find Eve," Lila said. "And see if Dat's arrived."

Rose nodded and closed her eyes. Even in her excitement she was tired, exhausted.

The next thing she knew Dat, Beth, and Shani were in the room, along with Lila, and it was past eight. She'd slept for a couple of hours.

"Have you seen the Bobbli?" Rose asked Shani. "Is she all right?"

Shani said they hadn't but offered to go and check.

"Denki," Rose said.

Beth stroked Rose's hair, while Dat stood at the end of the bed, not seeming to know what to say.

"The Bobbli's beautiful," Lila said. "I'm guessing she looks like Rose and Simon did. Lots of dark hair."

"What did you name her?" Dat asked.

Rose hesitated for a moment. Would the name be hurtful to her father? And she hadn't said the full name out loud yet, not the one she'd planned on. Would Lila approve of the middle name? It didn't matter. She was the mother. It was her responsibility. "Abra," she answered. "Abra Elizabeth." After both of her mothers.

An expression of confusion passed over Dat's face, but then he smiled.

"We'll call her Abrie," Rose said.

"That's perfect," Dat answered.

Beth didn't say anything, but her eyes were extra shiny.

"Where's Trudy?" Rose asked.

"Out in the waiting room," Dat answered. "With Adam and Zane. Your grandparents are there too."

That meant a lot to Rose. "Did you talk to Trudy?" Rose asked Lila. "And explain how I am and where the Bobbli is."

Lila nodded. Dat sat down, and Beth chatted away about how worried they'd all been. Rose knew they still were, about the Bobbli, but the sound of Beth's voice was comforting. The nurse came in, checked Rose's vitals, and then gave her juice to drink. "The anesthesia must be wearing off," the nurse said. "Are you ready for your pain meds?"

Rose nodded. She was definitely uncomfortable.

Shani returned and talked with the nurse quietly. Then the nurse said, "If you'd like you can go down to the NICU for a quick visit."

"Wunderbar," Rose answered, swinging her legs toward the side of the bed.

"Hold on." The nurse chuckled. "A transportation aide will wheel you down."

"Who else can see her?" Rose asked Shani as the nurse left the room.

"Your Dat and Beth. And Lila. For now. Depending on how long she stays in, others can see her, too, later."

"Did you see her?"

Shani shook her head. "I'd have to scrub to go in. I didn't take time for that. They said she's a fighter though. Believe me, they've taken care of babies much smaller."

Soon the transportation aide came for Rose. As he pushed her through the lobby, Rose asked him to stop. Trudy stepped up and gave her a hug, along with Mammi and Dawdi and then Zane.

"We're going to see the Bobbli," she said. "Will you be here when we get back?"

Her grandparents both nodded, and Eve and Shani said they'd stay too.

"May I go with you?" Trudy asked.

Rose shook her head. "Not tonight. But soon."

Trudy's face fell, but then Adam stepped to her side, and she gave Rose another hug.

The transportation aide began pushing again just as someone called out, "Rose!"

It was Reuben, although she couldn't see him. Her heart began to race as the aide stopped and turned the chair a little. Reuben stood in the middle of the hall, holding a slender vase with two white roses.

"For you," he said. "And the Bobbli."

She nodded, unable to speak for a moment. Dat stepped forward and shook his hand. So did Zane.

"Denki," Rose managed to say. "We're going to the NICU. Will you be here when we get back?"

Reuben shook his head. "I'll leave these."

Rose thanked him again, touched by his thoughtfulness. Then she swallowed hard and told the aide to continue. She'd given up so much—but she had little Abrie. That was who she needed to concentrate on.

She wouldn't call Trevor, after all—and she wouldn't ask anyone else to either. There was no reason to. She was one hundred percent sure of it.

Beth, Dat, and Lila trailed along beside her. When they reached the NICU, the nurse showed all of them how to scrub up and put gowns on. They had to wear a cover over their head, and Dat had to wear one over his beard. Then they were allowed to head in to see the Bobbli, Dat pushing Rose's chair.

"Good news," the nurse said. "The steroid shots worked. Her lungs are all right."

Rose sank against the chair in relief.

"This way," the nurse said as she led the way. They passed other babies in the tiny warming beds. Then they passed a woman, also in a wheelchair, wearing a gown and bathrobe too, holding a tiny Bobbli. A man stood behind her.

Rose realized, with all of them wearing the blue gowns, that maybe they weren't so obviously Amish. But then, by the way the woman and man stared at them, she smiled a little and figured they still were.

"She's right here," the nurse said. "We'll get you transferred to the rocking chair, and then you can hold her. We'll see if she'll nurse. If not, we'll show you how to pump. She'll need your colostrum."

Rose had read about that.

"Have you named her?" the nurse asked.

"Abra Elizabeth," Rose answered. "We'll call her Abrie."

"Great," the nurse said. "We'll fill out the birth certificate. We'll need your signature. Then we'll get it filed."

"Do I need to put the father on the certificate?" Rose asked. It was a question she'd wondered about but had thought she still had time to figure it out.

"No," the nurse said. "It's entirely up to you." Rose didn't sense any judgment in the woman's voice. Dat frowned, which surprised her—but she didn't have the energy to ask what he was thinking.

Rose could see the Bobbli now. She wore a diaper, but that was all—except for the tubes and wires hooked up to her. Once Rose was transferred to the rocking chair, the nurse wrapped the Bobbli in a blanket and placed her in Rose's arms. The tubes and wires were long enough to allow for that. The blanket was warm and the Bobbli incredibly light. Rose bent her head down and whispered, "Hello, Abrie."

The Bobbli looked up, her eyes bright.

"How much does she weigh?" Rose asked.

"Four pounds one ounce. She's a good size," the nurse said. "And she's eighteen inches long. She's been on an IV to hydrate her so she won't be hungry, but maybe she'll still nurse—it all depends on how developed her sucking reflex is." The nurse placed a pillow on Rose's lap, which helped support the Bobbli.

Lila and Beth both stepped closer. "Ah, she's so beautiful," Beth said. Then she turned toward Dat, "Come on, Tim."

Dat stepped closer too. "She's so tiny. I didn't know a Bobbli could be so small."

They all hovered over the little one, speaking to her and to each other. Soon she started to root against Rose's chest.

"That's a good sign," Dat said. "Perhaps I should leave."

"Good grief," Beth said, "you're a dairy farmer."

Dat nodded. "But Rose might mind."

"Dat," she said, "that's the least of my worries."

338

"I'll help you," the nurse said. She pulled open Rose's gown and helped move the Bobbli closer. She rooted around more and then latched on. Rose gazed down at her. It all felt so much more natural than she'd expected it to.

"Oh, you're doing great," Beth said.

Lila sat down in Rose's wheelchair.

Rose couldn't take her eyes off her Bobbli. She'd never felt such love. Lila rolled the wheelchair closer. "She's wonderful," Lila said. "I never imagined feeling this way. I can't even imagine what this is like for you, Rosey."

It had been so long since Lila had called her that. And there was no bitterness in her voice at all. No jealousy. Only joy.

The nurse explained that it was a good sign that the baby could suck. "That reflex doesn't usually kick in until thirty-four or thirty-five weeks."

Rose still couldn't take her eyes off the baby.

"We'll need to regulate her temperature until she can do that herself. And make sure she's gaining weight. She'll be in here for a few weeks."

Rose was too enthralled to answer.

"You'll need to make sure you take care of yourself too. You've just been through major surgery. You need to eat well and get a lot of rest so you can feed this baby."

"We'll make sure she does." Lila reached forward and put her hand on Rose's leg.

Something beeped, and the nurse said she'd be right back.

"What are you thinking?" Beth asked in a low voice.

Rose thought she was asking her, but when she glanced up, to her relief, Beth was addressing Dat.

He sighed. "I just got a glimpse of the past that I'd never really thought about, that I wasn't part of."

Beth stepped to his side. "What's that?"

Dat's gaze fell on Lila. "What it was like for your Mamm

when you and Daniel were born. Your Mamm was much stronger than I ever gave her credit for. You take after her." Then he turned to Rose. "And so do you. Don't either of you ever forget it."

Beth clasped her hands together but didn't say anything more.

Finally Dat did though. "It's amazing, isn't it, how the Lord brings healing. This Bobbli wasn't started the right way, but God will continue to use her to work his good. Just as he uses all of us."

Lila stood then, and with one hand on her cane, she wrapped her other one around Dat. He helped balance her as she hugged him.

Rose's watery eyes fell back on Abrie. She'd tell her about her father someday—but not today. She was grateful now that Trevor had never returned her phone calls, that he never came back to Lancaster County. It was for the best she didn't call him again. Dat had been right.

She wouldn't put Trevor's name on the birth certificate. There was no reason for Abrie to have the last name of Anderson if Trevor wasn't going to be in her life. Her name would be Abra Elizabeth Lehman. She breathed a sigh of relief, knowing it was settled. She'd never been so sure of anything in all of her life.

"What are *you* thinking?" Rose asked Lila, as her sister settled back down in the wheelchair.

"That I'm blessed to be Abrie's Aenti." She exhaled. "And that it's time for me to marry Zane. Even if we can't have children, we will still be a family. Just like you and this little one are a family, even now. I need to trust God with this."

26

The June rain clouds threatened as Reuben walked slowly from where he'd parked his buggy toward the Lehmans' house. He hadn't seen Rose since she'd given birth over a month ago. The Bobbli had come home the week before, and it sounded as if everything was going well.

Reuben had deliberately stayed away, but Tim had asked him to stop by and help finish their basement to make the space usable for Lila and Zane's wedding. They'd finally set a date for mid-July. A month away.

The rain started as Reuben headed up the steps and knocked on the back door. He was surprised when Rose answered it, holding the Bobbli against her shoulder.

"Reuben," she said. "Come in from the rain." She nodded toward the kitchen. "How have you been?"

"Fine," he answered, taking off his hat and hanging it on a peg in the mudroom. "How are you?" He stepped into the kitchen.

"*Gut*," she answered. Her eyes were bright, and her face was a little flushed. It was a warm day.

"How's the Bobbli?" he asked.

"Doing well," Rose said. "She's gaining weight and hitting her developmental markers. Considering she shouldn't even be born yet, she's doing great." Rose shifted the Bobbli from her shoulder to her arms with ease.

The little one had her eyes closed. She was tiny but had a head full of dark hair and a little indentation in her cheek. A dimple. A pain shot through Reuben's chest. He wished he hadn't come, but he couldn't turn around now.

"Denki for the flowers you brought to the hospital," Rose said. "That was thoughtful. It meant a lot."

He nodded, afraid to say anything more. Without responding or commenting on the Bobbli, he excused himself and headed to the basement. He wasn't sure if he should have taken the flowers or not, but he wanted to truly forgive Rose, to feel his forgiveness inside, and somehow he felt the gesture would help. Thankfully it had. He hadn't felt resentful of her since that night—even though his heart still hurt when he saw her.

"Tim?" he called out as he reached the bottom stair.

Trudy answered, "We're back here!"

Reuben headed toward her voice and found Trudy holding the frame of a wall. Reuben stepped to her side.

"Are you ready to take over?" she asked. "Because Dat's getting a little tired of me not knowing what to do to help."

"No," Tim said, "you were doing fine. Really." He winked at Reuben.

"I'll go play with Abrie," Trudy said.

"Play?" Tim asked. "Is she doing that already?"

"You know what I mean," she answered.

"You're going to go play she's a doll?"

"Jah. Something like that." Trudy grinned and waved good-bye as she skipped back through the basement.

Reuben was surprised at how relaxed everyone seemed. He'd

seen the stress and chaos of the Lehman house many times before. He was surprised it wasn't that way now.

Tim hadn't worked at the lumberyard for a few months. Reuben had missed the man's company and his expertise, but he was busy with his farm now and working on converting the Becks' barn. Soon he and Zane would expand the dairy herd.

"I should have done this basement work years ago." Tim shook his head. "Aside from needing the space for special occasions, we were all so cramped upstairs. We could have used the extra room."

"What all do you plan to do?" Reuben asked.

"Wall in the big area down here. Put in a stove over there, a sink, and a counter. We can set up the tables down here if the weather isn't good on the day of the wedding."

"Can Lila make it up and down the stairs?" Reuben asked.

"I've cleaned up the outdoor stairs," Tim said. "We'll use those. They're not as steep." He stepped back toward the frame. "She's doing better. She's gained more mobility in the last month, and she hopes to get rid of the cane soon so she will be able to carry Abrie."

Reuben smiled a little. It seemed both of the older Lehman girls were doing better.

⌒⌒⌒

A couple of hours later, Reuben went up to the kitchen to get two glasses of water. Lila and Beth sat at the table and Trudy stood at the window, holding the Bobbli. Rose was nowhere in sight. He expected that she was napping— after all she was less than a month past major surgery—but a minute later she came in with a basket of peas and radishes.

"Are you and Dat ready for a snack?" she asked Reuben. "And some coffee?"

"Maybe in a little bit." He quickly retreated to the basement.

They had worked for another half hour when Reuben heard a vehicle across the gravel outside. "Are you expecting anyone?" Reuben asked.

Tim shook his head. "No, but it's probably Shani. She stops by once a day or so to check on Rose and the Bobbli."

Reuben didn't hear anything more, but a few minutes later, footsteps fell on the stairs.

"Tim?" It was Beth. Tim put down his hammer and headed toward her. Reuben hesitated but then followed.

"Trevor's here." Beth's voice was low. "Rose wants you."

Tim paused for a moment but then took the stairs two at a time while Reuben froze. Trevor was the last person in the world Reuben wanted to see, and he decided to stay in the basement. But then Beth said, "Would you come up? Your presence might help keep . . . a balance."

Reuben couldn't imagine what help he could be, but Tim was his friend. He wouldn't abandon him now. He followed Beth up to the kitchen.

Trevor stood on the mud porch, his T-shirt sprinkled with raindrops, facing Rose. Lila still sat at the table, and Trudy was in the archway to the living room, holding the Bobbli. Abrie appeared to be sleeping.

"I had a brief note about the baby," Trevor said. "With your return address on the envelope."

Rose glanced around the room as if looking for an answer.

"I hadn't had an update from you for so long—"

"Update? That's not what those messages were. I needed to talk with you."

"Yeah, well, I intended to. But then I started to worry when you didn't call for a couple of months so the letter was a relief."

"What?"

"Yeah, the note said I should come see the baby. It was good timing. Sierra and I just broke up again."

"I don't know what you're talking about," Rose said. "I didn't want you to come. Was this note signed?"

Trevor shoved his hands into his pocket. "No."

Rose wrinkled her nose. Finally she said, "Well, the note obviously wasn't from me."

Before Trevor could answer, Tim stepped to Rose's side. "It was from me. I looked up Trevor's address at the library."

Reuben's hair bristled on the back of his neck. Why would Tim, of all people, do that? He'd been adamant, before, that he wished Rose hadn't told Trevor she was expecting.

"I suggested he come see you. And the Bobbli."

"Dat," Rose said, as if her heart were breaking. "Why?"

Trevor crossed his arms, staring at Rose. "I assumed you wanted me to come back."

Rose stepped back. "Jah, I did last winter. But then I stopped." She took another step backward, toward the table, toward Lila, leaving Tim and Reuben facing Trevor.

When Trevor saw Reuben, his expression went flat.

"Let's sit down and have some coffee," Beth said. "Come on in, Trevor."

Rose motioned for Trudy to go into the living room before Trevor reached the table. Trudy obeyed without a sound. Reuben heard the rocker going, barely, as if Trudy was doing her best not to make any noise.

Trevor locked eyes on Reuben as he sat down but didn't say anything. Reuben stayed standing.

Tim asked about Trevor's trip. It had been fine. Then Tim asked Trevor what work he'd found back home. "Construction," he answered.

Trevor crossed his arms and leaned back, looking as if he was weary of the small talk. "So why did you want me to come see Rose?" he asked Tim.

Reuben kept his eyes on Rose. She winced but didn't say anything.

"I figure as a human being you deserved to see your daughter," Tim answered.

"You could have asked me," Rose muttered.

"I knew what your response would be," Tim said. "I talked with your grandfather. I asked him what he would have done differently all those years ago, for your mother. And I thought of Lila's longing to know who her biological father was all these years. And I thought about Trevor, about what he deserved too." Tim shrugged. "I changed my mind from what I first believed."

Reuben couldn't help but admire Tim. The man had changed. He was right, that having Trevor visit now was better than if he showed up later—or if Abrie went looking for him as an adult as Lila had done.

Rose reached for Lila's hand, as if perhaps her sister could help her. But as Lila scooted closer to Rose, Reuben realized she simply needed the support. His heart swelled a little, thinking about how scared Rose might be. Did she think Trevor might try to take the baby?

Reuben stepped to the doorway of the living room. Trudy rocked the little one slowly. She'd woken up and was staring into her Aenti's face. Reuben quickly turned his attention back toward the adults at the table.

Beth passed mugs of coffee around.

Trevor didn't seem to know what to say and turned toward Lila. "How are you doing?" His voice was kind.

"Better," she said, pouring cream into her coffee.

"And how is Zane?"

"*Gut*," Lila answered. "He's probably on his way over." She glanced toward Dat.

Reuben stifled a groan, wondering how much more complicated the situation could get. This was the sort of drama he had come to expect at the Lehman house.

"Did you tell him you were coming?" Lila asked.

Trevor shook his head as a knock fell on the back door.

Beth placed a coffee cake, a knife, and a stack of plates on the table in front of Lila and then went to answer the door.

The first thing Zane said was, "Is that Trevor's car?"

"As a matter of fact, jah," Beth said. "Come on in."

Trevor stood and shook Zane's hand. Reuben couldn't help but remember their embrace last fall when Trevor had first come to Lancaster County. Clearly there was tension between the two now, and for good reason.

"Why did you come back?" Zane asked.

"I wanted to see Rose. And the baby. I'm trying to figure things out."

"What about Sierra?" Zane asked.

"We broke up." Trevor turned toward Rose as he spoke. "For good." He sat back down, keeping his eyes on Rose. "I really am sorry for not communicating for all these months. Sierra was angry, and I wasn't sure what to do. But when I got the letter, and assumed you wanted me to come, I started thinking about our time together. Of all the support here. Of how happy I was, really, while I was here. I'd been a little lost, until I got the note."

Rose nodded, just a little, but didn't say anything.

Trevor exhaled. "We have a baby. Wouldn't it be best for us to raise her together? I've changed in the last few months—honestly. I've stopped drinking. I'm entirely clean and sober."

The baby began to fuss, and Trudy stood with her, giving Reuben a panicked look. Reuben wasn't sure if he could help, but with eighteen nieces and nephews he'd had a lot of experience. He stepped back into the living room and reached for the baby, positioning himself where he could still see the table but Trevor couldn't see him. He put Abrie to his shoulder and patted her back, but by the way she began rooting around at his neck he wasn't going to keep her happy for long.

Rose glanced at Reuben and the baby and then back at Trevor. "Could we talk in private?" she asked.

"Around here?" he joked. "Does that exist?"

Reuben cringed.

"How about outside?" Rose asked. They both pushed their chairs back and headed out the back door.

Trudy had returned to the rocker. "Why is he here?" she whispered to Reuben.

Reuben shrugged, his heart racing.

"Is he going to take Rose and Abrie away?"

Reuben shrugged again, realizing he couldn't speak even if he knew what the answer was. He swallowed hard. The hollow feeling he'd had ever since he found out Rose was pregnant with Trevor's Bobbli was more intense than ever.

Trudy went to the window. "They're getting in his car." She turned toward Reuben. "Do you think they're leaving?"

"No," he managed to say. Rose wouldn't leave Abrie. "Is it still raining?"

Trudy nodded. "Just a drizzle though."

"They probably wanted somewhere dry to talk."

"I can't believe this," Lila said from the table.

Zane said, probably to Tim, "I'm so sorry about all of this. Really."

"I know," Tim answered. "Don't blame yourself anymore."

"Jah," Lila said. "Dat's the one who wrote Trevor an anonymous note that Abrie had been born." Lila's voice grew louder. "Go out there and talk to Rose, Dat. She can't get together with him. She'll listen to you."

Reuben joined Trudy at the window and peered through the sheer curtain. The car faced the house diagonally, with Rose closer to the window, so they had a pretty good view of her even through the rain on the windshield. Rose had turned toward Trevor and spoke rather animatedly. Trevor had his head down. When it appeared that Rose had begun to cry, Reuben turned away. It wasn't his business, not anymore, and he shouldn't be spying.

Trudy said, "She's getting something from the glove box."

"Maybe she's looking for a tissue," Reuben said.

"She has two bottles in her hands. Pill bottles. And now something silver."

Reuben wasn't going to speculate what that was all about. He kept his back to the window.

"She's getting out of the car," Trudy said. "And he is too. She's yelling at him."

Reuben could hear that, although he couldn't figure out what she was saying.

The sound of Lila's cane started toward the living room. Trudy pressed her nose to the glass.

"She just threw one of the bottles at him."

"What's going on?" Lila stepped closer to the window.

"Rose is really mad about something."

"What's in her hand?"

"A pill bottle. She just threw the other one."

"Oh," Lila said. "Is that a flask? She just threw it too." She shuddered and started back to the kitchen.

The Bobbli relaxed against Reuben, melting against his chest despite the drama. By some miracle, she'd fallen asleep again. He stepped into the kitchen. Lila was at the back door, with Zane right behind her. The door opened and Reuben could hear Rose yell, "You lied to me!"

"Okay, I took a few pain pills. And, yes, I took some of Lila's."

"That's a pathetic answer," Rose shouted. "You lied—back

then and just now too. And you were so vague about your girl-friend too—did you really break up with her before you came to Lancaster County? Or did you just tell me that?"

"Why would it have mattered?" Trevor was louder now. "You were cheating on Reuben."

"Jah, and it was the worst mistake of my life," Rose yelled.

Trudy stepped to Reuben's side as he stood beside the table, and then to the kitchen window. Reuben followed her.

"Go out there," Beth said to Tim. "No good is going to come from this."

Tim sighed and pushed his chair back as Rose kept yelling, still clutching the second pill bottle, asking if Trevor had lied to her also about wanting them to be a family.

"I thought I did," he said. "But obviously you're not in any sort of condition to make being a family work."

Rose erupted in a sardonic laugh. "Obviously you have some sort of drug problem. And a drinking problem."

"No, I don't." He crossed his arms. He lowered his voice a little. "Look, I do drink sometimes. And take prescription pills every once in a while." He shrugged. "But I'm not addicted to either."

Rose's voice grew louder. "Yet you steal and lie because of them."

Trevor didn't answer, but Beth nudged Tim. He stood and started for the back door.

Trevor still stood with his arms crossed, but now his shoulders were hunched. He wasn't the confident Englischer on the barn beam—no, he seemed more like a boy now. Or, more likely, a broken man. As he held little Abrie, Reuben felt a wave of compassion for him, realizing Trevor hadn't even asked to see his baby, let alone hold her. He had no idea what he was missing.

"I was so naïve." Rose's voice was lower now but still audible. "And foolish. Did you return just to see what your options were?

To see if it would be worth it to lie to me again? Did your father encourage you to do the right thing?"

"I haven't told my dad," Trevor said.

"Because you don't want your girlfriend to find out, right?" Rose yelled.

Trevor looked as if he might cry. "Ex-girlfriend. Honestly."

Tim stepped toward the two of them. "That's enough. If you need a mediator, come back in the house and talk this through, otherwise stop this yelling."

"Yeah," Trevor said. "We need to figure this out. If you don't want to give me a chance—"

"I don't," Rose said. "I was a fool to go as far as your car with you." Reuben could imagine how fiery her eyes were.

"Then we better talk about the legal side of things," Trevor said. "But first I want a paternity test."

"That's not necessary," Tim said. "I believe my daughter, one hundred percent. I didn't contact you to get child support. I'll take financial responsibility for the baby. But you're welcome to visit."

"Dat!" Rose said.

"It's the right thing to do," Tim said to his daughter. Then he turned back to Trevor. "But you need to have some sort of evaluation first, about your substance abuse. We don't need any more problems around here."

Trevor frowned, just a little, but he didn't say he wouldn't. He turned to Rose. "I won't stay where I'm not wanted, but I will be back to visit."

Reuben winced. Trevor was even more manipulative than he'd guessed. Poor Rose. Thankfully Tim could help her navigate what was ahead. Reuben wasn't sure if the man actually said good-bye to Rose or not. If he did, it was quietly.

Reuben stepped closer to the window. Rose stood with her arms crossed. She might have muttered a farewell but he couldn't hear it either. She spun around just as Lila came toward her and then thrust the remaining bottle into her hand. "Here," she said. "I'm so sorry I didn't listen to you back then."

Then Rose disappeared from sight as Tim stepped forward to talk with Trevor and then Zane did too. A moment later Rose came through the back door, and Reuben and Trudy both stepped away from the window. Rose's Kapp and dress were damp.

She hurried toward them. "Is Abrie all right?"

"She's fine," Reuben said, looking down at the sleeping baby.

"I'm sorry," Rose said. "For everything. Including"—she pointed toward the window—"that."

Reuben met her teary gaze.

"But I'll never be sorry for her." Her eyes fell on her baby.

"Of course not," Reuben said. He'd never ask her to, but he couldn't say that. Not yet. Ten minutes ago, Rose seemed to be thinking about leaving with Trevor. What was she thinking now? She met his eyes again but didn't say anything more.

"I need to go change into dry clothes," Rose said.

"Go ahead," Reuben said. "We'll be here when you get back."

<hr/>

They didn't talk any more that day or for the next two weeks. Reuben spent most of his evenings in the Lehmans' basement, helping Tim and Zane put up the walls, lay down a floor, and install a kitchen. He enjoyed the work and spending time with both men.

One day when Zane hadn't arrived yet, as Reuben worked with Tim, it seemed like old times, when they worked together at the lumberyard and talked about anything and everything—quite the feat for two men who were mostly quiet.

As Reuben held plasterboard in place, he asked Tim, "Do you ever wonder what your family's life would have been like if the Becks had never moved to Juneberry Lane?"

Tim had a nail in his mouth but took it out. "No." Then he smiled. "Well, sure, I used to. But I haven't for a few weeks at least." He grinned. "Why do you ask?"

Reuben shrugged. Zane and Trevor wouldn't have been in the picture. Simon wouldn't have been influenced by Joel's war stories and most likely wouldn't have joined the Army. The Lehmans would have been a normal Amish family. "It just seems things would have been so much simpler."

"Well, simple wasn't God's plan for us," Tim said. "He wanted us to love our neighbors. And let's not forget how they've loved us. How many times has Shani helped us out with her medical knowledge? Or brought a meal over. Or given us a ride. How many times did Joel give Simon wise counsel when he wouldn't listen to me? And I don't mean about the Army, which you probably don't realize Joel advised Simon *not* to join. And how many times has Shani mothered my girls?" Tim shuddered a little. "I actually hate to think about what our lives would have been like without them."

When Reuben didn't respond—he wasn't sure what to say—Tim continued. "I wish I could say my love for them truly comes from God. I hope it does. I hope I would have loved them even if they hadn't turned out to be good folks. But we've been blessed to have them as neighbors and as friends." It was quite the speech for Tim Lehman, but it turned out he wasn't done. "Sure, if I cared like I used to about what people thought, if I cared how those in our district were judging me, I might still regret that the Becks became our neighbors. I hope I'm past that. I really do. God willing, we'll share grandchildren someday. I want to keep being good friends to them."

As Tim put the nail back in his mouth and grabbed his hammer, Reuben thought about what he'd said and then about how Tim used to care about people judging him. Reuben understood that. But that was pride, plain and simple. When Tim gave that up, he gained so much more. His neighbors. His children. Eventually Beth. It had freed him. And humbled him.

The next day Reuben joined the Lehmans for supper before getting back to work on the basement. After the prayer, Zane announced that the lawyer he'd spoken to had called on his parents' phone.

Zane dished up a couple of chicken thighs as he spoke. "The insurance company determined Mr. Addison was at fault. They'll pay the medical bills and for the buggy." He added that the lawyer and the adjuster had met with Mr. Addison and, based on the evidence, convinced the man not to sue.

Lila's relief was evident as she smiled at Zane. Tim seemed relieved too, but then an expression of concern settled on his face. "Has Donald Addison lost his license because of this? Does he need our help?"

"Dat," Lila said. "What are we going to do? Give him rides in our buggies?"

"We could give him a list of our best drivers," Zane countered.

"Jah," Tim said. "And take over a pie."

Zane smiled and then said, "I think the thought is a good one, but he might feel we're rubbing salt in his wounds. Let's just see how it all works out. Maybe Gideon can find out if there's anything we can do to help."

"That's a good idea." Tim turned toward Lila. "You had a message today. From your brother."

"What? From Simon? Is he coming?"

"Not from Simon," Tim said. "And not from Daniel either."

"Oh, from Butch," Lila said.

"Jah," Tim answered. "He said that he and his mother would be honored to come to your wedding. They'll see you then."

No one spoke for a long moment, but then Lila said, "Denki. I better let Daniel know."

Tim nodded.

"Speaking of Simon," Tim said, "Lila didn't have a message from him, but I did." He grinned. "He'll be here for the wedding too. With Casey. And I'll go ahead and spoil their big news. They flew to Hawaii last week and got married."

"What?" Lila said. "They got married before Zane and me?"

"Apparently so," Tim said, turning to Trudy. "You know this isn't the way we do things, right? The way Simon has done things. The way Rose has—"

"Dat, I know," she answered. "Beth and I talk about this all the time."

Tim turned to Beth, at the end of the table. "Oh, is that right?"

"Jah, it absolutely is," Beth said. "But things seem to work out in spite of us."

"It's a paradox," Zane said to Trudy. "It means both things can be right at the same time." He glanced at Rose. She shrugged, giving him permission to go on. "God can work good from the wrong we do, but that doesn't make the wrong all right."

Trudy's face grew red. "Jah, I get it," she said.

Reuben tried to swallow his chicken but began coughing instead.

"What's the matter, Ru?" Zane asked, sounding a lot like Simon.

Reuben took a drink of water. "Tried to go down the wrong pipe," he said. "That's all."

Could he—should he—stand in the way of that good? He thought Rose loved him, but then she betrayed him. Now she had a Bobbli that he hadn't fathered, but she'd grown and matured in ways she probably never would have if she hadn't gone through the trials of the last nine months. Rose caught his eye, but he turned his head away, his heart racing.

Perhaps Beth sensed the awkwardness he felt, because she said, "We have peanut butter pie for dessert. Rose has been baking again."

Rose quickly stood and stepped to the counter, returning with the dessert. Reuben was stuffed, but he wouldn't refuse a piece of pie.

After supper, Reuben returned to the basement with Tim and Zane. He stayed later than usual to do some finishing work, and by the time he made his way upstairs, Tim was already in bed. Lila and Zane sat at the table. Reuben quickly told them good-bye and let himself out.

The sound of the Bobbli crying confused him as he hurried down the back steps. He followed the sound toward the field.

Rose walked in the moonlight, back and forth in front of the gate.

"What's going on?" Reuben asked.

"It's her fussy time," Rose said. "I don't want to keep Trudy awake. Or Dat and Beth."

"So you come out here every night?"

She shrugged. "It's been so warm this last week."

"You must be tired," Reuben said, thinking again that she wasn't that far past her surgery. "Want me to take a turn?" He reached out his hands for the Bobbli.

Rose passed the little one to him. "Denki," she said. "I appreciate it. Just for a moment. Then I'll take her back."

"It can get frustrating, jah?"

Rose nodded.

His sister Sarah's first Bobbli had been colicky. But she had her husband to share the responsibility. He knew Rose had a houseful of people to help her, but he doubted it was the same as having a husband.

He placed the Bobbli against his shoulder and began patting her back again. He hadn't held her since the day Trevor visited. Standing beside Rose, holding Abrie, the hollowness in him subsided some.

Rose stepped closer to him. "Denki," she said. "For everything."

Reuben nodded but couldn't seem to find his voice. Hopefully, in time, he would.

27

On the second Thursday of July, the morning of her wedding, Lila leaned against her cane and stood at the top step of the back stairs. Her grandparents, Eve and Charlie, and the Becks, including Zane's grandfather, had all arrived an hour ago. Now the sun was rising over the field, the men were all doing the milking, and half the women were in the basement finishing up the last of the meatballs while the others were making breakfast in the upstairs kitchen.

Dat had put a sink, two stoves, and a refrigerator in the new kitchen, as well as a long work counter that offered much more room than the upstairs kitchen did.

He was so happy with what he and Zane and Reuben had done that he said he'd remodel the upstairs kitchen next.

After the milking was done, the men would set up the benches and tables in the area between the driveway and the gate. The temperature was supposed to be just below eighty degrees for the day. Perfect for an outdoor wedding.

Lila walked carefully down the steps. Beth had planted annuals for the wedding—pink petunias, white impatiens, and pink and white geraniums—in whiskey barrels scattered around the outside of the house and along the driveway and fence line. The vegetable garden was also flourishing under Beth's care. Dat had cut the hay earlier in the week. Thankfully the dust had settled and all that the morning breeze carried was the fresh scent of the bales, drying in the field.

After she reached the driveway, she headed toward the gate, remembering the first time she'd seen Zane on the other side. She eased up on the cane as she approached the grassy area, visualizing what it would soon look like.

White and lime-green tablecloths would cover the tables. Beth had made the cake. It was all white except for thin green trim. Eve and Charlie were bringing flowers for the cake table, the only decorations they'd use, and her grandmother was contributing paper napkins and cups. The dishes from the church wagon, which was parked along the fence, would be used for the meal.

She held her cane with both hands and began walking toward the gate, imagining where the benches would be.

Lila had wanted to keep the invitation list small, but Dat and Beth kept adding names. She told them she and Zane couldn't afford that much, but they said they'd cover the expense of the wedding.

She reached the gate and put the cane back down. She'd be able to walk into the service without it, but she wasn't sure that she should.

Last night she'd managed to walk upstairs in the little house without her cane. Zane had taken her over, and carried her crazy quilt while she cautiously climbed the stairs. Once she made it to their room, she'd folded up her Mamm's quilt and then spread the crazy quilt she'd finished the year before over the bed. It was more appropriate for all that they'd been through. And scraps of blues and greens and purples brought life to the room in a way the traditional pattern didn't. Her Mamm would be pleased, Lila was sure. Besides, she had better plans for the shadow quilt.

She didn't open the door to the Bobbli's room when they left their own room. Instead she'd stood in front of it, frozen.

"I didn't take out the furniture," Zane said. "I'm not willing to give up on that yet. I don't think you should either." Always the optimist—jah, that was the man she was marrying.

"I won't," she said. "I'll do my best to trust God with . . ." She'd turned toward him. "This room." They both smiled, just a little, as she took the stairs down one at a time, and Zane carried her mother's quilt.

He'd start volunteering again at the fire station in another month. They'd be back where they'd expected to be before the accident, at least mostly.

"Lila?"

She turned to find Casey coming toward her. She wore jeans and an Army T-shirt. She and Simon had spent the night at Shani and Joel's but had come over to help with the preparations. "Breakfast is ready."

"Thank you." The house was already full, and it was still hours until the wedding would start.

"I'll go tell the men," Casey said, heading toward the barn. Her stride was long and confident, her head high and her back straight. Lila started toward the house, but as she reached the back stairs, Simon came running up behind her.

"Hey, sis," he said. "Today's your big day."

"Jah," she answered, turning toward him. "You robbed us of sharing yours."

"Would you have come to Hawaii?" he teased.

"I've always wanted to go there," she answered. "But you would have needed to tell us ahead of time."

"That's true," he said. They both knew there wasn't any

way any of them could have gone. It had been better not to know ahead of time.

He ducked, grabbed her, and lifted her off her feet and onto his shoulder.

She slapped his back with her free hand. "Put me down. You'll hurt me."

He laughed and said, "You're not as fragile as you think. Everyone's been too easy on you."

Lila hit him again, but she was glad he seemed so carefree. He'd been a sniper in Iraq, on the Syrian border, and she feared it would weigh heavy on him. But it didn't seem to. Strangely, the boy who had been raised Amish seemed not to have been affected by war, at least not badly. Time would tell.

He bounced up the stairs with her and through the mud porch into the kitchen, putting her down in the middle of the room.

Rose had the Bobbli in her arms and shot Simon a frown. "No horseplay," she said.

He flicked her on the arm and teased, "Aren't you the serious one now?"

"Or the responsible one," she said and then laughed, holding the Bobbli with one hand and flicking him back with the spit rag that had been draped over her shoulder.

As Simon headed to the bathroom to wash his hands, Lila sat down at the table, a little out of breath. She'd need to put her wedding dress on soon, while the men put the benches out. Or maybe they were doing that now. She stood and stepped to the window. Sure enough, Zane, Dat, and Joel were unloading the church wagon.

And Reuben.

Rose stepped to her side. "Why is he here so early?"

"I don't know," Lila said. But she was grateful.

"Rose, can you make the coffee?" Beth called out. "We need another pot."

"Sure," Rose said, glancing around, probably looking for Trudy. But then, through the window, she saw her little sister and Adam run by, headed for the chicken coop.

"I'll take her," Lila said, propping her cane against the wall.

"All right." Rose slid the Bobbli into her arms as Lila shifted her weight to her right leg.

Abrie cooed and reached up toward Lila's face. Lila lifted the Bobbli higher and rubbed her face against Abrie's cheek. Rose hadn't said another word about Trevor, and as far as she knew he hadn't called. She knew he hadn't visited.

She was surprised at the extent of Rose's anger when she found the pill bottles. In the past she was sure Rose would have justified his behavior in some way, but there wasn't even a hint of that. It seemed pretty foolish of Trevor to leave them there, but she could see how he might have overlooked them.

Zane was afraid he was getting pills from other places. Lila couldn't begin to guess how it would all turn out. Rose certainly seemed upset with him, enough not to ever trust him again, but Lila knew her sister could be irrational. At least she used to be. The truth was, Rose had changed.

Zane turned toward the house, and Lila stepped up to the window and waved, lifting the Bobbli up again.

He waved back and then pointed toward her. Reuben turned toward the house too and shielded his eyes. A minute later, as Zane and Tim put the last of the benches in place, Reuben started toward the house. By the time he washed his hands, Zane and Tim had come in too. Zane stood by her for a minute, sweet-talking Abrie, who blew a couple of bubbles. She was on the verge of smiling.

"Would you call Trudy and Adam in?" Lila asked Zane. "Breakfast is ready."

As Lila waited for him to return, the Bobbli began to fuss.

Rose was placing an egg casserole on the table as part of the buffet. "I'll take her in just a second," she said.

Lila didn't dare walk with the Bobbli. She was afraid her legs might buckle.

Reuben stepped to her side. "Mind if I take a turn?"

Relieved, Lila passed the Bobbli to him as Dat cleared his throat and then boomed, "Everyone gather around."

Zane stepped back into the house and to Lila's side. Across the room stood Shani and Joel, hand in hand, with Zane's grandfather next to them. Trudy and Adam stood in front, and Casey and Simon stood on the other side. Lila's grandparents stood in the archway to the living room, and Eve and Charlie, with Jackson, stood behind them. Rose stepped around the table, stopping beside Reuben, but she didn't take the Bobbli away from him. Everyone Lila loved most was in the room—except for Daniel, Jenny, and Brook. They should have arrived by now. She hoped Daniel wasn't angry with her for inviting Butch Jr. She'd tried to talk with him about it at church on Sunday, but he shook his head and walked away.

As everyone quieted down, Beth stepped to Dat's side. He cleared his throat again. "I'm very grateful for everyone in this room," he said. "For all of our family. For our neighbors." He nodded toward Joel and Shani. "For Zane." He smiled. "All those years ago I never would have guessed that cocky neighbor kid would become Amish—and now my son-in-law." Everyone laughed. "I guess we all know that none of us can predict what God will do in our lives." He paused for a moment, and Lila wondered if he'd choked up, but then he said, "And for that I'm grateful." He bowed his head. "Let's pray."

A minute later, after Dat said, "Amen," Beth began directing everyone through the buffet line. "Lila and Zane, you two go through first. There are chairs in the living room to sit on or tables in the basement. Everyone dish up quickly, because we still have a lot of work to do before our guests arrive."

Zane grabbed two plates and whispered to Lila, "Go find a place to sit in the living room. I'll be right there."

She complied, stopping at the window to look for Daniel and Jenny, but they were nowhere in sight.

⌒⌒⌒

By the time her brother and sister-in-law finally arrived, Lila was in her room putting on the new purple dress she had finished the week before. Jenny stepped in for a minute and said Brook had been up most of the night teething. "I told Daniel to come ahead without me," she said, "but he wanted to wait."

"Of course," Lila said, not wanting to ask Jenny how Daniel was doing. Or what he was thinking. He was here—that was what mattered.

Lila and Zane joined the congregation to praise God by singing "*Das Loblied*" at the beginning of the service, and then retreated back to the house for special instructions from Gideon. Zane looked so handsome in his straight-cut suit, holding his black hat in his hands.

The potato cooks laughed in the kitchen as they finished the peeling. They'd put the potatoes on to boil near the end of the service and then mash them for the dinner. The meatballs warmed in the basement ovens.

Zane and Lila sat down beside each other on the sofa in the living room and held hands. When Gideon came into the room, Lila pulled her hand away. Gideon asked how they were both feeling.

"Great!" Zane said, reaching for Lila's hand again.

"*Gut*," she answered, aware that she couldn't match Zane's excitement. That didn't matter. She was excited in her own way.

Gideon spoke to them about marriage, but Lila didn't listen

very well. She'd ask Zane later what he said. Something about not letting the sun go down on their anger and being willing to show the other grace.

"Ready to go?" Gideon finally asked.

Zane and Lila both nodded, and after Lila stood, placing her cane on the linoleum, Zane reached for her other hand. They followed Gideon out the front door, down the steps, and around the house.

The singing of the congregation sounded as if a choir of angels had descended on the farm. In many ways, one had. Everyone gathered would support Zane and Lila, want the best for them, and pray for them.

Rose held Abrie and sat in the last row on the women's side with Butch Jr.'s mother beside her. Across the aisle, on the last row of the men's side, sat Butch Jr. with Reuben beside him. Lila's heart filled with gratitude for Rose and Reuben's hospitality. When they passed Daniel, sitting beside Simon and Dat, she couldn't help but wonder if he'd met Butch. There was no way Daniel could miss recognizing their half brother if he saw him.

Zane took his place and Lila hers on benches facing each other at the front and settled in for the Scripture reading. It was 1 Corinthians 13, in English, in a translation she wasn't familiar with. Zane must have specifically asked Gideon to read it.

Zane had truly been patient with her. And kind. And gentle. She hoped she could love him in the same way, despite her brokenness. But perhaps Simon was right. Perhaps she wasn't as fragile as she'd let herself believe these last many months.

Gideon began the sermon. Lila was sure it would be long—and it was. It nearly lulled her to sleep as the morning grew warmer. Finally, Gideon said, "That's why we serve each other. Because Christ served us. And there's no relationship in life where we have the opportunity to serve another person as much as we do in marriage. No other relationship lasts, in a daily manner, as a marriage does. You care for a child for a short time. And you will care for your parents in their old age. But, God willing, Zane and Lila, you will care for each other for fifty or sixty years or more. Love each other. Cherish each other. Be honest with each other. Seek out each other's souls. Seek out each other's hearts. Build your relationship between who the two of you are on the inside. Love each other as you love yourselves. That's what counts."

Gideon smiled kindly. "Zane Beck. Lila Lehman." His eyes brightened even more. "I've known you both since you were children. I'm as pleased as I've ever been to marry a couple. Please come forward."

Lila left her cane propped against her bench, stood, and made her way to the front, stopping beside Zane. Gideon led them in their vows and then joined their hands together, pronouncing them man and wife.

Zane looked into Lila's eyes and squeezed her hand. She leaned against him. He kissed the top of her Kapp, in a show of affection uncommon for Amish men and definitely uncommon in Plain weddings. She didn't care. There were some things he'd never understand. And it didn't matter.

By the time they made their way up the aisle to the last bench, Monika was directing the men to set up the tables. An army of helpers soon transformed the space into a dining area.

As she and Zane mingled through the crowd, Lila greeted Connie and Butch Jr. and thanked them for coming. "Have you met Daniel?" she asked.

Butch shook his head.

Lila looked around for her brother. He stood beside Jenny next to the fence with a fussy Brook. She waved at him and motioned him over. She could tell, as he walked toward her, he wasn't happy about it. She hoped Butch couldn't guess at how Daniel was feeling.

When Daniel reached them, she introduced Butch Jr. "Hello," Daniel said. "I'm pleased to meet you." Then he nudged Butch's shoulder. "I figured it was you."

Butch nodded. "Yeah, I figured the same about you."

Daniel motioned to Jenny, and she joined them. Connie reached for the Bobbli. "May I hold her?"

"Jah, please," Jenny said. The circles under her eyes had grown even darker.

"Your family certainly is blessed with children," Connie said.

Lila swallowed hard at her words, reminding herself to trust. "Jah," she said. "God has been good to my family." And he was good to her and Zane too, regardless of what the future held. Through her hardships, she had finally come to trust him more.

Soon the corner table was set up and covered with a tablecloth, and Zane and Lila took their places. The table directly in front of them was for their two families, with Dat at one end and Joel at the other. Tears filled Lila's eyes. Zane, right beside her, was her person. And now everyone she cared about most, her people—including those who were missing at breakfast— were all right in front of them. Her parents. Her siblings. Her sisters-in-law. Her nieces. Her grandparents and Eve and Charlie. Butch and Connie were seated in the middle of the table. Rose stood off to the side in her new blue dress, in front of the pie table—heaped with pastries she had made for the occasion.

As Lila surveyed them all, she even had a sweet sense of her Mamm's presence. She still missed her sometimes, but life and love had continued, and Lila was thankful.

Monika must have had everything under control, because as the cooks marched out with the food, she took the Bobbli from Rose, cradling her against her bosom as she swooped her away.

Dat motioned to Reuben and directed him to the family table. On his way, he paused beside Rose, and for a moment, Lila saw the old playfulness in her sister as she gazed up at Reuben, a hint of a smile on her face.

Lila nudged Zane as Rose and Reuben stepped toward the table and then sat down.

"Do you think we can believe what we see?" Zane whispered.

"I hope so," Lila answered. Nothing would make her happier on her wedding day than to know that Rose and Reuben were getting back together. Then again, maybe it was just Dat trying his hand at matchmaking. Perhaps Rose and Reuben felt nothing for each other.

Once everyone was seated, Dat stood and led the entire congregation in a silent prayer.

Thank you, Lord, Lila prayed, as Zane wrapped his arm around her and pulled her close. *For your blessings. For your miracles. May we see them each day.*

28

Rose sat on her bed, propped against the headboard nursing Abrie, when Lila came in.

"We're getting ready to leave," she said. "We'll be back first thing in the morning." Usually a bride and groom spent their first night at the bride's house so they'd be available to clean up the next day, but there was no need for that when Lila and Zane's home was just across the field. There wasn't a lot Lila could do to clean, but Zane would be a big help.

"You must be exhausted," Rose answered.

Lila nodded. "So must you."

Rose stifled a yawn and then smiled. "I am."

"Most everyone has left. Monika and Gideon are still here, having a last cup of coffee. So are Shani and Joel."

"What about Reuben?" Rose asked. He'd been playing horseshoes when she came into the house.

"Why do you ask?" Lila teased.

Rose shrugged but smiled. "I thought I'd corral him into walking Abrie if she's fussy. He has a knack for calming her."

"He does seem to have the touch." Lila sat down on the bed and scooted up against the headboard. She touched Abrie's dark hair. "I'm going to miss you two."

"You won't be more than a quarter mile away."

"I know," Lila said. "But it won't be the same. These last couple of months have been . . . the best ever."

Rose felt the same way and nodded. "I guess we've both changed quite a bit, jah?"

"Jah," Lila answered. "Hard times make us stronger."

"And kinder," Rose added, leaning her head against her big sister's shoulder.

"And more understanding." Lila patted Rose's arm and then scooted off the bed. "Come visit us."

"Oh, we will," Rose said. And then joked, "Especially during her fussy times."

Zane had already taken most of Lila's things over to their little house, but she had one more bag. Instead of picking it up though, she bent down and pulled her Mamm's quilt out from under her bed. She turned to Rose. "This is for you."

"Lila! That's yours."

She shook her head. "I want you to have it. We put the crazy quilt I made on our bed last night. Mamm would want you—and Abrie—to have it." Lila's eyes nearly brimmed over with tears as she unfolded the quilt and placed it beside Rose.

"I can't," Rose said.

Lila laughed. "You don't have a choice." Rose knew Eve had given the quilt to Shani, who gave it back to Eve, who gave it to Lila.

"Denki," Rose said. And she meant it. Somehow being given the quilt drew her into the circle of women she most admired. She was a part of them.

The Bobbli had finished nursing, and Rose transferred her to her shoulder. "I'll be right out," she said, patting Abrie's back.

Lila picked her bag up off the bed and said she'd see Rose soon. As her sister left the room, tears stung Rose's eyes. She would miss Lila too, more than she let on. Lila had been the constant in her life all these years—even when she'd taken her for granted. She'd done the same thing with Reuben. It had really taken being a mother for her to start valuing others the way she should. It was as if her heart had expanded. It was as if, like Gideon had preached, she'd started to look at what was inside of people instead of what was on the outside.

Before, she'd thought about Reuben's job and his house. Of his income. Of all the outward things. But she'd seen him as ordinary. She winced at the memory. But it turned out Reuben was extraordinary when it came to his character, to what mattered. She couldn't fathom what she'd been thinking last fall.

Lord, she prayed, *help me to keep seeing what truly matters.* She put the Bobbli on the bed, pinned her dress, and then picked up the little one, wrapping a blanket around her.

Abrie mattered. How she worked things out with Trevor mattered, and she was very thankful to have Dat involved with that. He would be fair but firm. If it were up to her, she'd never see Trevor again. She couldn't believe she'd been willing to talk with him that day.

She could only imagine how much she'd hurt Reuben—again.

He definitely mattered too. Next to Abrie, he mattered most. She was one hundred percent sure of that, but she couldn't tell him. Not after what she'd done. She didn't want him to feel obligated to her, or for him to think she felt entitled to him, as some sort of consolation prize. That wasn't it at all.

She left the room, stepped into the empty kitchen, and then slipped out the back door. A couple of tables still remained by the gate where Dat and Beth, the Becks, Zane's grandfather, and Monika and Gideon all sat. Lila stood with her bag, most likely waiting for Zane to come around with the buggy. Daniel

371

and Jenny had already gone home. Simon and Casey, probably exhausted from their travels, had gone over to the Becks', and Butch and his mother had left hours ago. They seemed to have had a good time though, and it meant a lot to Lila to have them at her wedding.

Trudy and Adam swung on the gate. Surprisingly, Dat hadn't told them to stop.

Reuben wasn't in sight. Perhaps he'd gone home. Rose pulled Abrie a little closer. When she reached the others, both Monika and Beth stood to take the Bobbli, but then Monika laughed and deferred to Beth.

Reuben came walking out of the barn as Zane drove the buggy toward the group. Billie stopped, Zane hopped down, and then helped Lila up. Everyone clapped as they drove off.

"We better get the rest of these tables put away while we can still see," Dat said, standing. "And then it's off to bed for this old man." Dusk was falling quickly.

Rose sensed Reuben before she turned and saw him stopping behind her. "Could we talk?" he asked.

"Sure." She followed him over to the fence, expecting Abrie to start screaming any minute.

"I've been thinking . . ." Reuben said. "About us. Quite a bit."

She nodded. She had too.

"Do you plan to stay here, for good?"

"Are you asking if I plan to chase after Trevor?"

Reuben nodded.

"Never." She looked into his kind hazel eyes.

Reuben exhaled. "Would you consider courting me again then? In time?"

Rose's heart began to race. "First I have to know if you truly can forgive me for what I did and not hold it against me . . . or Abrie."

"I have forgiven you," he said. "I mean, I tried and tried,

and I suppose I did—I just couldn't feel it. But that night in the hospital, when I saw you . . ."

"When you brought the flowers?"

"Jah, that night, I knew what forgiveness felt like." He smiled a little. "But to be honest the first time I held Abrie, I still felt hollow from what happened. But then the second time holding her brought healing. And every time I see the two of you, I feel more whole."

Rose took another deep breath. "Do you feel you could be Abrie's father?"

"Of course," he answered. "No second thoughts. Ever."

"Even if Trevor ends up visiting? Even if he gets, heaven forbid, some sort of custody rights?"

"Jah," Reuben said. "No matter what."

She believed him. He'd been through a process Dat had never experienced. And besides, Reuben wasn't Dat. He was an entirely different man. He was gentler. More aware of what was going on inside of himself—and inside of her too.

He took her hand. "So will you court me again?"

"Absolutely," she answered.

Reuben led her through the gate to the field and then to the other side of the poplars, where they could hear the melody of the creek. He wrapped his arms around her and drew her close, first kissing her forehead, then her lips. His mouth was sweet and sure, and Rose kissed him back.

But then the Bobbli's screaming interrupted them.

"I'll go get her," Rose said.

"No, you stay here," Reuben answered. "I will." She stepped out from the trees and watched him jog toward Beth and scoop Abrie into his arms. As the moon rose, he started back toward Rose, surefooted, singing a lullaby to Abrie. Rose met him at the gate. The Bobbli stopped screaming for a moment, staring up at her mother in the dim light, but then started again, full force.

"Let's walk toward the lane," Reuben said, pulling the baby close and patting her back. "The three of us, together."

Rose stayed close to his side. By the time they reached June-berry Lane, Abrie had fallen asleep, and Reuben and Rose shared another kiss in the moonlight.

The two married on the second Thursday of November in Reuben's house. They hadn't had a chance to paint the inside, but they would. Someday. And they hadn't bought furniture yet either. But it didn't matter—they had everything they needed.

Only close family attended the service, and that morning, Lila confided she was pregnant. "I see the doctor tomorrow," she said. "He'll probably put me on bed rest."

"I'll help you, every day that I can," Rose said, hugging her sister. Nothing, besides marrying Reuben, could have made her happier. "You'll get through this."

Dat held Abrie through part of the service, and then passed her on to Beth. By the time Rose and Reuben exchanged their vows, Trudy had the Bobbli in the back of the living room, walking her back and forth.

As Gideon prayed a blessing over them, Rose had never felt so supported, or so loved.

She had a good man. A home. And a Bobbli. She hadn't gone the route she should have, that was for sure. But through the paradox of God's love, he'd blessed her anyway.

And for that she was eternally grateful.

ACKNOWLEDGMENTS

A big thank-you, as always, to my husband, Peter, for his encouragement, medical expertise, military expertise, and research assistance. I couldn't do this without you. I'm also grateful to our children, Kaleb, Taylor, Hana, and Thao, for their inspiration and motivation.

I'm deeply indebted to Marietta Couch for sharing her Amish experiences with me and for her friendship, encouragement, and care. I'm also very grateful to Laurie Snyder for reading early drafts of this story and for her feedback and support, and to John Jolliff for answering my questions about accident liability, determination of fault, and insurance coverage. (Any mistakes are my own.)

A big shout-out to my agent, Chip MacGregor, for taking a chance on me all those years ago and continuing to believe in my ability to tell a story.

I'm also very thankful for all of the good people at Bethany House, including my editor, Karen Schurrer. She adds so much to my stories, and it's always a pleasure to work with her. Thank you!

Most importantly, I'm grateful to God for inspiration, creativity, and endless grace.

Leslie Gould is the coauthor, with Mindy Starns Clark, of the #1 CBA bestseller *The Amish Midwife*, a 2012 Christy Award winner; CBA bestseller *Courting Cate*, first in the COURTSHIPS OF LANCASTER COUNTY series; and *Beyond the Blue*, winner of the *Romantic Times* Reviewers' Choice for Best Inspirational Novel, 2006. She holds an MFA in creative writing and lives in Portland, Oregon. She and her husband are the parents of four children.

Learn more about Leslie at www.lesliegould.com.

Sign up for Leslie's Newsletter!

Keep up to date with Leslie's news on book releases, signings, and other events by signing up for her email list at lesliegould.com.

You May Also Enjoy . . .

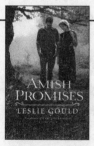

When Iraq veteran Joel Beck and his family move next door to an Amish family in Lancaster County, their lives are linked in unexpected ways. Eve Lehman, who keeps house for her brother, befriends their new neighbors, but life becomes complicated for both families when Joel's handsome army friend pays a visit.

Amish Promises by Leslie Gould
NEIGHBORS OF LANCASTER COUNTY #1
lesliegould.com

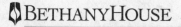

More from Leslie Gould...

Visit lesliegould.com for a full list of her books.

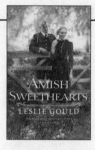

Though Zane Beck and Lila Lehman are neighbors, best friends, and sweethearts, they come from different worlds. When Lila's father arranges an Amish suitor to court her, Zane enlists in the army—unwilling to watch. Although separated by years and distance, their feelings, now hidden, have never faded. But will these two ever find a way to be together?

Amish Sweethearts
NEIGHBORS OF LANCASTER COUNTY #2

Betsy Miller has many would-be suitors, but she's not allowed to marry until her older sister Cate does. Unfortunately, Cate has scared off every man in Lancaster County—until Pete Treger comes to town. Could he be the one to finally tame the fiery Cate?

Courting Cate
THE COURTSHIPS OF LANCASTER COUNTY #1

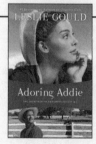

When Addie Cramer and Jonathan Mosier fall head over heels for each other, can their love finally end the feud between their two families?

Adoring Addie
THE COURTSHIPS OF LANCASTER COUNTY #2